Beach to the Baltic

Normandy to Schleswig

A Rifleman's Story

by
Albert Talbot

edited by
Paul Talbot

Dedicated
to
'London Town'

Her steadfastness, unquenchable optimism and
'never say die' spirit proved an inspiration
to the rest of the free world.

Albert Talbot

1914 –1994

Bren Carrier Rangefinder
'E' Support Company
8th Battalion – The Rifle Brigade

My father clearly remembered the occasion
when this photograph was taken, and he is the
man standing by the second Bren carrier.

Imperial War Museums Archive: Photo B8584. Bren
carriers of the Rifle Brigade (8th Battalion) move
cautiously along a lane south of Le Beny Bocage,
Normandy, France. The German positions
are in the high ground in the distance.

Table of Contents

Foreword

Albert Talbot, known to his family and friends as Bert, and his army pals as Loft or Lofty, wrote this account of his experiences during the Second World War as a way of exorcising his demons. His return to civilian life in 1946 was not easy for him, and for quite some time he found it hard to settle into civilian life.

His manuscript was a closely guarded secret until it came to light while clearing the family home. It then lay in my loft, but for the odd occasion when I read through the first half a dozen pages. I don't know why I didn't persevere. Finally, last week, I read it all the way through. Loving it so much, I felt the story needed to be shared with others. His use of army language, East End dialect and Cockney rhyming slang gives this semi-autobiographical novel a certain humorous quality. The respect he shows to those who endured so much during the London blitz also offers a unique insight into life in London at the time. Plus, how serving men and women came to terms with the fact their families were risking their lives each day. His liberal use of names and nicknames was done to help the reader identify with each character, and to make them appear real and vulnerable. The names he used are wholly fictitious and bear no resemblance to the actual lads he shared his war with.

As I read through his story, so realistic and traumatic, the years seemed to melt away, and I was again that small lad asking his father what he did during the war. My one abiding memory was when I asked that very question. He said, 'I went back to tidy up after Dunkirk'. And I in my innocence replied, 'you mean you went to pick up the helmets and rifles?' Many of the things he wrote about were just as he told them to me, plus others he omitted to put in his story, which I have taken the liberty of including. I am convinced that this story is a factual account of my father's war service from enlistment to demob, in the guise of a Londoner named Ronald Deakin.

I was determined to one day get it into the 'public domain', so I set about preparing it for eventual publication. I have stayed true to his work and memory and have kept all his original storyline. For me, this has been a labour of love, working through his manuscript, and making it accessible to others.

Paul Talbot

Chapter 1

'Reporting for duty'

As the nine-twenty from Waterloo came to a stop, a woman stepped from the guard's van and shouted, 'Wilchester! All change!'

Doors clanged and a mass of eager, jostling would-be recruits tumbled out of the carriages, pushing and shoving each other. The hotchpotch of civilians, many clutching small cases or bags, laughing and chattering, surged along the platform towards the exit. Assorted pinstripe suits, tweed jackets, silver-grey Oxford-bags, tightly belted off-white raincoats, with a couple of black and white Al Capone trilbies almost overwhelmed the ticket collector.

A hush settled as they emerged into bright sunlight, where three army lorries with tailboards down waited in the station forecourt. A tall, willowy soldier stood beside the first, looking stony and business-like in his best uniform. With three black and gold stripes on his right arm, he was trying to secure some semblance of order. The silver cap badge in the centre of his khaki forage cap, along with black regimental buttons and greenish-black lanyard complimented his splendid turnout.

'All men for the Rifle Depot this way,' he said, inviting them to climb aboard.

The metal benches down each side of the canvas-covered lorries quickly filled with chirpy civilians, eager to get the whole thing over and done with. A few, not so sure they wanted to give up their civilian status quite yet boldly walked down the station path in search of a pub.

'Let's 'ave a couple o' drinks first,' one of them said.

'Come on, Wilf,' Ron quickly added, urging the tall, fair-haired youngster to join him and Ernie.

'No need to bother,' the sergeant assured. 'We have a wet canteen at the barracks.'

Easily swayed, the new friends struggled aboard and sat next to each other. The driver, khaki shirt with sleeves rolled up, denim fatigue trousers, gaiters and highly polished toecaps eyed them as he fixed up the tailboard. Troublemakers if ever there were.

The lorries pulled onto the road, and a journey with feet slipping and sliding on metal floors got underway. They soon arrived at the depot, drove through a narrow archway designed for horse-drawn carriages, passed a sentry standing at ease outside the guardroom and made their way around a large parade-square. Redbrick barrack blocks bounded three sides of the square. Each block, honeycombed with row upon row of windows, gazed down judgmentally as several squads were being drilled. High castle-like turrets, topping the entrance arch, completed the depot's late Victorian architecture. Along the fourth side were wooden huts with concrete paths between each. In front of them was a canvas marquee with a sign over the entrance: RECEPTION.

At last, the green Bedford's came to a stop. Tailboards clanged down, and they were ordered to alight and pass through the marquee. Checking each man was a long process, with recruits needing to hang around for ages. The clerical staff asked the usual questions: name, date and place of birth, address, next of kin, civilian occupation, national insurance number and denomination.

Hugging their belongings, their last vestige of civilian life, they pushed through the door of what was to be their home for the foreseeable future. Down each side of the hut were iron-framed bedsteads, time-worn bedside cupboards and equally rundown lockers.

The three new friends made for beds in the far corner, taking in what was laid out on each. Arranged on top of a straw-filled palliasse were one striped pillow and two brown army blankets. At the foot of the bed, neatly laid out, were two mess tins, white enamel pint-sized mug, water bottle, knife, fork and spoon, a Bakelite hussif with spare buttons and needles and thread, an assortment of webbing straps, pouches, belt and a small and large valise.

Ron and his new friends swapped information about each other. Wilf Hall, a thatcher from Lickfield, East Sussex, had a wife and baby daughter. His strong hands, slim build and ruddy complexion showed he had spent a great deal of his work-a-day life perched on someone's roof. Ernie Price, an astute, beefy, quick-witted Cockney had light brown hair, hazel eyes and a small, well-trimmed Ronald Coleman moustache. Single and intending to stay so, he had been a porter at Smithfield Market.

With their chatter out of the way they staked a claim on one of the beds and had a closer look at their newly acquired possessions.

'Stand by your beds!' someone shouted. A sergeant entered with two junior NCOs in tow. They saw each man had a bed and none were vacant.

'Quiet everyone,' the sergeant ordered, 'and pay attention. My name is Sergeant Bevan, and this is Corporal Lowton and Lance Corporal Jinks. We are your platoon NCOs. For those of you without much nous that stands for none commissioned officer. People like us don't hold the King's Commission. Besides, we've never been shown how to hold a knife and fork properly. And we're not so gullible as officers. If you've got questions or have any problems, you come to *us*. Also, don't bleat to an officer if you feel put on. It'll only backfire on you. Lance Corporal Jinks is your hut NCO ...' He pointed out a door at the far end of the hut. 'That's his bunk, and he's a light sleeper.'

Ron eyed the NCOs. All wore battledress blouses with razor-sharp creases down each sleeve. The sergeant wore the already familiar black and gold stripes and a greenish-black lanyard on his right shoulder. The other two had emerald stripes with emerald lanyards. A forage cap was perched on each head, as if somehow defying gravity, with the corporals being khaki and the sergeant's rifle green.

'Listen carefully. You are now in C Platoon and will remain so for the next sixteen weeks while going through basic training. After that, you will move to a service battalion for yet more training. Hut twenty is your home in the meantime, so treat it with respect. Any barrack-room damage will come out of your pay. In ten minutes, you will form up outside and make your way to the dining hall. Lance Corporal Jinks will accompany you, and he tolerates no slouching. Bring your eating irons and mug. Parade after lunch will be at 1400 hours. That'll be for kit issue. We can then start the process of turning you into soldiers. God help us!' He paused for breath and then renewed his tirade. 'It's customary to spend the next few days settling in. It would also help if you got to know each other. By the end of your training, you will be the best of mates, or you'll hate each other's guts. Even if you can't stand the sight of someone, you'll lay down your life for them when the time comes, even Lance Corporal Jinks.' He looked at him and grinned. The corporal's stern expression barely changed. 'Your training starts Monday at 0800. That's eight o'clock in the morning for civilians, which you're not anymore. Leave your beds as they are until 1800. You'll be seeing a lot of me,' he cautioned before leaving, with the corporals following close at heel like obedient gun-dogs.

When they were well out of earshot, Alfie Neil, a tall skinny lad from Clapham, placed his thumbs in his ears. 'Oh Yeah,' he said, waggling his fingers. 'Get stuffed ya puerile twit.'

Fred Butcher, a stevedore from Limehouse, smiled at Alfie and said, 'Come on, matey, yuv made ya point. We daan't wanna be late for aahhhr kidney punch.'

Lance Corporal Jinks made a surprise entrance, hands on hips with legs splayed. He gave Alfie the evil eye then yelled, 'Grub up! Come on you lot,' he added when he saw one or two still sitting on their beds. 'Bring your eating irons and mug. Fall in outside. Lively does it.'

He looked at his civilian charges, formed up in three untidy ranks, scratched his head and tried to work out what order to give. 'Okay, lads, in your own time. Right turn and walk towards that monstrosity,' – he pointed at a structure so out of place in an army camp – 'and don't dawdle. Keep up with the man in front.'

After a few yards, the pace quickened at the thought of food. On cue the bugler blew 'cookhouse', sounding like *Come to the cookhouse door boys. Come to the cookhouse door.*

The recruits trooped into a noisy dining hall, a never to be forgotten experience. The 'other ranks mess' could hold, at a pinch, two-hundred and fifty, with two sittings at each meal. Officers and senior NCOs ate in their own mess, making over seven hundred at the depot.

When each table of twelve was full, a man at the end was given a chitty and told to procure everything from the kitchen supply hatch. Back he would traipse with three dixies, one holding meat and gravy, another of vegetables and a third with pudding. The lance corporal doled everything out. Starting cautiously, placing small amounts on each plate, it was possible with a bit of judgment to ensure each man had a fair share. This was called the family system. However, it was fatal to give large portions to start with, because no one liked the idea of giving anything back once it was on their plate.

Ron, unsettled by this pantomime, dwelt on home and all the lordly attention that his dear mother lavished on her loving, doting son.

Standing on a platform at the far end of the one-time circus big top was a stocky fellow who had obviously found his way to the depot via several pubs. He was busy auctioning his civilian clothes, swaying as he extolled the virtues of his Harris Tweed jacket. Ron and the others were not quite yet in the army, so the mess staff and NCOs were going along with this fun and hilarity. This comedic charade, however, didn't alter the food on their plate. For their first army meal, they were given two thin slices of bully beef, lumpy mash potatoes, colourless cabbage and watery gravy. Pudding was a chunk of rock-hard jam pastry and a dollop of thick, cloying custard. This was all washed down by a pint of sweet tea that met with everyone's approval.

Back in the hut one of the recruits strutted about, mimicking

Lance Corporal Jinks. 'Come on, lads. Get a move on. Let's be 'avin' ya. What a bleedin' shower. 'E's a twat that corporal,' he added for the benefit of everyone. 'An' a bastard.'

'Look aahhht, Jimbo, 'e's behind ya,' someone joked.

'Jankers fer you if 'e catches ya takin' bloomin' Gypsy Kiss,' said another.

'Orl right. Leave orf you lot. I'm only 'avin' a bit o' fun. This lot's gerrin too serious fer my likin'.'

'Who said join bleedin' army?' someone chipped in. 'It's gerrin worse by fuckin' second.'

'Who's gorra fag?' a scrounger quizzed.

'Why not ya tap the corporal, Ginge,' one of the lads ribbed, '... if ya dare?'

They sat on their beds, chatting and smoking. Most were Londoners, while four or five claimed they were born within the sound of Bow Bells, proudly proclaiming themselves true Cockneys. First names and nicknames were being used, along with a smattering of rhyming slang. In just a few hours these thirty strangers had banded together, turning into bosom buddies.

'Come on let's scarper,' someone teased.

'Too late, matey,' one sobering individual answered. 'Ya're in fer keeps.'

'Outside on parade!' roared the cocky little man once more, breaking up the harmless banter. Lance Corporal Jinks made his presence felt, and everyone stiffened, even the mouthy ones. 'Get a move on you lot. Kit issue in ten minutes. We're going to turn you into soldiers.'

'Come on, Ernie,' Ron said. 'Let's go an' ger our new whistle an' flute.'

Once more the ragtag of civilians struggled along, heading for the main barrack block, with Lance Corporal Jinks in close attendance. 'Okay, lads. Keep up,' he urged, hoping he wouldn't meet an officer or the regimental sergeant major.

Next to the main gate up two flights of stairs, they found the quarter master's clothing store. Sergeant Bevan and Corporal Lowton were already waiting. Now the real fun began as one by one they were issued with serge battledress and trousers, fatigues, braces, socks, boots, forage cap, steel helmet, underwear, shirts, plimsoles and PT strip. Before signing their record card, the stores NCO told them that any lost or stolen items would come out of their pay, along with the cost of the replacement. Once kitted out they made their way back to hut twenty, with a mass of army clothing in their arms, picking up any fallen items without dropping the rest.

As the last recruit entered the hut, the irksome lance corporal yelled once more, 'Outside on parade! Tea up!'

'Okay, 'ere's yer Toby Jug, Alfie,' said Fred Butcher.

'Daan't gerra bubble on, mate!' he barked, snatching his mug. 'I can manage fer m'self. I ain't no retard.'

Once more, they found themselves marching towards Oxford Circus, as everyone called the 'other ranks mess', inspired by the bugler's lively tune. 'Left, right, left, right, left!' the corporal sang out for the first time.

Tea was made up of cheese and potato pie, two slices of bread, a pat of margarine and a teaspoon of damson jam, with a pint of lusciously sweet tea. All wolfed down in double-quick time.

Later that evening, Sergeant Bevan leant his army bicycle against the hut and made an entrance. 'Listen for your name,' he said once he had their attention. He gave each man his AB64, part one and two. The reddish-brown part one contained personal and service details, while the buff part two was a record of payments made to the soldier.

Ron flicked through each page, looking for his service number. He noted the last three digits, 637. Having filled out his next of kin, he lay back and put his feet on the bed before lighting up.

A genial lad from Peckham, with a soft melodic voice, sang a refrain, summing up how he felt. '*I don't want to join the army. I don't want to go to war ...*' His song tailed off as the enormity of it all struck him. He cuffed a hand across his face to wipe away an imaginary tear. Everyone laughed at his antics.

Things quietened as each recruit became mindful that this was for real. It was evident the next few days were to be a relaxed affair, an informal introduction to army life. Still, they would be in for some tough training in the weeks ahead. Time was getting short. The Nazis, having invaded the Low Countries, now occupied The Hague and Amsterdam, forcing Holland to capitulate. German forces were now holding central Belgium, and the government had withdrawn to Ostend. German Panzers had also broken through in south-east France and were gaining pace as they pushed aside the hard-pressed defenders. Things were dire, and a sense of urgency and purpose prevailed.

Beds could now be made, with Ron and his new friends competing on the excellence of their bed making.

''E's definitely after a stripe, Wilf,' Ron teased, pointing at Ernie's bed.

'Pity he's got to lie on it.'

'I take nah notice o' you two wassocks,' Ernie replied, now strutting about, proudly wearing his forage cap. 'Wot ya fink?'

'It looks like a puddin' basin,' said Ron.

'Come on, stop takin' bloomin' Gyppo. Wot ya *really* fink?'

He studied his new pal, making it look like he was revising his opinion. After a brief pause, he said, 'Yeah, still looks like a puddin' basin. Though we're all gonna look chumps in *that* thing. At least I'll give mine a damn good scrub before I wear it.'

'Why, what's wrong wif it?' Ernie said, taking it off. 'Christ, it's filthy!' Hearing what was being said, the others picked up their forage caps and checked them over. 'Someone's worn it already,' he furthered. 'an' it looks loike they've puked in it.'

Ron started to attach the white metal badge with its split pin and brass plate to his cap, hoping the previous owner had nothing contagious.

From now on, uniforms were to be worn all the time, with no

exception. A poster of a smartly dressed soldier was pinned on the notice board, showing how the uniform should be worn. They gathered around the picture, discussing the merits of the drab, rough khaki and took the mickey out of each other as they tried them on for the first time. The NCOs had piled brown paper and balls of twine on the table for bundling up their case or bag, along with their civilian clothes, the last remnants of their former life. They would then be labelled and handed into company stores for sending home. Soon everything was wrapped up in an innocuous parcel, and they were wearing their uniform. It was a sobering experience, having one's civilian status stripped away within a matter of hours. Still, that was the forces way of dealing with the transition to service life, a quick sharp shock ... futilely resisted by some.

Two recruits, assigned as room orderlies, were fitting blackout boards to the windows.

Ron got off his bed, braces dangling, towel around his neck, with forage cap under his arm. He needed to find the ablutions to answer the call of nature and give his forage cap a good wash. 'Who's comin' fer a tomtit,' he invited to no one in particular. Two Midlander's on the other side of the hut got up and joined him.

The tented latrine was made up of a line of cubicles divided by hessian, with a telegraph pole down the centre to act as a seat. Duckboards ran the full length in front of these hutch-like cubicles. This Holy of Holy's was a place to which soldiers could escape and enjoy those rare moments of privacy, sitting like battery hens reading a newspaper or their most recent letter. Three waist-high troughs with cold water taps were the only facility for washing. Several zinc bowls were placed about, ready for use, along with a mirror over each.

He returned to the hut and joined his pals as they lay on their beds, smoking and chatting. Ernie was regaling everyone with his past exploits, bragging about girls he had scored with and the best technique for future conquests. 'Use yer napper wif 'em, lads,' he said. 'Love 'em an' leave 'em.'

'I knew a luvly bodger in Tootin',' someone chipped in from the other side of the hut. 'Worked at a bottlin' factory. 'Ad a smashin' chassis, she did.'

The shrillness and clarity of the bugler's 'last post' spelt silence in hut twenty. They listened as he deftly nursed each note from his bugle. It was now time to get between the rough, hairy blankets. Ten minutes later 'lights out' was blown. As the final note faded, the orderlies took down the blackout boards to let in what little light remained outside. Everyone was left to enter their own private world of thoughts, escaping to run over the day's events and mentally slip back home. Peace came as the laughter and chatter died down.

A distant train whistle reminded Ron of his beloved Camberwell. Suddenly, worried about what might happen and the pain it would cause his mother, a queasy feeling came over him. A tear trickled down his cheek. However, just thinking about all those thrilling tomorrows made his heart sing with delight. He turned over to settle himself, the blankets scratching his back.

Without warning a chaotic scene unfolded. The lights were switched on, and a loud voice yelled, 'Who the fuck took blackouts down?' Lance Corporal Jinks had returned from a merry jaunt in Wilchester. Darkness once more prevailed, but he still ranted and raved as he worked his way down the hut, scraping his shin on someone's bed and cussing blue murder.

'Oh, pipe down!' a voice yelled.

'Put bleedin' sock in it, Corp,' Fred Butcher whined, 'or I'll chuck ya through bloomin' thumb-sucking windaa.' And he was quite capable of doing so in the cloaked darkness.

Once the corporal was in his sack, someone said, 'Goodnight, mate. Sweet dreams.'

'Goodnight, Tosher,' said Beezer in the bed next to him. 'Wanna kiss?'

'Bollocks,' was his response. 'Ya come near me in the night an' I'll punch yer fuckin' 'ead. Savvy?'

Arthur Beezley wisely kept shtum.

One lad murmured to himself, 'God bless, Ma, wherever you arc?'

Gradually the noise of thirty virgin recruits changed to whispers and gentle laughter. At the same time, one or two savoured their last cigarette of the day. Soon they were fast asleep. All except Ron who dwelt on what had happened to him during the previous two weeks.

The postman's heavy rat-tat-tat disturbed Ron's lie-in and the peace of the small terraced house. His widowed mother, Olive, a happy buxom woman, brought up his morning cup of tea and an envelope marked OHMS.

'What is it, Luv?' she asked, somehow knowing it was bad news.

'Let's 'ave a butcher's, Ma.' He took the letter, tore at it and read the single sheet of paper:

RONALD HENRY DEAKIN
144 Old Queen Street, Camberwell, London. SE5.

You are hereby ordered to report to:
THE INFANTRY TRAINING CENTRE,
The Rifle Depot, Corruna Barracks, Wilchester, Hampshire. By 1200 hours on Thursday 16th May 1940.

Bring the following: A small case or bag with toiletries and personal effects, along with your National Insurance Card and Medical Certificate.

Enclosed: Travel warrant from Camberwell to Wilchester.

'Well, luvva duck,' he said excitedly. 'It's me reportin' papers, Ma. I gotta be at Wilchester Rifle Depot bloomin' next Thursday.' A broad smile spread across his face. 'Wot about that, Ma, I'm gonna be a soldier?'

His mother, lively and forthright, the sort of person who had an answer for everything, said nothing and went along with his newfound joy. However, she could not dispel the feeling of doubt, of what the future had in store for her boys. The Great War was never far from her thoughts. It was a time when boys became men and men became soldiers, marching to war with bands playing. Too many never returned, and more than a few came home marred by blindness, missing limbs and dreadful injuries. She could vividly remember those damaged Tommie's wearing their blue and white hospital suits, being wheeled around the streets.

Ron, her youngest, on reaching eighteen enlisted the day after his birthday, rather than waiting for his call-up papers. His brother, Jack, joined the Territorials well before the outbreak of war and was now serving with the BEF.

By the time he got to work, he was beside himself at the prospect of doing his bit for king and country. 'Mornin', guvnor,' he called as he made his way across the sawdust-strewn floor. There was a spring in his step, and his manager just knew something was up. Ron had been an apprentice at the Camberwell branch of a well-known chain of butchers, ever since leaving school at fourteen.

'Morning, Ron,' Dick replied as he looked after several customers.

Smartly dressed in white cow gown and rubber overshoes he made his way into the shop and stood next to his manager. 'I got me reportin' papers this mornin', guv,' he said breathlessly.

'Turn it up. That's quick.'

The queue of lady customers, chatting about the recent dire war news, stopped talking and looked at him in admiration. 'Ya're gonna be a soldier?' one of them asked.

'Yes, Missus Shepherd.'

'You'll make a luvly soldier, young Ronald,' cooed another. 'It's a shame they'll cut that dark wavy 'air of yours orf, you good looking bugger.' He flushed ever so slightly. 'Ya're the spit of ya Dad.'

'You're joking,' said Dick.

'Straight up, guv.'

'Blimey! You only had your medical last week.'

His medical had been at the Green Man public house in

Lewisham. The large upstairs function room was where candidates checked over by the medical officer and his NCOs. Numerous questions, coughing to order as the doctor cupped his testicles and providing enough urine for both bottles were all aimed at sorting out the men from the boys. He was thrilled when he passed A1, realising there was now no barrier to his joining up. The euphoria grew inside him as he thought of his fast-approaching 'call to arms'.

'Where they sendin' ya?' the errand boy asked.

'Wilchester, Hampshire. I gotta report next—'

His musings were interrupted by loud snoring from the other side of the corporal's door. Once more he was reminded that these men were to be his constant companions in the months ahead, along with the less than affable Lance Corporal Jinks.

A pang of regret, knowing he would not see his girlfriend for some time, started eating away at him. Her demure, perfumed presence could always make his heart skip a little faster. She was quite a looker, with her honey blonde hair and velvety skin. And her shapely figure always looked so alluring in the smart, stylish clothes she wore so elegantly.

The fetching image of Mavis slowly faded, and sleep crept upon him like a lover's caress.

Chapter 2

'Rifle Depot'

The sergeant sat at an old roll-topped desk, watching as two sentries got ready for guard duty. The remaining guards slept opposite the cells, in what had once been the mortuary.

On the desk were a set of standing orders, a pen, inkwell, well-used roller blotter and an incident book for recording everything that happened during his watch. The guardroom held little else: framed photos of the king and queen, a worn rug on scuffed floorboards, a rack with six rifles, glass-fronted key cabinet, two chairs, a gas hob and the makings for a cup of tea. Things had hardly changed since the depot was first built, except for today's mode of dress. During Queen Victoria's reign, they sported dark rifle green with a black leather belt, cross straps and a square pouch with a silver badge stapled to it. On their head, they wore a black shako with a green horsehair brush at the front.

The new sentries stood to attention in front of the sergeant as he briefed them on standing orders. When ready he ordered them to report to the entrance arch, following close behind. With rifle at the shoulder, they marched up to the old sentries either side of the main entrance and halted. They stood rock steady, awaiting his next order.

'About, tarn!' Both took up their dressing as the sergeant once again fussed over their appearance. 'Two paces to the left, march!' He then ordered the old sentries back to the guardroom for a mug of tea and the chance to put their feet up.

Each took it in turns to march up and down, watching for officers. Coming across a junior officer, they would salute at the shoulder by bringing their right arm across the chest and slapping the rifle stock. Senior officers were given a full-present-arms, while the commanding officer or armed party received a well-rehearsed shout of 'Stand by the guard!' followed straightaway by 'Guard turn out!'

With a black tasselled bugle by his side, the duty bugler headed for his first vantage point, to herald a new day. At six-thirty precisely he played 'Reveille', which sounded like *Charlie, Charlie get out of bed. Charlie, Charlie get out of bed.* This was a call for an instant spring to life, with NCOs charging into each hut. 'Wakey, wakey!' they would bellow. 'Rise and shine, you lucky lads!' It was not unknown for an NCO to double back, and woe betides any poor soul still clinging to his blankets.

Lance Corporal Jinks was up and about, nudging each man, waiting by his bed, insisting he place his feet on the floor. Close on his heels were Sergeant Bevan and Corporal Lowton.

'Have we got anyone Billy and Dick?' Corporal Lowton asked. Those excused duties would give their name, number and would be sent for an early breakfast. They would then be marched to the medical room in time for the MO's arrival. Malingerers were dealt with severely. No one stepped forward, which bode well for the day. 'Parade outside 0730. Don't dawdle and don't forget your small kit.

Ron and his pals were now fully awake, folding blankets and laying out their kit to the required standard. The laughter and banter in hut twenty at this early hour was not dissimilar to the London markets on a busy Christmas Eve morning.

''E's definitely an NCO in the makin',' Ron joked, nodding at Ernie.

'He'd be a right bastard with a tape,' answered Wilf.

'Oh, leave orf you two,' he said as he tried to get some semblance of order into his bed pack.

Once ready they formed up outside in three ranks, dressed in boots, gaiters, denim trousers and khaki angora shirt. Lance Corporal Jinks checked over each man, here and there wisecracking with them. 'You're wearing it on the wrong side, pillock brains,' he said to one recruit as he repositioned his forage cap. 'You wear it on the right. ... Hold your right hand up, son,' he added, checking if he knew his left from his right.' The lad dithered then raised his right hand. He moved to the next man. 'Do that button up, White! Where do you think you are, bleedin' Margate prom? Did you shave this morning, Molloy?'

'Yes, Corporal!'

'I suggest you take the paper off blade next time.' There were a few sniggers. 'Quiet!' he yelled. 'Haircut for you, Tonks. You might forget, but I won't.' He stepped back and cast his eyes over them. 'Soldiers?' he finally said with a mirthless grin. 'Good Gawd. What a bleedin' shower.'

The day's routine started with a swing, marching away, inspired by the lance corporal's, 'Left, right, left, right, left! Keep in step that man! Left, right, left, right, left!'

In pale blue vest, navy shorts, plimsolls and army socks rolled down, they entered the spacious gym. Its polished oak floor made it a daunting place, and, for many, a place of pain and torture.

Wearing his green and black striped jersey, the muscle-bound staff sergeant told them to begin running in a circle. After a short while, he shouted, 'Four lines in front of me! First exercise ... with me ... begin!' He started with a trunk circling motion, urging them to follow his lead. 'With me ... change!' He slipped into the next exercise. Trying to keep up, they struggled to match his fluid movements. A few ably stretched this way and that, while others overreached, almost collapsing. 'Right, keep it up, lads. You're getting the hang of it.' His sudden praise spurred them on. He then slipped into another routine, with arms straight out, legs together, knees bent. 'Down, up, down, up, down, up ...' he trotted out, all too quickly. More than a few crumpled on the floor, red in the face, sucking in air.

While all this was going on, two assistants busied themselves, fixing postures, timing and showing each move as and when required. The sergeant worked their legs, arms and trunk in a series of short, sharp, none stop exercises, sprinkling them every so often with fun inter-rank games.

The forty-five-minutes passed quickly. Once dismissed, Ron and the others made their way to the shower block, dragging their feet and showing how badly out of condition they were.

After a fifteen-minute break, they marched to the dental centre. Each man was given a thorough mouth inspection, noting any extractions. There was no pandering to soldiers. It was easier to remove an offending tooth if there was any doubt. The last thing they wanted was a soldier on active service with a raging toothache. They were then taken next door for injections against typhus and tetanus, with the promise of more at the weekend. This was the army's way of doing things, so in the case of ill effects, they could recover in their own time, over the weekend.

'Mus' fink we're bleedin' pin cushions,' Ernie moaned as he queued for his first jabs among many.

'Wotch they don't prick yer Khyber Pass,' Ron said, winking.

Back at the hut, they found the first week's training programme pinned to the notice board. There were four forty-five-minute training periods in the morning and three after lunch. Between each were a five-minute fag and pee break and a naafi break mid-afternoon. The list included foot drill, field training, rifle instruction, PT, bayonet practice and a route march at the end of the week.

'Wot abahhht this lot,' Ernie ranted to those around him.

'Bleedin' 'anover,' said another, ''ave a butcher's at all this square bashin' an' them lectures.'

'Ger yer ole daisy roots aahhht, Ron,' Alfie laughed.

'Look at this lot,' Beezer joined in, sizing up the list of parades and training sessions. '... 'Ang on,' he tersely added, 'they've only given us one naafi break all day. An' wiv only got fifteen minutes. It'll take that bloody long ta gerra the soddin' naafi.'

'Nah chance of a cuppa Rosie, Knocker,' someone chipped in. 'We might as well stretch aahhht an' 'ave a fag.'

All agreed they were in for a tough time, with a few suggesting they make a relaxing weekend of it. In the weeks ahead they wouldn't get much chance.

Friday's shots were nothing compared to what they were given on Saturday morning. Apart from a couple, they were off their feet, too ill to even go for lunch. Though by four o'clock all were hale and hearty, ready for a bit of fun and mischief. Some visited the naafi, while others took it easy. They enjoyed what might be their last free day for some time, larking about, smoking, reading, writing letters and finding out more about each other.

A photo of a baby boy was passed to Ron as he lay on his bed. "E's a cracker, Wilf,' he said. "Ow old is 'e?'

'Seven months and three days.'

'Come on, Wilf,' Steve Pugh said, stretched out on the next bed. 'Let's 'ave a butcher's.'

Ron handed the photograph of the chubby-faced baby back to Wilf. He then gave it to Steve and watched as it did the rounds, everyone agreeing his son was the bonniest kid they had ever seen.

Wilf's journey from Lickfield must have been hard for him. It was obvious he didn't want to be here, forever talking about his wife and son and harking back to family life. His pals also detected sadness and moments of quietness as if he were inwardly slipping back home. Unlike some of the boisterous occupants of hut twenty, he seemed somewhat unhappy, finding it hard to adjust to this new way of life, separated from his wife and child. No such trouble for Ernie, whose philosophy was love 'em an' leave 'em. Strictly no deep involvement was his maxim. He liked to think of himself as a wide boy, up to all the tricks and knowing all the dodges. He was forever boasting about his achievements, eager to impress that he had seen a bit of life. He maintained his best times were spent at the Blue Anchor in Bermondsey, his favourite pub.

Ron wrote a couple of letters, but it took some doing in the noisy hut, with its clamour of ribald laughter. One was to Mavis, giving her his army address and service number and penning a few words of endearment, asking her to visit him as soon as possible. The second was a brief, cheerful note to his mum, telling her how much he was missing her home cooking and the privacy of his bedroom.

Ernie's incessant chatter formed a constant background of noise in hut twenty. 'I've 'ad some luvly bodgers in me time,' he said. 'Some were a sight fer sore eyes ... silly cows,' he added less flatteringly. 'Now, Ron, if ya fancy a bit o' what does ya good, you stay wif ... wot ya doin'? Ah, cleanin' yer daisy roots.' He looked at the highly polished toecaps. 'Ya're makin' a grand job of 'em. Ya're a natural at this army lark. Where'd ya learn to do 'em so good?'

Ron smiled, recalling what his uncle had told him. 'Me Uncle Fred showed me ... 'e were in last lot ... on the Somme. 'E said: "if you get a good shine on your boots, Ronald, you'll not go far wrong". I don't know if it'll cut any ice with Jinksy, though. But at least it can do no 'arm tryin'. An' anyway, I find it relaxin'.'

'I get same feelin' when 'avin' sex,' Ernie offered for the amusement of everyone.

'Talkin' abahhht sex,' Alfie said, putting on his cap, 'any of you buggers fancy a cuppa an' a bit o' crumpet?'

Being Saturday night, the naafi was packed to the gunwales. The duty NCO, a pinch-faced lance corporal, tried his best to keep the peace, stopping swaddies jostling each other. The girls were kept busy, serving a never-ending queue.

'What's talent loike?' Ernie asked, peering over Ron's shoulder at a willowy, blonde bombshell. 'Stone'a bleedin' crows. Gerra load o' Greta Garbo.'

'Way out of your league, mate,' the man behind him said. 'Nearly every guy in the place has the hots for glamour puss. The muscle-bound, sergeant PTI has already staked his claim.'

'Jugs on that one ain't bad, though,' Ernie said, nodding at the girl on the tea urn.

'But she ain't a looker like Greta,' Ron observed.

'I know, but ya don't 'ave ta stare at bloomin' flames while ya poke fire, now do ya? Three gunfire's an' three rock cakes, Ducks,' he eventually said, using the army vernacular for a cup of tea. 'What time ya knock orf, Luv?' He leant over the counter and put his ear close to the maiden of his choice.

'Watch you don't singe your eyebrows, Sonny Jim,' she snapped as she filled a cup with steaming tea.

'Ah, that's put ya in yer place, Ern,' Alfie laughed. 'Ya don't stand a cat's ...'

She smiled and dropped Ernie's nine-pence in the till. Almost every soldier she served came onto her, and she well knew it was one of the more pleasing aspects of working in an army camp.

They found an empty table and piled cups and plates to one side, ready for the hard-pressed girls to collect.

A row of shelves behind the counter held a selection of items: cigarettes, matches, ink, writing paper, envelopes, razor blades, Brasso, khaki Blanco, boot polish and most other things required by your average swaddy at a minute's notice. A blackboard showed the sort of snacks on offer: five-pence for beans on toast, seven-pence for egg and chips, eight-pence for sausage and mash and ten-pence for fish, chips and mushy peas. Drinks to be had were tea, coffee, cocoa, Horlicks, Bovril, milk, Tizer and ginger beer, but no alcohol.

Butch stared at the mass of khaki gathered around tables or leaning against the wall. 'Bloody hell,' he said matter-of-factly, 'ya're in Kate Karney now, lads.'

Other members of hut twenty were sitting around another table. Whitey, or Eric White to give him his proper name was the hut comedian. Always full of pranks and jokes, he kept his pals in fits of laughter with his dry sense of humour. Benjamin (Benny or Solly) Solomon, a Jewish lad from Southwark, listened to Whitey's latest joke. Jimbo, name James Pretlow was adding up his loose change. Joseph Sharp from Lambeth, keeping his counsel sat in the corner eyeing a young girl as she flitted from table to table, joking with the swaddies and gathering up the dirties.

Someone switched on the wireless for the six o'clock news. When everyone realised how grim things had become a deathly hush settled on them. '... German Panzer troops' announced the newsreader, 'are sweeping through North-East France, driving a wedge between British and French forces ...'

As Ron listened, he thought about Chamberlain's efforts to avert war, and once it came, how things had changed beyond description. The diplomatic wrangling's and the 'peace for our time' pact of September nineteen thirty-eight, to appease the ranting despot was in the end to no avail. The invasion of Poland was one step too far. Many said that force was the only thing Hitler understood. But more than a few wanted to carry on appeasing him. Then that ill-fated Sunday morning when Big Ben's eleven o'clock chimes were followed by an announcement that the Prime Minister would shortly address the Nation. '... and so, consequently, *this* country *is* at war with Germany. ...' It was a sobering occasion, and it resonated through the Nation like the tolling of a funeral bell. Furthermore, quotes from His Majesty's inspiring speech were repeated in homes and public houses throughout Britain. '... We have been called, with our Allies, to meet this challenge. ... The task will be hard, and there will be dark days ahead. ...'

Severe restrictions were imposed. An air of despondency settled over Britain, from London's East End to the Gorbals of Glasgow. People learnt to grope about in unlit streets. They were plagued by ARP wardens, looking for chinks of light in blackout curtains. Barrage balloons sprang up all over the place, many moored to barges in the Thames and on the Clyde. Entrances to public buildings, sandbagged and manned by troops were ready and waiting to repel the Hun. Police officers patrolled the streets, wearing steel helmets and a respirator strapped to their chest. Children from London and other cities were moved to safe parts of the country. For many, it was the adventure of a lifetime. Their new homes in Wales or the picturesque villages of Wiltshire, Dorset and Devon would be a memory they would carry always. Parents were discouraged from accompanying children to the railway station in case they made a scene and refused to let them go. Lines of light-hearted children, holding hands with a sibling or friend would gaily trip along. Each carried a small case or paper parcel and a cardboard boxed gas mask, with a label tied to a button.

Despite all this the people in London were as cheerful as ever, voicing their rage at Hitler and singing their blues away:

'Run rabbit, run rabbit, run, run, run.'
'Don't let the farmer have his fun, fun, fun.'
'He'll get by without his rabbit pie.'
'So run rabbit, run rabbit, run, run, run.'

With all the dire war news, it was cheering to hear something positive for a change. Crowds of Londoners, needing a tonic to lift their spirits cheered the returning bluejackets from His Majesty's cruisers *Ajax* and *Exeter*. Together with *Achilles*, they had fought against Germany's surface raider, *Admiral Graf Spee* off Montevideo. Aside from this glorious event, the Royal Navy was still fending off packs of U-boats, set on causing maximum damage to Britain's vital supply lines. Before the outbreak of war their entire force had lain in wait to pounce on the woefully unprepared shipping.

It was shocking when *HMS Royal Oak* was sunk at anchor in Scapa Flow, with half its company killed or missing, presumed drowned. *Korvettenkaptän* Günther Prien, having slipped through the naval screen, fired all his bow tubes at this capital ship, sending her to the bottom in just thirteen minutes. This came on top of the previous month's calamity when the aircraft carrier *HMS Courageous* sank in the North Atlantic.

The announcer's steady voice brought Ron back to the present. '... A report has just come through,' he added during the news summary, 'saying the Germans now occupy Amiens and British forces are carrying out a tactical withdrawal towards the coast ...'

There was a gasp, and the chatter started up again.

'Bloody 'ell,' Ron said, frowning. 'That's a turn-up.' He went quiet as he thought about Jack in the East Surreys, wondering where he was in all this. Was he pulling back with the rest, or was he already a prisoner of war?

'Who wants another cuppa?' Wilf asked, trying to infuse a measure of cheer into the morbid proceedings and keen to get his mates a top-up now the queue had dwindled somewhat.

'Don't forget me an' Alf,' Ernie said as they chatted up the tea-earn-girl and her mate.

At the start of their first week of training, C Platoon formed up outside hut twenty. Corporal Lowton and Lance Corporal Jinks checked over each man, moving them from one place to another, sizing the ranks.

'At ease!' Corporal Lowton ordered. 'Stand to your front. Squad!' he bit down hard, followed quickly by, 'Stand at ease!' He shook his head. 'Let's try it again, lame brains. And this time wipe the sleep from your eyes.'

Sergeant Bevan moved forward to take over the platoon. 'At ease,' he warned. 'On the command "stand to your front", brace up smartly. At the command "squad", spring to attention.' He showed them what to do. When they had it near enough right in a loud voice, he ordered, 'Move to the right in threes, right tarn! By the right, quick march!'

As they marched towards the parade square, the corporals sang out the timing. 'Left, right, left, right, left! Keep your heads up! Swing those arms! Sort your feet out, Deakin! Left, right, left, right, left!'

Standing to attention, eyes straight ahead, thumbs down the seams of his trousers, Lance Corporal Jinks showed each drill move. The platoon then carried out each movement until the NCOs saw some signs of improvement. They then marched back and forth at the regimental pace of one-hundred and forty steps to the minute, each man picking up the timing like the tick-tock of a metronome.

'Who's that man bobbing up and down?' Sergeant Bevan yelled, pointing him out. 'That man there, Corporal, sort him out!'

'Pugh!' Lance Corporal Jinks screamed.' Friggin' hell. Keep yer head still, woodpecker. Pick your pace up. The man behind you will be up your arse soon. Get in step! Left, right, left, right, left!'

The RSM in best service dress, black lion and unicorn on his lower right arm, with an officer by his side watched as they switched between double-time and the regimental pace. Noting progress, he pointed with his silver-topped cane as he chatted to the captain.

After what seemed like ages, they marched off the parade square to the ding-dong of left, right, left, right, left!

Corporal Lowton halted in front of hut twenty. Thirty right boots smacked the tarmac as one. 'Fallout!' *Not bad*, he thought. *They learn fast.* 'Five minutes before we start field training. Smoke if you want,' – he moved closer to a lad with a twenty pack of Gold Flake – 'otherwise sharpish to the bog. I don't want some twat slipping off for a piss during the next session.'

'Look aahhht,' Ernie said, warning Ron and Wilf, 'the Corp's on bloomin' tap agin. That's second time 'e's cadged an oily rag off Shorty.'

'Me Uncle Fred said they were always on cadge when 'e were in. They never smoke their own if they can 'elp it. The lads'll get wise to 'im.'

The corporal lit his cigarette and laughed at something Shorty had said.

They next found themselves above the main barrack block. From this vantage point, each man learnt how to read the foreground, middle ground and distance. Between the depot and Upper Dawlston was open heathland and a couple of small hamlets, taken over by the army. Trenches and gun positions, with dummies and drainpipes painted grey, along with a few disguised vehicles created the illusion of war in this peaceful slice of England. They were next shown how to gauge distance and how to observe and record what they saw. This all-round view enabled them to watch other platoons being put through their paces on the parade square. To their right and rear sprawled open farmland with three or four farmhouses and outbuildings, surrounded by fields of varying colours.

The town of Wilchester, with its church spire, public buildings, shops and cinemas lay at peace. It was hard to believe that just across the Channel, a life and death struggle was being played out. After a lofty appraisal of their new home, they clambered down and doubled back to the hut for their next lecture.

Following a five-minute fag break, they settled down on a few beds, ready for an introduction to the Short Lee Enfield rifle. Corporal Lowton started by outlining each part on a blackboard balanced on the stove. 'To aim,' he said, again pointing at the chalk drawing, 'align the foresight with the back sight.' He picked up the rifle, pointing it away from them. 'The most important safety rule of all is never, repeat never, point it at anyone, loaded or unloaded. Unless you want to see them dead. You always hold your rifle this way.' He gripped the barrel with one hand and the stock with the other, keeping the muzzle pointed at the ceiling. He then passed it to Alfie, who gingerly took it, nervous it might go off in his hands. Each man then handled the rifle, many surprised at its nine-pound weight.

'Move yer friggin' arse, ya dozy bastard,' Jacko urged, trying to get a closer look.

'Watch your fuckin' language, Jackson!' Lance Corporal Jinks lambasted. 'There might be a lady present.' Everyone laughed at his wisecrack. Pleased with the response, he cracked a smile, the first they had seen from him.

Holding it at the point of balance, the corporal showed them how to remove the bolt. 'Push this lever forward,' he said, thumbing the safety catch. 'Lift the bolt and pull it back as far as it will go. Now press this small nipple.' There were a few smirks as he struggled to keep a straight face. 'Remove the bolt.' He placed it carefully on the bed. 'And keep it out of the dirt. If you lose it, you're well and truly buggered.' He explained about the escape of gas when it fired, the rifling that gave it its accuracy, its muzzle velocity and the highest point of culmination on the bullet's way to the target. 'This piece of kit is your best friend ... your bondook. Look after it, lads. Keep it clean.' He opened a brass flap on the end of the butt to reveal a piece of lead attached to a length of cord, a small bottle of oil and a square of red and white flannelette, known as four-by-two. 'It'll save your life one day,' he finally added, further stressing the need to look after it. Each man then went through the process of removing the bolt, with Jinksy rapidly firing questions at them.

'Smoke if you want,' Corporal Lowton said in conclusion while looking around for the lad he cadged a fag from earlier. 'The rest of the day's yours.'

'Cop, Ern.' Ron passed him a cigarette, along with Wilf and Alfie.

'In the bees an' honey, are we?' Ernie asked, taking one of his smokes.

Being the last session of the day, Ron was feeling rather generous. 'Anyone fancy goin' ta flicks tonight?' he said, sucking in a lungful of smoke.

'Sure, why not,' Ernie replied, taking him up on the offer. 'We'll gerra a move on after tea. I fancy a bit of darkness. Monday's usually me lucky night fer pickin' up a bit o' totty.'

Ernie prattled as they made their way towards the main gate. 'Keep yer mince pies open fer regimental peelers,' he said, marching with arms swinging high. 'Those two are right mean bastards. They'll do ya as soon as look at ya.'

Provost staff were forever on the lookout for untidy swaddies and un-rifleman-like behaviour. Provost Sergeant Killick was a time-serving soldier. His stocky, bull-necked figure and pugilistic features clearly showed he had once been the armies boxing light heavyweight champion in India. Provost Corporal Foster, chosen for his size, not his wit or intellect – he had little of either – was a giant of a man at six foot six. His most striking feature was his ham-fisted paws, somewhat overlarge, even for a man of his size. Dealing with defaulters, three or four times a day was their chief responsibility. They doled out a variety of tasks, some of which were of a filthy nature and quite demeaning.

It was best when near the main gate to conduct oneself with decorum. One or the other would always be on duty, taking names and service numbers and sending anyone back to smarten up. Officers also tended to be more prevalent around the main barrack block, as did the RSM.

Once clear of the depot they could relax, enjoying the scenery and ogling the talent. They walked past Woolworths and saw a couple of girls cashing up. The blonde smiled and waved. Ron and Ernie swelled with pride as they carried on their way, waving back at the girls. They now belonged to The Rifle Regiment, an elite fighting force whose battle honours went back one-hundred and fifty years. Its regimental colours, black and green, without doubt, were the finest in the British Army.

Wilchester sported three cinemas, the Regal, Plaza and Tivoli. *Wuthering Heights* with Lawrence Olivier and Merle Oberon were playing at the Plaza. Though they both agreed it was far too sombre and much too long. The Tivoli was now given over to live entertainment. They settled on the Regal, where the main feature was a Deanna Durbin movie, along with an old B movie called *The Frontier's Man*, starring Richard Dix.

After paying their tanner entrance fee, they found themselves helpless in darkness, until a winsome female with a torch said, 'Follow me, dearies.'

'Whatever ya say, ducks,' Ernie mumbled. 'I'm all yours.'

Feeling and fumbling along the row, they eventually fell into two empty seats and settled down to watch the film. The red Indian braves in war paint and feathers circled the wagons, firing flaming arrows at the hard-pressed settlers. Just as they were gaining the upper hand, a distant trumpet heralded the US Cavalry's timely arrival, forcing the bloodthirsty savages to call off the attack.

During the interval, Ron looked around at masses of khaki, spotting one or two familiar faces. There were only a handful of girls, snuggled up to a soldier of their choice.

Adverts flashed on the screen, showing a three-piece leather suite for thirteen guineas, nine square yards of Wilton carpet at eight guineas and a worsted three-piece suit for three pounds ten shillings from Foster Brothers. The cogs engaged on the next reel, causing the picture to jump before settling down to the British Movie-tone News. The first item showed British troops, weighed down with all manner of kit, hobbling up the gangway of a troopship. They were then shown lining the railings, smiling and waving goodbye, bound for some far distant part of the British Empire.

'Fuck that fer a game of soldiers,' Ernie prattled. 'Don't fink we'll be that 'appy when *we're* off ta war.' Next item was a group of Land Army girls kitted out in felt hats, green woollen sweaters and corduroy breeches, helping to produce food for the nation. 'They've got it made *them* farmers,' he blathered on. 'All that luvly crumpet. What a smashin'—'

'If you don't shut your mouth, gobshite,' someone warned, 'I'll shut it fer you.'

Ernie turned around, ready with a few choice words of his own, but all he saw in the half-light was Greta and her staff sergeant boyfriend, his arm protectively around her. He turned back to face the screen, sliding down in his seat as the opening title announced Deanna Durbin in *First Love.*

The make-believe world of romance and happiness, with college football players and girlfriends in the drugstore, was far removed from the British way of life. These dizzy blondes, redheads and brunettes, sweetly tasting their ice-cream sodas giggled and swooned over their hunky beaus. The scene faded to the honeyed voice of Deanna, with this romantic interlude briefly supplanting the wartime events of today.

Being soldiers of the king, Ron and Ernie stood to attention as the National Anthem played.

'Fancy a cuppa?' Ron asked as they made their way along the row. 'There's a Sally Army somewhere near 'ere. We might gerra Rosie an' a wad, buckshee.'

'Sure. There might even be a bit o' crumpet goin' spare.'

The Salvation Army canteen, a large villa type building, offered many home comforts for the vast number of troops that had swelled Wilchester in recent months. Table tennis and billiards, along with chess, draughts, dominoes and darts were to be had for the asking. The large room, swamped with khaki, was cloyingly thick with smoke and bursting at the seams. Sally Army soldiers, working at breakneck speed, were giving out gratis a cup of tea and a snack, either sandwich or cake.

They strolled back to the depot after their impromptu supper, smoking and chatting, once more relishing the freedom of a few hours away from the others. Reporting to the guardroom, they queued behind a dozen other swaddies and in due course gave their name and number to Corporal Foster.

Arriving at hut twenty they blindly made their way towards their beds.

'Yer beds are down there ya dozy basta'ds,' one sleepy form curtly advised.

'All right, tosspot,' Ron countered. 'I 'eard ya. Keep yer Barnet on.'

He reached his bed, barked his shin, cursed under his breath and removed his denim tunic and serge trousers, hanging them neatly in the locker. He then yawned, pulled back the covers and climbed into a lulling swathe of blankets, ready and waiting for him.

Chapter 3

'Soldierly Like'

With week one almost over, Ron and the others got ready for a fifteen-mile route march. This would be their first time away from the depot as a body of men. Keen to be on the way they formed up in plenty of time in front of hut twenty, ready to take in the rural delights of Hampshire and shake off what had been a testing baptism to army life.

Leaving through the rear gate, the NCOs headed towards Cobley. Tall hedgerows to their right veiled the depot's football and rugger pitches. On the opposite side of the narrow lane was a large grassed area where once officers played polo. Dressed in denim fatigues, they marched at a hearty pace, though somewhat bloated by their midday meal of beef stew and dumplings, followed by spotted dick and custard.

Ron and Ernie marched side by side in the middle file, with Wilf striding out in front. Ossie, surname Osmond was the third man in their file. Having a confident and quiet manner he had a beefy roundness, once topped by a mop of unruly blonde hair, before the depot barber got his hands on it.

'Pick yer feet up, Whipper,' Ernie said, geeing up Cyril Whipstone. 'I'll be on yer back in a dicky.' The lad was finding it hard to keep up. 'Bloody mornin' went quick,' he added for Ron's benefit. 'Thought we were gonna 'ave a bit o' fun wif Jinksy?'

'Oh, yeah,' Ron chortled. 'Ya mean when Butch lost 'is bondook?'

'Couple o' lads 'id it under some sandbags. Ole Jinksy nearly bust a gut, silly bugger. Butch wen' as white as a sheet. I fink 'e thought 'e were gonna be court marshalled, or worse, shot at dawn.'

Today's first session was bayonet-fighting, or sword fighting as it was known in The Rifle Regiment. Corporal Lowton showed them how to hold the rifle in a high port position, across the chest as they advanced. On the command 'on-guard' the rifle was brought down and pointed at the hanging target, followed by the order 'in'. Each man lunged at the hapless sandbag. The sword was then withdrawn and returned to the 'on-guard' position. Once they had dispatched the sandbag to the great builder's yard in the sky, they turned to the right so the next man could have a go. As they advanced at the double, the corporal encouraged them to scream like banshees. Still, all this madcap behaviour ceased when Lance Corporal Jinks arrived with their elevenses in a tea earn, which turned out to be as cold as a frigid woman.

The corporal next showed them how to maintain their balance and inflict a knockout blow by taking a half step and bringing the rifle butt under the chin. He then invited each man to attack him with all his strength, again showing how easy it was to get someone off balance.

Ron and the others decided early on in their training that discretion was the better part of valour, and they would let the NCOs handle them as per the army rule book. Lots of bruises and winded bodies were the outcome. His eagerness to inflict such pain convinced them he enjoyed this personal bit of tutelage, seeing how far he could push them until they snapped.

'Squad halt!' Corporal Lowton ordered. 'Righto, lads, fall out. Fifteen minutes rest.'

Wilf handed Ron and Ernie a cigarette each.

'Thanks, Pal,' Ron said, cupping his hand around the match so they could light their smokes. They drew on them, savouring the taste and slowly exhaled.

'When's your girlfriend coming to see you?' Wilf asked.

'Next Sunday, all being well.'

Each man found a spot to stretch out, making the most of this brief respite, joking and tickling each other with blades of grass.

'Come on you lot?' the corporal shouted after what seemed like five minutes. 'On your feet. Same place. By the right, quick march!'

They soon fell into the regimental pace again, clip-clopping along as mile after mile ticked by. Each man had his own way of fostering the relaxed mental state, needed to maintain this pace and endure such hardships in future.

A single-decker bus loomed around the corner. The squad peeled onto the grass verge, giving the driver room to pass. They resumed their place, again without being told to do so.

They passed a collection of farm buildings with an array of smells. Cows waiting to be milked were loudly complaining. The lads joined in, bellowing back and getting more than a few strange looks from the farmer and his wife.

An eye-watering pong from what was a pigsty wafted in their direction. 'Strewth,' said Beezer. 'Who's dropped their guts?'

'Rusk!' someone yelled. All eyes turned on him. Alfred Farley was usually the source of such smells.

'March to attention!' Lance Corporal Jinks yelled. 'Quiet that man! Left, right, left, right, left!'

Closing on the outskirts of Cobley, they opened the pace and thrust out their chests.

'Right wheel,' some wag said in a gruff voice as they passed the Hare and Hounds public house.

'Fancy a pint, Corp?' another comic chirped.

No such luck as they marched on. Its pleasant location, however, was noted and a few would soon sample its brews in the company of some delightful female. A signpost at the crossroads pointed to the nearby villages of Upper Dawlston and Paxton, with Wilchester seven miles back.

The next object of fun was a mouth-watering display of fruit and vegetables outside the village post office. 'Ripe bananas,' someone joked.

'Dream on,' Corporal Lowton said. 'They're as rare as rockin' horse shit.'

'Tanner fer ten-pound o' King Edwards,' carried on the ex-barrow boy. 'Get yer luvly cabbages 'ere!'

The corporals let them have their fun because they were marching so well, heads held high with arms swinging in unison.

The villagers looked on with pride at their khaki army. These were the lads who before long would stand between *them* and Hitler, and they looked as if they would give a good account for themselves when the time came.

A pretty country wife pushing a pram smiled as they passed.

'Wot time's ya're ole man go aahhht, ducks?' someone joked.

She grinned but said nothing.

'I'll be 'round later, darlin',' another quipped.

Again, no reply to their cheeky banter.

As two middle-aged women drew level, the lance corporal said in a firm voice, 'March to attention! Silence there! Come on, lads,' he added in a softer tone, a welcome change for Jinksy, 'don't take banter too far. You've got pride of the Rifle's to uphold. You're doing all right today ... so cut it out that man!' he screamed. 'Left, right, left, right, left!' Later they found out the one woman was the adjutant's wife and the NCOs were taking no chances with their Cockney charges.

'Nice place Cobley, Ron,' said Ernie. 'Not far from depot.'

'Looks bloomin' sort o' place ya could bring a nice girl fer a few 'ours. Might bring Mavis 'ere and 'ave a closer gander.'

Weary, back sore and thighs aching they smartened up when they saw the depot gates. Lance Corporal Jinks once more made his presence felt by shouting out the timing. 'Left, right, left, right, left!' Heads up! Swing those arms!'

At last, they arrived at hut twenty, spent and sweaty. 'Squad halt!' Corporal Lowton ordered. 'Into line, right tarn! Pick up your dressing. Wait for it. Squad dis-miss!'

Each man dived into the hut, changed into plimsolls and jogged up to the bathhouse. A quick soapy douse and they were ready for 'foot inspection'. Sergeant Bevan checked each man for blisters and chafing. Their first route march had produced no casualties, other than two or three cases of soreness, for which he advised a dab of surgical spirits.

Everyone agreed a stout pair of boots and a good pair of socks were the required trappings for route marching.

Plenty of food, unbroken sleep and route marches had indeed put a sparkle in their eyes. Regular visits to the gym, where they had progressed to vaulting horses, parallel bars and climbing ropes had also added to their physical health and well-being.

Leisure pastimes for more than a few were cards. The less adventurous preferred solo or whist, while the bolder types favoured pontoon, three card brag or poker. Sometimes large amounts of money changed hands, particularly after payday on Friday.

Weather permitting, pay-parade took place on the parade square, with an army blanket thrown over a well-scrubbed table. Saluting at the table was a drill move that Corporal Lowton had covered during a recent practice. Names were gone through in alphabetical order. Ron was thankful his name began with D because those with names such as Venables, Weston and Young would be hanging around all afternoon.

'Rifleman Deakin, 637!' the sergeant major called from behind the pay-table. The seated officer, with a ledger and piles of coins and ten-shilling notes sorted out his first week's pay.

'Sir!' he answered, striding up to the table. He halted, saluted, took a half pace forward and handed the officer his AB64 part two.

Having received his pay, taken back his pay book, he transferred the money to his left hand. He then stepped back, saluted, about turned and marched off the parade square with the sergeant major's words ringing in his ears. 'Get your haircut, Deakin!'

He fell in beside another rifleman as they made their way back to the hut line.

'Bleedin' 'anover,' Ron said, staring at his first week's pay. He shook his head in disbelief. 'Wot thumb-suckin' goods this?'

'Each week they hold back three and six ... tanner a day,' the other man said. 'Which they make up with two-bob a week recruit's pay.'

Ron arrived at the hut, mourning his fall in wages and status. As a trainee butcher, he was getting thirty-three shillings and nine-pence a week. He thought about his job, so rudely interrupted and hoped there would be one to go back to once the war was over. Next April, when finishing his apprenticeship, his weekly wage would have gone up to three pounds eleven shillings. He looked at the ten shillings and four-pence, realising that for the first time in his life he was a pauper.

'Wot's this bastard lark?' he said, looking over Butch's shoulder at the notice board. He put together a string of expletives and a few choice army expressions which seemed to sum up how he felt.

The new order read:

'EMERGENCY READINESS'

Owing to the threat of invasion, there will now be three states of readiness. 'Party 1' will be fully dressed and prepared to leave the depot at once. 'Party 2' will be allowed one hour to parade up to 'Party 1' readiness. 'Party 3' will be allowed out of barracks as normal. 'Party 1' will remain on duty for twenty-four hours and will be confined to the precincts of the indoor rifle range.

By order of the Depot Adjutant

Along with two other platoons C Platoon was chosen to commence this new security measure as 'Party One'.

Greatcoats and blankets were to be bundled and taken to the rifle range. Members of hut twenty had already been issued with new style greatcoats – calf-length, double-breasted variety. However, Butch drew the short straw and was given one of the quarter master's Great War relics which almost swept the floor.

After tea Butch was keen to begin greatcoat and blanket

bundling, hoping for a right royal mix-up. It was his chance to lose the mangy mantle and get one of the new ones. However, the others, seeing a glint in his eyes were just as keen to make sure he remained the rightful owner of this museum piece.

A fitful night was had on the rifle range floor, stretched out fully clothed, trying to get some sleep. At twenty past midnight, the 'general alarm' sounded, rousing the entire depot. The platoons quickly formed up in three lines, ready to board the coaches waiting outside the range, greatcoats and blankets already loaded.

As soon as Ron had taken his seat, he unlaced his boots and took them off, ready for a journey into the unknown. Eager to be on his way, the driver pulled away as soon as the last man was seated.

'Where too, Ron?' Ernie joked. 'Brighton or Soufend? Good job wiv gotta few crates o' brahn ale.'

The coach did one turn of the parade square and stopped in the same place. 'Everyone off!' the driver yelled over a chorus of raspberries.

'Just our perishin' Donald Duck,' Ron cursed under his breath as he put his boots back on, dismissing the thought of an evening's drive through the Hampshire countryside. 'Bloody Army!'

They were once more back to the floor of the rifle range, where a long night was had lying in fine-sifted sand that got everywhere. It proved wearying for the lads who until recently had enjoyed all the creature comforts of civilian life. As soon as 'Reveille' sounded, they hurried back to their billets. Each platoon was excused duties for twelve hours unless there was another alert. Much to Butch's disgust greatcoats were sorted without too much trouble. Each got their own back, along with two blankets at random, which were duly shaken out and folded into bed packs.

'Comin' fer a wash an' shave, Ern?' Ron asked. 'I could also do with a Gypsy Kiss.'

''Alf a mo, Ron, 'ang on a jiff,' he said, looking through his pockets for a ten pack of Players Weights.

'Look on yer locker, Nutty.'

'Oh yeah,' he said, picking them up, along with a box of matches. 'Okay me ole cock sparrer.' Ernie was first through the door, inviting a gentle jog.

After breakfast, Ron picked up his serge battledress blouse from the civilian tailor, after the neck had taken in to make it fit more snugly. He also sold badges, buttons and a few other odds and bobs. Ron bought a rifle green forage cap and a regimental tie with the rest of the money his mum had given him. While on his way back from the tailor, he picked up his laundry.

Sitting on his bed, he unfolded the freshly laundered towel. Inside was a pair of trunks, one pair of well-shrunk socks and his best angora shirt, sleeves still rolled up the way he had sent it to the laundry. Ron scratched his head, wondering why they had left them as they were. He collapsed on his bed, laughing and getting more than a few weird looks from his mates.

He lit a cigarette and picked up an unopened letter from his bedside cupboard. Mavis said how much she was missing him and wanted to know the train times from Waterloo. She also wrote about the good times they had had together, that she still loved him and was looking forward to seeing him in his uniform. She lovingly ended the letter. There was a post note, telling him that Jack had been in Maidstone when the German's started their big push; and that he had brought his new girlfriend, Kathy, to meet his mum. Ron tucked the letter into the breast pocket of his new blouse, meaning to have a more leisurely read later.

'Gor annovver bloke 'as she, Ron,' one of the wags called out.

'Never mind Deakin,' another said. 'There's plen'y o' skirt in Wilchester, jus' gaggin' fer it.'

Being on number two party meant they had to spend Saturday in barracks, in case of the real thing, or another snap rehearsal. They didn't object to a lazy day, writing, reading, cleaning boots, meal parades, playing cards, with the occasional trip to the naafi.

Good humour and endless pranks were the keynotes for the weekend.

Chapter 4

'Dunkirk'

Sunday was C Platoon's day for being allowed out of barracks, but not before they had attended church parade along with the rest from party three. Those who were Church of England formed up on the parade square at nine o'clock. When ready they marched to St Mary's, with the regimental band out in front, playing a selection of light military music. Roman Catholic's, Baptists and other creeds paraded half an hour later. The army was most particular when it came to a soldier's faith, giving him the means to worship God in whichever way he saw fit. However, dissenters were frowned upon; and still had to attend church parade as C of E.

Ron's first Godly moments were in Sunday school at the Wesleyan Hall in George Street, Camberwell. He had always been an ardent churchgoer, took great comfort from his faith and held to God's edicts, the best he could.

Having given himself the once over in a full-length mirror next to the door, he made his way to the parade square. The eight-strong squad of Baptists, in two ranks, were brought to attention by the duty sergeant and then checked over by an officer. In the absence of an NCO, the senior rifleman present took charge. The sergeant ordered him to proceed in a soldierly-like manner to the local Methodist church for their ten o'clock service. He marched them away, gave eyes right, a well-rehearsed salute and then passed through the entrance arch. Having wheeled onto the pavement, deserted this time on a Sunday morning, he marched in the direction indicated. He told his charges to 'march easy', clearly a time-serving soldier who knew the ropes.

They arrived at a modest chapel in a peaceful part of town. A notice at the end of the path announced this Sunday's speaker and services for the coming week. They entered the little chapel, two-thirds full. Ron walked down the centre aisle, with the rest sitting in one of the rear pews. He stopped, sat in the third row back, looked up at the carved organ loft and then at his mates, talking together. Above the pulpit was a hymn board with numbers for this morning's service. Hymnals and Bibles were already laid out, ready for use. He picked up a Bible, opened it at Deuteronomy and started reading about honouring thy mother and father until the service began.

As the minister gave his hell and damnation sermon, Ron thought of his childhood. His mum and dad had always been there, making him feel loved and needed. However, soon after starting junior school, his father died, turning his world upside down. He learnt to cope, fending for himself and fighting his corner. Sighing, he pushed away such thoughts and reflected on his current way of life, trying to lighten his mood. The past, with all its pain, seemed far removed and so unreal compared to what lay ahead. The prospect of going to war excited him, but at the same time made him nervous and anxious at what lay ahead once his war started in earnest. And where would he end up? Would it be a regular battalion or one of the newly formed ones? His thoughts flitted from one thing to another, seldom hearing what the speaker was saying, unable to settle his mind. The last hymn, with its simple but moving words, snapped him from his mawkish frame of mind.

Once the service was over, he placed a few coppers in an alms dish, queued behind other parishioners and then shook hands with the minister and speaker, thanking them for a lovely service and a thought-provoking sermon. Emerging into bright sunlight, he saw his chums smoking like chimneys further along the pavement.

The senior rifleman asked the proverbial question always on the tip of a soldier's tongue. 'Who fancies a cuppa an' wad?'

'What's chuffin' bird lime?' asked another.

'Nearly eleven,' Ron replied. 'I know a cafe just around the corner.'

They bundled into a little shop offering tea and cakes for one and six. A trim waitress, cute and elfin-like, wearing a black dress, frilly white apron and French maid's hat looked askance as they overran her tea shop.

'Hello, ducks,' the spokesman chirped. 'Can ya fix us up wif eight teas?'

She nodded amid a chorus of 'Good, gal!'

Each chose a cake and made the most of this Sunday morning tête-à-tête. In awe of these healthy, playful soldiers, she served them to all their wants. Finally, one lad gathered up the dirty crockery and placed it on the counter, no doubt trying to arrange a date with her, but nothing doing. They offered all-round thanks and then with further hints of meeting up later clomped out of the shop.

Ron bought a Sunday paper on the way back to the depot. The headlines read:

'Italy joins the war on Germany's side!'
'Germans only thirty miles from Paris!'

With a lack of civilian contact and limited access to newspapers, the common soldier had lost touch with the latest war news.

As they neared the main gate, the senior rifleman formed them up again and marched them passed the sentry, standing at ease outside the guardroom. They made their way around the parade square, halted in front of Oxford Circus and were dismissed.

Ron sat in his usual place. 'Where's everyone?' he asked before lighting up. 'I've never seen chuffin' place so empty.'

'Search me,' Ernie replied, drawing on a cigarette nub, nearly burning his fingers in the process. 'But food'll be plen'iful. We're bound ta ger loads o' buckshees. I've bin eyein' that rice puddin' fer ages.' He drooled, nudging him in the ribs. 'It were love at first sight.'

The dish in which it was made was the size of a dustbin lid and at least three inches deep. A golden skin, firm and succulent covered the entire pudding.

'Bed down when we get back, Ern.'

'You bet, Wilf.'

Mavis's one o'clock train gave Ron time to drop in at the Regal and see what was on offer the coming week. At the prospect of seeing Mae West and WC Fields in *My Little Chickadee*, he strolled along, thinking about his winsome, huggable Mavis. He wondered where they could go to be alone, so he could quench the yearning which almost consumed him.

As passengers wormed their way through the ticket barrier, he caught sight of a slim, golden-haired beauty tripping down the platform, getting looks from love-hungry soldiers going on leave.

He embraced her, then whispered, 'Hello, ducks.' Mavis wore a gold summer-weight two-piece suit, its small jacket curving over her shapely form. She was elegant in her neatness, having taken great pains over her appearance. He snuggled up close, pulling her close. 'You're a sight fer sore eyes.'

'Yer Mum wouldn't recognise ya, Ron,' she said, stroking his sleeve. Her bright, sparkling eyes conveyed her pride and pleasure at seeing him. And above all looking so upright and manly in his uniform. *How can someone change so much in ten days*, she thought as a warm feeling coursed through her body.

He held her at arm's length, taking in her radiant beauty. She smiled, took his arm and clinging to him walked away, arm in arm.

'Yer Mum an' Gran send their love. ... When will ya get leave?' she asked plaintively.

'Can't say,' he answered before changing the subject. 'Let's find the park, or do ya fancy a cuppa?'

They finally arrived at the park, made their way through a wrought iron gate and passed a red-brick house with a wealth of newly planted hanging baskets. Flower beds were laid out with what would soon be a blaze of colour. But how long would it stay that way before being turned over to growing food for the war effort? Something that was happening more and more to parks and open spaces.

Where two asphalt paths crossed, a Remembrance Memorial stood in the middle of a grassed island. Deeply carved on the front was *To The Glorious Dead of 1914-1918*. Below this was a list in alphabetical order of those who had paid the ultimate price. A bronze figure, showing a soldier in a typical warlike pose adorned the top, besmirched by bird droppings. Bunches of flowers slipped in half a dozen stone vases stood like sentries on the gravel either side. A tired collection of last year's wreaths and tributes from the mayor, councillors and others, resting against the memorial was a further reminder of those who gave their lives in 'the war to end all wars'.

The boating pool was a scene of intense activity. Stalwart oarsmen vied with each other, heaving away to impress their girlfriends as they sat demurely at the stern. Leaning over a waist-high railing, Ron and Mavis eyed these antics, grinning with delight. Swans, geese and other waterfowl darted hither and thither amongst the boats, snapping up pieces of bread thrown by children and their nanny's.

'Fancy a row, Luv?' Ron asked teasingly.

'Not on yer nelly.' She did not seem the boating sort.

'Come on, sweetheart, let's 'ave a Rosie,' he said, putting his arm around her and steering her towards a tea bar with canvas seats under a red and green striped awning.

'Pot of tea and cakes for two, please,' he said to a middle-aged woman.

'Ron, 'ow long will they keep ya 'ere?' she promptly asked. 'And where will they send ya once yer trainin's finished?' Her words tumbled out, questions she was dying to have an answer too. 'The BEF 'ave now left France. There's no stoppin' 'itler. Dunkirk were only good thing to come out of this God-awful mess. If it weren't fer Royal Navy an' them brave civvies with their little boats they'd be rowin' the … 'round this duck pond by now.'

'Can't say, Luv. Not that I won't. But I don't know. Once we've finished 'ere, I could be sent anywhere. It could be an infantry or a service battalion for special trainin'. I 'ope I end up in an armoured unit. I'd rather drive ta war than walk.' They both laughed. 'Anyway, don't let's dwell on that now. There are other things ta put our mind too. I know a lovely place, not far from 'ere. Come on,' he encouraged, standing and taking her hand, 'let's try bloomin' bus station.'

Half an hour later, they were in the village of Cobley, strolling around and looking for places of interest and somewhere to be alone. Soon there were fields on either side of a quiet country lane.

Arriving at a secluded copse, bounded by mature elm trees, they found a haven covered with a bed of moss, warm and inviting. They kissed and cuddled, looking lovingly into each other's eyes. Mavis took a square headscarf from her handbag and placed it on a particularly soft patch of moss. She sat down, legs to one side, facing him. He stroked her thigh through the silky fabric of her skirt. Lust and desire took over when he caught sight of pale skin above her stocking tops, along with pink French knickers. His petting ceased as passion took over. He spoke no words during their lovemaking and sated himself with little regard for her pleasures. The hedonistic act was soon over. She smiled with eyes that held love and sensually brushed grass and twigs from her skirt.

The young lovers smoked as they talked about what they had shared since first meeting at the local fleapit six months ago. Their talk once again got around to the war, making them maudlin. Saddened by what might happen, they were nevertheless resigned to an uncertain future. They agreed to carry on writing and swore to love one another forever.

'I've never seen so many soldiers,' Mavis maintained back in Wilchester, with soldier after soldier walking by, all intent on having fun.

Heads turned for a second look at the dazzling creature on that lucky bastard's arm. Some wolf-whistled, while one boldly cooed, 'Hiya, darlin'. Ya lookin' fer a *real* man?' Ron and Mavis gave him no heed as he strutted by, laughing and joking with his mates.

'Let's try in 'ere,' Ron hinted, smacking his lips. 'I could do with a pint an' a pack o' pork sctachin's. If they ain't on ration yet.'

As they entered the lounge bar of the Kings Head a sea of khaki, cloaked by half-timbered, mock Tudor walls, red leather stools and marble-topped tables warmly greeted them. Swaddies, NCOs, wives for those based in and around the town, or girlfriends, having secured a firm foothold, crammed themselves around tables piled with discarded glasses and half-finished drinks. Every bit of floor space was taken, and it hardly seemed possible it could hold any more, let alone two starstruck lovers in search of a drink. Soldiers, downing their beer as if it might soon be on ration, chattered away ten to the dozen. Eagerly they lined up in front of the bar, ordered drinks and quickly paid before someone jumped the queue. With glasses balanced on trays, they squeezed back to base and were greeted by cheers and hoots of laughter from their mates.

It was thirty minutes before departure and the train was already there. The young lovers lingered in the station bar, hugging and gazing into each other's eyes, only too mindful they would soon have to part.

A subdued feeling came over him as he entered the dismal hut, more depressing than a few hours ago. Loud, raucous laughter assailed his senses, lifting his spirits.

'Did she let ya 'ave yer wicked way, Deakin,' someone jeered from his bed. Three card players at the communal table shrieked at this tawdry crack.

Moments later, cloaked by the congenial atmosphere, Ron perked up and proposed, aided by the usual string of four-letter words that the said rifleman would do well to locate his mythical father. 'Come on Danny,' he furthered, 'did yer old man work bloomin' fairground?'

Everyone howled as Ron made his way over to the card players. He sat down next to a skinny lad from Whitechapel. 'Wotch ya,

Nobby,' he grinned, rubbing his shoulder against the one-time French polisher, almost knocking him off the bench.

'We're safe,' Nobby said, dropping a tosheroon in the pot, ''e's 'ad 'is oats.'

The kitty had plenty of silver amongst the coins, along with three crunched up ten-bob notes. Ron looked at Nobby's cards, pursed his lips, winced without conveying anything and watched as he scooped a tidy haul with the ace, two and three of clubs.

When Ron, Ernie and Wilf got back to the billet after tea Sergeant Bevan was waiting for them. 'Where the bloody hell have *you* three been?' he said before turning to the others. 'Right, *you* lot, form up outside. FSMO, as quick as you can.'

Wilf looked at Ron and shrugged. 'I understood some of that, but what the hell's FSMO?'

'Full-service marching order. We're on the move. Invasion's bloomin' started.'

They gathered up their kit and packed it in their small valise: towel, underwear, socks, spare shirt, mess tins, mug and eating irons, with folded groundsheet the regulation two inches below the flap. Everything else, greatcoat and webbing, they wore.

'Leave the rest as it is,' Sergeant Bevan growled, over-ruling any pleas or excuses. 'And don't fanny about. Quickly does it, lads.'

He formed them up outside, in a hurry, wanting to be on his way. 'Stand to your front. Squad! Move to the right in threes, right tarn! By the right, quick march!' As they marched up to the main gate, the members of hut twenty were clueless as to what lay in store for them.

With shiny, sweat-bathed faces, they marched down the busy High Street, ready for the next phase of this military adventure.

Swinging along, whistling at passing girls they now found themselves in a more salubrious part of town. A mixture of semi's and detached, fronted by neat lawns and herbaceous borders stood as a sentinel to domesticity.

'Squad halt!' the sergeant ordered. 'Stand at ease! Easy.'

A civilian, well in his seventies, wearing a belted raincoat and dark green trilby appeared from nowhere, standing beside the sergeant. They both walked up the crazy-paved path of the first house. Raising and rat-tat-tatting a brass, foxes-head knocker they stood and waited. After a brief pause, a harassed housewife loomed in the doorway, wiping her hands on her apron, listening to them as they told her what they wanted. She waved her arms as if to express some point, then grudgingly conceded to their request.

'First two!' Sergeant Bevan ordered.

They hurried up the path and went inside, leaving the woman scowling at the civilian before she slammed the door in his face.

Over the next hour, all but Ron and Ernie were put up in one's and two's in the remaining houses. Resigned to the fact they were about to be billeted in some stranger's house they agreed to stay together.

They found themselves in a small shop next to a police station. What was once the front parlour was now given over to selling sweets, though few were on offer these days, other than boiled sweets on ration. The bare stockroom, with a tabby cat sprawled on an armchair, was to be their new living quarters. The cat jumped down and started wrapping itself around the legs of a full-figured woman frying bacon on a small gas ring. With sweeping gestures, she explained her dilemma. How on earth, she said, could she take care of two strapping soldiers while at the same time looking after her shop? Having calmed down somewhat, the woman looked at Ron and Ernie as they shared the only armchair. She smiled then started to chuckle, her ample bosom jiggling as she tried to suppress a fit of the giggles.

'Not ta worry, ducks,' Ernie chirped as he stood up, leaving room for the cat to jump up beside Ron. 'Ya won't know we're 'ere. We'll be as quiet as church mice.'

'You can't share the same chair,' she suddenly announced. 'I'll pop upstairs and sort out another. You come with me young man,' she said to Ernie, 'and your nice friend can make sure your tea doesn't burn.' They both disappeared upstairs, giving Ron and the cat time to get to know each other.

Suddenly the bell over the door jangled, indicating someone had entered the shop. His instinct as a shop-worker was to get up right away and attend to the customer. Torn between disturbing the now snoozing cat and watching the frying pan, he decided to keep an eye on his second tea of the evening as the bacon turned golden brown and mouth-wateringly crisp. The smell was heavenly, and his stomach lurched at the prospect of more food.

As it turned out, the customer was the civilian billeting officer. He said they were to move to a house some distance away.

Before leaving the shop, they tucked into a bacon sandwich with lashings of brown sauce, regretting not being housed with the lady shopkeeper after all.

They stayed for just over a fortnight in their private quarters, sleeping and having meals there, loving all this lordly attention.

Later they found out the reason for their hasty after-tea upheaval. The troops, fleeing in their thousands from Dunkirk were being put up in depots around the country, for re-kitting, sending on leave and eventual return to their unit or a new posting.

Time blurred as their training carried on, unrelenting, rarely changing. Foot drill was always in the same squad position, staring at the back of the same head, knowing it as well as their own face. They sat with their mates at mealtimes, in the same place, eating the same tiresome food that they could hardly get enough of. The same jokes were aired, time and again, causing groans as an overused one-liner was told for the umpteenth time. The army seemed to thrive on routine, and each day was the same as the one before.

Strapped for cash much of the time meant naafi and pubs were frequented less than at the start of their training. Also, more than a few landlords had barred soldiers altogether, with the novelty of filling the bars with khaki wearing thin.

Quarrels broke out for the slightest reason, with fists sometimes flying. But things were quickly sorted, without intervention from NCOs. Unbeknown to them, they were starting to govern themselves. They were like brothers, watchful of each other when around those not of their family. Going about in close-knit groups, many had made lifetime friendships, despite how short that life might be in the service of one's king and country during wartime.

There were a few longed-for changes in training, with new lectures being added to replace those that had been on the timetable since day one. In their third week, they started rifle drill in preparation for guard duties. Some were from before The Great War, with more than a few having missing bolts, damaged back sights, barrels so bent you could hardly hit a barn door at twenty paces, and rifling rubbed smooth through years of use. The armourer assured them that once their training was over, they would be assigned a serviceable weapon. However, this was an army dreadfully short of equipment after Dunkirk.

The rifle went everywhere with them, even to the bog at times. Marching with one made quite a difference to route marches. At the trail, holding it at the point of balance was one way to carry a rifle. In the crook of the shoulder with the middle finger through the trigger guard was another. At the slope, balanced on the left shoulder is the most formal and could prove tiring for long periods. By far, the easiest way was to loop the sling over your shoulder and let it hang by your side.

One hundred and forty paces to the minute became second nature to these once clumsy recruits. Marches always followed the same route but were now longer and harder. They marched with a small valise, weighed down by three house bricks wrapped in a towel, pouches filled with stones to serve as ammunition and rifle and helmet. The most recent march had been forty miles in battlefield order, in a heat that could fry eggs on the pavement in minutes.

Map reading now featured strongly. Twice a week they were dropped off with nothing but a map, compass and canteen of water between each group of six. During one exercise they were dumped in the middle of Salisbury Plain, thirty-seven miles from the depot. They had to get back in ten hours, without being caught or using motor transport. A few got around this by stealing bicycles, which got the army in a whole lot of trouble.

At week eight, they started battlefield training. This involved live firing with Lee Enfield, Lewis, Brens, Sten submachine guns and sidearms. They practised on short, medium and long ranges, up to two hundred yards. With a Bren mounted on a carrier they fired at old Fords and Austin Seven's, peppering them to destruction. Ron proved to be one of the better shots and was awarded a marksman's badge and an extra fourpence in his pay. During this training, schemes and battlefield manoeuvres were always carried out in conjunction with light armour and artillery. Ron, having a good eye, was taken through the rudiments of range-finding by a helpful lieutenant in the Royal Artillery.

While staying at barracks in Salisbury C Platoon had to undertake guard duties at a stately home that had been taken over by the army early in nineteen-forty. Ron was on duty during one graveyard watch, midnight to four o'clock. He was tasked with guarding an imposing arch and a path leading to a Palladian Bridge spanning a river. The night was serene, with only the odd owl or bark of a fox. It was hard to believe there was a war going on. He felt calm, keeping guard with his happy thoughts for company. Suddenly, his musings were interrupted by the throaty snarl of heavy bombers. Just above the horizon was an orange glow in the direction of Southampton. From their loose formation and the occasional aircraft in trouble, he supposed they were coming away from a raid and were readying themselves for home. Again, it brought home to him that *his* own war was getting closer.

On another occasion, while on guard duty with Ron and Alfie on the Palladian bridge, Ernie got himself into a whole lot of trouble when he discharged his rifle. Bored out of his mind, he aimed at a large black bull some two hundred yards away and pretended to fire. To his amazement, the gun gave a loud crack, and the butt slammed into his shoulder. The bull bucked to one side took two or three drunken steps and then collapsed dead on its haunches. Called before the major, he was confined to barracks for fourteen days and fined a month's pay. The bull turned out to be the Earl's prized Welsh black and as a breeding animal was worth a small fortune, with the army making full reparation.

Ernie was the hero of the hour, getting his hands on some of the best cuts of beef in austerity Britain. At his next meal, the cooks gave him a large medium rare fillet of sirloin on a silver charger, to a round of cheering. Unable to eat even a quarter of it, he asked the mess staff to cut it into twelve equal portions and share it out between his mates, for which they were most grateful. They all agreed it was the best piece of steak they had ever tasted.

Next, they reported to the Brecon Beacons for what was loosely termed 'toughening up training', which involved living in two-man bivouacs for seven days of pure hell. An aloof captain tagged onto their platoon for the last few days. He went everywhere with them, rarely speaking and making copious notes.

Returning to Wilchester, they all agreed it had been the toughest four weeks of their life. Surely it could not get any harder. They were not to know.

C Platoon settled into the comparative luxury of barrack life, writing letters, reading, visiting the naafi and pubs, bulling boots and cleaning webbing. Once more, the highlight of each day was the card schools. A few of the more cautious types progressed to poker, making pots even bigger.

Some of the love-hungry jokers, whiling away their time, wrote anonymous love letters and slipped them in their washing, entreating the girls who washed their smalls to meet up with them. Some were quite successful with this approach, but a few ended up dating some of the plainer-Janes. And in one case a woman old enough to be his grandmother. The lark quickly died a death and was soon replaced by some other hair-brained scheme to while away the hours, until posted to a training battalion.

Mavis visited Ron twice more. The last time, because of travel restrictions and bomb damage to railway lines meant she arrived four hours late, only giving them enough time for a quick drink in the station bar. They both agreed it was best to wait until he came home on leave, whenever that would be.

Chapter 5

'The Blitz'

Sergeant Bevan spent most of the drill session switching between slow and quick march, in preparation for their passing out parade. In recent weeks, the NCOs had turned up the heat, drilling them two or three times a day and getting them to attend lectures from dawn until dusk, with only a short break to take on fuel. Any spare time was spent stretched out on their beds, resting their tired limbs and sore eyes.

'Phew!' Alfie puffed; wiping sweat from his brow. 'Thank Gawd that's over.'

Thirty riflemen tried to thread their way through the door, jostling each other to get to their bed so they could stretch out for a while before the next session.

'Rifleman Deakin!' an unfamiliar voice yelled.

'Over 'ere!' Ron shouted back.

'Ol' man Blakey wants ya,' said the duty corporal. 'An' at the double!'

'What for, Corp?'

'Ain't got a clue,' he grunted. 'I'm just chuffin' messenger. Move yer arse, son.'

'Wot's matter, Ron,' Ernie quizzed on behalf of the others, wondering why he was being summoned to the company office to see the adjutant.

'Fer Christ's sake, Ern, I don't know,' he sniped. 'I'll tell ya when I 'ave all the bloomin' gen.'

R Company headquarters had all the makings of a Wild West saloon, with its large wooden structure and porch-like shelter. Several swaddies were leaning on the rail, watching as Provost Sergeant Killick drilled four men, doubling them back and forth along the dusty road. The only thing missing from this mid-western scene were batwing doors and a couple of cow ponies tethered to a hitching post. Also, no sheriff was wanted here, only Company Sergeant Major Isherwood. He was quite capable of looking after all discipline matters hereabouts, keeping law and order in his part of town.

On either side of the adjutant's door were glass-fronted cabinets, holding battalion and company orders, along with shelf upon shelf of silver dating back to the regiment's formation.

The door opened and out trooped three men in single file, stamping their feet, so the hut shook at its foundations. 'Left, right, left, right, left! Prisoner and escort, halt!' the sergeant major barked. 'Fourteen days confined to barracks.' He frowned at the bareheaded rifleman. 'March him away, Corporal Dodds.'

'Next?' the sergeant major asked. Ron came to attention. 'What's your name, son?'

'Deakin, Sir! 637, Sir!'

'Stand at ease, Deakin. Just wait here.'

Ron marched into the office and was told by the CSM to salute. 'Rifleman Deakin, Sir,' the sergeant major said.

'Ah, yes. Stand at ease, Deakin,' the elderly captain said. 'I have a request for leave from your uncle. Apparently, your mother has been hurt in a recent air-raid.' After a few questions to confirm his home address, the officer said, 'Four days' compassionate leave. Carry on, sarn't major.'

Ron was given an advance in pay, ration allowance at two shillings and eleven pence a day and a return train ticket. The sergeant major dated his pass after duty on seventeenth of September to midnight on the twenty-first.

Since Dunkirk there had been a steady build-up of enemy shipping, landing barges and troops in the Pas-de-Calais and other French ports. The RAF tried to disrupt this force but made little headway against the Luftwaffe's efforts to protect their invasion troops. The London docks and the East End were heavily bombed. The damage was widespread, with hundreds of people rendered homeless. Air battles raged over Kent and the Thames Estuary, giving sightseers a chilling but memorable experience.

On leaving Waterloo, Ron saw first-hand the damage meted out by the Luftwaffe. The bus picked its way around deeply cratered roads, strewn with piles of rubble from buildings and shopfronts. It was a never-ending process of clear and repair, ready for the next raid when the whole process would begin again. Even with all this confusion, the bus made its way along unimpeded, showing it was business as usual. The High Street soon returned to some semblance of normality. Once the staff had swept up the glass, they placed witty, handwritten signs in the now open windows, alongside limbless manikins: 'Courtesy of Hitler'. 'Smashing times ahead'. 'Britain can take it, Adolf'. 'Are we downhearted – NO!'

From the top deck of a 37 to Herne Hill, Ron stared at the futility of it all, finding it hard to believe what was happening to his beloved London. As the bus made its way down Walworth Road, he saw furniture from former homes piled up at the side of the road. Much of it smashed beyond repair it waited to be reclaimed or burnt on one of the pyres which had sprung up all over the city. People hung around, sullen-faced, eager to know what plans had been made to rehouse them. Distraught mothers, nursing fractious babes conveyed their distress to their offspring. At the same time, young children happily played among the rubble, oblivious to their parent's terrible plight.

The conductress sat next to Ron, changing the destination sign from Camberwell Green to Brockwell Park. 'It's shocking, love,' she offered, brushing a wisp of hair from her face. 'Ya never know where they're gonna drop their bombs. Poor folk 'ave ta shelter all night. ... Where ya goin', soldier boy?'

'Old Queen Street, Camberwell.'

'Ah, they've 'ad one or two big un's there as well,' she said, laying it on thick. 'But not as bad as bloomin' dock area.'

She explained how anti-aircraft guns had been placed within the inner city. The crunch of the Ack-ack when an aircraft was caught in the crisscrossing beams of light shook the very earth. These unwelcome visitors, staying above the flak and diving when caught in the glare, flew on regardless.

When Ron arrived home, he found his mother was not badly hurt after all, though she did have her left arm in a sling. A house in the next street received a direct hit, with the shockwave throwing her to the floor.

144 Old Queen Street was a well-built terraced house, with an extensive cellar that had been reinforced by the council, so his mum and neighbours could share. Realising they would be spending a lot of time down there, his uncle and the others made it as homely as possible, with a table, chairs and four roughly hewn bunk beds.

Having spent time with his mum and grandmother, he suddenly announced, 'I'm jus' gonna pop an' see Mavis.'

'Tired of us already are ya, Ronald?' his gran said sagely.

'Never Mattie! Bloomin' earth'll freeze over first. Though I ain't clocked Mave fer weeks.'

'Young turtle dove,' she said, winking at him. 'Watch 'er old man don't catch ya. 'E'll skin ya alive.'

Mariah Matthews was the picture of a strait-laced Edwardian woman, embodying the era and the working class of London's East End. Her silver-grey hair – centre-parted and finished in a plaited bun – with her cheerful face and hazel eyes, showed proudly above her black crocheted shawl. The long gingham apron covered a wealth of petticoats and skirts, and her black side-button boots, and black lisle stockings gave the definitive touch to her daily attire. His Nanny Mattie, loved and worshipped by all, was a popular figure in Stepney. Known by young and old as Granny Matthews, she raised thirteen children, of which just five lived passed their teens. She was as tough as Harry Champion's old iron and had a heart of pure twenty-four-carat gold.

*

Ron surprised the Tonks's having tea.

'Cor blimey, Mave,' her father jollied. 'Look 'o's 'ere. Come in, son an' get stuck in. Ya look loike ya need a good feed.'

Once he had freed himself from Mavis's welcoming embrace, he sat between Sam and Hilda Tonks. Doreen, Mavis's younger sister, fussed like a bee around a rose bush, attending to his teatime needs. She worked at Woolworths on the Belgrave Road, Pimlico. As she poured his tea, she explained how each member of staff calmly guided customers to the nearest shelter in the event of an attack.

At dusk they heard the siren, warning of an imminent raid. Ron and the others hurried down the cellar steps for another night's vigil. Blankets and cushions were already down there, along with heaps of sandwiches and hot water in thermos flasks. If they were going to go, they would do so in comparative comfort and on a full stomach.

The desperate plight of London was bringing about a closeness within its citizens, unequalled anywhere in Britain, suffering and sharing the hardships together. One could only admire the courage of these people, whose acceptance of such things made them proud and tenacious. They settled for the simple things – food, friendship and security – needed to survive and live as normal a life as possible. Hitler's nightly raids were aimed at terrorising the people of London, and they would clearly bear the brunt for the immediate future.

Mavis's father explained how the first wave of bombers approached via the Thames Estuary, using the river and railway lines as a guide to the target. When in position, they unloaded thousands of flares and incendiaries, creating a beacon for the next wave. The heavy-laden bombers followed in their wake, with bomb doors open and bombs primed ready for release. Fires sprang up everywhere, gutting shops, offices and warehouses. Jangling bells from fire engines echoed throughout the night. Sam Tonks praised the fire services, who worked tirelessly as bombs and buildings fell around them. Begrimed, they struggled to quell firestorms running rampant, leaving charred, acrid remains. Mighty fires lit the sky, making it appear like day, tinting the clouds and horizon a blood-red-orange. Against this backdrop could be seen the ghostly shapes of gutted buildings and the occasional monument which somehow had escaped this welter of madness.

At first light, Ron made his way back to Camberwell, seeing for himself all the damage and the wretched souls as they sat outside their one-time homes, distraught and dejected. He was so proud of being a Londoner and so proud of its citizens, winning the praise of the entire world. His mood deepened into anger, making him steadfast to do *his* bit to end this lunacy. Street noises from traders grew louder, drowning out the terrible silence that always followed a raid. Horses stopping and starting, clanging milk churns and cheeky banter from chirpy tradesmen showed life still went on. People tried to be cheerful in the face of adversity. Yet, at times it was hard to keep smiling, especially with so much carnage around them.

Early evening Ron called on his Auntie Dorothy at her council flat in Deptford. 'How are ya, Ronald?' she asked, kissing him on the cheek. 'It's lovely ta see ya.'

'I'm fine thanks, Aunt Dot. Where's Uncle Fred?'

'Ya might know where 'e is this time o' day. 'E'll be proppin' up bar of 'is second 'ome.'

Ron arrived at the Cross Keys. His uncle's local.

'Well, look who's blown in,' Fred cried, grinning like a Cheshire cat. 'Give him a pint, Ethel. He looks like he needs one.'

Fred was in fine form, patting the seat by his side, urging Ron to join him once he had got his pint. He peered at his nephew from under his bushy eyebrows as he leant against the bar, pleased by his new-found confidence and splendid turnout. *Army life suits him*, he thought.

'You're a sight for sore eyes, my lad,' he finally said once his nephew had sat down. 'How much leave did they give you?' Uncle Fred, well versed in army ways, had sent a telegram to the depot, asking for compassionate leave so he could visit his injured mum.

'Four days, Uncle Fred,' he said, taking his first swig.

'Is Mum and Olive, okay?'

'Yeah, Mum's fine. A bit bruised. Nothin's broken. She were lucky. The doc said she could take sling off within the week. Mattie's 'er usual self. Fightin' fit an' 'avin' an answer fer everythin'.'

They soon got around to the fifteenth of September, when hordes of bombers, protected by as many fighters attacked the docks and East End. Burning barges were seen floating down the river, causing more damage as they drifted towards the estuary. At Silvertown, food stores, raised to the ground, discharged molten sugar into the Thames. Leaping blue flames devoured the oil and spirits flowing from the gutted warehouses. Woolwich Arsenal and nearby Plumstead suffered badly during the bombing, with troops being ordered back to barracks from cinemas, pubs and dance halls. Fred sometimes worked as a dockworker on Tripcock Pier and saw first-hand the damage caused to the Arsenal. The exact number of killed and injured had not yet been made public. Some said it was in the hundreds.

His uncle, enjoying his company – a lad he thought of more as a son than a nephew – became agreeably mellow as Courage's pale ale flowed through his veins. Grinning at Ron, whose clean-cut image and youth he envied, he was once more on his beloved subject – The Great War.

'The flower of British manhood,' he said without being prompted. 'Singing their patriotic songs and marching to their deaths. *Pack up yer troubles in yer old kit bag ...*' he sang for the benefit of Ethel and the others. The drinks he had imbibed before Ron arrived had removed any inhibitions ... though he had few to start with. 'Pack up be buggered,' he cursed. 'They never had a bloody chance, marching to their death.' He looked at his calloused hands, remembering better times, swallowed and sighed.

'Wot was it *really* like, Uncle?' he asked for the first time ever.

'You needed to live through it, to know what it was *really* like.

And I hope to God you never do. Not the way I did. The sights ... the things ...' He stopped and looked at his hands and then at his nephew. 'My clearest memory,' he said, starting afresh, 'was when I had to shoot one of our officers.' Ron put down his drink and stared at his uncle. 'Oh yes,' he said, seeing his look of surprise. 'But it was a blessed release for him. It still wakes me at night, even after all these years. The only person to know about it was your Dad. I've told no one else ... not even Dot.'

He fixed Ron with his steely grey eyes, resolved to tell him about the one thing that had haunted him for all these years.

'They made me up to sergeant two days before the Somme,' he carried on. 'By some miracle, I survived the initial attack while those around me were dying, horribly. There's nothing noble about death. It's messy, painful and final.' He shook his head to collect himself. 'When I jumped in a shell hole, I landed on top of one of our officers, Second Lieutenant the Honourable Edward Andrews. He was a good-looking kid, straight from England, only four months out of Marlborough College. In the next shell hole, we found four fusiliers, a corporal and three privates.

Under heavy fire, we went forward, taking cover every few yards. While holding up in a forward observation post, a whizzbang landed beside us, causing a large piece of shrapnel to rip across the officer's stomach, almost cutting him in half. He wasn't in any pain ... the shock you see. He just lay there looking peaceful, softly calling for his mother. It suddenly went quiet, as if I'd gone deaf. It was a weird feeling. I even thought I was dead, and the only one living was Andrews.' His words tumbled out, locked away for years. 'I heard someone say "please". The others looked at me, begging me to put him out of his misery. Then I heard it again, quite clear, a woman's voice. The officer was mouthing something as I cradled his head. When he looked away, I picked up his Browning and put it against his temple. As he turned and smiled at me, I pulled the trigger.' He shuddered and looked at his sleeve, expecting to see it once more besmirched with blood and brain. 'As soon as I fired the noise of battle started up again.

A few months later, I met up with the corporal. He said the sound of battle had been as loud as ever and he'd heard no woman's voice. He said I was off my rocker. I wrote to the officer's mother, telling her how brave her son had been and that he hadn't suffered. I received a letter back from his father, saying his wife had died while giving birth to Edward.' He paused, took a swig from a fresh pint, wiped the froth from his bushy moustache and carried on ridding himself of his pent-up misery. 'I went through hell after the war, drifting from job to job. I could never return to teaching English Literature. It didn't seem important anymore, being a teacher. The years I spent at Cambridge, trying to rid myself of my East End accent, to be accepted by the intelligentsia. In the end, it wasn't worth a jot. So many never came home. Out of my last year's tutorial, I was the only one to come back in one piece. Four died, two badly disfigured, one 'shot at dawn' and my roommate ended up in a lunatic asylum.

At the unveiling of the Cenotaph in Whitehall, by chance, I met the corporal again. It seemed fate that we should keep meeting like this. You were only a nipper when your Dad died.' He paused, thinking through what he would say next. '... I love you like a father ... always have done, ever since you were born. If you don't do anything else in this blasted war, Ron,' he said, drawing his musings to a close, 'keep your blessed head down and your eyes open. It's a cruel world.'

He explained that after all the horrors, he would not have missed it for the world, even with all the mixed emotions. The shock of seeing so many awful sights. The pain for all the things he had done. Love for his pals, many of whom never returned. And anger for the way the generals had perpetuated what ultimately became known as a costly and wasteful war.

'Your Dad's mob, the First Battalion Lancashire Fusiliers lost nearly five-hundred men on the first day of the Somme. Our top brass viewed twenty thousand killed as tolerable losses. Casualty lists were sent to Corps and Divisional Commanders in their fine chateaus, far from the front. It was a war of mutual annihilation,' he went on. 'Hungry, lousy, fed up and far from home, we spent four years of misery, shelling and terrible abuse. They were fine lads ... they were ... we won the war ... at what cost, though? Now we're going through the whole thing again. As if we hadn't had enough the first time. Mankind never learns from his mistakes.' He looked at the bar, remembering the many happy hours he had spent with Henry Deakin. 'Like me, your Dad had a bellyful of it. I'm sure his cancer was caused by being gassed in nineteen-seventeen. The wretchedness of winter in the trenches, all that mud and those horrid rats were hell on earth.' He paused and then said, 'No ... I hope your war's not like mine. Not by a long shot.'

He sighed, having divested himself of his pent-up anger, until the next time.

They were long lonely nights during the blitz, even though you were crammed in the shelters, shoulder to shoulder. It was the nightly pattern for Londoners, with 'alert' sounding at dusk and 'all clear' not going until dawn. Once morning came, everyone tried to put the horrors behind them and pick up where they had left off.

The hard-pressed RAF kept up their constant pressure on the bombers and fighters. Our brave pilots won the highest praise from the Nation. Winston Churchill called it '... their finest hour ...' and said they were '... the precious few ...'

The world over was praising the Londoner's stoicism and the doggedness of Britain not to buckle under the strain. The New York Times wrote, '... Britain stands today as a final line of defence against the worst form of aggression and everything free people detest ...' Churchill cautioned during one of his commons addresses, '... This may be zero-hour. ... Herr Hitler has lit a fire which will burn with a steady consuming flame until the last vestige of Nazi tyranny has been completely burned out ...' President Roosevelt said to Congress only a few days ago, '... America stands at the crossroads of its destiny. ... Time and distances have shortened. ... A few weeks have seen nations fall. ... We cannot remain indifferent to the philosophy of force now rampant in the world. ...'

The free world was voicing its support to those who fought against tyranny. However, words alone were not enough. What Britain and her allies needed more than anything was material support and in far much larger quantities than they were currently getting.

Chapter 6

'Dazzling Buggers'

The peace and quiet enjoyed by Wilchester differed markedly from the life and death struggle being played out in London. Ron breathed a sigh of relief as he handed his pass to the guardroom sergeant. He listened to the depot at dusk, taking pleasure from the familiar sounds. This life seemed to belong to another world. Its routine of bugle calls and khaki figures striding to and fro seemed to be welcoming him back.

There were only three platoon members in hut twenty. Two were stretched out on their beds reading, with a third at the table, wholly absorbed in writing that long-overdue letter.

'Wotch ya cock's,' Ron greeted.

Engrossed in their books and letter they briefly looked up and then carried on with what they were doing.

It seemed like ages since he had left the calmness of 144 and the madcap city with its churning noises. And he was now missing the solitude and comfort of having his childhood possessions around him. He liked to be with things that anchored him to the past, reminding him of the way it used to be. His bedroom, his own private space, had hardly changed since his father's death, and it had always been his haven of peace. A dark feeling came over him as he spread out his blankets, ready for a kip.

'Anythin' 'appen while I were away, Pete?' he asked, trying to draw some response from the letter writer.

'Laurel and Hardy have gone AWOL,' said Pete Draper.

Sam Olorenshaw, married with young twins, came from Bethnal Green. Born and bred in the East End, he worked as a tap-room-man at the Flying Scud on the Hackney Road. Twenty-nine years old, surly, hair as black as coal and more than a bit uncouth, it was unwise to joke with him because he was not too bright. If he failed to get your unique brand of humour, maybe thinking you were mickey-taking, then his fists would settle the matter. Before the war, he served in the Scots Guards. However, within a matter of months, he ended up in the glasshouse for nearly throttling a warrant officer to death. After serving two years, they discharged him in disgrace. A quick-tempered hard nut, no army rules would restrict him if he thought his family were in danger.

Sam and Stanley Coulsdon became good mates. No doubt hearing about the air raids, they would have hiked up to 'the smoke' to find out the extent of the problem for themselves. Stanley, a weedy twenty-year-old, looked up to him, lauding his hard-nosed, scrappy approach. He got on well with Sam, knowing his moods and fetching and carrying for him. There were no two ways about it, Olorenshaw would have dreamt up this little caper.

As his mates turned up, they made a beeline for Ron. Crowded around his bed, keen to find out what was happening in the city, they pressed him for information, concerned if their street or ward might have been affected in some way. He did his best to dispel their fears, playing down the danger.

The lively hubbub soon gave off a warmth that made him feel secure. He was back with his mates, once again part of his cherished platoon. And oh, how he had missed them.

The last three to arrive were Ernie, Wilf and Butch. 'Ernie, the Deacon's back!' Butch yelled, rushing towards his bed, then shaking it while grinning all over his face. Eager for news, all three flopped down, the springs twanging under their combined weight.

'Did ya getta bit o' love?' Ernie quizzed.

Ron smiled knowingly.

'Lucky bastard,' they all ribbed.

He answered all their questions, trying not to worry them too much about the Londoner's terrible plight. Slowly they drifted away to make their beds, ready for turning in.

The touch of army blankets, no sirens, raucous snoring and the company of his mates soon brought about a good night's kip for the Deacon, as some were now calling him.

The job of turning a bunch of civvies into an alert band of quick-thinking soldiers, requiring an instant response and mastery was a long process that could take anything up to a year. But due to the current climate, this had to be condensed into a much shorter period. For Ron's platoon and three others, this time would soon be up. They would shortly take on the full mantle of a rifleman and embark on their specialist training.

One lecture from a retired sergeant proved most enlightening. During any questions, Arthur Beezley asked about the battalions that made up The Rifles in peacetime. They learnt they usually had two, each manned by roughly eight hundred men.

The 1st Battalion spent early nineteen-forty with an armoured group, waiting for its full quota of vehicles, ready to support armoured units within a brigade. Engaged in building beach defences on the east coast they were sent to Dover as part of a small task force. They landed in France and were ordered to take up a position on the right flank of the BEF, around Lille, helping them to break out. However, a large armoured force thwarted their efforts. Instead, they focused on the defence of Lille, holding out for six days. This brave stand played a crucial part in taking over three-hundred thousand Allied troops off the beaches at Dunkirk, at a dreadful cost to the 1st, which was all but wiped out. The sergeant told them that a new battalion was being re-formed, somewhere up north.

The 2nd Battalion, about to return from Palestine after a two-year tour of duty remained in the Middle East on the outbreak of war. They were now with the 7th Armoured Division, fighting the Ities. As well as these two, they also had four London territorial battalions on the outbreak of war. Although woefully under strength, they soon increased their numbers and took on the role of motor battalions.

Riflemen were renowned for being self-reliant, courageous and tactically skilful. When they reviewed the command structure in nineteen-thirty-six, they naturally picked them for this new experimental role.

There were more than a few changes among R Company's NCOs in recent weeks. Jinksy now wore two stripes, Sergeant Bevan was transferred to the re-formed 1st Battalion, and Corporal Lowton took over C Platoon. They had a new one-striper, Lance Corporal Bagsley, a time-serving soldier in his mid-forties. Slight of build, somewhat clumsy, he was soon named 'mouth and trousers' because of his loud, noisy manner and luckless name. As soon as he came anywhere near them, you could always count on at least one East Ender mumbling, "ere cums mouff an' trousis.'

C Platoon's passing out parade drew near. It was hard to accept that these were the ill-assorted bunch of young, naive civvies who flocked into the station forecourt that sunny morning sixteen weeks ago.

Only one thing marred the peaceful, well-ordered routine of depot life, and that was the fear of what was happening back home. They craved news of families and came to rely heavily on those going up to 'the smoke'. And those all-important letters proved a valuable source of information, that was quickly passed on to others. But mail was now taking longer to arrive, sometimes up to a week. Each day they hung around the post-corporal, waiting for their name and turning away disgruntled if it was not among those called.

First thing Thursday, an order went up on the notice board, saying Friday morning would be a 'free from infection' check by the MO and full kit inspection by NCOs and QM stores.

Once their kit was checked against QM's records, they started Blancoing their small and large valise, cross straps, belt, pouches, sword scabbard, rifle strap and gaiters. They polished buttons and boots to a mirror finish and then set about cleaning their rifle and sword, checking for rust and grime and rubbing linseed oil into the butt and forestock.

Sergeant Lowton posted further orders, listing one-hundred and twelve names. Muster was set for 0700 on Saturday, with passing out parade at 1000 hours and CO's billet inspection an hour later. They all knew this called for ultra-cleanliness and perfect neatness. Late into the night, they set too, cleaning inside and outside hut twenty.

Next morning, with breakfast out of the way, they returned to hut twenty to give it the once-over. The stone edges around the stove, whitened by Rusk and painted with 'C PLATOON' in black – he was a signwriter in civvy street – made a focal point for their efforts, with brooms, mops and shiny pails arranged around it.

'Mouth and trousers' turned out to be worth his weight in gold. Like all the others he never went to bed, joining in bulling the hut. He walked up and down, casting an eye over each bed, with their kit deftly laid out. 'Fold that more neatly,' he would say at the drop of a hat. He went down on hands and knees, lining up the beds, telling the lads to 'move that one a touch forward' or 'push that one back a smidge.' At last, he called them outside, cast a keen eye over the billet once more and then closed and locked the door.

'Passing out' dress was to be best-serge, belt, sword scabbard, rifle and SD cap. All agreed to dress the same, with a few clubbing together to help those who could not afford to buy a rifle green forage cap.

Sergeant Lowton looked at them with glowing pride as he gave them a short pep talk. 'I want the best you've got this morning, lads. I'll not accept second best.' He paused, eyeing each one. 'I want plenty of swank, pride and bullshit. Call it what you will. I know I've got the best platoon *ever* to pass out of this place.' Each man threw out his chest. 'But I also want the others to bloody well know it. Get me?' They nodded as one. 'Now then,' he said, coming to attention. 'At ease, lads. Hands together. Push down hard. Feel the pull on those shoulders. Chests out, you bloody dazzling buggers.' They warmly smiled. 'Stand to your front. Squad!' As one they came to attention, giving him precisely what he wanted. A smile creased his face before he strode out to meet the platoon officer. He halted, saluted and informed him, 'Platoon present and correct, Sir! Ready for your inspection!'

The second lieutenant returned his salute and began to check over each man.

'For inspection, port arms!' the sergeant next ordered. The officer studied each rifle, pulling it away from the man and sometimes taking it out of his hands, intent on finding a smudge of oil or a speck of dirt. 'Examine arms!' the sergeant finally ordered. Each man slid back the bolt and pressed down the magazine spring with their thumb. The officer then put his eye to the business end to glimpse shiny rifling.

Forming up with three other platoons, they faced a white dais, level with the regimental headquarters main entrance. The door opened to reveal RSM Bowing and two officers. They came to attention, marched onto the parade square and halted beside the dais.

Lieutenant Colonel Pendleton, with his stocky, thickset aide-de-camp by his side nodded at the RSM. With pace stick under his right arm, the sergeant major took up station some way off, ready to call the parade to order. To one side stood the regimental band, playing an array of military music. He brought the waiting ranks to attention and dressed them in open order. When satisfied with their dressing, he marched up to the CO, saluted and handed the parade over to him.

Down each rank walked these smartly dressed career soldiers in their superfine SDs, black Sam Browne's, black rank badges and black buttons nodding here and pausing there. Once finished Colonel Pendleton and the major made their way back to the dais. The colonel briefly addressed the parade, thanking them for all their hard work and stressing The Rifles proud tradition. He then said they would be moving to a new camp to begin the next phase of their training.

In column-of-threes, they marched past the dais. Each rifleman, his forage cap perched over his right ear, on order from the platoon officer, snapped his head to the right, ready for the saluting colonel. They then marched passed the RSM, getting a nod of thanks from him and made their way off the parade square towards their huts.

The CO, platoon officer and RSM paused outside hut twenty, giving Sergeant Lowton time to bring C Platoon to order. 'Stand to your front.' he ordered. 'Squad!'. Thirty boots smacked the tongue and groove flooring, seemingly making the hut jump.

The colonel returned the sergeant's salute and then nodded at the RSM to take over, leaving him free to chat with each man as they lined up in front of their bed. This pleasant, aged warrior smiled and seemed to take a keen interest in his now departing young charges. Lieutenant Colonel Pendleton joined the army as a boy soldier in eighteen ninety-nine. Within a matter of months, he was fighting in the Second Boer War. By nineteen-fourteen Jasper Pendleton was a captain. On his left breast, he wore various campaign ribbons, along with an MBE, DSO and MC with bar.

Once their final inspection was over, they could relax, making up their beds and giving some thought to how they would spend their last weekend together. The post corporal waited until the CO had cleared the lines. Ron received a letter from Mavis. She said the raids were not as bad as they previously had been, though landmines were now being dropped, but none in Camberwell. Ration queues had become a daily part of life. Kathy and Jack were thinking of getting married. Also, Jack was stationed at Pirbright, Surrey and could get home most weekends.

Nobby said Stanley Coulsdon had been picked up and was in the guardroom. He had seen him taking empty dixies back to the cookhouse, guarded by Provost Corporal Foster. 'Talk abahhht David and Goliath,' he said. 'Stan's such a tiny bugger. The Corp dwarfed the poor little sod.' Apparently, they found him sleeping rough in Regents Park. Olorenshaw would be a different story. He would have got a no-questions-asked-job and moved a few times to muddy the waters.

Everyone agreed to have a few beers in town, now their time for departure was here. They also said they would try and stay together when they got to the new camp. But in the end, the decision was not theirs.

The talk of a few turned to their lady friends, whom they would have to leave behind, with friendships ripening into something more serious.

Countless riflemen would remember the Sentinel public house that faced the main gate. The roughly furnished pub the weekend of 'passing out' would be packed with khaki-clad youngsters, jostling with trays of beer and taking it in turns aiming blunt darts at a moth-eaten board. A few brave girls, joining in, coped well with these newly fledged riflemen.

Through the open door of the bar, a pianist could be heard playing the opening bars of *You Are My Heart's Delight*. Taffy Morgan, the depot's well-known sergeant cook, would soon render this delightful song in his polished tenor's voice. Taffy's presence in any pub ensured a great night.

Ron, Ernie, Whitey and Jimbo joined in, trying to keep up with Taffy in a hearty singsong. They sang with gusto, spurred on by the next chapter of their war.

Chapter 7

'Motorised'

During the winter Ron's new platoon carried out field training on the open, snow-clad hills and Plains surrounding Netheravon. This small Wiltshire town, two-thirds enclosed by the River Avon, lies three miles east of Salisbury Plain, four miles north of Amesbury and sixteen miles from Salisbury.

For the first quarter of the twentieth century, Netheravon camp housed many famous cavalry regiments. Proud names such as The Skins, The Bays, Death or Glory Boys, Cherry Pickers and The Greys in their turn trooped and wheeled to the trot, canter, gallop and charge across these broad Plains.

Barracks of that era had stables on the ground floor and trooper's quarters on the first, reached by robust iron stairways at each end. The camp bore names of Indian towns, Meerut, Simla and Multan.

A mounted regiment in those days would have consisted of around six hundred horses, with each having a detailed record card, covering its life in the army. It listed their number – branded on the front right hoof – its age, height in hands and colouring, any unique markings and veterinary notes. Most crucial though was its temperament and any bad habits. Lucky be the trooper who cares for a white-stockinged chestnut, white blaze between eyes, well-mannered and placid. While his mate, a few stalls away approached his jet-black mare with a broom in hand. Just in case it decided to lash out at him. During mucking out, horses would cock their ears at the string of abuse reeled off by their early morning grooms. The health and wellbeing of these noble creatures was a top priority for each trooper. The longer someone cared for an animal, the stronger the bond grew between them. Fanciful names thoughtfully chosen by the troopers would grace white-washed walls above their stalls.

Horses were always groomed to a high standard, even for a short canter across the Plains. The troopers – equally well turned out – in best SD, riding Bedford cords, buckskin strapped chaps, puttees and spurs would clip-clop along country lanes as if they owned the world.

The blood of most troopers would have run cold when forced to give up their trusted, almost human friends for those stolid armour-plated giants. They surely wondered how on earth they would master these whirring steel monsters with their grinding tracks. The wind of change had blown through the cavalry for years, sweeping away any thought of horses in a modern army, other than for ceremonial purposes.

The stables now became the motor transport line, with the Farrier-Sergeant taking on the duties of the Sergeant-Fitter.

The lads in 8 Platoon, A Company 3rd Motor Training Battalion, were quartered in Meerut Barracks. An iron-clad balcony stretched the full length of their billet, with Blancoed equipment and freshly washed kit draped over the railing once parades were out of the way.

The ablutions were below in what had been the stable wash house and could easily cater for the early morning rush. But it still meant crowds of jostling, khaki-shirted figures with white braces dangling, trying to shave in the dim light while holding a steel mirror and soaping up in cold water.

''Ere, mate,' Ossie moaned, 'yuv jus' baptised me bloomin' daisy roots.'

'Well keep yer chuffin' elbows ta yerself then,' Jimbo hit back. 'It'll give ya an excuse ta polish 'em.'

'Then ya can clean yours at same time, can't ya, 'Ossie said, tipping a bowl of scummy water over his pal's mirror-like boots.

As a posting, Netheravon, being quite remote, left a lot to be desired, with the nearest pub three miles away. Also, its single branch line was patrolled by MPs, checking leave passes before letting anyone board the train. There was no easy way out of this vast army camp, and even if there were the nearest pictures and dance hall were in Salisbury, with no transport to be had anywhere.

Distractions from the routine of training were few and far between. The Garrison Theatre offered a sprinkling of fresh faces with each change of concert. Crown and Anchor, bingo and shove ha'penny took place after pay parade on Friday night in the 'other ranks mess'. Games such as these proved costly on a soldier's meagre pay. The fortnightly Garrison theatre show was the highlight of the week and was looked forward to by all. A milling crowd of tank wallahs, gunners and riflemen jostled each other, waiting for the single door to open. Cries of joy would announce the start of a frenzied dash to get in and secure a front-row seat, so they could ogle the girls.

'Friggin' 'e'll, mate,' Ernie cussed, turning on a gunner behind him. 'Wotch it! That's me bleedin' arm yuv just bashed. I use it m'self sometimes ... loike ta keep it in good workin' order.'

Having got himself out of what could have turned into a punch up, Ernie clumped along the row, trying to find a vantage point away from the pillars. Anyone finding themselves stuck behind one would have to ask the man by his side for a running commentary.

The sound of instruments warming up announced the show was about to start, which was duly greeted by a chorus of clapping, foot-stamping and cheering in the hope of a good night's entertainment.

The compère, getting everyone in a receptive mood, started with a raucous singsong. Ron, Ernie, Whitey, Alfie and Benny launched with gusto into a much-loved Gene Autry song:

> *'Mexicali Rose stop crying*
> *I'll come back to you some sunny day*
> *Every night you'll know that I'll be pining*
> *Every hour a year while I'm away*
> *Dry those big brown eyes and smile dear*
> *Banish all those tears and please don't sigh*
> *Kiss me once again and hold me*
> *Mexicali Rose, goodbye' ...'*

Once they had belted out *Mexicali Rose* a couple of times, the tenor changed, and the band struck up another old favourite:

'If you were the only girl in the world
And I were the only boy
Nothing else would matter in the world today
We would go on lovin' in the same old way
A garden of Eden just made for two
With nothing to mar our joy
I would say such wonderful things to you
There would be such wonderful things to do
If you were the only girl in the world
And I were the only boy ...'

After the final bow, the door clattered open, and there was a mad dash for the naafi before closing.

'Come on, Ron.' Ernie elbowed his way to the counter. 'Let's be 'avin' ya. Yer in chair. ... Two teas an' two Eccles cakes please, Luv,' he eventually said to a rather cute brunette no older than sixteen.

'Not a bad show tonight,' Ron ventured, cutting his cake into quarters. 'Bit of a giggle. The blonde dancer 'ad a sugar and spice figure and a leggy pair of gams. Though 'er boat race weren't up ta much.' He took a piece of cake and after swilling it down with a mouthful of tea added, 'I'm glad they've kept a few of the old gang in 8 Platoon.'

'Me too. Though I don't know 'ow long that'll last. But I 'ope you an' me can stay together. If I'm gonna feel the 'eat of action, I'd rather 'ave you by me side.'

Ron said nothing, smiled and rested his hand on his arm. They had become good friends. He also hoped they could stay together, shoulder to shoulder. One day, when old in the tooth and crotchety, they would brag about their war over a pint at the Blue Anchor, just like his dad and Uncle Fred used to do.

Field training now included river crossing, laying and detecting mines and the use of barbed wire. They carried out each exercise by day and then by night. Moonlit nights, however, were rarely picked because it was just not pukka.

When river crossing, boat crews were detailed first, with Bren gunners setting up on each flank to give covering fire. If any were lucky enough to stay dry – a miracle in itself – there were always a few so-called mates to egg on the others to dunk the poor swaddy.

In the pitch-black they carried the boat shoulder high, bobbing up and down as per terrain, with one end dropping as Benny's foot found a rabbit hole. 'Hold on, Sol,' Ossie cussed, 'ya're all over fuckin' place. Sort yer flamin' plates aahhht ya thrupenny bit. Keep yer friggin' end up. I'm losin' mine.'

As soon as the boat was grounded, the fun began. 'Heave ya lazy sods!' Sergeant Wesson yelled. 'Get yer bleedin' backs into it. Come on you idle buggers. Push you, wankers.' There was no way the twelve-man boat would move in the shallows, even though it was only made from wooden struts and canvas. He added his weight, pushing and shoving. 'Come on! Put yer fuckin' backs into it! Push! … An' again, push!' The mud briefly gave up its hold, and the boat moved a tad. 'That's it.' It moved again, helped by more water under its keel. 'Okay,' said the sergeant, 'in ya go, Whip.' Now floating freely, with a few guys holding it back, he ordered the rest to jump in and start paddling like mad. Ron thought of his holiday in Cliftonville when his Uncle Fred would hire a canoe and paddle Jack and him far from the beach. The madness of thinking about such a thing at a time like this, cold, fingers rubbed raw, muscles aching and soaked to the skin by pelting rain.

Laying and lifting mines could prove a ticklish business, where one careless slip could prove fatal. Sappers laid mines from the major datum-line, with a plan being made to record their position. When trying to locate mines, a steady probing with a sword and feeling with fingertips was the favoured method, by choice on your stomach to spread the weight. Mines tended to be more prevalent in ploughed fields and dirt tracks. Any disturbed ground was a sure-fire sign Teller or anti-personnel mine was just under the surface. If speed was of the essence, and they were not to be lifted straight away, then white tape was used to show any laying patterns. As you probed, it was also advisable to keep an eye open for tripwires, checking if they were a push or pull variety. While all this was going on, especially when you were less proficient, it was reassuring to know the mines were not armed.

When some dipstick forgot his thick gloves and the coils of barbed wire had to be untied and stretched, he could be heard cursing his stupidity. 'Come on ya bastard, open up,' he fumed, urging the stubborn coil, bouncing it up and down, hands torn to shreds. 'Whose thumb-suckin' idea's this, anyway?'

'Watch it, mate,' a voice softly called. 'Brownie's only over there.' Lieutenant Browning was their platoon officer and had the hearing of a barn owl. 'He'll string you up by your balls if he catches you talking like that.'

'Fuck 'im,' the now angry undoer softly cussed.

Platoon in strike and defence over various types of ground and making the best use of cover was practised time and again. Before attacking one first had to decide whether to place a light machine gun on the flank and advance from the front; or leave the Bren facing and attack from the sides, so encircling the defenders. When putting in their final charge, each man would scream the worst oaths and invectives imaginable. 'Charge, you loathsome bastards!' they would cry. 'At 'em you Cowson's buggers!'

Even though they were fully-fledged riflemen, their training never stopped. A number were put through a transport course, learning how to drive and maintain fifteen hundred-weight trucks. Others were given instruction on the Bren-gun carrier or personnel carrier. Their sergeant and officer graded each man by questions and skill tests, so they could apply what they had learnt when posted to an operational unit.

Of those who had been at Wilchester, only ten remained in 8 Platoon, and to a man, they were all Londoners. This included Ron, Alfie, Jimbo, Whitey, Ossie, Whipper, Ernie, Rusk, Benny and Sharpy. It was reassuring to have a few of the old crowd around them. Taking comfort from this, they hung around each other, living in each other's pockets and going everywhere together.

Every so often a platoon would be warned for an overseas draft. After returning from fourteen day's embarkation leave, they could be seen coming away from the QM stores, loaded down with a white sea bag, holding khaki drill shirts, shorts, hose tops and other kit needed in a climate that could top one-hundred degrees Fahrenheit in the cool season.

'Annovver George Raft went aahhht today,' Ernie told his pals. 'Middle East, I fink? Warm an' sticky. Not bloomin' sort I loike.'

'How'd ya know?' Ron asked, knowing full well where they were heading.

'None of 'em were smilin'. The poor sods looked loike they'd won second prize for two weeks in Brummingham when first prize were fer one. Anyway, they'd a white topee under their arm. ... I'd loike ta get me knees brahn,' he shortly added. 'An' they say them dusky eyed bints learn abahhht sex from a right early age. It's because of chuffin' warm-blood, ya know.'

'That aside, me ole cocker, you'll soon know when it's your turn,' Ron told him, fed up with all this overseas draft talk.

'Shall we put his name down for a Middle East posting?' Sharpy teased.

'Yeah, good idea, Joe. We could say 'e wanted ta gerra bit of a tan.'

'Turn it orf, you two,' Ernie hit back. 'Stop takin' the—'

'Ah, he's turning Charlie,' Sharpy said, egging Ron on. 'No bottle. That's his problem.'

By now Ron and Ernie were scrabbling about on the floor, trying to get a headlock on each other.

'Come on ya ugly bugger,' Ron urged as he got the upper hand. 'Give us a kiss, you old Mullock, an' I'll let ya go.'

It took up to three months to reach the Middle East, starting from Liverpool or the Clyde. It was a long, fraught journey around the Cape in crowded troopships. They would stop at Cape Town and Durban before arriving at Suez, where North Africa was giving Britain its only successes.

The BBC announced daily of Britons gains in the Middle East. Bardia, Tobruk, Sidi Barani were the names of these cut and thrust battles. British forces squared up to the Ities south of Benghazi. The newly termed Eighth Army routed 250,000 – eight times its size – and drove them back five-hundred miles. Taking 130,000 prisoners, eight-hundred artillery pieces, four-hundred tanks and eight generals. Despite this crushing defeat for the Axis forces, *Generalfeldmarschall* Erwin Rommel soon took charge, pushing British and Commonwealth troops all the way back to Tobruk.

They were fortunate indeed to be taught by some of those who had so recently seen action. The officer in charge of their training was a company commander from the ill-fated 1st Battalion. He lost his right arm during the stand at Lille and was awarded a Bar to his MC. Thomas Wesson, 8 Platoons sergeant, another time-serving soldier had seen action in the desert with the 2nd Battalion. After the death of his wife and daughter in an air raid, he was sent home. As an experienced soldier, he was a safe pair of hands to have around. The lads thought highly of him, hoping he would be with them when they saw action for the first time. However, for all that, he had a maddening habit that got on everyone's nerves. When briefing the men while on exercise, he would forever be in a crouching position, as if he were still in action, fearful of being spotted.

'Reminds me of a bleedin' diddycoy,' Ernie mouthed, nodding at the sergeant as he addressed his section leaders. 'Always squattin' on 'is bleedin' 'aunches. 'E finks 'e's still close ta chuffin' action.'

'It's 'is trainin',' Ron surmised. 'But he knows 'is stuff. An' I hope 'e's with us when we get *our* baptism of fire.'

'Do ya know, pal—'

'What?'

'—ya make me guts turn over wif such talk. I'm poppin' ta the bog. Ya comin, tosspot?'

Company Sergeant Major Cope, a competent old warhorse of sixty-three, was also an ex-2nd Battalion man. He had a spreading waistline, bald head and bushy, greying moustache. He started his service life as a boy soldier, took part in the Boxer Rebellion in Peking and was with the BEF in The Great War. Like many old soldiers, he was brought out of retirement on the outbreak of war. After Saturday muster parade he would oversee a drill session, making his presence felt, checking if any had neglected their drill or misplaced some sharpness. After the CO's inspection, he would mete out a small measure of punishment if a billet was below standard. After final dismissal, except for those on guard duty or cleaning their billet, everyone was free for the weekend.

'Come on, slowcoach!' Ron yelled back at Ernie as he made his way along the iron-clad balcony. 'Ger a move—'

'Keep yer 'air on, lightening.'

'Yer a shiftless sod at—'

'Wot abahhht Jimbo and Oz?' Ernie butted in, ignoring him.

'Are they comin' as well?'

'Of course, they are, pillock-brains.'

'Will their Mum let 'em come an' play?'

'Bollocks, ya clever arse,' he hit back. ... 'I'll just check.'

All four made their way towards the motor pool, ready for a grand outing. Half a dozen Bedford's were lined up outside the transport office, ready to ferry their cargo of mischief to nearby towns. Having no benches, they rode standing up. Each man held onto the metal frame, or the man by his side, swaying about like stalks of wheat in the wind while at the same time trying to avoid being tipped out the back when the lorry accelerated. A pleasant time would be had in these busy Wiltshire towns, offering anything to delight and amuse the happy-go-lucky riflemen.

Now their training was over, they would soon learn to which battle zone they were to be sent. So, who could blame them for seizing these last few moments of pleasure?

They knew their toughest challenge was yet to come.

As they wiled away their time, it was hard not to think of those back home, living through the terrible raids that had started up again. Other cities were now suffering as London had, such as Cardiff, Hull and Sheffield. They were not only bombing places of industrial importance, but also urban areas where the workers lived. For the time being a unique situation occurred, with fully trained soldiers cosseted away in relative safety. While at the same time their loved ones battled for their lives, standing up to Hitler's merciless raids.

Each rifleman had his own story to tell about the bombing, the endless loss of life and having to spend their precious leave in air raid shelters with strangers. Stories of Londoners using the tube stations, sleeping side by side, tightly packed on the platforms quickly spread, adding further heroism to these stalwart citizens. This banding together, sharing each other's sorrows and singing each other's praises was proving an inspiration for the free world.

Britain and her allies were surely going it alone.

Chapter 8

'The 5th Battalion'

Three members of 8 Platoon had already been picked as section leaders, with another made up to lance corporal. Rumours were rife, and everyone reckoned these promotions were in advance of moving to an operational unit.

'Nah bleedin' tapes fer me, matey,' Ossie announced. 'I've gotta bloomin' nuff ta look aahhht for.' He thumbed his chest.

'Jealous are we, Oz?' asked Whitey.

'Nah bleedin' way. I'd rather 'ave bloomin' clap.'

'I thought you'd already got it,' Whitey countered, laughing at his own wisecrack.

'Bollocks, fishcake.'

For weeks, the talk had been about the fact that their relaxed way of life would soon be at an end. All the toing and froing finally bore fruit, when a list went up on the notice board, telling 8 and 9 Platoon of kit inspection by QM stores and a 'free from infection' check by the MO.

Two days later a party of sixty formed up on the parade square in full-service marching order, ready for counting and checking. Large valises and kitbags with names and service numbers stencilled in black were piled up outside Meerut Barracks, in preparation for loading onto a Bedford.

With a final look at the place that had been home for eight months, Ron and the others headed for the railway station aboard two charabancs.

'We're off ta Middle East, Ron,' Ernie said, nodding as if he already knew where they were heading. 'Lock up yer women, Mustafa.' He rubbed his hands together, thinking of brown knees and Mustafa's dusky daughters. 'Ernie Price is on 'is way.'

'If 'e catches ya sniffing 'round 'is women 'e'll chop yer John Thomas off with a blunt carvin' knife. You'll end up a eunuch, servin' 'is harem jellied eels.'

'Ouch! That'd bring tears ta me mince pies.'

'Wot, 'avin' yer Hampton Wick chopped off or servin' jellied eels? Anyway, numskull, where's yer tropical kit?' Ron furthered. 'You ain't goin' anywhere warm. Not until we meet up with Fritz. Come on, Ern, ya useless clod, use yer 'eadpiece.'

They climbed aboard three carriages on the single track, waiting for the engines return. Taking off their ton-weight valise, they heaved them onto the luggage racks to be forgotten until the last minute. They then stacked their kitbags on the floor, sat back with their legs resting on them, took out their cigarettes and gave some thought to their destination. A shrill whistle and clanging of couplings announced the engine had returned. Ron promised himself that if he were ever a civvy again, he would never get on a train or bus without at least knowing in advance where it was going.

Low and behold, they headed nonstop for London. Thrilled at the prospect of a few hours in the city of their birth they chatted idly about their favourite pub and dancehall.

'Guard duties in London, Ern,' Whitey joked. 'Just think, home every night. Utter bliss.'

'Bliss! Piss more loike! Yuv got more chance kissin' chuffin' Pope on 'is—'

'Price!'

'Yes, Corp?'

'Button it! We wanna rest from your incessant rabbitin'.'

'Whatever ya say, Lance Corporal Ru' ... Farley.'

They finally arrived at Waterloo. Any thought of home visits or pub crawls were well and truly out of the question. The NCOs were watchful of their charges, keeping their eyes peeled just in case someone was planning to nip off for a few hours. As soon as they were counted, they were marched towards the concourse. Once more a Bedford and two charabancs were waiting to take them to Kings Cross for the next leg of their journey.

More stations flashed by as they sped north, stopping at Hitchin and then Grantham where rations and mugs of tea were handed out by a sourfaced sergeant WRAC and her chatty girls. Next stop was Newark, followed by Leeds and lastly York. The officer ordered them to debark, warning not to leave so much as a toothbrush behind.

Riflemen and junior NCOs were formed up by the sergeants, and the roster was gone through, checking each man in alphabetical order. Relieved they had not lost anyone they marched them to platform three, where yet another train waited for the jostling, overloaded soldiers.

'In ya go, Alfie,' Ernie said, holding the door open. 'Give us yer portmanteau. Ladies first.' He lifted his kit bag and placed it on the luggage rack.

'Thank you, young man,' Alfie answered, matching his infectious banter. 'So, so kind. It's nice ta meet a soldier wif such lovely manners. Instead o' the course, loathsome twats ya come across nowadays.' He took some shrapnel from his trouser pocket and handed him a shiny farthing. ''Ere, young man.' He dropped it in Ernie's proffered hand. 'Go and buy a nice big gobstopper—'

'Thank you, miss,' he said, shuffling his feet like Charlie Chaplin and doffing his cap before giving him the finger.

'—an' fer Gaud's sake choke on the blessed thing.'

They finally arrived at Pickering, North Riding, Yorkshire, where more lorries waited.

The Bedford's raced along dry-stonewall-lined roads, up hills and down dales, before turning down a track that disappeared into the mist. After a ten-minute rutted drive, they came upon a sheltered clearing in the middle of a large wood. Holding sway was a block of offices, so out of place with its surroundings. To the side and rear sprawled a series of corrugated Nissen huts. A black and green sign said:

COMPANY HEADQUARTERS
J SUPPORT
5th BATTALION – THE RIFLE REGIMENT

The senior sergeant ordered them to get down and place their kit in a pile, ready to be marched to the dining hall for a late lunch.

White-capped, overall-clad cooks filled plates pushed forward and poured into tea-stained mugs a thrifty measure of scalding, weak, sugarless tea.

As their hunger pains lessened, Ron and Ernie questioned a couple of mess staff. They learnt their new home was a mile from the village of Croftleigh, which lay at the heart of the North Yorkshire Moors. The nearest decent sized town was twelve miles away. Shocked by its isolation and the fact Croftleigh had no pub, they were more than a bit miffed by the absence of a ready watering hole.

Battalion HQ was housed in the main buildings, while J Support bunked down in Nissen huts to the side and rear. This maze of buildings had once been an agricultural college for North Yorkshire. The rest of the Fifth was based six miles away at Saxton Hall, a large manor house commandeered on the outbreak of war.

After their sparse meal, half found themselves in an empty Nissen hut with two rows of wooden bunk beds and little else. A monster of a stove, breathing and roaring like a blast furnace stood in the middle of the hut. Its soot-blackened pipe disappeared through the ceiling, smoking like mad at the joints. Blankets, palliasse and pillow were already laid out on each bed. The hut NCO told them to unpack because this was to be their billet from now on. Ron, Sharpy, Ossie and Jimbo were the only ones still together. The rest were told to bed down in a spare hut, ready for taking to Saxton Hall the next day.

'Nice place,' Ron said, flapping his blouse. 'It'll do me. Though it's as warm as Gypsy Nell in 'ere. Let's take bloomin' bunks over there,' he added, hoisting his kitbag and valise. They made their way over to the furthest corner, as far from the stove as possible.

Next morning the battalion adjutant explained that thirty men were to join J Support, with the remainder going to L Motor Company at Saxton Hall.

The commanding officer, Major Sloan, a tall, bespectacled figure in his early thirties took charge. He explained that until a few months ago, they had been a motor company. But during early clashes in Belgium and France it was apparent they lacked support from anti-tank and medium machine guns.

The company's second in command, Captain Jamieson, read out each man's name, letting him know to which platoon he was to be attached. Ron and Sharpy found themselves in 15 Machine-Gun Platoon, with Ossie and Jimbo in 14 Anti-Tank Platoon.

Machine-gun platoons were made up of eight Bren carriers, with each being manned by up to four men. Platoon members took on the role of either driver, machine gunner, rangefinder, wireless operator or despatch rider, with all others being designated as gunners. Anti-tank platoons had six tank personnel carriers. Each was equipped with a quick-firing anti-tank gun and being larger than a Bren carrier could carry ten men with their gear. In the case of someone being taken out during an action, their duties were carried out by someone else until they were once more back up to strength.

Ron and Sharpy, lined up with the other gun crews were being taken through the quick-firing, water-cooled Vickers machine gun. Each hand-fed belt held two-hundred and fifty rounds of .303 ammunition, with one in six being a tracer.

Seated behind their guns, Gunnery Sergeant Cox ordered, 'All guns! Range four hundred yards! Target to your front, rapid-fire!' They simulated firing for twenty seconds, then put up their right hand to show they had a stoppage. On the command 'clear jam', each gunner pulled back the cocking handle and let it fly forward with a metallic clunk. 'Carry on firing!' the sergeant freshly ordered.

Stoppages ranged from the simplest, which were soon sorted, to those of a more complex nature. Serious jams could put a gun out of action at a crucial time, and it was essential to know how to clear them as soon as possible. The only downside of the Vickers was its tendency to jam when fired nonstop. To avoid this happening, one had to apply five-second bursts followed by a two-second pause. Apart from this, it was a robust medium machine gun that had stood the test of time, since before The Great War.

When firing, a light tap either side of the butt would adjust its aim by one degree. More taps would produce a higher angle of fire. Experienced gunners could aim with ease, placing rounds squarely on the target. Guns would be set on fixed lines during the daytime, on an exposed position or a break in a hedge through which an enemy might advance. If the attack came at night gunners could traverse back and forth across the gap, with tracers showing the line of fire.

Everyone received training on the Vickers. As soon as each session finished, they were free to focus on their other duties. Drivers worked on their carriers, while wireless operators fussed and tinkered with their sets. Rangefinders practised with their scopes and dispatch riders cleaned and maintained their motorbikes in perfect working order. Each soldier absorbed their primary role and learnt a second in the way an actor would learn an understudy part, knowing both to perfection. Throughout history, the British Army had prided itself on its ability to adapt, and riflemen more than any other were masters of their trade.

Ron became one of two rangefinders in 15 Platoon and followed training on the Barr and Stroud scope. This was mounted on a short stand and used lying down, with its three-foot tube parallel to the ground. The right-hand viewer showed a split image, while the other displayed range scales. To take a reading a straight edge on a tree, tank, building or bridge was selected. By rolling the top and bottom image inwards, until they lined up, he was then able to read off the range in the left-hand viewer. A higher number of readings produced a greater degree of accuracy, thereby enabling gunners to place their rounds on target. When firing the rangefinder-rifleman would observe the strike, telling gunners to raise or lower their aim. On taking up a new position, he would also make a range card, sketching the terrain, checking and rechecking each object and feature, giving a range and heading for each.

While all this training was going on the anti-tank platoon practised with their six-pounders. They manhandled them across the terrain, to position, range, fire and later strip and clean, ready for the next training session, or the real thing.

They soon settled into their new and hopefully temporary home. Hopefully temporary because they wanted to move somewhere else, so they could get some half-decent food. What was on offer, thrifty and tasteless left a lot to be desired. Breakfast was one scrawny banger, a pat of rancid butter, two thin slices of bread and discoloured water that barely passed as tea. All other meals were just as meagre.

A few weeks later they found out the reason for this penny-pinching. Just by chance, a few of the lads were having a quiet drink at the Cock and Feathers in the next village. Without asking, a woman sat down beside Ron.

'You don't mind if I sit by you, pet?' the redhead asked, moving closer.

'Of course not,' Ron obliged. She seemed too forward for his liking and assumed she was 'on the game'. 'Would ya like a drink?' he asked civilly.

'Don't mind if I do, pet. A port and lemon will do nicely.' After a bit of small talk, which Ron thought was leading up to something she said, 'I know another of you lot – in The Rifles.'

'Ere it comes. 'Oh Yeah,' Ron said guardedly.

'He's really good to the other girls and me.' Ron was more convinced she was a fully paid-up member of the oldest profession in the world. 'He brings us a nice bit of meat each week, which ekes out our meagre rations. He also gives us margarine, jam, tea and sugar. Nothing's too much trouble for him. He's a good-hearted sort.'

''E sounds it.'

'He—'

'Wot's 'is name? I might know 'im.'

'Harry Summers,' she said after a brief pause.

'Oh, yeah, I know 'im,' he said, placing the name straightaway. *Bloomin' bastard. So that's where our grub's goin' ... ta feed this greasy trollop's maw.*

Ron later passed on what he had learnt to the others.

'Harry-bleedin'-bastard-Summers,' Ossie said. 'Nah wonder nosh is sorry an' sad. 'E's givin' it away in exchange fer friggin' favours. I bet 'e's givin' 'er plen'y o' meat.' They all grinned, knowing full well what he was getting at. 'Bleedin' bobagee's!' He looked around in case there were other cooks in the bar. 'Bastard wankers.'

'A right old fiddle,' said Sharpy. 'We'll put the word around. Let everyone know what he's been up too. The lads'll go berserk. They'll hang the bastard. We're starving to death, and he's giving our grub away to renter bender and her mates.'

Ron leant forward, urging everyone into a huddle. 'Our best bet,' he whispered, 'would be ta 'ave a word with Mister Summers. The name of that ... were Sheila Bryant. She cleared off sharpish like when she saw I weren't impressed with what she were sayin'.'

Next morning, talk soon got around to Sergeant Harry Summers, head cook and chief handler of the camp's rations.

'Let's put the frighteners on him,' Sharpy said, chuckling. 'He'll only get six months. He'll love it. We could have a word with Dicky Crouch and Arthur Stone.'

'Yeah, good idea, Joe,' Ossie agreed.

In pre-army days, Crouch and Stone had skulked around Kings Cross with a gang of hard nuts who gave many a rival gang member a short, painful stay in the local hospital. Once they had finished with Summers, he would agree to anything. But if he were foolish enough to call their bluff, the only outcome would be being broken to the ranks and given six-months at Catterick Barracks, Detention Centre. Evil in thought and deed the provost staff competed to see who could inflict the worst inhuman treatment on their so-called comrades. The constant doubling in full kit and endless abuse from these cruel brothers in arms was renowned.

A swaddy turning up at the guardroom, with kitbag and webbing scrubbed white, was a sure-fire sign his sentence had ended, and he was returning to his unit. While at Netheravon posters were plastered all over the place, asking men to transfer to the Army Provost Corps, with an assured promotion to corporal. No self-respecting soldier would ally himself to the Royal Cypher cap badge of this unit, even though it spelt safety away from the carnage of war. No wonder they sat alone in silent shame when making their way home on leave.

After Sergeant Summers' ill-fated meeting with 15 Platoon's very own Mafia, the amount and variety of food improved beyond expectations.

Chapter 9

'Nursemaids'

The handsome, fair-haired Donald Bowkett was a loyal and efficient officer, a perfect leader for 15 Platoon. When training with machine guns, he showed first-class knowledge and a natural ability to teach others. He came over as a modest individual, who would impose his will with a minimum of fuss and words. His sky-blue eyes were fixing, and his movements cautious and measured. When machine gun training, he would rap out orders as if taking a maths lesson with a group of sixth formers.

'All guns, six hundred yards!' he barked. 'Enemy to your front! Rapid-fire!' The sound of eight Vickers firing on a narrow front was the loudest thing Ron had ever heard, next to his mum yelling at him when he had done something wrong. After twenty or so rounds Mr Bowkett saw the strikes falling short of two Mark Vs from The Great War. His words rang out again. 'Stop! Up fifty yards! Same target! Rapid-fire!' Once they had finished, he ordered, 'Cease fire! Unload!'

With the practice over they set too stripping and cleaning their machine guns. As each man worked Lieutenant Bowkett and Sergeant Cox mingled, watching as they set about putting it back together. If they were going to have trouble, it was best to work it out during a practice, rather than the real thing. The same clear-cut commands and readiness to help showed when he checked over the Bren carriers in the motor pool and oversaw the training of wireless operators, despatch riders and rangefinders.

Cloddy, as most officers were fondly known, but not to their face was well thought of and took a keen interest in his men's welfare. Anyone having problems, at home or in the platoon would simply have a quiet word with Sergeant Frazer. As senior NCO, Wally oversaw all discipline and would soon arrange a cosy little chat with their officer. Mr Bowkett was their link with higher command, a man they would one day follow into action and obey no matter how hopeless his orders might be at the time.

Each motor company at Saxton Hall was made up of three motor platoons, a scout platoon and a mortar platoon. J Support had two medium machine-gun platoons and an anti-tank platoon, lodged next to the headquarters building in the ex-college barns and huts. The 5th Battalion, The Rifle Regiment, functioned as a close-knit, fighting force, making it a free-thinking battle group of some eight hundred men.

Battle training took place on the bleak North Yorkshire Moors. Through such schemes the role of a motor battalion was made clear to all, helping each man understand the part he played in the overall stratagem. A motor battalion was a pivot from which the big boys could swing and overcome opposition. With rifles, light and medium machine guns, mortars and anti-tank weapons, and cunning, they could overwhelm most anything obstructing an armoured advance. They would clear woods and villages, hold captured ground and round up prisoners after a breakthrough. At night, their job was to protect tank leagers and carry out listening patrols. Motor battalions were known as the nursemaids. With their 15cwt lorries, half-tracks, Bren carriers and scout cars, they kept up with the armoured advance until the very last moment. On the command 'ground action' they would leave their vehicles, deploy their firepower and engage the enemy.

The sixth and final company in the Fifth was Battalion HQ. Housed in the office block, along with the CO, adjutant, padre, senior medical officer and quartermaster they were responsible for the supply and spiritual and bodily welfare of every soldier under their control. Further support units were in the same building. The Light Aid Detachment Platoon dealt with the recovery and minor repairs of light vehicles, with a few REMEs to help with more complex tasks. Backing up the Comms Platoon, which oversaw all aspects of communication was a Royal Corps of Signals section.

Those at headquarters were amazed when they heard that Germany had invaded Russia, sending the battalion into a frenzy of excitement. The Nazi jackboot, having swarmed over most of Europe and the Balkans now shocked the world by launching a dawn attack on an eighteen-hundred-mile front, from Finland to the Black Sea. It was an astonishing turn of events, meaning they were now fighting on two fronts.

Joe Sharpe, having passed top of his driver and maintenance course was assigned as a Bren driver. As a budding mechanic – far removed from his civilian occupation – most days he could be found with sleeves rolled up, greased to the elbows, helping other drivers tinker with their Brens, or working with a REME to strip down an engine. Today he was with Sergeant Fitter Knight, refitting a track on a tank personnel carrier, having replaced a cracked link.

'Hold it tight, Wack,' the sergeant said. Sharpy grunted and groaned as he dragged the links together. 'Back slightly. Now Pull.' They both heaved, and the heavy steel track rolled over the bogie wheel.

'Got it, Sarge.'

'And about bloody time. The links are lined up nicely, son. The pin should slip in as easy as your pork chop on your wedding night.' Sharpy picked up the large cotter pin and pushed it in as far as it would go. 'That's it. Now give it a wack, Wack.'

He hefted the sergeant's prized blacksmith hammer and tapped it home. 'Phew, that was a job an' a half,' he said, wiping his forehead and leaving a smear of grease to show he was a fully paid-up member of the guild of mechanics.

'Yeah. A tough bugger,' the sergeant said, wiping grease from his hands with an old shirt.

Charlie Knight was one of the rare survivors who had taken part in the last ever cavalry charge at Moreuil Wood on thirtieth of March nineteen-eighteen. Canadian by birth, having served in the Royal Canadian Dragoons, he married an English girl after the war. Joining the Blues and Royals, he served in Northern Ireland, India, Palestine and finally Egypt. He hung up his uniform five years before Neville Chamberlain's 'peace for our time' speech. On the outbreak of war, he was working at a garage in Brent Cross and offered his help to REME as a skilled mechanic, with over twenty years' army service.

'What's the time, Charlie?'

'You're a cheeky pup!' he chided. 'It's Sarge to you when we're in uniform. You're not my bleedin' officer, you know. Anyway, squirt, why do you want to know? Have you got something better to do than help the chap who's teaching you everything he knows?'

Charlie and Joe got to know each other at Netheravon. The old-timer saw in him the makings of a mechanic and helped him to get his hands dirty at every opportunity.

He unclipped the leather cover on his wristwatch and checked the time. 'Ten minutes to three.'

'Fancy a cup of tea and a bacon sarnie, Sergeant Knight?'

'That's better, Pipsqueak.' He never called him Sharpy, but Joe or any other quirky name that came into his head. It was a game with him, as life was. The Great War had taught him not to take things too seriously. 'Don't mind if I do. But I'm buyin'. You poor sods never have the spondulics. You're always spending money on beer and totty.' He slapped him on the back, almost knocking him off his feet. 'Come on then, son, let's scrub up. An' over a cuppa I'll tell you what it was *really* like to serve in the cavalry and have a thoroughbred between your legs as you charge the enemy.'

The Bren carrier, built from three-eighths inch plating, first came into being in nineteen thirty-four. This full-tracked, sturdy warhorse, with its Ford V8 engine, was in its element gambolling across open fields like a frisky colt. Independent and self-contained, Bren carriers acted as a mobile force that could hit the enemy hard, while at the same time using its agility to get out of trouble. Its bogies and solid drive would pick out every bump, jarring the driver's spine and causing constant backache. The low driving position meant his legs were almost at right angles to his body, making it a taxing vehicle to drive. On the plus side though it was easy to maintain and could carry the crew's kit, bedding, groundsheets, tarps, food for up to five days, weapons, ammo, jerry cans with water and reserve petrol, tools, spares and thirty-two gallons of fuel in two tanks. Riflemen, free-thinking and proud of their heritage thought of their vehicles as home; and loved the freedom to brew up whenever the chance presented itself.

Highly mobile, it flew along at a top speed of thirty miles an hour. However, on roads, they had to keep below fifteen. The reason for this low speed was because of its complex steering system, which on tarmac roads made it somewhat fickle. To steer a full-tracked vehicle, all a driver had to do was lock one track and the carrier after two or three little bucks would face a new direction. With practice drivers became adept at steering tracked vehicles and sometimes found it difficult to change back to 'rack and pinion'.

Sergeant Frazer, getting the lads used to their vehicles, at the slightest excuse would take them out in convoy, bombing along country lanes, and, of course, breaking the speed limit. Needing to keep up, the drivers had no choice but to match his breakneck speed.

'What's chuffin' speedo say, Joe?' Ron asked, holding on for grim death as the carrier bucked and slewed around each bend on the Pickering to Kingsthorpe Road. 'I'm scared ta look.'

'Just nudging thirty.'

'Bloody hell,' Lew Taylor said, looking at Ron as they stood behind Sharpy. It was better to stand at this speed. 'Ease off the gas, mate. You'll kill us all if ya role this darn thing.'

'It won't be my fault,' Sharpy hit back.

'*You're* bleedin' drivin'!' Ron yelled.

'Not in the least, Deak. Wally's setting the pace. If he sees me slow down, he'll put me on a fizzer. I've got to keep on his tail. Don't worry, you girl's blouses,' he said anew. 'I know what I'm doing.'

'See, Dad,' Ron said, looking up at the cobalt blue sky. ''Itler never got me, but some twat of a West Ham supporter did.'

After what turned out to be the longest spell in one place, J Support moved from the bleak Yorkshire moors to the breezy seafront of Lowestoft, with the rest of the Fifth staying at Saxton Hall.

Spread out along the promenade they stayed in guesthouses that had been taken over by the MOD. The happy holiday crowds, laughing mums and dads and strings of lively, fractious children were now nowhere to be seen. The sideshows, ever-churning noises and pull of the pleasure beach ceased long ago, leaving only an echo of happier times. If you were lucky and chosen to stay in one of the larger guesthouses, your whole platoon could shack up together. You then shared with just one or two others, giving loads of space. However, it was mostly potluck as to where the billeting officer put you.

The Company HQ and dining hall were in the once-grand Pleasure Garden's theatre. Parades were held in the larger hotel car parks, while drill took place on Lowestoft's wide roads. Lorries and carriers were lined up along the now lifeless promenade, facing the barbed wire beach.

15 Platoons billet, The Balmoral – faded sign left as a token of better days – boasted hot and cold running water in every room, with two lavatories and a large bathroom on each floor. Ron, Sharpy and another guy settled on a large bedroom facing the choppy North

Sea. Cracked lino covered by small threadbare rugs, timeworn wardrobes, ageing bedspreads, old-fashioned curtains and pictures hanging on grimy walls gave it a shabby but homely feel.

"'Ose bin leavin' dog ends abahhht?' the section corporal moaned.

The room orderly, lying on his bed, looked up from his tattered paperback. 'Search me, Corp.'

'Well, sweep chuffin' floor,' the NCO said, not to be denied.

'What agin?' the reading soldier moaned.

As soon as the NCO left, Ron and Sharpy swept the floor for the first and not the last time. The room-orderly, ignoring them, lay back reading his well-thumbed copy of Agatha Christie's *Murder on the Orient Express*.

The onetime resort offered plenty of pubs and cafes, a snooker hall over Montague Burtons, two flea-bit cinemas, a dancehall and a small theatre on South Pier. Most were still open, catering to thousands of soldiers in and around the town. A lucky few were billeted away from the seafront and the biting wind that lashed the promenade, setting windows rattling in the former guesthouses.

Crowds of carefree, black buttoned soldiers, fleeing the cold winds, invaded the warm pleasure palaces. They mixed freely with the locals, singing their lively Cockney songs and teaching the girls how to do the *Lambeth Walk*:

> *'Anytime you're Lambeth way,*
> *Any evening, any day,*
> *You'll find us all doin' the Lambeth walk.*
> *Every little Lambeth gal,*
> *With her little Lambeth pal,*
> *You'll find 'em all doin' the Lambeth walk.*
> *Everything's free and easy,*
> *Do as you darn well pleasey,*
> *Why don't you make your way there?*
> *Go there, stay there ...'*

The smoke room crowd, spilling onto the grass in front of the pub were over the moon when the gifted Matlow started banging out another old favourite on his tuneless upright:

'Come, come, come and make eyes at me
down at the Old Bull and Bush,
Da, da, da, da, da,
Come, come, drink some port wine with me,
Down at the Old Bull and Bush,
Hear the little German Band,
Da, da, da, da, da,
Just let me hold your hand dear,
Do, do come and have a drink or two
down at the Old Bull and Bush ...'

After *The Old Bull and Bush* had been sung, three times, the never to be missed hell-raising *Knees up Mother Brown* energised the Sparrow's Nest:

'Knees up Mother Brown
Knees up Mother Brown
Under the table you must go
Ee-aye, Ee-aye, Ee-aye-oh
If I catch you bending
I'll saw your legs right off
Knees up, knees up
don't get the breeze up
Knees up Mother Brown ...'

Dating back to seventeen-eighty, Lowestoft's Sparrow was the local Auxiliary Navy's haunt, along with their brothers in arms from the army. It was their first point of call for a great night out and was a magnet for girls in search of a good time.

Before the war, trawlers sailed out of this seaside resort-cum-fishing port. Deep-sea fisherman now worked as fleet auxiliaries, helping the Royal Navy to sweep for mines and other sea duties. Its stockyards held vast amounts of raw materials. Mountains of seasoned timber, African Blackwood, Australian Red Cedar and Walnut from Brazil lay in great roofed, stockyards around the town, waiting for peace to reign once more.

The company leave roster rolled around every four months, giving each man five days. Ron and Sharpy had already been home once, but this was the first time on-leave together.

Arriving at Kings Cross, ratty and tired, they spent most of the journey standing up. The platforms and walkways were choked with service personnel, running for trains or racing for the nearest exit.

Every newspaper at the WH Smiths kiosk displayed a similar headline: 'LIBYA – 50 MILES'. The German war machine fed off the Allies failures and was momentarily silenced by their successes. But of late these were few and far between. For weeks talk had been about the sinking of *HMS Ark Royal*, torpedoed off Gibraltar with no fatalities – a miracle if ever there was. This capital ship was homeward bound after giving air support to Malta, which for months had been under constant attack. A further news item that broke a few days ago concerned a British commando raid on Rommel's desert headquarters. But fortunately, for him, he was in Rome at the time. Not able to achieve their primary objective, which was to capture or eliminate the man, they nevertheless gained valuable information during the raid.

The narrow platform, crowded, hemmed Ron in, making him feel rattled. He waited, shoulder to shoulder with fellow passengers, watching as elderly businessmen studiously studied their broadsheets. Soldiers, sailors and airmen chit-chatted ten to the dozen. Women dressed in warm coats, wearing headscarves, looked as if they had just clocked off from the arms factory. A ginger-haired second lieutenant was snogging with a Wren in an alcove, hand hidden from view in the folds of her coat. A few, happy with their own company gazed at propaganda signs where once ads for Colgate toothpaste, Woodbine cigarettes and Lambs Navy Rum adorned the walls. The new-fangled posters warned people to be careful when talking in public. Signs such as 'Careless talk costs lives', showing a ship's keel slipping below the waves; a shapely blonde doing up her suspender clips, captioned 'Keep mum ... she's not so dumb'; fingers touching lips as they whispered 'Watch out ... the enemies about', were plastered all over the place.

The train was packed, with standing room only. Ron held onto a leather strap as the carriage swayed from side to side. A pilot officer, the top button of his tunic undone to show he was one of Churchill's Few, leant against the carriage door, reading *The London Evening Standard*. As he folded his paper, before getting off at Angel, Ron just had time to read the sub-headline:

'British Army opens a broad front in Libya, and
advances fifty miles, capturing Sidi Rezgh ...'

Stopping at Old Street, he saw a sea of faces staring at the carriage, looking for an empty seat or space where they could stand. They jostled to get through the doors, quiet with newspapers folded. The next station, Bank, people were talking in small groups, city gents, service personnel and women alike. It was as if the social barriers of previous stations had been stripped away. At London Bridge, he again saw them waiting on the platform, but no one was attempting to board. Once more, they were talking freely, sharing some snippet of information. Those in the carriage saw all the fervour and wondered if something had happened? As the doors opened a smartly dressed man in a pinstripe suit and bowler hat got on. He spoke to a pregnant woman, seated, reading her *Woman's Weekly*. She turned to a man by her side and said something. The man leant forward and spoke to a sub-lieutenant, relaying what the woman had told him. The naval officer turned and addressed three swaddies.

The startling news of Japan's attack on Pearl Harbour and Guam rolled down the carriage like a heavy swell slapping against a ship's hull. The attack had taken place at eight o'clock that very morning, local time. The USA straightaway declared war on Japan, followed by Britain and her Dominions. News of fatalities was vague, but some ships had been sunk, including the *US Arizona*, with most of its crew entombed in its upturned hull. Luckily, if you can say such a thing amidst so much tragedy, the fleets three aircraft carriers (Japan's primary targets) were already at sea.

Ron found his mother and Jack standing outside 144, talking with everyone else. It looked as if the whole street was out. He had never seen the like before.

His mother whooped with joy and ran into his arms. 'Ain't it wonderful news, Luv,' she bubbled, grinning from ear to ear.

Jack slapped him on the back. 'At last! America 'as just declared war on Germany. Now we 'ave the bas'!' he exclaimed, short of swearing. He had already done so in front of his mother and had had his ears boxed for his profanity. Most serviceman's every other word was an expletive, and it was hard to get out of the habit when around family. ''Itler's as good as beat, an'—'

'Not quite,' Ron censored sagely.

Ron and Jack went to Uncle Fred's for tea and ended up at a full and rowdy Cross Keys until early next morning, drunk as lords.

Things were very much the same at home, with people working or hanging around in never-ending ration queues. The drab December weather, along with the blackouts, did little to lighten the mood in London, with Christmas only three weeks away. It was as if people were barely ticking over, going through the motions, waiting for something to happen. Then the news about America joining the fight. What a blessing. It galvanised the city, sending it into a fizz.

Not to be denied, Ron spent a great deal of his leave sampling London's many brews, drinking with Uncle Fred and Jack, or anyone else who happened to be around. During this leave he and Mavis had their first big row, showing that in their case absence was not making the heart grow fonder.

All too soon he caught the surging, rattling tube train to Kings Cross to meet up with Joe.

'Watch it, Ron,' he greeted. 'We have an hour to kill before the train arrives,' he added artfully. 'There's only one thing for it.' He nodded at the station buffet bar. 'You're buying. Yours truly's skint.'

'Yer always boracic, ya bleedin' spendthrift.'

Sharpy put his arm around his shoulder as they strolled towards the bar.

'Ya can't fool me,' Ron said, shrugging it off. 'Ya tight-fisted jam rag.'

It was a relief to be back after such a wearying journey. They soon slipped once more into the routine of weapon training, mine-laying and foot drill, with the odd sentry duty, guarding the seafront while dreamily gazing out to sea.

At the *Palais de Danse*, Ron and Sharpy spotted two cracking girls dancing together. They both agreed it was a sin to let such creatures partner each other. So, they set up a plan to split them up. Their tactics were well worked out, or so they thought. Firstly, on this occasion, no machine gun was needed. Secondly, Ron would carry out a frontal attack and make eye contact with them when he got nearer. Thirdly, Sharpy, outflanking them, would start chatting up the blonde. Ron had already marked his target, the well-stacked lass with the wispy waistline and shoulder-length brunette hair. This two-pronged attack, they both agreed could not fail.

They began like chess players making their opening gambit. As he threaded his way between jitterbugging dancers, Ron made eye contact with the girl of his choice. He kept a lookout for flailing arms, kicking legs and over-enthusiastic dancers out to impress. The brunette coyly looked at him and then teasingly turned away. Despite this apparent snub, she smiled before showing him her back, with its cascade of tresses.

With no sign of Sharpy, he said in his best BBC voice, 'Hello. My name is Ron. I've got no one to dance with, other than my pal. And guys shouldn't dance together, and neither should girls.'

'It looks like you've lost him,' she said, giggling while looking around.

'He's on another mission,' he replied, staring into her eyes. Suddenly, lost for words, he said the first thing that came into his head. 'You've got the loveliest eyes. They're the colour of a South Sea lagoon.' *'Ell, Deakin, where'd ya dredge that from?*

Suddenly there was a crashing sound, and someone swore blue murder. 'Yow brainless twat,' yelled a Royal Navy petty officer. Sharpy, lying on his back had his feet in the air, stranded like a scarab beetle. The whole dancehall turned and looked at his antics.

'New dance, mate?' one wag joked.

'At least 'e won't get bunions,' ribbed another.

The sweet-natured blonde, taking pity on the soldier, said, 'Are you all right, pet?'

Pet 'e ain't, miss. An' 'e ain't bin 'ouse trained either. With his posh voice gone, he said, 'That's Sharpy. 'E's me mate. 'E were dancin' on 'is own 'cause he ain't gotta partner.'

By now, Joe was on his feet, talking to the girl who had shown such concern. 'Joe Sharp,' he said, holding out his hand, 'Bren gun carrier driver and onetime lady's hairdresser.' She took it and smiled – a smile that thumped him in the solar plexus.

Ron looked at him in surprise, mouth open, hardly believing what he had just heard. 'What?' he said, coming to his senses. 'Did I 'ear right ... are my ears ... *lady's* 'airdresser?'

'You tell anyone, and I'll punch your head,' Sharpy said, still holding the girl's hand.

'But a *lady's* 'airdresser—'

'It's a damn good job. My Dad and his Dad were lady's

hairdressers. I'm the third generation.'

'That's nice, but a *lady's* 'airdresser?'

'It's better than being a butcher!' Sharpy hit back.

'Yeah, but butcherin's a proper man's job.'

'Don't say another word' – he stabbed a finger at him – 'or you'll end up on your back.'

'Well, I think a lady's hairdresser is a lovely job,' said Miss Gallant, coming to his rescue. 'Would you like to dance, Joe?'

'Sure ... so long as your friend dances with' – he stretched out a hand towards his so-called mate – 'Ronald Henry Deakin, rangefinder and *onetime* apprentice butcher. I think he can work out his left from his right, just about.'

He turned and spoke to Ron as the band struck up again. 'Mission accomplished, Deacon. We'll slay 'em when we get ta—'

'Or they'll slay us.'

Margaret Kenna, or Maggie as she was known, was a shapely Suffolk girl with whirlpool green eyes, pale blemish-free skin, with just a hint of makeup and the lushest head of hair Ron had ever seen. She took an instant shine to him.

As they walked back to The Balmoral, Sharpy tackled him about his recent remark. 'What did you mean by a butcher being a proper man's job, compared to a lady's hairdresser?'

'Ya know ... well ... the impression they give.'

'Hmm, the impression *they* give. And what sort of impression would *that* be?'

Ron quickly changed the subject. ''Ow'd ya get on with Jackie? She seemed a nice kid. Too good fer bloomin' likes o' you.'

'We're meeting up tomorrow night, outside the Palace.'

'Oh yeah! What's on?'

'*How Green was my Valley* with Maureen O'Hara and Walter ... thingamabob.'

'You said ya were gonna give that a miss. ... An' its Pidgeon, bird brain.'

Joe ignored his cutting reply. 'I did, but Jackie likes that sort of thing.'

'Mm, goodness. You are getting' on well, findin' out 'er taste in films so soon.'

'What about you and Margaret?'

'Maggie, *actually*, Joe Sharp, onetime *lady's* 'airdresser. Ya barmpot, pillock! Why'd ya come out with that load o' crap?'

'Me ... my mind went blank. That was my chat-up line before I threw my lot in with you scabby buggers. It makes a girl feel safe, knowing she's dating a hairdresser. My father went mad when he saw how coarse I'd become,' he said, changing the subject. 'During my last leave, I went to the salon to speak to him. I thought it would help, him seeing me in uniform. We ended up having an almighty bust-up. I even swore in front of him.

'I bet that pissed 'im off?'

'I'm even startin' to talk like you,' he said, ignoring him. Just talking about his father was enough to sharpen his diction. 'He has paid a fortune for my schooling, sending me to some of the best private schools that money can buy.'

'Ya poor sod. ... Blimey, who'd 'ave believed it. Ronald 'enry Deakin sleepin' with a toff. An' a *lady's* 'airdresser ta boot?'

'I'd watch who you say—'

'Is it yer ole man's shop?'

'Yeah, but—'

'An' you'll inherit it one day?'

'You're a mercenary sod! ... My sisters and I will. But it's not one shop ... it's three.'

'Three!'

'Can you hear an echo?' He looked around jokingly. 'Yes, *three*! One in Knightsbridge, one in Mayfair and one in Piccadilly, opposite the Ritz.'

'Jesus Christ! I thought ya lived in Lambef and yer old man were a barber?'

'Not me ... my Dad, but my Great-grandfather were ... was a

barber. He married an English girl and came to live in England, settling in London.'

'Where'd 'e come from?'

'Vienna.'

'Oh, 'e were German? That makes—'

'Austrian, you ignoramus. There's quite a difference.'

'Not ta 'itler.'

'He lived in Lambeth and opened a barber's shop in Derby Gate, behind the House of Commons. In nineteen-seventeen, when the old king changed his name to Windsor, Grandfather changed the family name from Schwab to Sharp.'

'Who'd 'ave believed it. Joseph Sharp earnin' a livin' rubbin' 'is 'ands through woman's locks? Ya wouldn't 'ave ta pay me. I'd do it fer buckshee's.'

'And that's why I kept it to myself. To avoid such obtuse comments.'

'Yer secret's safe with me, kiddo,' Ron said, winking at him. 'By bloomin' way what's obtuz mean?'

'It's French for dick.'

'Ya speak French?'

'*Bien sûr, je peux vous sans cervelle* obtuz.'

'Bloody Gypsy Nell! That'll be useful when we get ta France. ... By the way, what did ya say?'

'I said, "of course I do, you brainless dick". Father expects all his staff to converse in French. Many of our clients use it as a second language.'

'Wot's French fer kiss me obtuz?'

'*Kiss mon* obtuz.'

'I'll remember that. It might come in useful one day. Do ya still live in Lambef?'

'No, Holland Park. I said Lambeth because I didn't want any of you lot knowing the truth. It wouldn't do my standing in the platoon much good.'

'Wot, bein' a *lady's* 'airdresser or a toff?' Ron took out his key and opened the front door. 'Don't worry, Joe, yer secret's safe with me. But I need a good night's kip ta get me 'ead 'round what yuv jus' told me.' He pushed the door open. 'An' anovver thing,' he further asked, 'why are ya always skint? Yer family must be rollin' in the stuff.'

'I earn the same as you. Twenty-nine bob a week. And before you say it ... no, I don't have a bank account. My father went mad when I enlisted. He told me to wait until I was called up. He was going to pull strings to get me a safe posting in London.'

'Hardly safe with all the bombing.'

'He was not—'

'Could 'e do that sort of thing?'

'He can do anything he wants; he knows people. I didn't want that. I wanted to do my bit. He said, "Joseph" – he's the only one to call me that – "if you volunteer before they call you up, you'll get nothing from me". He froze my bank account.'

'He can't do that!'

'He *can* if his brother owns the bank.'

'Blimey! Ya poor deluded sod. A penniless toff, *lady's* 'airdresser ta boot and yer in bloomin' Kate Karney.' He studied him, then grinned. 'Ya realise from now on yuv gotta stay on me good side.'

Sharpy shrugged and gave as good as he got. ''Ave you got one, butcher boy?'

'Yes! And don't drop yer aitches, Quiffy.'

Ron and Maggie became good friends, as did Joe and Jackie. Maggie was just like her youthful-looking mother, May. He had never been in the situation before of fancying the mother as well as the daughter. Maggie had a younger brother, Eric, but he didn't fancy him in the least. The obnoxious little toad thought all soldiers were thick and stupid.

Christmas week, Ron was given a three-day sleeping out pass and spent a delightful time at the Kenna's, treated as one of the family.

The cold northeasterly was a minor discomfort during the many happy hours spent in Maggie's warm, encompassing embrace.

Before the war, Maggie's father, Tom Kenna, had been a deep-sea fisherman. When war broke out, he became a naval auxiliary, serving on his trawler, *Maggie May*, sweeping for mines off Lowestoft. Throughout the many yarns with him, when he happened to be on leave, Ron learnt something of the tough, brave and somewhat undisciplined seaman who crowded the Sparrows Nest.

Chapter 10

'Johnny Doughboy'

Everyone was thrilled when Sergeant Frazer told them of their impending move to Brighton, especially with it only being a short train journey from Victoria. Ron hoped the oyster and shellfish bars were still open. But somehow, he knew that would not be the case as such places closed soon after holidaymakers deserted coastal resorts on the outbreak of war. Within a matter of months, troops arrived in their stead, swelling towns to bursting point.

The other companies, now based at Freckenham, Suffolk would shortly join them. This long-awaited merger would prove telling in the months ahead.

Being a full-scale movement, with support units, J Support set out on their journey in high spirits. There was now a steady flow of men and military hardware throughout England, more so since the Yanks had arrived. It was a mammoth task, finding places for so many troops and their equipment, sometimes moving them arbitrarily. Heavy armour and low loaders clogged villages and towns, snarling up main routes. The south of England had turned into a vast army camp, and surely it would sink below the waves with the steady build-up of men and material for what was now being called the 'second front'.

The ocean of tears and sad goodbyes as they headed south was palpable. Tommy Atkins knew the army's way of doing things. It was a case of 'don't let him get too complacent', keep him guessing and on the move, and don't let him make any strong attachments. A lovesick soldier can affect the fighting efficiency of a unit and could be bad for morale. Ron and Maggie's chance encounter, with no ties, was there for one reason only ... to satiate their sexual appetite. They both agreed to keep in touch, promising to remember the good times. Throughout their relationship, love was seldom mentioned, except on those rare occasions during intense lovemaking. However, it was different for Joe and Jackie who, on parting, talked about getting married.

Rumours persisted for some time, guesswork as to where the battalion would be sent now it was fully operational. Because of the looming merger with the other companies, many said it was in preparation for the Middle East. Two sister battalions were already in Libya, while another was currently sailing from the Clyde to join them. Fortunately, no Rifle Regiment battalion had been sent to the Far East. In that theatre of war, things were going terribly wrong, with Singapore surrendering to the Imperial Japanese Army in February forty-two. A few days before this happened several troopships sailed into Singaporean waters. Hundreds of RAF and Army personnel were taken prisoner before they even had a chance to fire a shot in anger. Olive was not to know for some time, but her youngest brother, Jack, was one of those on board. She was distraught that they had not put into a neutral port when news of Japan's attack on Singapore became public knowledge. Many poor souls would have lived, and the ones who survived could have been spared years of cruelty at the hands of their captors.

Once more, they were put up in empty hotels and guesthouses. It was like a dream, paid for doing little, free digs and food and an extended holiday in Brighton courtesy of the British taxpayer. Army life was sometimes peppered with such delights, and this one was supremely idyllic. Their billet was the notable Grand Hotel. However, its name might be grand and its fame once noteworthy, but it now resembled a seedy, flea-ridden dosshouse. Parades were held on hotel car parks and a school playground, with vehicles parked away from prying eyes on a churned-up recreation ground behind the town. Each company was assigned a section of promenade and told to keep it clean and tidy, making sure it passed muster at a minute's notice. PT and games were played on what had once been a bowling green and rose garden, with a stiff sea breeze almost bursting their lungs. All they needed to complete this picture of bliss was a few ice-cream stalls and fish bars, but each was boarded up for the duration. Donkeys were not required either as noisy swaddies raced pick-a-back on parts of the beach set aside for recreation.

'Use yer whip, Lenny!' one of the lads jeered as half a dozen plimsoll shod donkeys and their jiggling riders raced each other.

'Give it wot for, Cyril!' another yelled. 'I've gotta tanner ridin' on ya!'

The going was heavy, and Cyril and his donkey collapsed on the surf dampened shingle, rolling about in fits of laughter.

Here too a few boarded-up hotels, bearing names such as the Carlton, Gladstone, Mayfair and Belgrave gazed down at loud rumbling vehicles as they encroached on this once opulent splendour.

Beach wiring was now one of those fatigues meted out by provost staff. Though to these healthy, suntanned riflemen, this was sheer paradise and not even those ardent custodians could sour things for them. Sunny days, plenty of talent and joyous pastimes for off-duty hours was sublime. They hoped this life would last forever, but rumours still filtered out of the company orderly room.

By the end of their second week, they received fresh orders.

'Someone's fucked up,' Ron said, sitting on the seawall with the others. 'I bet some twat of a pencil pusher 'as moved our little green pin ta sunny Brighton by mistake.' He broke the seal on a fresh pack of Capstans and passed them around, lit up and inhaled deeply, drawing in the acrid smoke. 'Only ta find two-thousand US Marines need puttin' up in a hurry. An' us poor sods a' used ta travellin'. ... Soddin' 'ell,' he cursed afresh, 'I feel like a chuffin' nomad sometimes.'

'Where will they send us?' Jimbo asked plaintively.

Ron pinched a speck of tobacco off the tip of his tongue. 'God knows.'

'Back to Lowestoft?' Sharpy asked, hopefully.

'Up north again I suppose,' Ron opined.

'Scotland?' Jimbo put in afresh.

'If it is, an' it's anywhere near the Clyde,' Ron furthered, 'it'll be in preparation fer the Middle East. They'll use us now or save us fer 'second front', whenever that'll be.'

'Whatever,' Ossie carped, 'we're on bastard move agin. An' I were lookin' forward ta spendin' chuffin' summer in Brighton. It ain't so warm when ya ger past St Albans.

Ron looked out to sea, flicked his nub in the briny and said, 'At least they can't send us south ... other than France. 'It's gotta be north again. I'm pissed off with this goin' up and down ruddy England. I'm beginnin' ta feel like a friggin' yo-yo.'

J Support loaded their gear and for the second time headed north, but this time they were in for a real treat. Mindful of not carving up the roads with their heavy tracks they carefully made their way along Bermondsey High Street, rattled over Tower Bridge and waved at crowds lining the streets of Whitechapel and Shoreditch. Breaking their journey, they stopped for lunch in Victoria Park. For months J Support would be talking about 'their tour of the capital', as they called it.

Housewives in Hackney cheered their Cockney kinsman as they rolled by. 'Are ya comin' in fer a cuppa, soldier boy?' joked one peroxide-blonde as she scrubbed the step of her two-up-and-two-down terrace.

'Yeah! But not ta much sugar fer me, darlin',' a comic teased. '... Wot abahhht a knee's up, ducks? Somethin' ta send us on our way.'

She obliged by lifting her skirt and kicking out her leg, showing her cami-knickers and stocking tops.

The lads cheered in thanks.

It was kisses and cups of tea all the way.

With the city and suburbs far behind, they threaded their way through open countryside, past farms, fields of ripe corn, cart horses and hay wagons with the occasional tractor. The convoy of wheeled and tracked vehicles moved along tree-lined roads, most of the time empty of traffic. Slowing to a more sedate pace when encountering a quintessential English village, they drove down narrow lanes, trying not to disturb the quietness of England.

Land Army girls, eating their mid-day meal waved as lorry after lorryload of soldiers drove by. 'Want any 'elp, lass,' a rifleman yelled through cupped hands. A cheering girl beckoned, encouraging him to join her. 'Let's scarper, George,' he added for his mate's benefit, jokingly swinging his leg over the side of the three-tonner. 'I've always fancied bein' a farmer's Rob Roy.'

The ribald banter persisted as the convoy progressed, with chaps in each lorry and carrier adding their unique brand of humour to this memorable scene.

The battalion's large Nissen hut camp at Freckenham, Suffolk, became J Support's new home. The merger with the Fifth's remaining companies, long overdue, proved a milestone in their training as a unified force that would soon have its mettle tested.

Ron, Joe, Ossie and Jimbo were able to catch up with the other two members of C Platoon still serving in the Fifth. Over a few beers at the Bell in Thetford, Ernie, now a lance corporal told them about rest who had been at Netheravon with them. Whitey, an ex-forestry worker, like Wilf, transferred to the Pioneer Corps. Benny lost his right leg below the knee during training and was discharged on full war pension. Whipper, on leave in Bridlington, went out on a minesweeper. The vessel was sunk by an E-boat, with all hands lost. Ron also went out with Maggie's father to relieve the boredom that most soldiers suffered from at times. Rusk, now a second lieutenant was in the Middle East with his platoon. Peter Draper, one of the original members of C Platoon trained as a commando and was now serving with a secret group in the Libyan Desert. He had recently been awarded the Military Medal for saving the life of his officer and sergeant while under heavy fire, even though he was himself severely wounded.

Field training was now carried out in woodlands and copses surrounding the market town of Thetford. Its blood-red marble cross to those who died during The Great War, standing as a landmark was a constant reminder of the sacrifice that some might soon have to make. The tough but thrilling training around Barton Mills, Soham and Ely, with weekend visits to Cambridge and Newmarket, proved perfect living. This life was soldiering at its best, peppered with leave in London and helping farmers harvest sugar beet and potatoes to feed the nation.

As they bided their time in this outpost, the skies were forever full of aircraft. Seeing bombers labouring to get airborne, watching them form up in their squadrons was profoundly moving. At dawn, these same aircraft could be seen limping home to places such as Lakenheath, Mildenhall and Scampton, or any other airfield if they could not make it back to base. These brave airmen, British and American alike were taking the fight to Germany. This sustained bombing campaign was, without doubt, a turning point, setting the wheels in motion for the next crucial phase.

Yet again they were on the move, back to the north-east coast. Staying in empty hotels and guest houses, they found themselves in the onetime-bustling seaside resort of Bridlington. The rest of the Fifth was eight miles away at Reighton Gap, a purpose-built army camp that one day would house a holiday park.

'Don't fink I'll bovver next year, Gladys,' one wag joked as he carried his kitbag through the lobby of the Esplanade. 'It's gerrin a bit crowded this time o' year.'

'Pr'aps we should try Soufend next time, Bert?'

'Nah, it's full o' septic tanks.'

'Pr'aps we could go abroad?'

'Yeah! Good idea, Glad. We could spend a couple o' months in France, aye, an' then pop an' clock Uncle Adolf in Berlin.'

They soon settled into their new billets, getting acquainted with the pubs and a few local attractions – mostly female.

Infantry platoons were now attached to motor companies, requiring a rethink on transport. Each company was issued with American M2 half-tracks, commonly known as White Internationals. This nine-ton beast with its powerful engine and sturdy gearbox could cross open country at an impressive lick of speed. Crew members, of which there were three, were taught to drive and maintain this armour-plated monster.

Battle tactics with live firing were now the norm, with gunners deploying machine guns on fixed limits. As barrels seesawed from side to side, the staccato rat-tat-tat and zip-zip-zip of rounds whizzing four-foot overhead and the occasional thunder flashes gave the realistic sounds of battle. House clearing, kicking in doors, slinging in a live grenade, charging in after the blast to silence any opposition was a white-knuckle experience. The only snag came when you had to deal with a 'blind' because some clod forgot to clean away the grease from around the detonator sleeve. But letting off another close by would soon remedy the problem without much risk to life and limb.

Another piece of kit they were introduced to, was the projectile infantry anti-tank gun. Known as a PIAT, it was modelled on a spigot mortar system and launched a small bomb using a strong spring with a charge in its tail. If you didn't want a nasty smack under the chin, or worse a broken jaw, it was best to grip it tightly with both hands. Its effective range was under one hundred and fifteen yards, which is rather close to an enemy tank that is lethal up to two thousand. German tanks, such as Panthers and Tigers were formidable beasts and hard to put out of action. All AFVs had soft underbellies which could be breached quite easily by mines. Likewise, their tracks were also vulnerable. However, it was better to disable the gun first by firing at where the turret joined the body.

But should your aim be less than perfect, the gunner, alerted to your presence, in the blink of an eye would send a high explosive shell in your direction. And a shell landing twenty feet away was sure to kill or seriously maim.

The NCOs, pressing the men to higher levels of fitness, introduced 'run and walk' marches. Each began with quick-march, and after two telegraph poles, without pausing, they would run the next two and then alternate between marching and running.

'Yuv bin on bleedin' nest agin me ole wanker,' one jogging rifleman said, urging his breathless pal. While at the same time trying to ignore sweaty, khaki serge between his legs, feeling like two pieces of sandpaper rubbing against his thighs.

There was nothing like a 'run and walk' followed by an assault course with its array of obstacles, all aimed at testing one's staying power to breaking point. The fast pace, with a sustained rhythm, made these jaunts a pushover for super-fit Tommy Atkins. A relaxed mental state was the keynote, letting one's mind dwell on some after duty treat.

Full-scale war games lasting twenty-one days took place in February forty-four. Ron and his pals sensed their easy-going way of life would soon be over, and this was surely a prelude to the 'second front'.

They crammed every piece of kit in their large valise and kitbag, loading them on their Brens ready for the off. Berets, now favoured instead of forage caps, were likewise packed away and steel helmets had to be worn from now on. Everyone was told not to discuss the exercise and all leave was cancelled.

Each motor company was attached to an armoured unit, with J Support in reserve. To simulate battle conditions umpires raced around on bicycles, waving coloured flags. They would appear from nowhere, shouting things such as 'You, man, you're out of action!

You three are dead! Your tank has lost a track!' and 'Your unit has just been wiped out!' But it was not easy to replicate tank and infantry clashes, and things soon went awry.

'You look like shit,' said Ossie, picking up the dixie.

'I feel like shit,' replied Ron.

'I thought ya were brahn bread, Deacon?' he chirped while pouring freshly made gunfire into his mate's mug.

'I am,' he said, chewing his tea.

Ossie could make a passable brew from piping hot radiator water. No open fires were allowed in case they gave away their position. The British swaddy was a master of invention, and his daily cuppa was not to be missed for anything.

'But yuv bin walkin' 'round. An' bloomin' Sarge said anyone brahn bread 'ad ta merge inta background loike an' not be seen.'

'Wot would 'e 'ave me do? Turn into an effin' tree an' disappear up me own arse?'

'Ya could sit in yer Bren?'

'Ya must be off yer bleedin' rocker, Oz. The ole girl'll be as cold as Dick's freezer.'

'Dick, 'o's Dick?'

'Oh, a guy I knew, who—'

'I dint know ya were like that, Deak.'

Ron ignored his quip. '... It's bleedin' brass monkey weather,' he instead added, cradling his scalding mug. 'Me fingers 'ave lost all feelin'. Cut 'em off an' I wouldn't feel a bloody thing.'

'Wrap a few blankets 'round yerself.'

'That tosser of a second lieutenant's kippin' in Bert's Bren, huggin' our blankets to 'imself ... cosy like. 'E's as warm as friggin' toast in there. An' 'e ain't gonna let me 'ave any.'

'Is 'e brahn bread?'

''E thumb-suckin' will be if 'e don't get 'is digit out, skivin' bastard. I'll give 'im a piece of my mind before this lots over an'—'

'Can you afford it.'

'I've got plenty to say to that bastard. ... Shortly we'll be following that wanker into action. Next time he crosses my path the feathers'll fly, believe me.'

'I'll sell tickets to it.'

'You do, Oz.'

The brigade's tanks churned everywhere into a claggy mess, in places reminiscent of Passchendaele at its worst. Escaping from the rain and mud was impossible. The endless wind howled across flat, open moors, cutting everyone to the quick. Ron's section, giving up sleeping beneath tarpaulins on the muddy ground spent two nights standing up in a railway worker's hut that providence had placed nearby.

Once relieved, each man tied his bedroll in his groundsheet with a piece of frayed rope, fingers numb. Hungry and cheesed off they waited as drivers revved their engines. Within no time they would wash and shave in scalding hot water. But pity the poor sod who was last, skimming away grey scum before starting his morning ablutions.

They were soon greeted on this drab, overcast morning by a welcome roar from petrol cookers in a field kitchen. Half a dozen cooks worked by storm lamps, shielded from the elements with huge awnings. Juggling with mess tins while gulping down tea the cooks doled out Burgoo topped with a slick of treacle, bangers and mash and a wedge of freshly baked bread smothered with marge and strawberry jam.

With food inside them, hands cupping a steaming mug life took on a new meaning. But no words can describe the feeling, having stuffed oneself silly when your guts start complaining. A few lads trooped towards the field-latrine. Stripping a mud-encrusted leather jerkin, greatcoat, denim blouse, pulling down your denim serge trousers, drawers, lifting one's angora shirttails and squatting in the pitch black was beyond most people's ken. Once you had all but disrobed you would then grasp a young sapling and with a stiff breeze whistling around your arse let nature take its course. All this discomfort was a sure-fire remedy for constipation, especially with the noise of battle going on around you, along with the occasional stonk close by.

The 'red flag' went up at first light, and someone yelled, 'Prepare to move!'

Once more, the thrill of chasing each other, bombing across open country and striking the fear of God into a slippery, fast fleeing enemy.

The next evening, after yet another day of utter confusion – when all you wanted to do was stay warm – the sheer delight of sheltering in a straw-filled barn. No matter if a couple of carthorses in the next stall whickered all night, now and then kicking the wall for good measure. Plus, a pair of friendly mice playing in the straw only inches from your head.

That same night Ron queued behind known teetotallers, hoping the platoon sergeant would take pity on him and slip their quota in his mug. With his extra tot, he made his way back to the warm barn and his rough blankets for a night's well-earned kip.

Returning to the billet after making his will, which was duly witnessed by two lance corporals, Ron sat on his bed reading Mavis's latest letter.

'Bad news, Deakin?' his sergeant asked, seeing his grumpy expression.

'The bitch 'as blown me out, Sarge,' he whined, screwing it up and flinging it on the floor. 'She's got annovver bloke. I bet it's a bleedin' septic tank. Bloomin' bastard. Not Mavis, but the toe-rag 'o's screwin' 'er.' In truth, he was not surprised she had given him the push. He knew only too well how she must feel. Someone like Mavis always needed a bloke to show her a good time and being posted to the north-east meant his visits to London were few and far between.

'Never mind, son,' his sergeant said, picking up the letter before making his way over to the stove. He lifted the cover and looked at

Ron, who nodded. 'There's plenty of nice girls about,' he added, consigning it to the flames, 'eager to give a soldier boy a bit of love. Why only last week the Imperial owner's wife came onto me. Best couple of hours I've had in ages.'

'You're better off without her,' Sharpy said, adding his own views on the matter. 'With all these bleeding Yanks about ... sure as hell you'd cop a packet.'

Every three months, CSM Dawson formed everyone up and read out a paragraph from King's Regulations. It stated that it was not a crime to catch VD, but it *was* to conceal it. Subsequently, it was the duty of every soldier to visit the 'early treatment room' after a night out. Sessions were held on how to avoid contracting the disease and the warning signs to look for. Your average rifleman when seeing the symptoms, would straightaway report sick. Medical orderlies sometimes carried out snap inspections during muster parade. Everyone was ordered to take out their 'old man' for what was called a 'short-arm inspection' – a rare treat for any female in the vicinity. Soldiers did their utmost to keep themselves fighting fit. During The Great War, wilfully contracting the disease was deemed to be a self-inflicted wound and could be classed as cowardice.

Ron knew dating Mavis was not the most sensible thing to do, especially with all those Yanks putting themselves around. On the other hand, being dumped by her was of no concern to him now because he already had a new girlfriend. Betty, a sweet-natured seventeen-year-old, worked in a shoe shop next to Dick's. Things were different for him this time. There was something rather special about her, and he had never felt this way about a girl before.

They met by chance, though somewhat of a wet one. During his last leave, he went to see his manager, to ask if he could have his job back once the army was done with him. Dick told him his apprenticeship had already been cancelled. Ron was beside himself, realising he had no job to go back too. His onetime manager, and so-called friend, said nothing more, leaving him standing in the middle of the shop, open-mouthed. Once Dick had finished serving his customer, he called him over, grinning all over his face. He confirmed that his apprenticeship had indeed ended. But from the day he joined up, there was a job waiting for him. Over the moon, Ron put on his old white cow gown, still hanging in its usual place, plus a blue striped apron, the sign of a qualified butcher. He worked until closing time, relishing his newfound status.

By mid-afternoon, he went into the yard to burn some cardboard which had been hanging around for days. Being slightly damp the rubbish took some burning, causing smoke to billow all over the place. Someone yelled, telling him to put the fire out. Out of sheer pig-headedness, he heaped on more cardboard. The shrill voice suddenly shouted, 'you asked for it!' A deluge of water was thrown over the fence, drenching him from head to foot.

He barged into the shop next door and then into the yard. A girl was standing there, a firebrand in more ways than one, holding an empty fire bucket. Her hair was vibrant auburn, she had a petite figure, shapely legs, pleasingly eye-catching and came up to his shoulder. He was smitten as soon as he laid eyes on her.

'Wot ya do that for, Fire Bucket,' he said, looking down at his wet coat.

'Yow 'alf-baked dollop o' lard,' she answered, spitting like a roaring fire. He took a step back. 'That smoke were guin everywhere.'

'I can burn stuff if I want. I don't 'ave ta ask—'

'Now mister ... if yow want an argy-bargy, yow've cum ta right place.'

Taken aback, he hesitated. '... Ya talk funny, Fire Bucket,' he eventually said, once more using her impromptu nickname. 'Are—'

'So, da yow, soldier boy!' she came back sharply.

'—ya from Brummingham?'

'What if I am? An' it's Burminum.'

'I've never met a Brummingham lass before.'

'Well, yow 'ave now. So, stop gorpin', yow saft bugger.'

He found out she lived with a cousin and her husband (an

airframe fitter at RAF Croydon) in Catford, after arriving from Blackpool three months earlier. Her mother died in childbirth when she was just eighteen months old, and her father passed away when she was eleven. Her story melted his heart. Neither of them knew it, but this chance meeting lit a fire which would burn brightly for years to come.

Before leaving work, Dick handed him his indenture papers, along with a five-pound note. Ron asked what the money was for. He said it was because his apprenticeship had been terminated before time. He doubted that somehow because his mum only paid seven pounds ten shillings at the start of his training.

It turned out to be a special day in more ways than one.

American troops and vast quantities of arms and supplies were now crossing the Atlantic in huge convoys, running the gauntlet against U-boats and surface raiders. The British people soon warmed to Johnny Doughboy, as he was affectionately known. His zest for life added a cheerful note in these days of rationing and want.

The Americans took over towns and barracks in the southern counties, joining their Canadian cousins who had been here since the start of the war. American camps drew girls like bees to a honeypot. Crowds of love-hungry GI's, with names such as Top Sergeant Antonio Gomez, Master Sergeant Zeke Medina and Private First-Class Eugene Miller filled our towns, villages, pubs, dancehalls and brothels. They put themselves about with their packs of Chesterfield cigarettes, bottles of bourbon, Coca-Cola, nylons, gum and their famous Hershey bars. How could anyone in austerity Britain resist these lovable newcomers, loaded down with their endless treats from their PX stores? They came from every State, marked by their diverse drawls: the deep south, the Midwest, the east coast and the boroughs of New York.

Without question, it was no contest between Tommy Atkins and his cousin from across the pond. Not only did Johnny Doughboy earn more than his British counterpart, but his walking-out-dress was far smarter than our boy's drab khaki serge. He sported the finest worsted service jacket with a narrow waist and matching belt, hipster slacks, shiny peak cap, slim-fitting poplin shirt with tie and coarse brown crepe-soled shoes. What a contrast to time-worn Tommy Atkins. Dressed in his four-year-old blouse, he looked like he had spent too many nights sleeping rough and recently had the misfortune of being dragged through a hedge backwards.

But they were comrades in arms, waiting for the gathering storm.

While out on the town these newcomers kept themselves to themselves, intent on chatting up anything in a skirt. When drinking, they would collect at one end of the bar, with the Brits at the other. A cultural divide existed between Joe and Tommy, and it needed to be bridged. There was a saying that the Yanks were 'over-sexed, over-paid and over here'.

'Say, Rube,' a master sergeant from Staten Island yelled, 'what about a toon?'

'Yeah, let's give the Limey's a toon,' echoed an ex-hack driver from Queens.

'Youse gonna give our British buddies a toon, Rube?' yelled another.

'Okay, fellas,' the black guy said, slipping onto a piano stool.

The bar erupted to the sound of Tin Pan Alley. The Yanks shrieked as the tempo hotted up, with Rube's fingers ably picking out each note.

The slick-haired ex-hack driver, leaning against the bar gestured to a few British guys. 'Hey, Limeys!' he yelled. 'Ya wanna drink?' A bomber pilot and his crew made their way over. 'Set 'em up, Joe,' the Yank said, slapping a fiver down. 'Drinks fer everyone. Uncle Sam's buyin'. An' this time put some ice in ma *beeeer*.'

They mingled, talking about the war, weighing up how soon it would be over now they were once more comrades in arms. Hours passed, and the beer flowed like water over a weir. Without knowing it, they had so much in common: family, girls back home, fear of what might happen and the desire to live life to the full. But why worry? Tomorrow will look after itself. Live for today was everyone's axiom.

'Youse Limeys ain't bad,' the master sergeant said, slapping the pilot on his back and spilling his beer.

'I'm pleased you think so,' the pilot replied, wiping his sleeve. 'Whatever, ole boy, we're glad you're with us on this one. We've been going it alone for far too long.'

'Together we'll show that little jumped up corporal. Hey, Rubinstein!' he yelled at the black guy. 'Let's make this place rock so much that ole Adolf'll hear us in his nest of vipers!'

'Rock indeed, Yank,' the pilot said, swilling the rest of his beer before picking up the next pint. 'Here's to Anglo American cordial. And an end to the war.'

'Yeah, I'll drink ta that, flyboy.' He smiled. '... But I prefer *beeeer* ma'self. Even this stuff.'

Chapter 11

'The 6th Commandment'

For weeks talk had been about the Brigadier's forthcoming review. As soon as orders went up on the notice board, NCOs started running around like headless chickens. Each man was checked over, with sub-standard clothing exchanged for new ... something unheard of in the British Army. It must be something especially important to go to all this trouble, the grapevine was saying. Galvanised into action, everyone started bulling up their kit, from beret badge to SD boots.

Ron and his mates passed from bed to bed, ruling on each other's efforts, praising or finding fault as the mood took them.

'Aye, Joe,' Ron said, looking at the mirror-like finish on Harold Whiteman's boots, 'ger a load o' Chalkie's daisies.'

'Bloody hell!' Sharpy exclaimed. 'They're brilliant.'

'Show 'im yer polisher, Chalk,' Ron furthered.

The bubbly East Ender held up a pair of frilly French knickers. 'She never put 'em on agin,' he said, grinning all over his face. 'I walked back wiv 'em in me skyrocket. Ya gerra luvly shine.'

Satisfied with their turnout, Captain Jamieson ordered J Support to mount and move off in 'column of route'. Meeting up with the rest of the battalion they formed up in front of Bridlington's wide beach. Deserted but for barbed wire, crisscrossed, iron staked, strung out to break up the barren stretch of sand it would have been a daunting prospect for invading troops.

Once vehicles were parked, everyone was ordered to 'fall in'. More checks followed with officers and NCOs fussing and clucking like mother hens. Ron and the others stood to attention for a good twenty minutes, before, at last, three cars drove down the promenade.

Ron was amazed to see four important personages get out of the second car. The colonel saluted His Majesty and invited him to inspect the troops.

Ron stood rock steady, eyes straight ahead as the king walked down the line of soldiers. He felt a nervous flutter in his stomach, hoping no one would speak to him. The king, taller than his wife, wore the uniform of a Field Marshall with Sam Browne belt, five rows of ribbons on his chest, RAF pilot's wings and a cloth peaked cap. Passing only a foot in front of Ron, he was amazed to see touches of makeup around the king's eyes and lips. The matronly queen trailed behind, looking at the troops while chatting with the colonel. Behind their mother were the princesses, in matching tweed suits and felt cloche hats, listening to General Bernard Montgomery as he explained something to them.

Inspection over, the royal party returned to their car, a midnight blue Rolls Royce. It rapidly drove away with their escort in tow, leaving Monty and the others to make their way to the officer's mess in a nearby hotel.

At last, the order came to 'stand at ease', followed straightaway by 'stand easy'.

Half an hour later, General Montgomery made his way down the hotel steps with the colonel by his side. Monty walked to the front of the parade and climbed aboard Ron's carrier. He waved his arms, urging them to break ranks and gather around. This small, composed figure waited for the chatter to die down. In the meantime, he calmly gauged those nearest to him, looking thoughtful and somehow conveying how much each man meant to him. As if on cue, he cleared his throat, smiled softly and won them over. In short, clipped words, he said, 'I like the look of you fellows … I really do. You show great style and promise,' he resumed after a brief pause. 'Yes, indeed, you do. I've decided you're the chaps for me.' His steely eyes danced from man to man. The soldiers' chests swelled as they gazed open-mouthed at Monty, the hero of El

Alamein. Each man agreed he was ready. This private chat by their general had fired them up, making them eager to take the fight to Hitler.

After lunch, a section from each company spread out in training groups. The king and queen were then given a brief display on how each weapon worked.

Her Majesty, standing in front of Alfie Bell, a short, thickset lad from Bermondsey, asked what he would do if his machine gun jammed.

He smiled a toothless grin. 'Jus' pull back this knob, Missus Queen an' carry on firin',' he answered with a lisp.

She beamed at the East Ender. The colonel quickly whisked her away before the grinning man could say more.

Alfie's number two, Lofty from Kingswinford, Staffordshire was aghast. 'Yow bloody ignoramus ... Missus Queen,' he said through the side of his mouth. 'Bloody 'ell, yow 'alf-baked-dollop-of-useless—'

'She should never 'ave bloomin' asked,' he answered, now they were well out of earshot.

Alfie was never allowed to forget his gaffe. His mates would be talking about it for a long time, and perhaps someday one of them would write about it in his memoirs.

After all this time, four years, Ron sensed he would soon see action. It was hard to say what made him feel this way, but something had changed in his well-ordered world, and he just knew things would never be the same again.

Within a couple of weeks of the king's visit, they were on the move, heading south once more. Military vehicles monopolised the roads, causing mayhem as more and more soldiers headed for the south coast.

Tanks from D Company 7th Queen's Own Hussars squealed and scuttled by, taking great chunks out of the worn tarmac. Ron sat at the side of the road, drinking tea with the others, reading what was painted on the side of each Cruiser Mark III. It was obvious to which company they belonged. Devine Discontent led the way, shadowed by Dead-eyed Dick and then Delightful Delores. Desperate Dan and Dan Dare followed up the rear. Ron thought J Support should do the same but gave up after coming up with just two, Juno and Juliet. The tanks skirted a village pond beneath ancient spreading oaks and elms, churning up the verges of this sublime, rural setting.

They now found themselves in old cavalry barracks next to Aldershot garrison church. Catering almost exclusively for the military, the army's association with this Hampshire town dated back to the Crimean War. Just like Netheravon, it was laid out in a series of two-story buildings which once housed horses and troopers. 15 Platoons billet had an open veranda with iron railings on all three sides. On the ground floor was an old stable block, now turned into a clean and whitewashed dining hall. Next door was a disused entrance gate with regimental badges in relief on the arch. Beside this stood a Victorian guardroom, abandoned long ago.

The platoon received orders to fit metal plates to the sides of their Brens, waterproofing them with white sealing Bostik. It could only mean one thing; a beach landing was imminent.

In case of sudden movement, twenty-four-hour permits were issued instead of standard leave passes. They increased the amount of food in each mess. Seconds were offered, and mess staff pushed trolleys around doling out yet more portions, even though swaddies complained about being stuffed. Many said the 'powers that be' were fattening them up for the kill. NCOs likewise became less exact with their daily rum ration, and their gunfire grew stronger and sweeter, as the time to go got nearer and nearer.

'Me gut stands aahhht a bleedin' mile, Micky,' one lad said, slapping his waistline. 'All this lovely grub,' he further chuntered as his mates savoured their after-meal cigarette.

'Ya sure ya're not preggers?' one of his mates asked. 'Yuv not bin buckshee wif yer favours ta some good lookin' septic tank?'

'Nah! I get 'em ta use a Frenchie, or rubber as they call 'em'

'Why,' his mate blurted out, ''ave they made a mistake?' He laughed at his own wisecrack while opening a fresh pack of Senior Service. He lit one and inhaled. 'Bloody marvellous. Life's grand.'

'Do us a favour, Stubbs,' another said, not feeling in a warlike mood, 'shut yer bleedin' cakehole. Let's enjoy our smoke.'

'It's gotta be soon,' someone said, getting up with the rest and trooping out of the dining hall to empty their leftovers in a swill bin. 'We'd better pack our bags.' He dunked his plate in a soapy vat, then rinsed it in what had once been clean water. 'I 'ear Yanks are gerrin windy.'

'Tell us somethin' new,' Stubbs quipped, having the last word.

A couple of tattooists in the town vied with each other in adorning soldier's bodies with all manner of fancy designs, along with names of loved ones and regimental mottoes. Ron heard of one lad having his old man tattooed with an erect penis and the words 'be rough with me', which it was said was only readable when he was fully aroused. The lengths some chaps will go too. It would have been a strange request to adorn such an appendage. Then again, maybe it was done by a girlfriend or bosom buddy, as a sign of undying love.

Aldershot boasted three cinemas, showing *Cover Girl* with Rita Hayworth, *The Fighting Seabees* with John Wayne and Joan Fontaine and Orson Welles in *Jane Eyre*. The Theatre Royal played twice daily to a packed auditorium.

After tea on Friday, they started queuing for their weekly cigarette and chocolate ration, then raced to tag onto long lines of khaki outside the cinemas and theatre.

The dated, Victorian barracks in The Shot, as Tommy Atkins called Aldershot, housed thousands of healthy, robust soldiers, of which most were from the Armoured Division. The Canadians, having pulled out months ago, left behind goodwill messages on the barrack walls. Alongside these were stirring images of local girls, barely clad and in risqué poses. Each was well drawn and showed the same hand. A large cap badge, next to one curvy long-haired beauty called 'good-time Glenda', belonged to the Royal Canadian Mounted Police. Other proud regiments, Princess Patricia's Canadian Light Infantry (Princess Pat's) and The Toronto Scottish had also left their mark with cap badges and caricatures of some of their officers, along with messages such as 'see you on the beach'.

The padre toured the barracks after lunch each Sunday, urging the dozing men to join his evening service and partake in a free cup of tea and a rock cake. Though most of the time he was fighting a losing battle. To put off the lustful longings that most soldiers had every waking hour, even for an hour or two to sing a few hymns was too much for some. They felt their life was but sand running through an hourglass and all too soon the precious grains would be gone. However, there were a few more each week attending services. The thought of dying in battle tended to focus one's mind.

Despite group talks and debates with the padre, a burning question plagued Ron. How would he react under fire and could he, in fact, kill someone when it came to the put? No amount of thinking about it would ease his mind. Being an ardent churchgoer, he dwelt on this a lot. The sixth commandment says *Though Shalt Not Kill*. He kept running it over and over in his mind, making his fret more about it. But soldiers were trained to precisely do that, without thought of God and retribution. Moreover, if he wavered for just a second, it would be him communing with his Maker.

To these misguided swaddies, it was all too obvious the padre was there to give comfort to the wounded, give those who were dying the last rites and read the burial service over them. He would be far too busy to listen to the ramblings of someone with ethical doubts. So, like many, Ron kept his misgivings to himself.

Ron and a platoon mate, Curtis Sates, known as Cadger because of his habit of cadging everything in sight, applied for twenty-four-hour permits. They weren't issued with a travel warrant because the adjutant didn't want them travelling out of the area, just in case they had to get back quickly. Getting around this, they hiked to London, even though it would only mean spending a few hours with the family. It might be their last chance before going to war. In no time they got a lift in a three-tonner to Chertsey. Within minutes of being dropped off, a London Brick Company lorry came along and took them to Charing Cross.

'Butcher's at all them bleedin' septic tanks, Ron? They're all over the place, like a bleedin' rash. Wot ya know, Joe?' he said to three gum-chewing doughboys, larking about and prancing along the pavement on Westminster Bridge.

All three laughed and waved at Cadger as if he were a long-lost cousin. The mouthy one, tunic spattered with what looked like puke, said in a broad Texan drawl, 'Hiya, Limey. We're gonna have tea with tha queen.' Fuelled by an excess of alcohol, they laughed even louder.

'Oh yeah, which queen's that, mate?'

Ron chuckled at Cadger's reply. Out of earshot, he said, 'To 'ear 'em talk you'd think they'd all got soddin' ranches an' oil wells.'

'Ya can't blame chuffin' silly cows,' Cadger said, lighting a cigarette.

'Who cares anyway. We'd be chuffin' same, lordin' it down Fifth Avenue.'

They parted at The Oval, planning to meet up later outside The Duke of Wellington on the Great Western Road.

On their return, they flagged down a truck known as a DUKW, or Duck to Tommy Atkins. The sergeant and his mate were on their way to Weymouth and said they would drop them off at Aldershot.

'Everythin' all right at 'ome?' Cadger screeched above the wind.

They clung to the sloping, coffin-like top of the speeding Duck.

'Could be worse, Cadge,' Ron replied, trying to light a cigarette. 'Me Mum knew summit were up when I said I could only stay fer kidney punch.

'Same wif my lot. You'd fink chuffin' Pope 'ad died, seein' their long airs and graces.'

'Not such a good idea after all,' Ron said, sighing. 'But it were worth all the effort. It might be bloomin' last time they see us.' He wiped away a tear, perchance caused by the wind whipping across his face. He turned to look at Cadger and saw he was similarly afflicted, using an old rag to wipe his eyes and blow his nose.

On Friday morning they reported to the rifle range, which true to form was as wet as a Saturday night in Manchester.

The standard practice was for each man to fire five rounds grouping, five rounds application and five rounds snap, either prone, kneeling or sitting. Your pals in the butts, knowing your firing detail and aided by a pencil, pot of glue and strips of white paper could deftly inflate your score. Thereby helping you get a marksman's badge, along with a few extra pennies in your pay.

'Okay, Lofty!' one of his mates yelled. 'Firing point three!'

Buster, a dark, swarthy lad from Staines put his head above the butts and waved to show he had seen where Lofty was in the firing detail.

'Down,' Sergeant Cox ordered. 'Load! Twenty-five yards grouping, fire!'

Within thirty seconds of his last shot, Lofty's target was lifted again, showing a tight grouping right of the bull at four o'clock. Likewise, if he wanted, he could frustrate a lordly officer who had high hopes of taking part in the next Bisley shoot. One such officer, a second lieutenant from Preston with a double-barrelled name sent for the armourer. The officer insisted he move the rear sight to the left. He fired five more rounds and found he was out even more. A neat group on the left-hand edge of the target. The armourer moved it back to its original position, and the officer fired a further five rounds. Buster duly taped them over and put five scattered pencil holes on the edge of the target. By now Ponsonby-Browne was beside himself, saying the rifle was useless and should be withdrawn. His efforts were in vain. Buster just wanted to have a bit of fun with this officer.

As they marched back to the billet, little did they know the next time they fired their rifles, it would be in anger.

A few 'old sweats', having served in the Western Desert were now finding their way into J Support. These tough, unruly swaddies brought new words and phrases into barrack-room chatter, briefly supplanting the torrent of four-letter words that peppered a soldier's banter. It was now shufti cush, alakefic and saida bint as these 'old sweats' kept up their endless desert, Arabic babble, and sang their engaging songs:

> *'Saida bint I like your charming manner.*
> *To live with you, would be my one desire.*
> *I think I'll call you Tina.*
> *It rhymes with talla.*
> *My swain gyppo bint and cush cateer.'*

'Be a pal, Topper,' one scruffy old-timer called. 'Bring a cuppa cha back wif ya!' Frank Male stopped a bullet in Tobruk and once fit found himself in The Rifles.

'Sod orf,' Topper refused less politely.

'Wot wif, Maley?' a good-natured youngster obliged, flexing his fingers. 'Give us yer lolly then, ya old scrotum.' Male emptied a pocket of shrapnel on his bed and selected four halfpenny pieces.

'Where's yer slinger?' he pressed as he took the money, urging him to get his backside off the bed.

'Arf a mo,' Male said, getting up. 'Don't do yer nut, kiddo.' He handed over his mug and smiled, knowing full well he had conned another roommate into bringing his tea back from the naafi. 'That's trouble today,' Male said once the lad and his mates left, 'there's nah bleedin' muckin' in spirit these days wif these wet-behind-the-ears youngsters.'

Male's less than agreeable manner was the exception to the rule, with most 'old sweats' being quite affable. There was one thing for sure, though, Ron and the others had been taught well, and when the time came, they would give their life for each other. Nevertheless, during the heat of battle, they would not be far from Male's side, providing courage under fire to those less experienced.

Ron and the others attended a lecture on the kinds of German uniforms they would shortly encounter. An aged captain they had not seen before showed them a half-sized cut-out of a soldier in field grey, wearing a coal-scuttle helmet, black webbing and jackboots. The NCOs gave each man a booklet showing German ranks for the army, navy and air force. The officer next took them through the uniform worn by Panzer troops, saying they used to wear black before changing to field grey. He picked up another cut-out, a paratrooper in a grey jumping smock with large patch pockets for stick grenades. Around his neck was a Mauser sub-machine gun, along with a cape and water bottle hanging from his waist. He wore calf-length boots, laced at the side and a double-strapped helmet with a winged emblem on the side. He also wore his brevet for six parachute jumps during training, an eagle in flight with a cluster of laurel leaves. The lecture concluded with the Gestapo and *Schutzstaffel*.

After lunch, an RAF Flight Sergeant, aided by a rather cute

WRAF with several posters took them through the features of various German fighters and bombers. First was the Messerschmitt bf109, touching on its characteristic's and its destructive firepower from a 20mm cannon in its nose and two machine guns in the wings. Then he covered the Focke-Wulf 190, another low winged plane. But this time with two cannons in the nose and once again two machine guns. Next were Dornier and Heinkel bombers. They also had retractable undercarriages, but with quite distinctive egg-shaped tailplanes. It was a great deal to absorb in just a few hours, but he pressed on, ignoring their glazed expressions.

All these facts were to help them form a picture of an enemy waiting behind the Atlantic Wall. German soldiers, having been used to 'good living' during their war, now found life a struggle, with food shortages and the bombing of their cities. Also, letters from home were few and far between, plus there was always fear for their loved one's safety. Likewise, casualty lists in newspapers made for depressing reading.

Allied command was also mindful that the enemy had a distinct advantage over them, entrenched behind their well-prepared defences. Each command station and gun post were linked by tunnels and telephone, so reserves could be sent to those sectors under attack. Having time on their hands, they built up strong positions, disguising them, so they blended in with their surroundings. Each post was counter-ranged, ready for direct fire orders should a 'position' be over-run. As soon as their troops withdrew there would be a pinpoint barrage on the new occupants. Hence the golden rule to always consolidate 'over and off' a captured position. They also had plenty of time to prepare clear fields of fire, using obstacles to throw attackers into their killing zones. They would also conceal heavy armour, ready to support their infantry when the time came. Concrete tank traps, where armoured vehicles would get bogged down, needed to be breached first by the infantry. The sheer cliffs and reinforced gun emplacements, covered by machine gun turrets, swinging freely to provide a deadly field of fire made the Atlantic Wall a seemingly impregnable fortress, stretching from Spain to Finland.

The Germans also had another advantage. Their troops, toughened by years of combat, had honed their killing abilities during the Spanish Civil War, the nineteen-forty Blitzkrieg, North Africa and the Russian Front. But they were now being pushed back in the east and were all but ousted in North Africa, Sicily and much of Italy. Also, Anglo-American navies now had mastery on the high seas, cutting Germany's supply routes and slowly starving them into submission. That great feeling of victory when trouncing weak, ill-equipped nations was a distant memory. Left now was the nagging doubt of themselves, one day, being the vanquished. The Allies were now threatening the very heart of Germany, and soon would be fighting for their very existence. And maybe, within months defending the Fatherland itself.

But Adolf Hitler and his minions claimed victory was still within their grasp. Then again, some of his Generals would gladly depose him and sue for peace. During his reign of terror, there were several attempts on his life, and his revenge was brutal and unforgiving.

They would be watching and waiting in their dugouts and gun pits, knowing only too well it was a matter of time before the Allies came. So, Willi, Franz, Seipp and Otto watched and waited for signs of invasion, reading their last letter from home, over and over.

The command structure of a motor platoon was of paramount importance for its success. Mr Bowkett lead 15 Platoon, and his word was law, with Sergeant Frazer acting as number two, followed by Sergeant Cox. Should all three be 'taken out' during an action, the next senior NCO would take charge. Each section was made up of two vehicles and led by a corporal. All drivers became the lead crew member, with NCOs seldom taking on a driver's role.

Mr Bowkett and his sergeants had been working these three years to turn thirty guys into a bunch of brave and resourceful warriors. During training, they moved men around to increase fighting efficiency, so creating an ideal team mix. Doing so allowed them to recrew and work with others in the event of someone being taken out during an action.

While all this was going on the sergeants watched for signs of friction. If they thought it was affecting morale in a crew, section or even the platoon itself they would warn Mr Bowkett of the need to move men around.

By now, they were trained to perfection. Nevertheless, the sergeants still switched drivers within each section every few months. Ron and Pat Iverson from Derby, known to all as Ginger was once more teamed up with Charlie Squires, a fourth-generation costermonger from Spitalfields Market. Once waterproofing was finished, with metal sides stored away ready for fitting later, they could give some thought to loading and stowing their gear on the Bren. Ron and the other two, with help from Sergeant Cox, discussed where everything should go. Belts of ammo for the Vickers, pouches of .303 rounds, rifle's, mills and incendiary grenades were to receive special attention. Without doubt, though, as far as they were concerned, the most precious item was the toolbox, loaded with food. The tommy cooker, equally important needed to be ready at a minute's notice for a brew. Big things were lashed on the outside, while bedding rolls, tarpaulins, groundsheets and kit bags were tied off for comfort and protection. Two four-gallon Jerry cans – water and petrol – were also strapped on the back next to the toolbox. Another precious item was the platoon's rum ration in a stoneware jar. They stored this on Ron's Bren, under the watchful eye of Sergeant Cox, who issued it on the orders of Mr Bowkett.

As time slipped by, they enjoyed their semi-relaxed lifestyle, trekking into town, taking in what was on at the Royal and cinemas, vying for places in the never-ending queues of khaki. The routine of camp life stayed very much the same, disturbed only by bugle calls, parades and visits to the mess. The lads passed the long hours by writing letters, playing cards and going to the naafi and pubs.

There was not much else to do, other than wait.

Chapter 12

'Firm Foothold'

Sports day, with its inter-company rivalry this year was held in Aldershot Park, with races taking place on a cinder track owned by a local athletics club. Budding Olympians pitted themselves against other hopefuls at running, high jump, long jump, shot put and discus.

A cloudless sky with sun beating down put everyone in a positive frame of mind. Today was a marked contrast to the last two when squally showers and high winds pounded Aldershot.

It's the first decent day in weeks, thought Ron as he warmed up for the four-hundred relay with Jimbo, Lance Corporal McBain and Corporal Farrell. Having come second in the one-hundred yards, Captain Jamieson put him down as anchorman.

'Now don't drop bloomin' baton, Ern,' Ron said, digging him in the ribs.

Ernie, having beaten him by a whisker in the one hundred, was running for his own company. 'Don't worry, lad,' he said, punching his arm.

'Lad!' He looked aghast. 'You're four months older than me ya dopey pillock.'

'Hey, watch yer language, son. Don't forget yer talkin' to a Corporal.'

Ron made a grab for him. 'Come 'ere ya great lummox.' Ernie wasn't quick enough, and within seconds he was sitting on his chest, arms pinned by his side. 'Got ya at me mercy, Price,' he said, hawking up spit.

'You dare, Deakin,' he threatened. 'You'll be on a charge quicker than ya can swalla that bloomin' muck ya're gonna dribble in me face.' He taunted, daring him, but he knew he wouldn't do it. Not because of the threat, but because you don't do that sort of thing to a mate.

Suddenly the relay was announced. Captain Slater stopped halfway through his address. The next voice they heard was the colonels. 'Stand by for an announcement,' he said from a raised dais. 'Great news!' He paused for a moment to get everyone's attention. '... We have just heard that the Allies have landed in northern France.'

An almighty cheer went up.

At last! The long-awaited day had arrived.

It was a good five minutes before he spoke again. 'I don't have much detail, other than to say British, Canadian and American troops have secured a firm foothold on the French coast.' Another cheer went up. 'All leave is cancelled, forthwith. We will shortly be called on to join the fray. Enjoy your day, chaps. And don't tire yourself out. You'll need all your energy and wits about you in the weeks ahead.'

Captain Slater took back the microphone and called for the relay teams to form up in their lanes.

Mess staff handed a paper bag to each man, along with a mug of tea, for taking away and consuming in small, gossiping groups. A Spam sandwich as thick as a doorstep, one suspect sausage roll and a piece of dry, tasteless fruitcake was quickly devoured amidst happy, carefree chatter.

Where and when will it be? This was the question on the tip of everyone's tongue. *No time ta practice now*, Ron mused. *This war larks for real, an' no second chance if ya get it wrong.*

A few joyful swaddies hung around a three-tonner from the comms platoon, trying to glean more up to the minute news from the harassed crew, being bombarded from all sides.

'Wot ya fink, Barney?' one old sweat asked, no doubt working out the odds of getting through it all unscathed.

'Nah more dodgin' orf, me ole cocker,' another said in jest.

'Get aahhht of it,' Barney replied, grinning slyly. 'Plen'y o' nickel-an'-dime. Ya worry too much, Sid.'

Medals were given out at the close, just before returning to barracks. J Support took third place in the relay. They were leading after the second change but bungled the final one when Ron dropped the baton. Ernie ribbed him over tea, swearing he would never let him forget his new nickname, 'baton brain'.

After tea, where the chatter still pulsated above the sound of scraping chairs and clinking crockery, Lieutenant Bowkett visited them for a final check on any shortages. 'Speak up now, lads,' he cautioned, 'if you're short of anything—'

'A few more pees would have been nice, Sir.'

'I've marked *your* card, Smith,' said Corporal Farrell.

'—otherwise, forget it.' He gave Smith a look that could curdle milk. 'Sergeant Frazer,' he continued, 'give me a list by muster parade tomorrow of how much ammo we have on each vehicle.'

'Very good, Sir.'

What followed was a relaxed update on the invasion. Mr Bowkett, better informed than your average swaddy, explained that British and Canadian forces had secured a solid bridgehead on three beaches, Gold, Juno and Sword. Ron's face drained of colour when he heard what the one beach was called. Fortunately, the others were dead against his choice of name for their beloved Bren, settling on his further suggestion of Betsy.

The Allies were now driving forward, exploiting their gains. The Americans, meeting stiff opposition on *their* beaches, Utah and Omaha, were pinned down for hours, with heavy losses on Omaha. They were now heading inland but were behind schedule.

'Quick, you lot!' someone yelled. 'Come an' 'ave a gander at this lot!'

Everyone rushed outside and gazed at hundreds of aircraft, towing clumsy-looking gliders. The sky was black with them, all heading south. *Good luck me ole lads*, Ron wished, knowing full-well up there were the real heroes. The airborne glider infantry, packed side by side, restless, cheerful, afraid – very afraid – were ready for any eventuality. On this warm summer's evening, he watched, deeply moved by the awe-inspiring sight he was privileged to witness.

'Wouldn't fancy their chances, Jock,' one lad mused.

'Nae,' his mate nodded. 'Ye would'na get me up in one of them ... cannae abide heights.

With much curiosity, each man before leaving Aldershot was told to change notes and silver into French francs. They were also given a pocket-sized booklet with a picture of the *Arc de Triumph* on the cover. It gave details on the country, codes of behaviour and a few basic French phrases:

'Parler anglais Madame' – *'Mon petite Cherrie'*
'Comment vas-tu ma chérie' – *'Sil vous plait'*
'Bonjour, mon ami' – *'Combien Madame'*
'Bonjour Monsieur' – *'Mercia beaucoup'*

All guesswork was at an end. It wasn't a secret anymore. Each man knew where he was going, after four years of waiting.

'It's gonna be gay Paree,' one joker cooed when they gave him his francs and booklet.

'Prepare to move! Load vehicles!' The order went around like quicksilver.

15 Platoon stowed their gear, careful to spread the load and tie everything down. Ron and the others attached more than average importance to the food box, filling it with tins, Huntley & Palmers biscuits, cigarettes and a dozen large bars of Cadburys Dairy Milk. Iron rations were also given out, stored in a wooden box lashed to the side of the Bren. Made from chocolate, beef and oatmeal, these were to be grated, tipped in water and boiled to provide a nutritional drink while on the move.

The Fifth eventually pulled out of the old cavalry barracks. The array of vehicles looked fearsome enough to take on anything the

Germans dared to throw at them, and the crews were in high spirits with the prospect of at last meeting Fritz.

The roads were now given over entirely to military transport, all bearing down on ports in their correct sequence, ready for loading on thousands of ships waiting on the south coast. As they made their way along predetermined routes, MPs and civil police kept the roads clear of non-essential traffic. Closing on the outer suburbs of London, Ron's platoon stopped for a quick brew, parking on the pavement to avoid blocking the highway. Shortly children surrounded each carrier, trying to see what they could cadge.

'Git bloomin' compo aahhht, Ginge,' Charlie said, setting up the tommy cooker with a large billy-can on top. He opened an airtight tin, took out two gel tablets, placed them on the burner, lit each one and then slid the plate across when they were burning nicely. '... Come on ya bastard,' he cursed, watching for tell-tale bubbles.

'Yuv got ta much water, Chaz,' Ron said, kneeling beside him. 'There's only bloomin' three of us. Not whole chuffin' army. Chuck some away. The bleedin' war'll be over by time it's boiled.'

'Wotch it, nipper,' Charlie urged, steering a couple of ragamuffins out of the way. The eldest, in shrunken jersey and coarse tweed shorts, marched on the spot, lifting his knees high to impress the soldiers. He quickly snapped to attention and saluted Ron and Charlie with a grubby hand that looked like it had not seen water in months. With knees just as dirty, stockings slipping down over badly scuffed, half-laced boots he looked a comical sight.

'You'd make a damn good soldier, kiddo?' Ron said, returning his salute. 'Wot's yer name, son?'

'Tommy Danks, mister,' he answered, brushing a shock of blonde hair from his forehead. 'This is me mate, Sidney.' A runny-nosed six-year-old with cold sores around his mouth stood stiffly to attention.

'Oh yeah,' Charlie said, sizing them up. 'I suppose you'll be wantin' some Rosie Lee?'

'Yes please, mister,' they both replied.

''Ere, Deak, pop 'round back and gerra few squares o' that stuff wiv bin savin', he added without letting on he was talking about their private stash of chocolate.

''Ere, kids,' Ron said, handing each a square. 'If ya go an' blab ya won't get bloomin' rest.' They popped the chocolate in their mouth and then drank tea from Ron's mug, so it melted into a soupy mess.

Ron felt at peace as he sat on the pavement, drinking tea with his mates and two young urchins watching him as if he were a hero. A warm glow spread through his stomach when he realised, for the first time since leaving Aldershot, he was at last on his way to war.

Within minutes the 'red flag' went up, telling everyone to load, ready to move. 'Okay, Chaz, in ya go,' Ron said, slinging the slops in the gutter. Before climbing aboard, he ruffled the hair of their young guests and handed each two squares of chocolate. 'Tarrah, kids. Wotch the road an' keep out of trouble,' he added as a Sherman clipped the kerb.

'Sure, mister,' Tommy said, popping the last piece of Dairy Milk in his mouth. He shouted as they pulled away, 'Good luck, mister! Kill a German fer me!'

Much to everyone's disgust as they drove through the suburbs, they were told to stay with their vehicles and not to slip off to say goodbye to families. Even though many home districts passed by tantalisingly close.

This time they stopped at Rainham for another brew and something to eat. Sergeant Frazer said they would be moving within an hour to a holding camp to bed down for the night, ready for Tilbury Docks next morning, and loading for Normandy.

Harold Woods sat in his half-track with a pained look on his face. 'Wot's up, Sticks?' one of his mates asked.

'I live two streets down on the right, an' I can't even go an' say goodbye ta me Ma.'

'Course ya can, dipstick,' Corporal Price said, having overheard what Woods said. 'Ya're all right, Sticks. Nip orf, sharpish loike. We'll cover fer ya. But be back in 'alf an 'our if ya know what's good fer ya. Otherwise, yer plates won't touch the ground.' Woods gawked at him, open-mouthed, hardly trusting what Ernie was saying. 'Get bloody lead aahhht yer daisy roots, son. That's an order. Go and clock yer Ma.'

It was dusk when they reached the makeshift camp, and then the bother of hanging around, waiting for orders. Standing next to Sergeant Frazer, with too much time on his hands, Ron found himself detailed for picket duty.

Row upon row of army bell tents crowded the council sports ground at Thurrock. Knowing his kit was safe on Betsy he took one last look at the tent he would later bed down in, noting where it was among so many. He turned away and went to patrol up and down the transport lines, with only a battle-scarred pickaxe handle for company.

After what turned out to be a tiring journey, he was more than pleased when his two hours of aimless watching ended. Finding his tent, he threw himself into the first available space, slipping instantly into dreamland.

Waking a few hours later, he looked around, sorting out his bearings. He caught sight of a white mackintosh and two battledress blouses. On the shoulder of one was a major's crown, while the other bore three pips. Moving closer, he saw K Company commander and his number two, Captain Swan, fast asleep like children on the eve of a great adventure. In fear of being put on a charge for sleeping with officers, in army parlance, he made a silent, speedy and orderly withdrawal. It was hardly surprising he had bedded down in the wrong tent, because each looked the same as its neighbour.

He told Charlie what had happened. 'I spent last night with Courtney an' Vesta Tilley,' he confessed, treating it as a grand wheeze.

'Hob knobbin' wif motor companies now, aye, Rip Van Winkle?' his mate joked.

'It were a mistake. No lights. Midnight. Black as a coal 'ole. Ya can 'ardly blame me. It could 'ave 'appened ta any of us.'

'Ah, but it didn't, Snoozy,' Ginger said on the cusp of laughing. 'It happened to you.'

'We're not good enough fer 'im now,' Charlie added for good measure. 'Jus' shows wot a China plate'll do if 'e gets 'alf a chance.'

His mates roared with laughter when they saw Ron's sullen face. 'Bastards,' he said, laughing with them. 'Ya scabby bunch of toe-rags.'

Within an hour the drivers took their carriers and half-tracks to Purfleet for final waterproofing and then onto Tilbury.

The morning news came over the tannoy saying enemy forces, though initially taken by surprise were now putting up stiff resistance. Still, the Allies were pushing forward to enlarge their bridgehead, in preparation for landing more troops.

Late afternoon everyone made their way to Tilbury Docks in Bedford's, cheered on by hordes of children, all yelling 'come on mister chuck us yer loose change!' The lads duly obliged, knowing full well they would have no need of English money for some time, if ever again.

A constant line of soldiers struggled up the gangway of an American liberty ship. Each was bent on finding a berth, so they could heave off their pack, squatting, settling for a bit of unclaimed space and prepared to wait for orders. After a while, once the last man was settled, the ships engines started to vibrate through the hull like a giant waking. As if fearful of what might happen, she warily moved away from the quay, placing herself in the running tide. A couple of tugs, fussing around her like a doting mother sounded their foghorns in salute. Amidst frantic thoughts of U-boats and dive bombers, she moved towards the estuary, flanked on either side by an untidy sprawl of warehouses, huge capstans and ships being unloaded by stevedores, thronging all over the jetty like worker ants.

At first light they found themselves anchored off Southend, nestled in the middle of similar vessels. Two frigates and a motor torpedo launch kept them company, being their escort across the channel. To pass the time the ship's captain called for a boat drill. Wearing life jackets – those able to find them – they were told to walk in a calm and orderly manner to their lifeboat station. Ron thought if ever they were in danger of sinking, the last thing he would see would be calm and orderliness.

Having moved into position, three lines of ships got underway, veiled by a smokescreen from the frigates. All ranks, except seamen and a few naval auxiliaries manning fire hoses, were told to stay below deck until they were well out of sight of land. They sailed past the Isle of Sheppey, on towards Margate, Broadstairs, Ramsgate and finally Dover. The white cliffs slipped by unheralded, with soldiers huddled together in the crowded hold. Many would have liked to see these chalk, white cliffs as they turned south towards Normandy, as more than a few would never again behold their iconic image.

Below deck, away from officers and NCOs, Paddy and George from 14 Platoon ran a Bingo-style version of Crown and Anchor. Using the gaming dice and makeshift cards, numbered three to eighteen they had already made a tidy profit of one and nine-pence on each card of ten games.

'Eyes down an' look in, lads,' Paddy warned, rolling three dice. 'Ernest Bevan ... number eleven.'

'Coalface Jonnies,' the men chorused in reply.

He rolled again. This time three crowns showed. 'One and eight ... give us a date.' Everyone softly cheered. Then another role. This time it was a crown, heart and anchor. 'Useless bod ... unlucky sod ... number thirteen.' A couple of guys groaned. The last role was six. 'Trip to the flicks ... number six.'

'House!' someone yelled.

'Keep yer voice down, arsehole,' a lad cussed from the driving seat of a Bren.

'Over here, Tilley,' the winner softly called.

George Tillman picked his way amongst boots and gaiters stuck out at all angles and then checked the winning card. Right,' he said, winking at Paddy, 'we have another winner,'

'Bottom line, guys,' his mate warned. 'Look in. Here we go again.' They all bent to the task, eager to win a tin of fifty Players Navy Cut.

There was a deathly hush as the duty officer and sergeant threaded their way through a sprawl of legs to reach Paddy and George. After a brief exchange, they put a kybosh on any further thought of going on with this illicit game. Disgruntled murmurs showed what they would like to do with these two busybodies. King's Regulations, however, made it quite clear that Crown and Anchor board games, in any form, can only be played under supervision of an officer.

Returning to their small groups they sulked at their lot, wishing for some much-needed action. Waiting around and kept in the dark was sending more than a few around the bend.

From deep in the bowels of the ship a group of soldiers were singing, tugging at everyone's heartstrings and whisking them back home to their sweethearts and families:

'We'll meet again
Don't know where
Don't know when
But I know we'll meet again some sunny day
Keep smiling through
Just like you always do
Till the blue skies drive the dark clouds far away...'

They seemed to have been sailing for days but were in fact only nine hours out of Southend.

Well, this is it, Ron mused. *No more excuses. This is for real. Though I'll feel better when I get off this vomit ridden tub.* A nauseous feeling grew in his stomach. Was it nerves or seasickness? A few guys were honking up below deck. He had a strong stomach but hearing someone retch was a sure-fire way of setting him off. He stared at the mass of khaki, lying, stooping, standing, filling all vantage points on the crowded deck and wondered if they were having the same twinges of doubt. He hoped he would equip himself well and not let his friends down. Still sweating out his silent doubts, coming to grips with his fears – fear of disgrace and losing respect for himself and from others – he tried to shrug off this negative feeling.

To everyone's relief, the flotilla finally anchored off Normandy. Ron was amazed by what he saw, realising the battered coastline a few days ago was part of Hitler's Atlantic Wall.

There was now plenty of time to view this incredible sight. Hundreds of ships, all sizes and classes, from troop and cargo transports to heavy cruisers and corvettes rested at anchor. Tank and infantry landing craft weaved in and out of the larger ships, before making their way towards the beach to unload men and equipment. On their flank, Royal Navy frigates zipped back and forth, drawing U- and E-boats away from invading troops. Squadrons of Spitfires and Typhoons gave a constant curtain of air cover, keeping enemy aircraft at bay. It was D-Day plus four, but there was a long way to go before Tommy Atkins could hang up his uniform.

'Grub up,' someone yelled. For a British Tommy, this was the best news ever, giving him relief from the boredom of having to hang around for orders, plus a chance to gripe about the quantity and quality of food on offer. Ron, Charlie and Ginger picked up their mess tins and followed everyone else to the stern. With a hefty portion of bully stew, a large chunk of fresh bread and roly-poly and custard, they made their way back to Betsy, squatting down beside her tracks.

With their meal out of the way Ginger started to brew up.

'Give us a sup,' Company Sergeant Major Dawson asked as he chanced to be standing nearby. 'Is it a good brew, mate?'

We're gonna be China plates are we, Droopy Draws? 'Rifleman Iverson makes a mean gunfire, Sir,' he said, handing him his untouched mug. He would never forget the verbal basting and an hour's drill practice by the incomparable Mr Dawson. Worst of all at six o'clock, while everyone else was out enjoying the delights of Aldershot. 'That'll teach you to be late for muster parade, Deakin?' Dawson thundered, taking delight in flexing his power over a poor swaddy who happened to be caught short at the wrong time. *We'll see, mate,* Ron thought as he was marched back to the duty office.

'Nice brew, Deakin,' the sergeant major said, handing back his mug.

'Anytime, Sir,' *an' bleedin' next time, matey, I'll be sure ta tip somethin' nasty in it before I give it ta ya.*

Drivers were told to report to their vehicles, ready for loading. On a given signal they mounted and waited for further orders. The Royal Engineers started to busy themselves by hooking up carriers and sending them twisting and twirling above the deck. When over the landing craft they lowered them onto the ducking and diving flat-top with a loud thud. They worked like beavers, having little respect for these lovingly cared for vehicles. When four were loaded, the crews and countless infantry wallahs swarmed down rope netting. Having no keel, it bounced around like a cork in a barrel in a force ten gale, making it hard to climb down with any degree of safety. Ron held on for grim death, watching transfixed as vaporous, pink water lapped between the vessels. Each wave saw the landing craft lift to within three feet and then fall away like a runaway lift. He needed to time his jump on the next surge. If he missed his footing, he would fall and break something, or worse still end up between the hulls and get crushed to death. Next time the landing craft was close, he made a panicked lunge towards what he hoped would be salvation. He let out an audible sigh as he straightened up and then threaded his way between each carrier, making for Betsy and a grinning Charlie. Taking his seat, he heard laughter as more men jumped down and realised for the first, and not the last time that this was a form of nervous release. Each man was dealing with things the way best he could, knowing full well he would soon be fighting for his life.

Waiting offshore in the churning swell was pure agony, being tossed all over the place, making oneself black and blue. Once each craft was ordered to go, it would pick its way through jetsam, nudging ever closer to the crowded beach, hopefully without mishap. To come all this way and fall at the first hurdle would be just too much. An hour later, they were still waiting. Orders were being given by naval officers, telling drivers to start engines and cast off. Ron thought if they didn't get going soon, on to dry land, he would lose his breakfast, as many had already done, making the deck awash with everyone's last meal. A young ensign in cap and white submarine jersey stood on his platform, waiting for orders to go.

At long last, the order came!

'Ahoy, number fifty-one!' someone yelled. 'In you go!'

A cheer went up.

A light naval craft appeared around the stern of the liberty ship. Without slowing, it ploughed on. The bearded officer lowered his megaphone and gave them a cheery wave. The flat-top's engines whirred into life, and it lurched forward, its bell announcing it was on its way. Overhead a solitary Spitfire observed what was going on, haughtily.

Down went the ramp with a thwapping sound. Charlie edged Betsy towards what looked like a sheer drop. He moved forward, felt the carrier shudder, then her nose went down like a ton of bricks, ready to meet the crushing weight of water. Ron, standing on the passenger seat with hand raised, gave him instructions. 'Take it steady, Chaz. You're okay, China. Easy does it. Touch ta yer left. Enough. Keep it like that.' He felt the carrier touch sandy bottom, sinking a little and then finding its footing. 'Welcome to France!' he yelled, slapping Charlie on his back. 'Fer Christ's sake let's find somewhere ta brew up. Me mouff's feelin' like a parrot's crotch.'

Jeeps, carriers, tanks and lorry's, upended, half-submerged and pitching in the swell made it difficult for drivers to get off the beach. Large shell holes formed natural vehicle traps, being the downfall of many. The best thing to do thought Charlie was to follow someone else or the tracks of a vehicle which had not come to grief.

Two lines of Brens from J Support loomed larger as they struggled on, picking their way around a few dead Germans. A structure ripped apart by a massive explosion stood in the now fading light, its shape clearly identifying it as a heavy gun emplacement.

Once off the beach, Charlie was told to spend the night in the first field he came to, ready to join his unit at their muster point next morning.

Betsy's crew, dead on their feet, giving up on checking if there were any Boche about, agreed *their* war could wait a bit longer.

The next few days were spent in a small village, north-east of Bayeux, leagering in an orchard.

Music from a tannoy belted out, sometimes stopping for the BBC news. Drivers de-waterproofed their vehicles, stacking metal plates on top of a huge pile. Everyone bathed in a village pond – to the amusement of a few locals, mostly women – to wash away the 'chatty' feeling that was a constant companion for soldiers on the move.

They set up their bivvies by stretching a rope between two trees, throwing a tarp over the top, tucking in the ends and holding it down with a few bricks from a bombed-out farmhouse. Kit and bedrolls were arranged at the closed end, with a cooking and brew-up space by the entrance for ease of access. Rifles and machine guns, close at hand, were loaded and ready.

Paddy Lomas and George Tillman ran a book on the St. Leger. Everyone sat around listening to the race blaring out over the tannoy, making them feel close to their family while at the same time homesick.

The lads enjoyed this camping spirit, playing football and cricket and cooking for themselves from their ample supply of pack rations. The Fifth was ready, awaiting their first battle orders.

Chapter 13

'D-Day plus five'

15 Platoon mustered in front of what was left of the village school. A few sat on infants' chairs – those not smashed in this welter of madness – while others perched on ammo boxes. The rest lounged about on the brick-strewn grass, keenly waiting to be brought up to date by their officer.

'Righto, lads, settle down,' Sergeant Frazer warned. 'Mr Bowkett's going to tell us a bedtime story.' He grinned then added, 'So, no rabbitin'. They're all yours, Sir.'

'Thank you, Sergeant ... though you'll have to tuck them in when I've finished. Okay, chaps, smoke if you want,' he said, lighting up, 'and come closer. I don't want to have to shout.' A few dragged their chairs and improvised seats closer, eager for news.

He started by telling them that Eisenhower was the supreme commander with Monty being accountable for all land forces. He then went into detail about the planning of Operation Overlord and the deceptions aimed at wrong-footing the Germans into thinking an attack would come through Calais. They already had first-hand knowledge of what went on in England during the build-up. Amazed by the amount of material and number of troops thrown into Overlord, they listened in awe as their officer detailed each aspect. Warships, troop transports and landing craft totalled some seven thousand, with air support from eleven-thousand aircraft. On the sixth of June, one hundred and fifty-six thousand soldiers landed on or behind the beaches. He talked about the hard months of training. A few mumbles were heard but they were soon quiet again. He further touched on the amassing of vast supplies to support what was arguably the largest seaborne invasion in world history. He told them of a floating harbour which had already been towed piecemeal across the channel. Mulberry would soon be dealing with hundreds of thousands of tons of armour, supplies and troops direct from the ships.

Cloddy talked about secret landings on the French coast to survey the terrain, tides, defences, depth of anti-tank traps, and even to what sort of sand there was on each beach. Next, he explained how troops would flow once they had built a solid bridgehead. He then told them of the undercover work, and a programme of sabotage and subterfuge to weaken their ability to respond once the attack came. He covered the low-level bombing of bridges and rail yards to hamper them further. He also touched on how they contrived to have a bogus force in Kent, under the command of General Patton, giving credence of an attack coming through Calais. The critical thing, though, was the weather. The Allies window of opportunity had been shrinking for weeks. And if they didn't go soon it would put the whole invasion in jeopardy for this year. Eisenhower, after much deliberation, settled on the sixth. Overlord was a resounding success, and they were now mixing it with the Boche on equal terms.

Lance Corporal Mick Timmins put up an easel and blackboard from one of the shattered classrooms. On it was drawn the French coast from Rennes to Le Harve. Coloured chalk showed the American and British sectors. Utah ran up the Cherbourg peninsula to a place called Quinéville. Omaha, the other American beach butted onto Gold. Between Gold and Sword were the Canadian's on Juno.

Not a single word escaped them as he briefed them in his customary way, in such fine detail. It made them feel proud to be part of such a grand scheme. He explained how they landed on each beach and faced varying degrees of resistance. Hitler's Atlantic Wall was soon breached, and troops courageously pushed forward. The British and Canadians suffered light losses, with a much higher number on Omaha and Utah.

'Our armoured division,' Mr Bowkett said, lighting another cigarette, 'to which we belong came in on the second floating wave of D-Day plus four. Thanks to many brave men, a door has been opened for us. They have now moved on and are dealing with some tough opposition. But we're slowly edging forward. I know you're gutted not to have been in the first wave' – a few choice words issued forth – 'but don't worry, chaps,' he added, ignoring them, 'your time will come to prove your worth.' He managed a broad smile, which they responded to with chuckling, wincing and stirring from their somewhat awed state.

From the major's earlier briefing Mr Bowkett started by saying the American airborne troops the night before D-Day had landed on the Cherbourg peninsular. Their job was to knock out coastal guns protecting the sea lanes, capture road junctions and be ready to harass Jerry from the rear once the invasion came. Having achieved their objectives, they would then link up with their seaborne force.

In the British sector, an airborne division and a paratroop brigade under cover of darkness dropped east of Caen. Their goal was to capture bridges over the River Orne and the Caen canal, destroy heavy coastal guns and wait for their invasion troops at first light. Under cover of darkness, Royal Marines cleared explosive charges from the shoreline.

At first light on the sixth, there was an immense naval barrage. Seven battleships, five heavy cruisers, seventeen light cruisers, three dozen destroyers and a melange of smaller warships, rained down thousands of tons of high explosives on the enemy coast.

On Utah combat infantry finally made it ashore. Although harassed by small arms fire they pushed forward. Given close support by combat units and DDs, which were launched three-thousand yards out they secured a firm foothold. When ready, they set out for La Madelaine to link up with their airborne boys. Omaha was another story. Sent in from a greater distance than Utah DDs floundered, and landing craft got swamped by rough seas. Hundreds of men drowned when their equipment dragged them below the waves. Fire from bunkers, pillboxes and gun positions was intense, pinning men on the beach. Unable to advance, heavy mortar and machine-gun fire trapped them against the sea wall. More troops landed, swelling numbers even further, which led to higher losses than expected.

On the British sector, brigades from Wessex, Staffordshire, Yorkshire Ridings, Highlands, Lowlands and Canadian Provinces stormed the beaches, taking a small amount of fire. Where possible, they made use of Crabs (anti-mine flail tanks) and Crocs (flame-belching Churchills) and the Royal Engineers mortar tanks. These were known as the 'funnies' and belonged to Hobart's 79th Armoured Division. They proved their worth when used in conjunction with infantry, playing no small part on the British and Canadian beaches.

'Well, that's as I understand it, chaps,' Mr Bowkett added for good measure. 'I know it's a bit sketchy but anything I've missed you'll soon pick up from others. Our forces are now heading inland to push Fritz out of France, Belgium and Holland. And at the same time give him a thrashing he'll never forget.'

He glanced at his watch to show the briefing was over. 'Thank you for your patience. Dismiss the men, Sergeant Frazer.'

'Sir,' he answered, coming to attention.

At long last they were on the move, heading inland to make room for the next wave of landings. Ron, Charlie and Ginger were Betsy's permanent crew, with Sergeant Freddie Cox acting as fourth member for the meantime. Their place in 'column of route' was third in line behind Mr Bowkett. They had taken great care in stowing and tying everything down, knowing only too well when the rough stuff started, ease of access would be a lifesaver.

By late afternoon they were seven miles nearer to Saint-Lô, on the edge of a newly liberated village. They were ordered to set up their leager in a war-torn orchard and await further orders.

'Fancy dobiein' yer smalls, Ron,' Charlie asked expectantly.

'Okay, me ole shiner. It'll give me somethin' ta do. I suppose an oily rag for each would be fair?'

'You'd better ger 'em whiter than white fer that price?'

'They'll be as good as yer Ma does 'em,' he said, setting up the tommy cooker. 'Aye, Ginge, ya got anythin' needs washin'?'

'No,' he replied, 'I'll wait until I meet some sweet-natured *mademoiselle.*'

'Suit yer bloomin' self,' Ron said, scraping what was left of a gel tablet from the tommy's burner plate. He picked up the tin and chose two lozenge-shaped tablets. Placing them on the plate, he lit each one, using half a dozen matches. They were hard to light, but once going they would burn fiercely, and woe betide if you got any on your fingers. He placed a large Huntley & Palmers biscuit tin on top, three-quarters full of water with a few shavings of carbolic.

As soon as the water bubbled and frothed, Charlie dropped a pair of socks in the tin. 'Ya daffy-dahn-dilly-clod,' Ron cussed, pinching at them before they had time to sink, burning his fingers in the process. 'Ya know nuffin', birdbrain. We do our whites first.'

Charlie looked at him as if he'd gone off his rocker, shrugged and started stripping down to his underwear. He pulled his vest over his head and passed it to him, along with his drawers.

Ron held them at arm's length. 'Though, in your case, China,' he said, dropping them in the tin, 'I don't think it'll make much difference. Next nickel-an'-dime it'll be two oily rags, pretty Rob Roy.' He pursed his lips and made a smooching sound. Without a stitch on, Charlie hunkered down, watching him taking on the duties of an old washerwoman. 'We do our whites first,' he explained, 'then our dicky dirt's, an' then our almond rocks.' Charlie passed him a lit cigarette and stuck one behind his ear. 'Thanks, Chaz,' he said, stirring his smalls with a large spanner as if making a tasty stew.'

'Come on,' Charlie chided, 'they must be done by now?'

'Calm down, Trigger. Ya can't rush a thing like this. Me ole gal takes whole day ta do me an' me bruv's stuff. ... 'Ere, Pinkie,' he said, looking him up and down, 'you'd better put some clothes on in case

Fritz catches ya stark-bollock. If 'e does jus' rabbit an' pork gibberish. Yer surprisingly good at that. He'll think you've escaped from the loony ...'

'Ha, ha, fuckin' ha!' Charlie countered as he put on fresh underwear.

Like a couple of suburban housewives, they placed their washing on a line stretched between Betsy and a shell busted apple tree, stood back and admired their labours.

Children from the nearby village came to inspect *les soldats anglaise*, now living among them, having no doubt bid a not too fond farewell to the Boche. The tiny mites came into view, paying their respects at each awning. A pale, sweet, half-starved girl of some seven or eight-years-old was bravest in confronting these red-faced, chirpy soldiers. She wore a long black dress a couple of sizes too big, covered by a clean white smock trimmed with lace. She held the hand of a little boy no older than three, who kept sneaking behind her back, scared of these khaki giants. One could hardly blame him as anyone in uniform ostensibly posed a threat. She smiled a timid welcome at Ron and Charlie.

'*Parly vous anglaise, mon petite Cherie?*' Ron said in his best army-French. He had attended lessons every Tuesday night for over a year, ready for just such an occasion. His teacher said he had got an aptitude for languages.

She shook her head. '*Je ne parle pas Anglais.*'

Charlie asked in English, with a French accent, 'What is your name, love?' She frowned and shrugged. 'Charlie,' he said, pointing at himself and then at her. 'Marie,' – again that dreadful accent – 'Fifi, Jeanette, Madeline?'

'*Ah, oui.*' She smiled, lighting up their day. 'Janine,' she said, pushing the small boy forward. 'Andre.' He shrank away again, but less fearful when hearing his name. His winsome smile melted their hearts.

'Poor little sods,' Ron said, looking at the ghostlike figures around each bivvy.

'Let's see wot wiv got 'ere,' Charlie teased while rummaging through the food box. 'Chocolate ... sweeties?' Most soldiers hated tinned sardines, and he saw it as a heaven-sent opportunity to unload them as surplus to requirements. 'Sardines fer mama,' he said, stacking them in her arms, 'cigarettes fer papa, an' chocolate and sweeties fer Andre an' Janine.' The children smiled at all these lovely things. Charlie shrugged, returned their smile and promptly ruffled Andre's hair.

'Poor little sods,' Ron said once more. 'I bet they've never 'ad a proper feed.'

Charlie, misty-eyed, was quiet, maybe thinking of his daughter, safe at home he hoped in her mother's arms. 'Let's 'ave a ball o' chalk, Ron,' he said, shrugging off his gloomy air and emotional trip back home.

They strolled around the village, seeing for themselves the gaunt faces at each door, nodding but rarely smiling.

'*Bonjour*,' they both said, flexing their social skills.

In the village square, there was a poster on a pockmarked wall. Hard to read because of the Gothic text it was probably a list of rules which the populous must obey, on pain of transportation or death by firing squad. Signed by District Commandant *Oberstleutnant* Wilhelm Eiermann, it was dated as recently as June third nineteen forty-four. It now carried a Cross of Lorraine in streaky, red paint.

A short walk brought them to some better class houses, built with wrought iron gates and windows secured by wooden shutters. As they wandered around like tourists, looking at the now peaceful village, they talked about the future and what life would have in store for them once the war was over.

As they passed a farmyard, Ron noted the rusting tools and drabness of the farmhouse, with its unkempt barns. It spoke volumes about how lean times had been. Next to what he supposed was once a stable block was a large three-story house with many windows, by far the grandest they had seen so far. In the courtyard cowered a cat, ducking to and fro as a swallow dive-bombed it. They chuckled, amused at this strange turn of events, once more showing some of the wonders of nature on this dreamy summer's day. Under this cloak of stillness, it was hard to believe this village had been under the German yoke for four years.

The door of the chateau-style house opened, and a well-dressed woman walked towards them, a basket in her arms. It wasn't easy to tell her true age because of her undernourished appearance and ravaged look. Time had not been kind to this once attractive woman, and she might be in her late forties or early sixties.

'*Bonjour, Madame,*' Ron said, taking off his helmet.

'Hello, Tommie,' she replied with a soft Scottish burr.

He looked at her in surprise. 'You speak English, *Madame*?'

'I most certainly do, young man. But I don't get much chance these days. My name is Madelaine Broussard. My Granddaughter told me of your kindness towards her and Andre.'

'Janine is your Granddaughter?' Charlie asked, also taking off his helmet.

The lady nodded, a haunted look coming into her grey, lifeless eyes. 'She saw you walking around and came to tell me.' She handed Charlie the basket. He saw a dozen or so eggs. 'A gift from the Broussard's. For all your kindness. We have plenty. Chickens are the only things to thrive these days. Scrabbling about for food they are too quick to catch. They forever seem wary ... like they might end up in the pot. They seem to know. ... So, we let them live' – again that look – 'and use their eggs to sustain us. The villagers would never dream of taking the *Comtesse's* chickens.'

Both stiffened when they realised that she was a titled lady.

'Are there just the three of you?' Ron asked, trying not to make it sound like he was prying.

'Yes.' Yet again that look, though this time etched with pain. 'Andre, my husband ... the Boche took him in May nineteen forty-two. I have not seen or heard from him since. We met at St Andrew's

University, fell in love, married and came back here to be with his mother and father. My daughter, Christelle and her husband, Albert, were *La Résistance*. They were caught last year ... and shot. There are now only three of us. ... Janine came in crying. She and Andre have never known such kindness. The Boche never gave us anything. They just took ... as if it was their divine right.' She smiled wailfully, came closer and kissed them both. 'May God go with you, Tommies,' she said before turning away.

Ron watched as she walked back to her once-grand house. *And may God be with you also, fine lady.*

On their return, Ron and Charlie were in time to witness their second issue of pack rations from the back of a three-tonner.

All manner of foodstuffs went into these packs, plus other things Tommy Atkins would need to keep up his spirits. Such as cigarettes, pipe tobacco, matches, boiled sweets, chocolate, even lavatory paper which the humblest of soldier would use at times. These tasty meals, mixed fruit cocktail, steamed puddings, powdered custard, condensed milk, tinned sausage and bacon, beef stew and dumplings, steak and kidney puddings were a delight to behold. Soldiers lived well when on active service. They would spend ages choosing what to have and swap with other units as the mood took them.

Before every meal, they would have a lengthy confab on the merits of each item. Only then would it go on the menu.

'Oh no, Chaz,' Ginger moaned. 'Let's have steak and kidney and mixed—'

'But we 'ad that last night,' Ron countered, shoving a tin of sausage and bacon under his nose.

'—veg and plum steam pudding.'

'I agree wif steak and Sidney,' said Charlie, 'fair an' square. But I can't keep me bleedin' eyes open after them puddin's o' yours.'

'We'll vote on it,' said Freddie, acting as mediator. 'Those in favour of plum pudding.' Only Ginger put up his hand. '... All in favour of mixed fruit cocktail and condensed milk?' Three hands shot up, quicker than a ferret out of a bucket. 'Motion carried.'

'Talkin' about motions,' Ron quipped, 'while you lot get tommy goin', I'm poppin' ta chuffin' khazi.'

Chapter 14

'Break Out'

The Fifth finally received their first battle orders.

The night before the attack Ron lay in his bivvy listening to the skirl of pipes, a tell-tale sign their Scottish cousins were getting their blood up. Laments played all night as Lowland, and Highland pipers went through their stock of rousing tunes. There would be little sleep as these proud regiments with long traditions, and famed battle honours roused their warlike spirits. Royal Scots, Black Watch, Gordons, Cameron's and Seaforth's danced and whooped their lively reels till the early hours.

At first light, an immense barrage of some six-hundred guns called the brigade to order.

During this action 14 Platoon was attached to L Motor Company, with machine-gun platoons and a troop of Priest self-propelled guns under the command of Major Sloan. The Fifth was ordered to capture and hold high ground north-east of their starting point. This would enable their armoured regiments to use them as a pivot so they could put in a full-scale attack on both flanks.

Ron and the rest of the platoon crouched in their Brens, waiting to move into the affray. Shells screamed overhead on their journey of destruction, with luck carving a path through the German lines. A green flare climbed skywards, and a dozen pipers primed their khaki covered bagpipes and bravely leading the way.

The battle, intense, bloody and savage needed flame belching Crocs to clear the last vestiges of resistance. At last, they carried the day and in heavy rain rumbled passed the old Canadian lines of a few days ago. Cheerless rows of newly killed riflemen and Scots infantry covered by gas capes placed side by side were a stark reminder of what war can do to a human body. Brown woollen socks, gaiters, green Highland hose with cherished *Sgian-dubh's* and studded boots complained bitterly at the indignity of their owner's death.

Soon a sickly-sweet odour of rotting flesh from naked, swollen corpses of Canadian soldiers, weathered grey and waiting for burial began to fill their nostrils. This charnel house had been no man's land for over a week. The German night patrols looted their uniforms, leaving them naked and deprived of their last vestige of dignity.

Everyone who gazed on this parade of death, powerless to turn away had the same sickly feeling. The lads overcome by what they saw again realised that war was not to be taken lightly. Ashen-faced and speechless, exercises and schemes were a thing of the past. It was nothing like playing at warfare, when an umpire would cycle around the battlefield, telling soldiers to 'lie down, son, you've just been killed'. There was no getting up from this. War was real, and for keeps.

The Scots, many of whom had never seen action fought like demons, giving themselves an instant place of honour. Their red and yellow badge, gracing each vehicle, filled the leager where Ron's platoon bedded down in hastily prepared trenches. Everyone was shocked and not surprisingly quiet, even Mr Bowkett.

Nobby Hale, sensing the cheerlessness tried to lighten the mood. "O's fer a cuppa cha?' he said, holding up his mug in salute. 'Me mouff feels loike floor of Uncle Ted's pigeon loft.'

A few 'old sweats' laughed.

While tommy cookers boiled water, cooking sausage and mixed veg, or anything else which took their fancy (though few were hungry) a couple of lads started singing:

'Any old iron? Any old iron?
Any, any, any old iron?
You look neat. Talk about a treat!
You look so dapper from your napper to your feet.'

Not to be outdone two or three others took up the refrain:

'Dressed in style, brand-new tile,
And your father's old green tie on.
But I wouldn't give you tuppence for your
old watch and chain,
Old iron, old iron ...'

With their minds on home and a full stomach, their first taste of war gradually faded. It would never get any easier, that was for sure, but each time they saw a dead body, it would be less shocking than the time before. They weren't hard-hearted in any way, far from it, but it was the only way they could deal with the horrors of war. Training could only teach them so much. The rest was down to them. Each needed to come to terms with it in their own way.

Next day, the Fifth crossed the River Odon. Leading the way J Support was tasked with taking ground forward of the Scots position. Within minutes of crossing the Odon, one of N Company's half-tracks ran over a Teller mine, killing one and wounding three, the first of many.

After sorting some fierce opposition, J Support found themselves on a ridge with orders to protect the flank from counterattack.

Ron made a range card, taking readings on the terrain to his fore, while the rest took turns keeping guard or digging trenches. Both machine-gun platoons set up their Vickers along a ridge, with a couple of Priests in support.

An Army Air Corps spotter plane flitted over their lines, waggling its wings in greeting. Almost at once two 109s came out of the sun, ready to strafe J Support. The Auster dropped as low as it could in a bid to escape the kill-hungry fighters. Seeing the spotter plane, they started harrowing it like a bully picking on his victim. A dirty squirt of black trailed from the aircraft as cannon shells struck home. A split-second later there was a loud explosion as it broke up, spreading debris over a wide area. A Bren carrier from 16 Platoon burst into flames with grenades and rounds popping. To make it even more exciting (that's what it seemed like ... like you were watching John Wayne in *Flying Tigers*) five light-enemy tanks nosed out of a thicket that Ron had ranged at nine-hundred yards. The Priests opened-up, knocking out four and sending the last one scurrying back into the protection of the trees. Not to be outdone the machine gunners gave each crew a few difficult moments as they bailed out of their damaged vehicle. The surviving crewmen chased after the remaining tank, leaving behind a handful of dead and wounded.

Soon they were moving again, driving through a village and out into open country beyond. After a series of halts to clean up isolated pockets of resistance they at last settled into a leager, ready for a night's well-earned rest.

Ron, Charlie and Ginger decided on a large slit trench in which to bed down. Taking a break, they propped themselves against the back of the half-finished trench with a fresh brew and a fag. Together they chin wagged about how things had gone and how lucky they were in getting through the day unscathed. To remind them they were living in the middle of a war zone, there was a loud whip-like crack followed immediately by a loud explosion. A stray AP shell had gone through one of 15 Platoon's carriers, lightly wounding Corporal Farrell, Lance Corporal Hicks, Blacky Coleman and Steve Mascall. They were lucky, as was their Bren, but for a hole in both sides, missing the engine housing by a hair's breadth.

By now everyone was digging like crazy to get below ground.

A few days later 14 Platoon ran into trouble while helping M Company take Hill 112. Heavily mortared and machine-gunned, they suffered many casualties. But for Sergeant Bill Porter and one of his corporals, more would have died.

Coming to their rescue, 15 Platoon also got in trouble when Mr Bowkett took them in the wrong direction. As they sped through the hostile country shots rang out from several houses, catching the lead Bren and lightly wounding Sergeant Frazer. They fanned out across a ploughed field and pulled up sharply when they saw a line of tanks a mile away. Fortunately, they were Sherman's and the platoon carried on towards a village at the base of the hill. Within no time at all, the gut-wrenching sound of 'moaning minnies' forced everyone to bail out of their Brens and run for cover. These multi-barrelled monsters fired all their rockets at once, their fins screaming like banshees.

'Look aahhht, lads!' Charlie yelled, leaping into a ditch with Ginger and Freddie, 'annovver load o' shit comin' our way.'

Ron flung himself into the same ditch, clawing at the stinking mud in terror. He counted each explosion as they fell all around, choking him with the stink of cordite. Clods of earth and stones rained down, hitting him on the back and pinging off his helmet. In this stonk, four riflemen were injured, including Alfie Bell and the man who had given him so much grief about his Mrs Queen gaffe. Alfie, severely wounded, cried as he held a large field dressing against a ragged hole in his stomach. He looked at Ron, concern all over his face, knowing full well they needed to get him to an aid post as soon as possible; otherwise, he would bleed to death. Lofty sat on the ground against their wrecked carrier, in shock. Grinning lopsidedly, he dragged on a cigarette, his right ear and cheek cleaved away by a piece of shrapnel.

Ron, losing his rifle in this stonk, took Alfie's while helping him aboard a Loyd carrier on its way to the RAP. He lit a cigarette for him, made sure he was comfy and promised he would soon be back in Blighty.

The enemy was reluctant to give ground, fighting for every inch. A steady stream of shells rained down, causing the platoon to withdraw pell-mell across open country.

Charlie acted as lead Bren, with Mr Bowkett following up the rear. He told himself they weren't running away, just pulling back to regroup. 'Come on, Ron!' he yelled, opening the throttle as far as it would go. 'Fuck this fer soldierin'. It's gerrin too hot fer my likin'!'

Freddie, wedged by his side, agreed, only too willing to be heading back to their lines. They pelted across fields like a scared jackrabbit, with Ron hanging on for dear life. Ginger, bouncing up and down on one of the tarps, was hugging the Vickers mounting frame for his dear life. Ron got up and made a lunge for it as well, intent on finding a better purchase. Suddenly he had the weirdest feeling he should role himself in a tight little ball. Instinctively he ducked his head just in time to miss a strand of barbed wire running along the top of a hedge, feeling it graze his helmet. The carrier dropped with a bone-jarring crash onto a cobbled road.

'Fuck me! That were close, Chaz,' he said, laughing hysterically. 'Ya nearly took me bleedin' 'ead orf.'

Later, when he was waiting for the folds of sleep to take him, he would realise just how close he came to a Portland headstone in Normandy. It would not have taken much for him to hightail it back to the beach, but for the steady influence of a Royal Warwicks sergeant, who admitted spending most of the day scared shitless.

J Support took up position on Hill 112, overlooking Carpiquiet airfield. They started digging in forward of a tall hedgerow running from one end of the hill to the other. Within minutes they were pinned down by intense mortar fire, causing yet more casualties, one of which proved fatal.

Why not me? Ron cringed inside the shallow trench, snuggling close to Charlie as if his very life depended on it. *Someone up there must be watchin' over me. Weavin' 'is magic spell.* He was really perplexed. How on earth could he survive with all these shells landing around him? His gut-wrenching fear mounted, causing an awful dryness which made his tongue stick to the roof of his mouth. His faith was strong, and it always helped to say the Lord's prayer at moments like this. Except that this time he was yelling it over and over at the top of his voice.

The shelling eventually stopped and normality – as normal as it could be – returned to the trenches.

A Sherman, gun pointed at the Jerry lines, reversed away from the hedge. 'Gawd almighty 'is leavin' us,' Charlie said with a shocked look. '... I wish I could sod orf so easily.'

'Fuck our luck, Chuck,' Ginger replied, his face steely in stoic acceptance.

A few minutes later another tank took up station in the recently vacated spot. The routine of refuelling and rearming never failed to alarm footsloggers. They would remain edgy until they were back again, giving them a feeling of security that heavy armour gave the ever anxious swaddies.

Taking the tommy off Betsy, Charlie and Ron set about making a brew in the trench. Things had calmed down somewhat, with Jerry probably doing the same in his own front line.

'Would ya like Earl Grey or Darjeelin'?' Ron asked Ginger and Freddie. His Uncle Fred always had a liking for fancy teas, as Ron called them, and would bring them out whenever he had company.

'Any Lapsang, Deak?' asked Freddie, showing he also knew his teas.

''Fraid not, Sarge. We used rest of it yesterday when colonel come over fer Tiffin.'

'Anything'll do, son. As long as it's sweet and wet.'

'I used to know her!' Ginger nimbly exclaimed.

'What you gabblin' about, Iverson?' Freddie asked, somewhat confused as to where this line of banter was going.

'Sweet and wet! ... Sweet because she worked at Cadburys in Bournville and wet because—'

'She lived in Brummingham!' Ron roared, grinning.

'Do you know, mate,' Ginger countered, 'for a crack shot and one of the best rangefinders in the battalion you can miss the bleeding obvious at times.'

'Oh, yeah,' Ron said, grasping what he was getting at.

'Pack it up, Iverson,' the sergeant said, spitting in his mug to dissolve a blob of iron ration from their morning's hastily prepared meal. 'You're making me horny.'

'A drop o' gold watch'll do the trick, Sarge,' Ron said, holding up his mug. 'It'll spice up yer cha.'

'The only thing that'll spice up this mug, Deakin,' he said, tossing it to him, 'is a hefty quota of strong, sweet, mashed gunfire. And *that* whisky's for emergencies only.'

'Today's been an emergency, Sarge,' Ginger said, pointing at two bodies covered by gas capes. 'A bloody humongous one.'

'You'll know when real trouble bites you on the arse, Iverson,' the sergeant censured. 'You'll then have leave to raid my kit. And if it's me leaching my lifeblood away, you open that bloody bottle and pour it down my throat until I choke to death. Whatever any do-goody officer says about giving the wounded alcohol.'

Mr Bowkett took Ron away from his mates to one of the Sherman's. The tank commander outlined his concerns, saying he could pick out an enemy tank in the twilight.

At his officer's request – it was not an order as Ron would be putting his life on the line – he struggled aboard the Sherman and set up his rangefinder on top of the turret. Scanning the terrain, he spotted a couple of irregular shapes on the edge of a wood. Quickly working out the range, he passed his scope to Mr Bowkett and dropped down into cover. Never had he felt so exposed in his entire life, with those hungry 88s lurking, searching for easy kills. Any second he expected a blinding flash, followed by a pitch-black void.

'They can 'ave this army lark, Chaz,' he later told his mate over a mug of tea. 'I'm on me bleedin' bike when this lots over an' done with. The only bloomin' thing I want now is a peaceful life, a pretty trouble an' strife and a couple o' bright kids ta look after their ole man in 'is dotage. Fer me it's too bleedin' dodgy,' he further confided. 'We don't stand an earthly gettin' through this lot in one piece. Look at those around us,' – he eyed the bodies once more – 'droppin' like flies.'

'Gerrin windy are we, Ron?' Charlie joshed.

'You bet!' he said in disbelief. 'It's playin' Gypsy Nell with me guts. I can't even raspberry tart without cackin' me pants.'

Charlie grinned. 'Earlier,' he finally said, 'when we were lyin' next to each other in that 'alf finished trench—'

'Yeah, cosy, weren't it?'

'—I dropped an almighty one.' He laughed. 'But with the noise of the bloomin' shellin', an' you screamin' yer 'ead orf like a nutter on Speakers' Corner ya never 'eard me.'

'Wot of it, thunder guts?'

'I think it's my turn ta do washin'...'

'Oh!' Ron exclaimed when he saw Charlie grinning once more. 'Well, if ya 'ave ... you'd better do yer washin' separate ta mine, cacky pants.'

'Look who's talkin'.'

'Ah, but I ain't done it yet, Sunshine. Ya beat me to it.'

16 Platoon rejoined the company after seeing Jerry blitzed by a flight of rocket firing Tiffies. They took up station on their sister platoon's right. Within minutes of setting up their Vickers heavy shelling rained down, causing one death and one slightly wounded.

While all this was going on 14 Platoon on K Company's right flank spotted a Tiger dug in on a small rise half a mile away. They managed to put the tank out of action, but not before Jimbo was wounded in the right hip by a shell fragment. Ossie put him on a passing Loyd that was taking the injured to an advanced dressing station.

Shortly after this enemy fire caught K Company, with shells and mortars dropping on top of them. But as luck would have it, they were well dug in and kept their heads down. They spent a hellish time stretched out in the bottom of their trenches. The sergeant major visited them during the night to keep up their spirits and give them stout hearts.

The threat of being surrounded was real, and Ron and the other three thought they would soon be 'in the bag'. Choosing to look the part they changed into SD's and best boots. In the end, J Support retired in an orderly fashion, later collecting in a potato field where they spent three days resting and rearming.

That hateful hill was their baptism to the horrors of war. The constant shelling, mortaring and machine-gun fire swathing the lines gave everyone their first real blooding. It was 'dig for your lives and get below ground to outlive the deadliest fire'. A salutary lesson which would stand them in good stead in the months ahead.

One learns quickly when one's life is at stake.

Chapter 15

'Battle of Normandy'

Betsy's crew, having gone without proper sleep for a week, was woken by the driver of a three-tonner. 'Petrol an' ammo!' he called, kicking the guide rope of their bivvy. 'Come on you lazy buggers!'

All four staggered into the harsh glare – sun already high in the sky – half-drugged with sleep and half-dressed. 'Oh, sod off!' they all cried.

'No peace fer wicked,' Charlie said, rubbing a hand across the stubble on his chin. He yawned, scratched under his armpit and farted. '... An' I bet 'e were a knocker-upper in a former life?'

The driver stacked Jerry cans of petrol and water, ammo and pack rations. But best of all a freshly baked loaf, warm and crisp and a large piece of bung wrapped in greaseproof paper – just like at the Coop.

Charlie sliced the bread, coated it with Marg and carved the cheese into thick wedges.

'I know you lot ... greedy bastards,' Ron said, wolfing it down while keeping an eye on the other slices. 'I don't trust you, gannets.' He smiled as Marg and slaver dribbled down his chin onto a clean vest. This was a real treat. However, it made it harder to get back to the linseed oil flavoured biscuits in their pack rations. Which had the consistency of dried sawdust and tasted of bat droppings. Hence the sheer delight of freshly baked bread and Cheddar cheese.

In the rest camp west of Caen, they endured the noise of a barrage as it pounded the city, ready for what all being well would be the final assault. Since early July, the none stop bombing had all but flattened the city, leaving only the Cathedral and hospital standing. During one of these raids, a half-track from L Company got caught by 'friendly fire', killing seven riflemen and one officer. Another vehicle alongside took some of the blast, killing three more and wounding five.

The lads endured the noise from a nearby battery, making it hard to sleep above or below ground. With each recoil, Ron felt the ground flex beneath his tired body. He turned over and thanked God he was not on the receiving end of these shells, whistling overhead in the dark heavens.

Next day they heard the Germans in Caen had surrendered to the 3rd British Division and the Canadians.

With the pressure off them for a while, they enjoyed a spell of cleaning and resting, giving them a chance to recover some semblance of order. With such splendid weather, they began to sunbath, making each leager look more like a nudist colony than an army camp. The top brass soon put a stop to these antics, saying enemy aircraft would spot hundreds of milk-white bodies lying around like Blackpool holidaymakers during Wakes Week.

Those inclined to do so caught up on letter's home, giving them a chance to focus on something other than the horrors around them. However, officers were now vetting mail and the men had to keep to mere basics. Save it was not a problem for most, as the last thing they wanted to do was write about where they were, what hell it was and who had recently died.

Ginger and Ron looked over a knocked out 88mm gun. Items belonging to the crew, jackboots, webbing, letters and photographs lay scattered about. It was a sharp reminder of the human tragedy which now blighted this once peaceful part of Calvados. Next to a pile of shell cases were four freshly dug graves, with coal-scuttle helmets resting on Mauser rifles pushed into the soft earth.

A hundred yards away was a wrecked Cruiser from the 4th Royal Dragoon Guards. Making their way over to the tank they worked out the driver must have moved into 'line of sight' of an AP shell.

Looking inside the blackened hull, they were suddenly overcome by the smell of seared flesh and the image of a terrible death. Feeling nauseous, Ginger stepped back and trod on a patch of newly turned earth. Realising this was the crew's remains he quickly righted a cross made from an ammo box. There were five names on the crosspiece, with rank and service number. The shell would have punched clean through the half-inch armour plating like a hot knife through butter. Deflected by something or someone it would have whizzed round and round, igniting fuel tanks and setting off rounds in the bins. If they were lucky, death would have been instantaneous. If not, it hardly bore thinking about.

The Bocage country, dressed in its summer majesty, with its woods and tall hedgerows circling fields of corn made it hard to spot Jerry as he lay in wait. Sudden death stalked the high corn. German and Allied corpses lay amongst this golden crop, alone and unclaimed. Through want of care, they would soon die, leaving a putrid smell to mark their final resting place.

Ron and the others promised that if any of them were killed, the others would drag them to the base of a large tree, so the 'body removal squad' could give them a decent burial. The German soldier, seemingly a lifetime ago, but, in fact, only the day before yesterday was still fresh in everyone's mind. His form splayed across the road, almost twice as wide and twice as tall as he was in life, would be a constant reminder of the awfulness of war. Except for drivers, everyone was told to look away. However, this was the last thing you should say to an inquisitive swaddy. To a man, they gazed on the haunting image of war at its most bestial. Most troops had a morbid fear of bodies in the road, being run over by column after column of armour. You could hardly drag it out of the way because to leave your vehicle for such a Christian act would put your own life in jeopardy.

Back at the leager Ron and Ginger found Bert Moule, one of 15 Platoon's despatch riders showing a group of swaddies how to ride his motorbike. Even though they were keen to have a go, they did not envy a despatch rider's lot. Because when on the move he had the unenviable job of being out in the open, with no armour plating around him. To confirm this fact the battalion's first two deaths were despatch riders from N Company, with helmets and goggles adorning their makeshift crosses at the side of the road.

Once rested, repairs made, rearmed and with fresh troops they were ordered to the Caen area. Netting and greenery now covered most vehicles to break up their outline, making them harder to spot from a distance.

Rumours of a new offensive started to spread as soon as Major Sloan headed for the Corps Commander's briefing. The platoon was a buzz of excitement. What would happen next? How many more would have to die? And will it be me next time? These were the questions everyone was asking. However, their anxiety was soon forgotten when a more significant event occurred, namely the arrival of their first beer and cigarettes for over a month.

'All right, lads,' Company Sergeant Major Dawson warned. 'Settle down,'

Each platoon sergeant kept an eye on his men, making sure there was no talking in the loosely formed ranks. Sergeant Frazer saw Sharp and Deakin standing next to each other. He gave them a warning look.

'Easy, men,' Major Sloan said, looking at a chest of drawers someone had dragged from an abandoned farmhouse. He opened the bottom drawer, still full of lacey underwear, sat on top and put his boots on the drawer while trying to avoid getting dirt on the silk lingerie. 'The ground's dry,' the major furthered, lighting up, 'so park yourself somewhere. Smoke if you want,' he warmly added. 'This is an informal chat, so don't stand on ceremony. The Colonel has asked each commander to address his men.'

He looked at his notes one last time then started. 'Well, as you know, the last few weeks have been rather tough on us all. But we've acquitted ourselves well. The Corps Commander has mentioned us in glowing terms several times in his war diary. The Fifth's casualty figures, though, have been higher than anticipated, with forty-nine killed and one-hundred and fifty-six wounded, nearly a quarter of our strength. J Support is once more back to normal – if things will ever be normal again – and so is the battalion. We've had our rest. So, you will be pleased to know we'll shortly be joining the fight again.' Mumbling rose from the ranks. Sergeants noted names, ready for the rough edge of their tongue once the briefing was over. 'I won't go into too much detail. I'll leave that to your officers.'

Ron gave Sharpy a look, showing how he felt. Sergeant Frazer, seeing them, mouthed, 'You dare.'

'It's not going to get any easier,' the major carried on. 'Not for some time, anyway. Fritz has untwisted his knickers and is now putting up one hell of a fight. The slippery little bastard.' A few sniggers escaped. NCOs scowled, hoping the men would not see it as an invitation to chatter. But there was no need to worry. They were all ears. 'Our division, plus the famous desert rats and a newly arrived Scottish armoured division will cross the River Orne via two bridges that the Yanks captured intact. Good old Johnny! Once on the other side, we will attack on a broad front. Recon has told us Fritz's first line of defence is made up of two infantry divisions, with armoured reserves in support. These consist of a Panzer brigade and a heavy tank battalion ... Tigers and Panthers no doubt. Their next line of defence consists of 88s and 'moaning minnies', Waffen-SS panzergrenadiers and a battalion of SS Panzers. There's also an armoured battle group – numbers yet unknown – and two more Panzer battalions in reserve. We're in for a tough time, I'll be bound. But we have lots going for us. Our three armoured divisions will cross the Orne at 0500 to the accompaniment of a creeping barrage, which will cover our advance towards the main railway line from Rouen to Brest. The Fifth is tasked with taking and holding all high ground in the vicinity. The sterling work we did on Hill 112 convinced the general we were the boys for this little caper.'

Ron felt his stomach lurch as the cramps started up again. Was it his diarrhoea returning, or the mention of that damnable hill?

'This barrage is to be known as the Atlantic Roller,' carried on the major. 'Our three divisions will fan out, one to the left one to the right and one in the centre. This tactic will create a broad spearhead for driving into the enemy's soft underbelly. Your officers will brief you on movements, timings, ammo and other details relevant to your unit. RAF and American medium bombers will drop several thousand tons one hour before the main bombardment.'

'Much good that'll do,' someone mumbled. Another name was taken.

'For some of you, this will be your first time in action.' He knew most of J Support and could easily pick out the replacements spread through the ranks. 'It's vital *you* 'old sweats',' he said, searching for a few familiar faces, 'take the new chaps under your wing. And *you* newbies should look towards those who have already seen action.'

Ron looked at the fair-haired Dafydd (Duck) Griffiths from Swansea, now teamed up with Ossie. He smiled, hoping to belay his fears. The Welshman smiled back, a tick at the side of his mouth betraying his nervous state.

The major finished his briefing and then embarked on some small talk. 'The jungle drums tell me you've had some beer brought up this morning?'

'Och aye, sairrr,' answered one rifleman near the front. 'Ya ken it'll noo go ta waste.'

His sergeant nearly jumped on him, but the major quickly asked, 'You're a bit far from home?'

'Och aye, sairrr. Aberdeen.'

'Well, Rifleman ...'

'Campbell, sairrr.'

'Well, Rifleman Campbell, enjoy your pint and keep a clear head. And if you come across someone in field grey don't offer him any. And don't under any circumstances tell him what we're up too. ... This goes for all of you,' he clearly stated, addressing the entire company. 'Keep your mouths shut. Don't discuss it among yourselves. And don't even talk about it in your sleep.' He paused for emphasis. '... Thank you, Sergeant Major.'

'Company, attention!' he bellowed, saluting the CO.

Mr Bowkett turned towards Sergeant Frazer. 'Wally,' he said after a pause. He always called him Wally when he wanted a favour.

'Sir?'

'Keep your eyes on the lads tonight. Let them have their fun. They've earned it. But limit them to two-pints each. I don't want any thick heads tomorrow morning. We have a lot to do, ready for 0500 the day after. Get a couple of level-headed ones to keep an eye on them. They'll more than likely listen to one of their own. Deakin and Sharp have their heads screwed on right. Have a quiet word with them?'

'Of course, Sir,' the sergeant said, surprised by his choice of moral guardians. 'I'll have a word in their shell-likes.'

Whichever way Ron chanced to look, tanks from the armoured brigade were arrayed alongside Brens and half-tracks from the Fifth. This display of firepower, waiting for orders to go, was an impressive sight. A green flare soared towards a rain-leaden sky, and a tremendous barrage rained down on the far bank, advancing with each salvo.

Meeting light resistance, J Support rolled passed their first waypoint, picking up their pace as tank commanders itched to fire their guns. Still reeling from the air attack and now living through a hellish bombardment the enemy's forward troops laid down their arms in droves, the will to fight seemingly gone from them.

During the barrage, a rogue shell landed in Fresné-la-Mère, destroying a water pipe in the middle of the main road. Within minutes a half-track from 14 Platoon found itself stuck in the hole. The driver, a burly lad from Cleethorpes, cursed as he struggled to right his carrier. As the rest drove by each driver expressed their views on his carelessness. One rifleman with a ready wit said, 'What's yer name, mate, death?'

Moments later, the self-same driver, having extricated himself from his watery grave forced his way into a line of stationary of vehicles. Metal scraped on metal as he nudged a Bren carrier out of the way, waving his thanks.

'We din't 'ave much fuckin' choice, hairy-arse!' yelled the driver's mate while showing two fingers.

One of the half-track's passengers turned around and roared, 'And same to you, Rifleman!'

'Oh, nobs ta ya uncle,' Ron mumbled under his breath.

The Divisional General in a black beret and red collar tabs of a brass hat, not happy with the rate of advance had taken the first means of transport to see for himself what was holding them up. His willingness to visit the frontline made Ron think of his dad and Uncle Fred. How different it must have been then, with their staff officers cosseted away in their chateau's miles from the front, barely concerned with their soldier's welfare. To hear of a general visiting his troops raised the fighting man's morale, making him in awe of his leaders.

To slow down their advance they had slaughtered horses and cattle at crossroads, junctions and vantage points where a platoon might deploy. The recent warm weather made it hard to approach them, even with a wet cloth over one's mouth. Each breath brought a scent of foul decay.

The general ordered tank-dozers to push the rotting carcasses out of the way so they could carry on with their advance. Close on their heels were Crocs who would soon turn them into a mass of charred meat – giving a smell just as bad but with fewer flies.

Ron spent his forty-eight-hours as company runner at battalion headquarters. He bedded down in an ex-Jerry dugout, saving him digging a three-foot-wide hole the size of a grave.

The Germans, having departed in great haste, left all manner of stuff behind. A broken-down lorry loaded with fur coats, spiced sausages, smoked hams, cases of schnapps, Cognac, Calvados and wine was abandoned in the middle of the road. Piled up on the grass verge were suitcases full of the spoils of war, along with half a dozen crates of fine worsted cloth from Solomon Cohen and Sons of Warsaw, mildewed and now fit for rags.

He set off on this beautiful summer afternoon at a brisk pace, running then walking towards Delta Sector where J Company was leaguered. Coming to a railway bank, facing miles of open ground he saw a field of fire which in army parlance was called a 'natural killing ground'. Only too aware of Sherman's nestling behind the manmade ridge, the enemy shelled their position without mercy.

Taking cover every few yards, he threw himself into each space, running the gauntlet and judging the distance to cover each time, harkening the sound of shells. He scuttled along, heeding his instincts, which by now were finely tuned.

Pleased to find the major so quickly he retraced his bobbing, weaving way back to headquarters. As he passed one ex-Jerry trench, he heard someone yell, 'Ya look loike a bleedin' Jack-in-a-box wiv a dose o' clap!'

There was an almighty explosion on the far side of the trench, sounding like a foundry drop hammer, throwing up tons of earth and a partially buried body.

'Hiya, Chaz,' Ron said with ringing in his ears. He got off his stomach and closed the gap before the next stonk. 'You okay, mate?' he added when he saw his terror-stricken look.

The humour of a few moments ago was gone. 'No!' Charlie screamed, brushing earth from his blouse. 'I ain't ... dropped a near un they did. If I'd 'ad me Uncle Ned up any furver they'd o' knocked it orf. ... Nah thumb-suckin' joke,' he added when he saw Ron grin.

Joining Charlie in his straw-lined abode – a discarded comb and a pair of false teeth on a shelf – he stretched out his legs, easing his itchy ankles. 'Decent billet, Chaz,' he said, removing a salami and a freshly baked French stick from his valise. 'Better than my place.' Having torn the bread in half, he cut the salami into chunks with his sword and gave Charlie his share. 'I think they used mine as a latrine.'

'Talkin' about shit ... is it *this* that pen and inks,' Charlie said, holding up a wedge of salami between two pieces of bread. He whiffed the air. 'Or 'ave ya bin sleepin' wiv a dead Kraut?'

'The salami's courtesy of 'itler,' he replied, brushing off the insult like flies from a piece of meat. 'The rooty I got at an *estaminet*, 'alf a mile from headquarters. The food's pukka. It's me that stinks. I took socks off last night, an' by time I woke' – he removed his gaiters and lifted his trousers to show off his powdery pink, swollen ankles – 'I were a war casualty. The little bastards 'ad bin wolfin' on me all night. I asked Doc fer a blood transfusion, but all 'e give me were a bottle of calamine. ... Yeah, yer billets a palace compared to my hovel,' he furthered, munching on bread and pork meat. Another crop of rockets whistled overhead. 'But it'd be nicer without bloomin' musical accompaniment.'

Suddenly there was a shrill cry. Ron chanced a look in the direction of the noise. He saw a man and woman coming from the German lines, dragging a small handcart behind them. Blood poured down the man's right thigh. The woman, blonde and in her mid-twenties, kept looking over her shoulder. They made straight for Charlie's trench, cackling with joy. '*Bonjour, mon ami* ... whisky?' The man took a bottle of Haig from his cart. '*Les Allemands*,' he laughed, proudly boasting Jerry had missed this prize.

Ron sorted out his battle-scarred mug. Loathed to turn down the offer of a drink he removed some tea leaves from an earlier brew, inviting the man to tip a measure in his mug.

With the man and woman sent to the rear, bread and salami consumed, Ron gave Charlie a bottle of Martell brandy. He beamed all over his face, cradling the bottle like a new-born baby. 'Too good fer drinking' in this 'ole. ... An' anyway, yuv gotta keep yer Uncle Ned clear. We'll save it fer a special occasion.' He took his spare shirt, folded it around the bottle and then carefully placed it in his valise.

'Keep yerself safe, Chaz,' he said, sliding over the lip of the trench. He crouched low, not wanting to draw attention to himself and looked back at his mate, fearful of what might happen in his absence.

'See ya later!' he shouted as Ron doubled towards the nearest tank. He watched as he bobbed and weaved his way between vehicles, praying he would soon be back.

Ron was only six when his father died and was devastated at the loss of his pal. They shared so much together. When decorating his home – Henry Deakin was a painter and decorator by profession – he would give Ron a jar of water and a paintbrush so he could help. It took years to get used to the fact that his dad was not with him anymore. Even now after all this time, he could hardly believe it. One moment he was there, reading him stories, tickling and cuddling him, wrestling on the lawn at the top of their long garden, taking him fishing and to football matches. The next, he was no more. A memory which all too soon faded, leaving him to dart into his dreams without warning, making him feel warm and secure in his slumbers. Only too aware those he loved might be taken from him at any moment, there one minute, gone the next he started building up a store of memories to draw on in the future.

Soon after landing on the sixth, he began doing the same with his army pals, noting their quirky ways. Without knowing it, he would watch them, building up a detailed picture of each. To start with they treated it as a lark, saying he probably fancied them. Eventually, cheesed off with this odd behaviour, they started ribbing him, cruelly. Also, he thought there was something wrong with him, watching them all the time, fearing for their safety. He even doubted his own masculinity, thinking this long-term exposure to a 'man's only world' was turning his head. The warmth towards his pals went deeper than meer matily friendship – feelings sometimes bordering on love. He also thought his obsession with death was morbid, sick, weird. But for most soldiers, living with it each day was not by any means unusual. During the horrors of war, the Grim Reaper was never far from one's side, waiting to stake a claim.

Grieved by Ernie's death from of 'friendly fire' while taking Caen he started writing everything down about his first army pal, to act as a reminder of the good times they had shared. Saddened by his death and the death of others, without warning his eyes would flood with tears, streaming down his cheeks. Those around him knew how he was feeling, having themselves shed tears for lost pals. New friends, those who swelled their ranks every few weeks, remained just that – friends. No close ties sprang up between them and the 'old sweat's'. It was best not to get too close just in case you got hurt all over again.

The Fifth was ordered to support an attack by the Royal Tanks and the Fife and Forfar Yeomanry on a heavily defended ridge. This battle proved a textbook success, ending in many captives from Adolf Hitler's 1st SS Panzer Division. These arrogant troops, mentally shackled, sat in silence. What would happen to them? They would not be too optimistic if their own brutal behaviour were anything to go by. To blend in with other troops they had removed their collar tabs and badges and had thrown away their helmet with its tell-tale SS emblem.

A group of about forty waited to be moved down the line. Not out of trouble yet, because of their own shells landing precariously close they huddled together, somehow thinking this would offer protection. Corporal Rowlands, a tough bandy-legged ex-dustman from 16 Platoon prowled back and forth, daring them to make a move. He had a good reason to hate these evil bastards. Born and bred in Coventry, his wife and twin daughters died when the city was bombed in nineteen-forty. A few guys said he was waging a private war, keeping a tally on those he had personally killed. It could just be talk, but if his manner were anything to go by – a hard, uncouth bugger with a mean streak – there might be an element of truth in the rumour. His charges watched as he stalked them like a wild animal, fearing for their safety. When ordered to move, they doubled away, with the corporal chasing them down the road, snarling and pointing his rifle.

There were still plenty of Germans fighting back though, using tricks such as tucking a primed grenade inside a sling. Caught out a few times Tommy Atkins soon realised that a white flag and hands in the air did not necessarily mean they were ready to surrender. Itchy fingers and the desire to hit back sometimes meant it was easier to fire first.

Snipers volunteered to stay behind, hiding in empty houses or church spires, knowing full well they would never see their families and friends again. While others, desperate to take as many with them as possible perched in trees, carrying on the fight. Even the dead fought on with a primed grenade wedged under the body, so when moved another death would follow.

The platoon leaguered in a farmyard, which had recently seen heavy fighting. 'Dig in lads!' Mr Bowkett yelled. 'Counterattack expected!'

'Come on, Chaz,' Ron urged, eager to get below ground. 'We'll take it in turns.'

'I've heard that before,' Ginger said, walking to the back of the Bren. He handed Charlie a trenching tool. They started digging, throwing soil forward of their position, making good progress in what must have been an old vegetable patch. Ron and Freddie lay beside Betsy, keeping a lookout for snipers. The other two groaned, heaving spadeful after spadeful on a steady growing mound, which would form their parapet.

Ron chuckled, thinking of his bucket and spade on Cliftonville beach with Jack, seeing who could dig the biggest hole. His Uncle Fred stretched out on his deckchair would give the winner a sixpenny piece. So long as they left him alone with his *Daily Mirror*.

'Wot's so bloody effin funny?' Charlie grunted as he dug the spade in once more.

Ron was about to reply when a couple of shots rang out from a farmhouse some three-hundred yards away. Two gunners from 16 Platoon put ten-second bursts through windows, doorway and under the eaves. As if by magic, an elderly woman appeared, pinning up her hair and making her way around the back of the house, or was it a sniper disguised to give them the slip? All at once they heard the whistle of shells. Charlie and Ginger, having got down about four foot, flattened themselves in the trench, quickly followed by Ron and Freddie diving on top. Their trench leapt like a fairground Cake Walk as a stonk of five or six shells landed on the position.

'Platoon officer and sergeant!' someone screamed. There were cries from other half-finished trenches, showing there were more casualties.

Mr Bowkett received a nasty wound in his groin, along with a mangled left hand. White-faced with shock he swooned. On hearing Charlie's whispered remark, 'I fink 'e's goin',' he roused himself, trying to struggle to his feet. Lance Corporal Timmins, wounded in both knees, lay on his back groaning and tossing his head from side to side. Robbo, Mr Bowkett's driver, was bleeding profusely from his forearms. Wally Frazer was hit in the lower back by a shell fragment.

Ron stuck a field dressing up his blouse, careful not to cause more pain and assured him it was only a flea bite.

Ginger fetched the bottle of whisky from Freddie's kit bag. 'What about it, Fred?' he asked, dropping his rank around the others. 'Is this emergency enough?'

'Okay, Ginge,' he shouted back, more concerned with his efforts to stop Robbo bleeding to death.

'Don't give a wounded man whisky!' balled Major Sloan, who happened to be visiting their position. Though not before Cloddy mouthed a couple of welcome gulps.

They arranged the stretchers on Betsy, with injured arms and legs bandaged and T for tourniquet on Robbo's forehead. They wished them all the best, patted them without causing more pain and waved them off as Charlie and Ginger drove to the nearest aid post.

Now under the command of Sergeant Cox, 15 Platoon, barely able to muster a driver and gunner for each vehicle quickly withdrew.

Ron waited for Charlie's return, but there was no sign of him by dusk. Eventually, he cadged a lift in a half-track from Ernie's old platoon. He spent several hours chewing the fat with Rifleman Woods, who talked mostly about Ernie. Sharing his precious memories, Ron told him about some of the larks they got up to during basic training. The driver said Ernie had been a rough diamond and one day would have made a first-rate career soldier. This pleased Ron no end, knowing his pal had turned into someone rather special. War had been the making of him and at the same time, the cause of his death.

For J Support this was one of the worst encounters so far, with seven killed and twenty-two wounded, a quarter of their strength. Not only were they taken out of the line, but the battalion was as well. The last eight weeks had given them a terrible mauling, and they needed time to resupply in arms and men and recover.

On the road from Falaise to Caen, a unique situation occurred when the Fifth met up with their sister battalion, the First. They exchanged ribald comments as they passed each other, but Ron's lot wasted no time in hurrying for a long-overdue rest in Caen.

Chapter 16

'Closing the gap'

Ron finally arrived at the inland port on the Canal de Caen à la Mer. Full of naval vessels and enormous barges it was teeming with freshly landed troops. He cursed as he wandered around, trying to locate his platoon among so many. In the end, he gave up and made his way over to a group of GI tank wallahs. Taking pity on him, they gave him a mess tin of tomato soup, smoky pork with Boston beans, enough coffee to float his kidneys, a hearty tot of bourbon and a bed for the night.

The last two months had taught him to take each day as it came, not asking for much: a place to sleep, food in his belly and the friendship of his mates. During periods of melancholy, which occurred more so these days, he dwelt on things other than the war: home, mom and nan, Betty, Uncle Fred and his job. Before going to sleep, he had got into the habit of thanking God for allowing him to live through another day.

He lay next to an M3 Stuart light tank, with four guys from Kansas and mentally slipped back home. Very soon he was fast asleep, dead to the orange flashes in the eastern sky.

Just before dawn, Charlie and Ginger rumbled into the port. Pleased to see them he soon remembered how he had felt the night before and could not resist a friendly blast, telling them how he'd suffered.

'Daan't bleedin' start on me, matey!' Charlie blasted. 'I've only bin drivin' all night ta reunite ya wif yer thumb-suckin' kit. At least I bet yuv 'ad some chuffin' shuteye? Kippin' yer soddin' 'ead orf all night.'

'Sorry, Chaz,' he said contritely as Ginger tried to warn him that Charlie was not feeling his best, due to a recurring bout of diarrhoea. 'I didn't—'

'Oh, fillet of cod orf,' Charlie said before checking Betsy over.

A week later they found themselves once again in Carpiquiet, where the weather had changed to heavy rain, gusting winds and high humidity.

"'Ere it comes, Deak,' Charlie said, making a dash for the bivvy. 'I've never seen it pour so much.'

It danced on the roof of the tarp like marbles, filling their half-finished trench and soaking their clothes and blankets. No matter where they went, they got soaked and ratty. The torrent at times was horizontal, turning the floor of their bivvy into a viscous mess. What's more, it was Charlie's birthday, the worst ever.

Next day the sky was a cerulean blue, without a cloud in sight. By mid-afternoon, the previous day's rain was a distant memory. A tarp stretched between two trees and held down with an ample supply of bricks – seldom a shortage these days – proved a first-rate billet and a haven of peace. As they dried their bedding and shook out their kit, fresh rations arrived. For the first time in weeks parcels and mail caught up with them, now they were in one place for a while. Amazingly they were given last Friday's *Evening Standard* and *Daily Mirror*.

After lunch, Ron and Charlie caught up on what was happening back home, amused by all the tittle-tattle in each district. They read through the scant sports section, wishing they could watch a proper game of soccer. League football, an obsession for most males from eight to eighty, on the outbreak of war was cancelled for the duration. Going through Craven Cottage's turnstiles would be a grand tonic, they both agreed. To once more have a regular job, meals at home, trips to the pub and do all the things they once took for granted seemed a pipe dream. Still, they couldn't complain, having just tucked into rump steak and chips and a stoneware jar of young wine just out of its cradle. To finish off, they had tinned pears with fresh cream, a whole brie and crusty *pain de campagne* from a nearby *estaminet*. And best of all real cow's milk in real tea, instead of powdered compo and goat's milk from a kindly farmer.

With waistbands loosened and flies undone, they sat back dragging on an after-feast cigarette. A familiar figure, hound dog in appearance, stood under the canvas awning, waiting to be invited in.

'Come in, Missus Moule,' Charlie's humour oozed as Bert, one of only three despatch riders left in J Support stood on the threshold.

'Mornin', Missus Squires,' he said, matching his light-hearted banter.

'Your Fred agin?'

'That's right, me dear,' Bert countered, playing along. ''E went ta pub last night an' spent all 'is blitherin' wages. The little—'

''E were probably with my Ron, an' that scroungin' bastard Ginger Iverson from down the road. 'Anyway, Missus Moule, 'ow can I 'elp?'

'Ya couldn't let me 'ave a bit of sugar until payday, could ya, Misses Squires?'

'So long as I ger it back, dearie. Me ole man keeps me short these days.'

By now Ron and Ginger were in fits of laughter, tears running down their cheeks at this Saturday afternoon charade of Mrs Moule and Mrs Squires running down their spendthrift husbands. This instant was one of those occasions when the war was forgotten for just a moment, and the memory of it would stay with them long after the fighting had ended.

Rested, secure, away from the horrors of battle, they discussed civilian life, what the folks were doing back home, and what they would do once this blasted war was over. Clean and dry, a surfeit of food in their bellies and having caught up on lost sleep, it was possible to picture another way of life.

A corporal PTI in red and black striped jersey and navy shorts emerged from his bivvy, trying to win them over. 'Now then, lads,' he said, running on the spot, urging them to join in. 'Let's warm up the ole muscles, an' we'll 'ave a game of soccer.'

'Gertcher,' one lad scoffed. 'It's warm enough in this sweaty 'ole.'

'Hark at muscles,' someone gibed.

'Come on, lads,' he urged once more, 'let's be 'avin' ya. Let's 'ave a kick 'round. After all its Saturday afternoon. What else is there ta do? If we can't be at Loftus, let's bring Loftus 'ere.'

A few got up and went to get changed, having made up their mind to have a game of soccer. 'But no physical jerks, Corp,' one of them challenged. 'A kick around, you said.'

'Just so. A kick 'round. ... That's more like it!' the corporal exclaimed when he saw more returning to their bivvies. 'We can use the edge of the aerodrome.'

Even those who had told him to get lost were now kitted up, paired into teams, running on the spot. Soon there were about forty, all dressed for a proper game of football.

Loftus Road *had* come to Normandy, and it was QPR v Fulham all over again.

With the arrival of a new platoon officer and eight fresh-faced swaddies, Captain Jamieson moved men around in 15 Platoon, spreading battle-hardened troops through the ranks. He made Charlie up to lance corporal, assigning him to 14 Platoon to replace several injured NCOs. It was standard practice when someone was promoted to move them to another platoon so they could get used to their new rank away from their erstwhile friends.

Ron was pleased when he heard he was once more being teamed up with Joe Sharp and a pimply-faced youth from Bristol called Joe Page. There was much talk about what they should call the new lad – he not having a say in the matter – as the last thing they wanted was 'Joe' being bandied all over the place in the heat of battle. In the end, they settled on JP or Beaky.

A couple of days later Ron and the others were ordered to the rear for some much-needed vehicle spares. This allowed them to see first-hand the vast amount of supplies needed to sustain such an army. Teeming troops transferred thousands of boxes to colossal storage areas, ready for moving to the 'front'. Ron could only envy these guys their comfortable billets with real beds, disturbed only by the occasional tête à tête with some sweet-natured *mademoiselle*. To supply such an army was an incredible feat, never equalled before in the annals of war. Tommy Atkins could now call on all types of meat, fresh veg, newly baked bread, cheese, butter, milk, newspapers, beer, cigarettes and tobacco. Not only were these at hand to keep up his spirits, but also the latest movies and safe places to go during leave periods. Shower units were also available, along with the chance to launder clothes that by now stood up on their own. Every few weeks delousing was arranged as most privates, NCOs and officers were as lousy as cuckoos.

Even if battles were savage and costly, they at least knew they would be given time to relax and recover, as best they could. Once again, Ron thought of his father and uncle, weighing up their war against his. There was no doubt the young officers who survived that dreadful war, to become this war's senior officers, had learnt their lessons well.

'You're in the wrong mob, Ron,' Sharpy said, seeing his downcast visage. 'You should have joined the Supply Corps when you had the chance. I remember you saying at the time, "Not fer me, China,' he mimicked, 'I wanna see some action,"'

'I've seen that all right. Enough ta last a lifetime.'

Three privates sat around an open fire, frying bacon and chuffing on doorsteps crammed with rashers, making breakfast for their mates as they stacked and restacked boxes.

A corporal with two bullocks, showing their displeasure – or relief at once more being on dry land – led them towards a large marquee with skins stacked as high as a man.

'You can't get much fresher than that,' JP fancied.

'That's 'ow I feel sometimes,' Ron said, sizing up the beasts.
'In what way?'
'Bein' led ta the slaughter.'

A trip to Bayeux, strolling around the city, where red caps patrolled in pairs had been arranged by their new officer, Lieutenant Lyle. Ron immediately recognised the man. He was the bastard who slept all night in his Bren with the platoon's blankets swathed around him, while his men froze their balls off on the bleak Yorkshire Moors. Ron spoke to him at the time but might as well have saved his breath. War is about sharing hardships, whatever your rank, he said to the officer just before being put on a charge for insubordination.

After Major Sloan's briefing, Mr Lyle made a point of speaking to Ron. He apologised for his behaviour that night and asked if they could put the whole episode behind them, as they needed to focus on the job in hand. They cleared the air and dismissed it as an unfortunate incident that should be forgotten.

The petite *mademoiselle* in silk stockings, high heel shoes and chic dress waited outside the cathedral's main entrance for her British soldier boy – having no doubt dated scores of Germans before their hasty retreat. Two women walking up and down, making their intentions more obvious, chatted up soldiers, promising them a good time. Wherever they went, they were forever plagued by Toms, plying their trade, offering whatever for the right price. Some were quite pretty. But most were far from pleasing, having been on the game since Methuselah was in short trousers. Their painted faces, charmless figures, lack of personal hygiene and drab, beat-up clothes left little to the imagination, robbing you of any desire. Only those swaddies who were desperate would frequent such ladies. It could be lonely at times, starved of female company. But the one saving grace was there was always a few nice girls about, not on the game, to give a soldier boy a bit of love and attention in return for a few luxuries. Mankind and his views on morality rarely changed, only the conquering army and the goods on offer.

Ron and the others found themselves in a bar where a stone-faced *madame* served a weak concoction of sugared water, laced with piffling amounts of Calvados. For some, it seemed everything was poorly timed, downright inconvenient, putting an end to a cosy arrangement with the Germans. This lady, ankle-deep in five-franc notes was one such instance of French *bonhomie* at its worst. She looked down her nose, snickering with her regulars while giving these liberating soldiers dirty looks. Taking enough insults for one day, they walked out of the charmless bar, spending the afternoon looking for Bayeux's very own *Folies-Bergère*.

Early evening, they came across a bar in a market square. The genial owner and a few locals welcomed them with open arms. They spent a pleasant couple of hours drinking and making merry with their new friends. On parting, after refusing to take any money, the patron promised to visit each of them in London after the war. They swapped names and addresses and pledged lifelong friendship.

As soon as they returned to camp, they heard the Falaise Gap had finally been closed, resulting in the encirclement of the Wehrmacht 7th Army and the 5th Panzer Army. The ensuing battle all but brought about the destruction of Army Group B west of the Seine. This now gave the Allies unfettered access to Paris and the borders of Germany. It proved to be a turning point in the war.

Bombers, *carte blanche*, started flying over Caen in large numbers to clobber Jerry as he fled north with his tail between his legs.

'That'll wake the bastards up, Joe,' Ron said as more B17s flew over at twenty plus thousand feet.

'Lovely stuff, me old cocker,' Sharpy chirped.

'It'll make our job easier,' JP opined.

'One hopes ...' said Sharpy wisely. 'But remember, Beaky, where war is concerned, take nothing for granted.'

As the column raced through thickly wooded countryside, Ron and the others enjoyed the lovely weather, swanning along in this idyllic setting. Having been involved in the bitter struggles around Caen, it made a change to see parts of France untouched by war and receive such warmth from these once oppressed people.

A rear-guard action, being played out in a small village required 15 Platoon to remain in a shady lane, listening to the exchange of shells between friend and foe.

Ron strolled up to Georgie and Jimmy in front, offered them a smoke each and leant on their Bren for a chat. 'Well, wot ya think's causin' 'old up, Jimmy?' he asked before taking a lungful of smoke.

George Pearson and Jimmy East, miffed at having their breezy drive so rudely curtailed started fooling around, chatting like two brigadiers running over their battle plans. 'Ah, yes, Robin,' George said in a plummy voice, 'bring up your brigade, and I'll support you on the left flank with the twenty-first and twenty-second.'

'Good wheeze, Chesney, old bean,' Jimmy guffawed.

'Damn good show,' Georgie said, placing his pretend map in an imaginary briefcase and then pushing his glasses up the bridge of his nose. 'Synchronise watches, Robin. ... 1400 hours.'

'Spot on, Chesney.'

These two clowns were born comedians. Georgie, swarthy with an ever-present five o'clock shadow was in his mid-thirties. Jimmy, a young Tyron Power lookalike, hailing from Mansfield, was a real ladies' man. There were no two ways about it some sweet-natured girl would be missing his good looks, bright, sparkling eyes and cheeky, ready wit.

Cedric Wilmot, a war correspondent attached to the Fifth, with his Leica around his neck walked by as Georgie and Jimmy gabbled on. He glanced at them, thinking these casualties of war had somehow slipped through the net.

'Red flag up!' Sharpy yelled. Each man started running towards their vehicle.

They pulled away and shortly came across the newly liberated village. Each Bren drove around the debris of collapsed buildings and soon drew level with two knocked out 88s guarding the main road. A dozen dead Germans, sprawled about, ripped apart by heavy fire had fought and died in this vicious rear-guard action.

To avoid being shelled, they quickly passed through the village and then called for a halt. Ron's section started brewing up next to a German Great War cemetery, with twenty or so graves. The Teutonic crosses gave their name, rank, date of birth and death. The grenadiers, youngest fifteen and eldest sixty-two had made the ultimate sacrifice for their Kaiser.

Not much 'as changed, thought Ron.

15 Platoon took up station in a recently harvested cornfield, using a hedgerow as camouflage. Their officer told them that if Jerry showed his hand, a barrage would be laid down two-hundred-yards to their front. Conscious of how close it would be, also knowing how inaccurate artillery could be at the best of times, Ron and Sharpy set too digging a deep trench.

With machine guns set, ranges taken, orders issued, and watches assigned, they settled in for the night, ready for a well-earned stodge and brew. After feeding the inner man, they sat back and loosened their bootlaces. Otherwise, it felt like a tourniquet around each instep, making it nigh impossible to sleep. Boots and clothing had to be worn all the time, unless in a rest area. Undoing your laces was the only concession to comfort.

It was soon clear Jerry had withdrawn to a better-defended position. The moonlit landscape was eerily quiet, leaving ghostly forms cast by stacked sheaves of corn. It turned out to be a creepy night, but a new day finally bubbled above the horizon.

The order 'prepare to move in twenty minutes' was passed around the company, giving each crew time to make a quick brew and wad. A large billy-can with two or three pints of water over a dixie of sand and a mug of petrol soon got the water boiling nicely. Though you quickly learnt to stand back when the match was lit. Because it was not only the sand that ignited but the fume-laden air as well. This new wrinkle had been picked up from Male and other desert wallahs. It soon became the norm for making a quick brew.

As they drove down chalky-white roads, people started appearing with all manner of drinks. '*Vive la Angleterre,*' one elderly gentleman said, pressing Calvados apple brandy on Ron and JP.

'*Vive la France,*' they replied, tendering their mugs for a mouthful of this potent brew.

Joyous inebriated civilians, lining the roads, encouraged the soldiers to imbibe. Needing to keep a clear head, they held out their mugs and once talking to their hosts tipped the contents in a dixie at their feet, for later consumption. This led to some weird concoctions, but not a drop was wasted.

There was yet another holdup when an armoured unit engaged tanks that remained behind to slow down the advance. Sharpy pulled up behind a Mark IV Churchill, switched off his engine and waited for orders to proceed. The tank commander, microphone pressed to his mouth, chattered to other tanks in the vicinity. With the internal speaker switched on his crew could hear what was happening, keeping abreast of things.

'Sunray calling Baker Group ... over,' the officer said, looking through his binoculars at three tanks making their way along a ridge on the skyline, firing as they went.

'Receiving, Sunray. Strength six ... over.'

'Muzzle flashes north of your position, Baker. There are three enemy AFVs two-thousand yards out.'

'Roger, Sunray. I have sight of them ... Panthers ... several dozen troops on foot. Engaging!'

One of the tanks exploded, ripping its turret clean off. A pillar of fire belched skywards. A split-second later, Ron heard a loud whooof.

'Kill confirmed, Baker. Good shooting.' The captain once more raised his binoculars. What remained of the tank was on its right side, bodies spewing out of a gaping maw.

'Thank you, Sunray ... over.'

'Anytime, Baker. Happy shooting. Over and out.'

These carefree tankmen treated the whole thing as if it were a game. But to Ron and the others a game it was not. The thought of being enclosed in one of those iron coffins was totally alien to them. They preferred to take their chances out in the open, with small arms, mortars and shells. To be fried to death in a steel box was not their idea of fun. Infantrymen, fleet of foot, thought of tanks as slow, awkward beasts that were far too vulnerable to armour-piercing shells. They had seen too many fall prey to a well-placed round. The shell would punch clean through the hull and then whiz around like the blades of a harvest thresher. If the crew survived and the hatch wasn't jammed, they would bail out with nothing worse than concussion, loss of hearing and scorched clothing and skin. Save a busted turret meant escape was impossible. High octane fuel and bursting shells yielded some terrible results, sometimes peeling back armour with absolute ease.

AFVs depended on infantry as their warlike partners and the infantry looked on tanks as their big brothers, and neither would swap.

Arriving at their overnight leagering point Ron and JP got down for a chinwag with a tank wallah, leaving Sharpy to put Betsy to bed. He positioned her between two Sherman's from the Royal Horse Guards, to which they were now attached.

Parked in the middle of the road, with its engine running was a Humber scout car from O Group. The second lieutenant, seeing them approach stuck his head up from the hull and told Ron to sod off. His driver said something about having time for a brew, but the officer refused, saying they had a job to do. With nerves frayed, they headed towards the German lines. Before bedding down recce wallahs would take a swift belt up the road to draw any fire. This was to ascertain the enemy's strength, relying on their speed and agility to escape any *panzerfausts* lurking in ditches.

Ron looked at Ginger. No words were exchanged, but both knew what the other was thinking. *Rather them than me.*

Next day the convoy threaded its way through the outskirts of a medium-sized town, untouched by war. Street after street of semi-detached houses made them think of home. Each house had a neatly laid out garden, trim lawns and newly turned borders, ready for autumn planting. Once again, this seemed to belong to another world.

Facing another holdup, one that would last some time, Sharpy and the other drivers parked their carriers and started brewing up.

The rumble of tracks and the distinctive growl of a German heavy tank caused everyone to drop their cha and bully-beef butties. Ron and Sharpy grabbed their rifles and a satchel of Mills grenades. They slid into a muddy ditch, leaving Ginger squirming behind Betsy, ready to repel the attack with a loaded PIAT. They waited, heart pounding, the taste of bile at the back of their throat. A Tiger hove into view, gun depressed to show it was no threat. The Horse Guards officer cheerily waved as he passed, making his way down the line with his new toy.

'Cocky bastard,' Ginger mouthed, grinding his butty in the mud. 'I hope his knob falls off.'

As they waited for the 'red flag' an elderly Frenchman in mayoral red, white and blue sash, with a dozen or so locals in tow wooed Ron and the others with a jug of cider. '*Homme d'artillerie,*' he said, proudly stabbing his chest with his finger. '*Artillerie sergent.*' Having convinced them he had served as a gunner in The Great War, with his boom, boom, booms, he explained that their church had a large crypt where leading citizens would shelter in the case of a raid. Some ten yards away stood three girls with shorn heads. Being found guilty of fraternising with the enemy, with the Germans gone the townsfolk had hacked off their hair, leaving clots of blood where the blade had cut deep.

The mayor saw the Tommies looking at the girls no older than eighteen. *'Ils ont collaboré avec le boche,'* he said, slicing a finger across his throat.

The Fifth drove down the main high street, past a Gothic revival-style church and then wended its way onto some high ground beyond. They soon came across a burnt-out motor coach with a red cross on its roof and sides, and a few dead Germans tended by rats.

The force that took up station, a small armoured group and half the Fifth had a one-hundred-and-eighty-degree arc of fire. Made up of tanks, machine guns, mortars and Priests it soon drew the enemy's attention, shelling without mercy and making life unpleasant above ground. Just after midnight, Panthers, Tigers and a battalion of Waffen-SS panzergrenadiers entered the town and encircled the hill. Having set up their stronghold they would no doubt be waiting to rough up our soft skins as they brought up supplies, while at the same time trying to locate reserve troops, now cut off and tightly bottled up.

The pain in his guts could not be put off any longer. When digging the latrines, Ron thought the spot was perfect. Nice and close to the trenches. Though, with all this shelling, they now seemed rather exposed. Taking a deep breath, he sprang from his trench, creating a world record for a tomtit.

Casualties began to rise, and the RAP was soon under pressure. They tended the seriously wounded first, and once stable kept them below ground to protect them from further harm. Those not likely to live through the night were moved to a remote part of the post and given a hefty dose of morphine. The padre comforted them as they drifted in and out of consciousness, taking details of next of kin and promising to write. Early the following day, those who had survived would be transferred to an ADS.

Having returned from the khazi an almighty explosion and blinding flash filled Ron's world, shoving him and Sharpy against the rear wall of the shallow trench, tipping them backwards. They slithered back into the hole, crouched low and waited for cries of help.

'What the fuck was that?' Sharpy pressed while struggling to breathe in the hot, cordite infused air.

'You okay?' Ron smirked.

'No! he snapped. 'I fuckin' ain't!'

'Don't get a bubble on, mate. Yer still in land o' the livin'.'

'Only fuckin' just.'

''Ave a shufti ... an' clock what's 'appened?' Ron asked as he lit a cigarette to steady his nerves.

'Lost the use of your legs again, butcher boy?'

'But wotch yer bonce, Quiff,' he said, ignoring his acerbic remark.

A high explosive shell had scored a direct hit on a three-tonner loaded with anti-tank rounds. A few seconds earlier Corporal Paddy Walsh, recent recipient of a Military Medal, and his new officer were yarning and drinking tea beside the Bedford. Neither body was found. Not so much as a dog tag. Chalkie (pinkie) Whitlow caught it in the backside, while another rifleman refused help, fighting the stretcher-bearers. Harold (chick or coop) Cooper, with his constant good humour, would be sadly missed. The nasty stomach wound required him to be moved carefully to avoid excessive blood loss. After a while, he relented, taking them up on the offer of a lift. Sadly, this ex-toolmaker from Hartlepool died on his way to the RAP.

Ron's section was ordered to set up a listening post fifty yards closer to the German lines. It proved a long night, with each rifleman peering into stacked corn sheaves, thinking the phantom shapes were attacking troops.

Waking at first light, Ron saw the barrel of a Sherman Firefly above his head, its right track only inches from the trench. He turned and shook Lance Corporal McBain awake, grimaced and said, 'Friend of yours, Willy?' McBain looked at the tank, went the colour of parchment and spewed up in the bottom of the trench.

'What's up with him?' Sharpy asked.

'Somethin's upset 'is stomach,' he said, nodding at the tank.

'Oh, it turned up just after midnight.'

'Ya could 'ave warned me.'

'I didn't want to wake you. You were sleeping like a new-born babe.'

Breakfast over they paid their respects to Cyril Benton from East Cheam and his new buddy of four days, Sandy Browne from Rugely. They covered them with anti-gas capes and stood saying a soldier's prayer. The padre, drawn and red-eyed arrived from burying Harold Cooper, just in time to commit two more brave lads to the earth. Once the burial service was over, he left to do the same for four more from K Company. Three riflemen from Cyril's platoon shovelled in the earth which had once formed the parapet of their trench.

Major Courtney, the Fifth's new second in command, walked about in his white mackintosh, checking on the position and asking each soldier how he was faring. Stopping in front of Rifleman Sharp he praised him on having shaved and asked how he was doing.

'Okay, Sir,' he replied, looking at the freshly filled graves. 'I could be worse.'

He followed his gaze, made no comment and then walked away.

'Do us a favour, Ron,' he said once the major was out of earshot, 'shave my friggin' arse ... silly bastard.'

As they made their way back to the trench line, a flight of Tiffies nosedived, ready to strafe their own troops. The signal wallahs ran to put out recognition flags, but not before the lead aircraft fired his rockets. Fortunately, his aim was high, peppering a field behind J Support's headquarters.

That same evening a battalion from a Midland County regiment retook the town after a terrific barrage, with a few rogue shells landing close to the Fifth's forward lines.

Ron thought about the mayor, who supposed his war was over. Also, the townspeople cowering in the church, wondering if they had survived. He further thought of what the Boche would have done to punish those who so brutally hacked off the women's hair?

Thirty-six hours after the start of this operation a line of ambulances, protected by a single Sherman made their way down the hill to take the wounded to the nearest ADS.

Later they heard their long-awaited replacement would relieve them the next day. But the enemy, not letting up, again counter-attacked, giving 15 Platoon's gunners more target practice, which they gladly took advantage of.

Chapter 17

'Race to Antwerp'

The Fifth's relief force, badly mauled by three Focke-Wulf 190s at Bourguébus took time to sort themselves out, licking their wounds and sourcing replacements from a sister unit. The Coldstream Guards, having arrived a week ago at Ouistreham finally got underway, three days behind schedule.

The guardees marched either side of the road, some laughing while others caterwauled at German prisoners heading in the opposite direction. More than a few were quiet, tense, withdrawn and shocked by their recent baptism of fire. With helmets pushed back on heads, reserve ammo draped around their neck, and light machine guns slung over their shoulder they marched briskly now their forced march was nearly over.

The small village, choked with tanks, half-tracks and carriers was overrun by hundreds of prisoners with hands placed on heads, picking their way between vehicles and troops on their way to the front.

'*Hände* fuckin' *hoch*!' a Welsh fusilier barked, urging his charges with a jab of his rifle. '*Schnell*! *Schnell*! Come on you dozy bastards.' Angry at being picked as their nursemaid he lashed out with his boot at a hobbling SS private, causing him to stumble. 'Get up you, little shitehawk!' he screamed. 'And keep up you pigs. *Zusammenhalten, sie Kraut Schweine!*'

Prisoners were of all ages: pimply-faced Hitler *Jugend*, not yet old enough to shave, to thickly whiskered grandfathers from the *Volksturm*. They stared blindly ahead, finding it hard to believe such a thing could happen to them. Dressed in dirty, threadbare uniforms, dragging their feet or tripping along after stopping for a call of nature, they were a pitiful sight. This ragtag of humanity, from all over Germany and Eastern Europe had fervently followed the same flawed cause. Even though they were from all walks of life, they had one thing in common, their immense relief at being out of the fighting, but for the occasional shell from their own side.

Four Wehrmacht privates, carrying a fallen comrade, kept looking at the ashen face of their childhood friend. His head lolled back, almost touching the ground. With each shell burst, they crouched lower, causing his head to graze the dusty road.

As the line of vehicles ground to a halt, a few POWs stepped forward, trying to scrounge cigarettes from the soldiers. A panzergrenadier, his right arm in a sling and a field dressing around his throat, singled out a wiry looking sergeant who was trying to direct his driver around the milling throng. The burly *Obergefreiter* placed two fingers to his lips as if smoking, pretending to inhale, smiling and showing extreme pleasure. '*Deutschland kaput,*' the corporal said, left arm outstretched, seeking some sympathy from his vanquisher. '*Kreig nicht gut.*' He shrugged his shoulders, a wince of pain showing fleetingly in his pale blue eyes.

'Arf a mo, Fritz,' the sergeant countered, pointing his finger accusingly. 'Yuv changed yer bleedin' tune. I bet ya weren't sayin' that when ya were goose-steppin' inta Poland?'

'Adolf Hitler *nicht mehr. Er ist fertig,*' he blustered, saying Hitler was finished.

'Well, whatever ya jus' lingoed ... still don't alter fact ya want one of me smokes.'

'*Ya! Ya!* Smoke,' he said keenly, again placing fingers to his lips and nodding.

The sergeant delved into his pocket for a nearly full pack of cigarettes. Three more POWs, seeing him take them out crowded around the carrier, thrusting out hands. He gave each a cigarette. They held them up, looking at their whiteness and then put them to their nose, smelling real tobacco.

'*Vielen Dank,*' each thanked, nodding. A fair-haired Luftwaffe officer added in perfect English, 'Thank you, sergeant.'

They dragged down a lungful of smoke, enjoying one of his Gold Flake. It made a change from the dry horse-manuric-weed they usually smoked. Its aroma lingered in their vacated trenches for days, tainting the air with the sourness of unwashed feet. A few hours earlier, these men would have given each other little quarter. Frontline troops had a healthy respect for their opposite number, discounting, of course, the reviled SS. It was easy to join these august ranks, but far from easy to resign or retire, unless fate tips the balance.

For several days J Support leaguered in a field on the other side of the village, where long-range shelling rarely gave over. Thanks to a complex trench system, courtesy of Jerry, casualties were few.

Due to the threat of counterattack, the men endured long periods of 'stand-to'. This proved tiring for those who had gone without proper sleep for weeks. 'Stand-to' harked back to the Boer War and Great War. It was customary to launch an attack at dusk, or just before dawn, to catch the enemy in a state of flux. Troops were required to be ready an hour before with rifles loaded and machine gun posts manned.

Ron and Sharpy, standing on wooden duckboards strained their eyes and ears for signs of an attack. Being early morning wildlife was stirring, causing the dawn chorus to play havoc with these jumpy watchers. Any slight noise and they would have the whole company on their feet, amidst oaths and curses that would make a sailor blush.

'Ya windy cunt-faced bastards!' one irate ranker exclaimed after yet again being woken from his slumbers.

'Yer scared witless ya turd-faced tosser's,' griped another, minus his boots and over trousers. 'I'll get me own back,' he added, standing on one foot while tucking in his shirt, a loaded rifle clamped between his knees. 'Nah sleep for you ... ya, poxy bastards.'

It was a mild form of torture when dog tired, stretched out in a muddy hole, to be shaken time after time when off duty.

'I'm up an' down loike a fuckin' yo-yo,' another moaned, making his views known. 'I daan't kna if I'm on me Khyber Pass or me bleedin' Spanish archer.'

On hearing netting being taken off one of the Brens, Ron and Sharpy ducked down in their trench, ready for a few choice-gifts from Jerry. The carrier headed for the fuel dump to pick up some much-needed supplies. This pre-dawn routine made everyone nervous because of the noise it created. The enemy, hearing a vehicle startup, would call their artillery to order. Within minutes a couple of shells were fired, to remind us they were still there.

The Coldstream's finally took over from the Fifth, giving them leave to pull back to a 'rest area' ten miles south of Caen.

Rested and resupplied, the Fifth now attached to a newly arrived armoured brigade started their push towards Antwerp, with K Company leading the way. In their wake was a squadron of Sherman's and behind them the rest of the force. J Support and the 1st Hussars formed the rear echelon. To begin with the advance was cautious, not wanting to weaken their position by stringing themselves out. But as the brigade's confidence grew, so did the pace. After a while J Support was ordered to take up a position on the left flank. It was not long before a carrier from 14 Platoon was hit, killing two and wounding several others.

Despatch riders relayed fresh orders, telling everyone to hold tight while an American division crossed the centre line, to cover the right flank.

'Trust bleedin' Yanks,' Ron said, hawking and gobbing in the bushes. 'Same as last lot. Late fer party, scoffed all the grub, swigged all the beer an' nicked all the birds.'

'At least it'll make our job easier now the Fourth Cavalry's arrived,' Sharpy reckoned as he pretended to lasso Major Sloan's half-track.

'Red flag up!' someone yelled.

Ron doused the petrol fire and clambered aboard. He rested the billy-can on his knees, heat scorching his legs as he tried to keep it level, avoiding getting compo on his best trousers. 'No jerkin', Joe—'

'Don't talk dirty, Ronald,' he said, making like a censoring mother.

'—otherwise, I'll scald me privates.'

Betsy suspiciously bucked back and forth, sloshing compo all over the place. A mile further on there was another stop. Ron handed JP the still warm billy-can, leapt down and eased wet serge away from his crotch. Within minutes the mixture was boiling, and they had their third brew in as many hours.

Sharpy, now an inveterate chain-smoker rarely removed his cigarette, except to light another or take a sip from his mug. 'Ron, you make a lovely cuppa,' he chided, letting another mouthful swill around his smoke-dried mouth. 'You'll make someone a lovely wife one day.'

'Bollocks, tosspot.'

Suddenly the flag went up.

Joe gulped down what was left and passed his mug to Ron. 'Anymore in the pot, Doreen?' he said, grinning.

Ron gave him what was left, dregs and all. 'You an' yer bleedin' Rosie Lee,' he cracked, slinging the fire dixie aboard. The Bren behind them gave Betsy a playful nudge, easing her along.

On the outskirts of a large town, many houses, gutted in a recent air raid spilt on the road, forming an obstacle course for the drivers. They gingerly made their way around the piles of rubble and at last arrived at a crossroads where people were pressed up against the vehicles, making it impossible to move forward. Men and women pushed out hands towards their saviours, holding out posies, crying babies to be kissed, bunches of grapes and bottles of wine. The crowd finally parted, and the mayor in his red, white and blue sash walked up to Major Sloan's half-track. The major, now standing, ignored the man and tried to get the people to move away from his vehicle.

'*Vive la France!*' the mayor shouted. The crowd went wild. '*Vive la Grande-Bretagne!*' They cheered again. '*Vive la Amérique!*' More shouting. '*Mort à la Boche!*' Death to the Boche got the loudest cheer. He handed Major Sloan a bottle of champagne, a bunch of red roses and kissed him on both cheeks. The major, leaning over the side of his half-track tepidly returned his thanks. If it hadn't been for Captain Jamieson keeping hold of the folds of his blouse he would have overbalanced and landed on top of the verbose mayor.

'*Je ... je vous re ... re mer ... mercie, Monsieur M-Maire,*' the major said, reading from his phrasebook.

'Lucky 'e dint say *kiss mon* obtuz, Quiffy,' Ron said, sneering at his mate.

'Well said, Ronald Henry Deakin, *onetime* apprentice butcher.' Sharpy recalled the moment as if it were yesterday. So much water had gone under the bridge since then, and they were still together. The Gods were looking after them. And long may They continue to do so. 'Have you had chance to use it yet, lover boy?'

'What?'

'*Kiss mon* obtuz,' he said on the cusp of laughing.

'No! An' I don't intend to, you evil bastard. What ya told me were a load of Jackson Pollock's. ... Anyway,' he furthered, 'I'm a one-girl-guy now.'

'Bloody hell! Someone's tamed the Deacon,' he said, ignoring the affront.

'Wot about you an' Jackie? Is it as strong as ever?'

'Stronger!'

Major Sloan leafed through his phrasebook in a bid to find the right words for such an occasion. He turned to Captain Jamieson and said something. The captain shook his head and shrugged. The major once more made frantic sweeping gestures, trying to get them to move away from his vehicle. The crowd, acting as one, cheered and waved back. Knowing his efforts were futile he swung around and yelled, 'Do any of you lot speak French?'

Sharpy stood on his seat and shouted, 'I do, Sir!'

'Rifleman, tell this ... to disperse the crowd and let us carry on with the blasted war.'

'Of course, Sir!' Putting his fingers to his lips he blew a loud wolf whistle, cutting through the noise. Everyone was now looking at him. '*Nous sommes pressés d'aller à Paris,*' he said. '*Nous avons une table réservée chez Maxim's pour huit personnes et nous ne voulons pas qu'Adolf la pince.*'

The people started laughing, even the mayor. Slowly they backed away from the vehicles. Shells began falling on the other side of town, encouraging the crowd to disperse. At last, the major's half-track freed itself and resumed its journey to Antwerp.

'Hey, Joe,' JP asked after they had gone a couple of miles, 'what did you say back there to make them move so quick?'

'I told them to shift because we were in a hurry to get to Paris.'

'What's so funny about that?'

'Nothing. But I also said we'd got a table booked at Maxim's for eight o'clock. And I didn't want Adolf nicking it.'

'I 'ope Irish an' Sloan Square don't find out wot ya said,' Ron quipped, passing them both a cigarette, 'otherwise Droopy Drawers'll put ya on a fizzer.'

'I used my initiative,' he said, lighting up from a cigarette butt. 'Anyway, it cleared the crowd.'

'That weren't you! That were bleedin' Boche!' Ron howled scornfully. 'They must 'ave bin listenin' ta ya, an' thought they'd give ya an 'elpin' hand. ... All very dodgy if ya ask me.'

'What is?'

'That salvo comin' at chuffin' right time.'

'A mere coincidence.'

'Coincidence, me arse. Yer a fifth columnist.'

'Oh, bollocks,' he hit back. 'You talk a load of cod's wallop at times, Deakin.'

'Well, yer one-sixth German.'

'I've told you before, birdbrain, my Great Grandfather came from Vienna. He was Austrian. That aside, me old cocker … coming back to a more cognizant—'

'Cogni-whatsit. What's that when it's at 'ome, Quiff?'

'It's French for pillock, butcher boy. Anyway, I didn't lie … just bent the truth a bit. One day I will eat at Maxim's … Jackie and I will.'

'Wot twaddle.'

'Play your cards right, porkchop, and I'll treat you to *your* dinner one day.'

Ron checked his watch. 'Ya will, sooner than ya think. It's your turn ta cook, sweetheart.'

The number of vehicles and heavy ordnance left behind had increased dramatically in recent weeks. Many were broken down, and others just too cumbersome to take with them. A few miles south of the Orne, near a village called Ménil-Gondouin, a heavy howitzer plus hundreds of rounds were found abandoned by the roadside. The charges set to destroy this cache of arms failed to explode. This chance find was rather pleasing, as shortly it would be turned on their prior owners. All agreed this was by far the best way to receive arms and ammo, direct from the enemy.

Just as they reached the Orne, a rail bridge was blown, sending tons of rubble high in the air. It rained down, peppering their forward troops and killing M Company's second in command. They were then thwapped by mortar fire, with more deaths, including an officer and two medics tending wounded on the riverbank.

Machine gun and mortar platoons, tasked with supporting the Royal Engineers as they worked to span the river, sited their weapons by the light of a full moon. In response to their gunfire, there was a burst from half a dozen Spandau machine guns, catching sappers and forward troops. Things worsened when shells and mortars started raining down. The sappers, taking heavy fire, lost one-third of their number as they tried to span the river with a Bailey Bridge. A mortar platoon, mercilessly thwapped, was pinned down close to the bank. With the moon obscured by cloud, they eventually withdrew to a tree line some six hundred yards away, where the senior MO had set up the RAP. Thankfully there were no deaths, but many were injured, a few seriously.

Ron's platoon gave covering fire to an amphibious crossing by a Welsh territorial battalion. To start with things went well, but soon fire from Tigers and 88s stopped any further advance, pinning the Taffy's in a dip two hundred yards from where they landed. Once Priests, artillery, mortars and rocket firing Mustangs had hammered Jerry, they carried on with their advance and secured a firm bridgehead.

As soon as the bridge was ready, heavy armour pushed forward amidst scenes of utter chaos. Burned out enemy AFVs and transports littered the battlefield, along with hundreds of dead Germans. Macerated bodies of horses from an earlier raid, along with the bloated remains of their drivers were a squirming mass of white. The air, thick with flies was dense enough to cut. They crawled over the living, getting inside clothes and in every facial orifice. The smell was bad enough, but flies in their millions were worse. It was a dreadful sight, showing war at its basest.

15 Platoon took the lead, braving the stink that clung to every piece of kit for days, flooding their senses and giving rise to violent retching. As they threaded their way between these dreadful scenes, shocked, weary troops, many wounded, gave themselves up. Even the reviled SS was now only too willing to 'throw in the towel', not caring what happened to them. But there were still plenty of ardent Nazi's about to make life difficult at times.

During what was a dreadfully wet night they formed a close leager against die-hard SS troops, whom it was said were roaming the woods in search of easy kills. Was it true, or scaremongering? Who knows, but no one was taking the chance.

Next day the sun was shining, putting everyone in a positive frame of mind. Orders came through to rest for a few days, giving them the chance to recover. The battalion took over a disused brewery, arranging bathing in enormous vats, just like Tommy Atkins did in The Great War. There was once more a sense of routine, with each man revelling in this unexpected break. Some riflemen accepted offers from the locals to put them up, opening their homes and showing immense kindness. In return, they shared their rations and other foodstuffs from a mobile naafi. It seemed strange to be once more living in a house, being part of a family unit, going to dances, chatting up girls, and walking about without fear of being shelled.

The strangeness of war ... what madness it all was.

The column pushed on towards Antwerp, little by little sweeping away what resistance remained behind to slow down their advance.

They soon crossed the River Risle, via a repaired bridge courtesy of the Royal Marines, only a hundred miles south-west of Paris. Once on the other side, any thought of keeping up this swift pace was out of the question, when they came up against a large Panzer group, well dug in. The attack proved fierce and costly, but eventually, they carried the day. Swathes of prisoners, along with a Wehrmacht General and two high-ranking SS officers in civilian clothes gave themselves up.

On the move again, a *Raupenschlepper* transport towing a 105mm howitzer tried to tag onto 16 Platoon. The corporal in the rear Bren, taking exception to this, got his driver to slew to one side. He turned his Vickers on the caterpillar tractor, knocking out the windscreen and killing both occupants. No doubt, getting fed up with life in the German Army the Wehrmacht *Obergefreiter* and *Gefreiter* was more than likely trying to 'work their ticket' into our mob.

As the miles ticked by both machine-gun platoons, shielding the column's right flank travelled at a fair lick of speed, ever closer to Antwerp. This fast pace was fraught with danger, keeping in touch with a fast-moving column. Running into small pockets of resistance each Vickers cut a swathe through them like a farmer toppling hay. It was a risky business pelting along at such a madcap speed, blindly sliding around corners and launching across fields.

Sharpy drove with confidence, while the others, struggling to keep an eye on the column watched for signs of an ambush. 'Where are they, Deak?' he asked.

'Can't see them,' Ginger replied. The week before JP had copped a Blighty while on patrol, and Ginger was once more teamed up with Ron and Joe, making Betsy's crew one of the most experienced in 15 Platoon.

'Keep ta yer left, Joe,' Ron said, tapping him on his shoulder, 'an' stop witterin' ya nervy bugger. You're making me jumpy. They can't be far ahead.'

'They've pushed away from us,' Sharpy said. 'We've lost them.'

'Don't worry,' Ron assured. 'They'll only be a few hundred yards ahead. They're more than likely brewin' up by now. ... Though gerra a move on, fearless. Otherwise, we'll be mincemeat fer an eighty-eight.'

'Bear right!' Ginger yelled. 'They must be 'round the next bend.'

'I hope your fuckin' right!' Sharpy hit back angrily. He locked the track and slewed right, nearly tipping out Ron and Ginger at the same time. The pebbled road clearly showed AFVs had travelled this way ... who's though?

'There's the Quad,' Ginger said as Sharpy fell in behind two carriers, now running parallel to the main body of armour.

'What did I tell ya?' Ron said smugly.

'If you bastards carry on this way ... get us all fuckin' killed!' Sharpy screamed, his hands shaking as he lit a cigarette.

By now everyone's nerves were shot. It was getting harder as they got luckier and luckier. Living through scrape after scrape, while those around you died, was taking its toll on men like Ron. The odds seemed to be shortening each day, as those whom you thought had charmed lives were lucky no more.

Chapter 18

'The ultimate test'

After what turned out to be a gruelling drive of some fifty miles, J Support's lead vehicle took the wrong turning, resulting in the company getting hopelessly lost. The next few hours proved fraught with danger, culminating in 16 Platoon having to turn around in a slumbering village. Even though it was well past midnight, an *estaminet* opened its doors and lights came on in all the houses, casting a warm glow on the main road. The villagers gave them a heartfelt welcome, urging them to get down from their vehicles and join in the celebrations.

Knowing it was rude to snub such friendliness they joined in the party spirit, cavorting in the road, downing a cocktail of drinks. A few instruments appeared: a ukulele, several mouth organs, a French horn and a battered old squeezebox. The ad hoc band struck up, and everyone started singing Flanagan and Allen's iconic song:

> *'We're going to hang out the washing on the Siegfried Line.*
> *Have you any dirty washing, mother dear?*
> *We're gonna hang out the washing on the Siegfried Line*
> *'cos the washing day is here.*
> *Whether the weather may be wet or fine*
> *we'll just rub along without a care.*
> *We're going to hang out the washing on the Siegfried Line*
> *if the Siegfried Lines still there.'*

All too soon they were ordered to remount and carry on with the war, leaving their friends to drink themselves silly. Bottles of wine were pressed on them, along with hugs and kisses from sweet mademoiselle's and their equally shameless mothers.

Within a couple of miles, they ran into two German horse-drawn wagons. A one-sided fight ensued, no doubt sending villagers back to the safety of their homes.

They found their right route and caught up with the brigade, who were mixing it with heavy armour and massed troops. So much confusion reigned that a sergeant from K Company captured the ex-commander of what was once the 7th Army as he sat eating his breakfast in a parked car.

All-day long horse-drawn transports arrived with distraught civilians, fleeing the bombing and the advancing Russians, even though they were still hundreds of miles away. Bemused German soldiers, marching west towards the safety of a POW camp stared in awe as tanks and half-tracks trundled by, ever closer to the borders of their beloved Fatherland.

How the mighty had fallen.

Betsy and her crew now motored through places made famous by The Great War. The landscape, with its cluster of war graves every few miles, showed several slag heaps that over the years had turned into verdure hillocks, making them look as if they had always been there. One could also make out the twin columns of the Vimy Ridge Memorial. Inscribed with the names of over eleven thousand Canadian soldiers – no known grave – it was unveiled in nineteen-thirty-six by King Edward VIII. It hardly bore thinking about, only three years before World War Two. For the first half of the twentieth century, Europe had been in turmoil. What would the second half be like and would it be any better? Only time would tell. But against all the odds, life still went on, even with the world tearing itself apart. In the distance, smoke could be seen rising from tall chimneys, showing, come what may, things had survived the last four years.

Each time they stopped, cheering crowds gathered around their vehicles. The people embraced and kissed their liberators, giving them handfuls of fruit and bottles of wine. Nearly all were weeping with joy. Ron politely excused himself from one especially clingy female, before nodding at Sharpy, who was egging him on. Betsy lurched forward just as she jumped down to join her parents. He assumed it was her mother and father, but nothing could be *that* certain these days.

The brigade pushed on, skirting battlefields of The Great War: Cambrai, Loos, Mons, Messines, Ypres. New battle honours would grace regimental banners, Dieppe, Caen, Tobruk, Monte Cassino. Other historic events, such as Dunkirk, Burma, London Blitz, Battle of Britain, Pearl Harbour, would echo around the world for years, spawning numerous books and films. This war was just as bloody as The Great War. And would be just as haunting for those who had lived through it.

They sped north between avenues of trees, across miles of flat, featureless landscape. It made for nervous motoring, waiting to run into a well dug in Tiger or a party of grenadiers with *panzerfausts*.

'I bet me ole man were 'round 'ere in last lot!' Ron yelled as they rolled along in dazzling sunshine. 'He might even 'ave marched down this *very* road.'

That war was so out of step with today's, with mud-splattered riders from the Royal Artillery urging their teams along shell-cratered roads against a bleak landscape, devoid of nature's loving hand. They would thunder passed ranks of Tommie's, belting out their songs as they marched to the front, or weary and mindful as they returned for a few days' rest. Always bogged down in the same place, but for a few hundred yards gained during some costly action, time seemed to have stopped for Tommy Atkins and the cloud of despair over the entire world hardly dissipated.

The swiftness of today's advance was a marked contrast to *that* war.

J Support dug in and watched hordes of grey falling back. Thinking it was a feint Major Sloan ordered 16 Platoon to find out if Jerry was pulling out. Having gone half a mile, they were in the process of turning around when the officer saw a large force a thousand yards out, formed up, ready and waiting.

The company was brought 'to order'.

Both machine-gun platoons and a troop of Priests moved forward in line abreast, holding their fire for as long as possible. With the enemy made up chiefly of infantry, it would have been a slaughterhouse. The grey hoard headed straight for them in what seemed a death or glory charge. When they saw what was arrayed before them, they dropped their weapons and yielded without firing a shot.

At the close of the day, J Support leaguered in an abandoned enemy harbour. They found fire cinders still warm, showing how recently Jerry had left. As soon as they started cooking their evening meal, people from a nearby village joined them. They had with them bottles of Belgium beer, stoneware jugs of wine and bunches of grapes. Not the tart variety for making wine but black dessert grapes, large and succulent.

Tommy cookers stayed burning all night as they opened pack ration after pack ration, sharing everything with their new friends. They sat around chatting, eating and drinking to the point of bursting. Their guests ate everything put in front of them as if it was to be their last meal. Cedric Wilmot, drunk as a lord recorded the occasion with his Leica. Before turning in, Ron and the others made a fruit salad with grapes, topped with oodles of condensed milk.

Next morning, Cedric gathered Ron and a few others by the side of the road. War Correspondents were forever coaxing soldiers into posing for those back home, showing how the war was going and in what fine shape they were. This time they stood in front of an SS Panzer Group sign attached to a telegraph pole. At the start of a new day, perhaps their last, they were dazed and speechless, putting on a brave face as Cedric clicked away.

Much of the time, it was like a dream. It was as if your thoughts were detached from your body. Each burnt out tank, each mutilated corpse, each gaunt civilian, was like seeing them through someone else's eyes, watching the misery, devoid of all emotion. You were blameless – carrying out orders – innocent of crimes against humanity and God. Ron could hardly remember the last time he had said the Lord's Prayer. His faith, or lack of, was battle-weary, as he was. The risk of death, living each day as if it was his last and at the end of it, breathing a sigh of relief tinged with guilt was putting a terrible strain on him. If he were to survive the horrors, it would be years before he could once more lead a normal, balanced life.

War had a lot to answer for, and Ron was one among many.

Twenty miles south of Brussels, Ron came face to face with his worst nightmare, forcing him to confront his demons. As 15 Platoon moved forward to link up with L Company, they came across a great many *Volksgrenadiers*, backed by a 4.75mm anti-tank gun and two armoured half-tracks. They were first alerted to their presence when a *panzerfaust* rocket took off the right track of the lead Bren, causing it to slew to a halt some four hundred yards from the enemy. The half-tracks took this as a signal to advance, edging forward with a few men taking cover behind each vehicle. A few fields, not yet harvested, made it difficult to pick out the remaining troops.

The platoon formed up in line abreast, ready to meet the onslaught. Mr Lyle could have left the damaged Bren behind and pulled back, putting it down to a greater force. But he chose to hold his ground, knowing full well their AFVs would be close at hand. Those not manning the Vickers lay behind clumps of stubble left behind after reaping, with rifles cocked and ready. No range finding this time, just fire and adjust your aim accordingly.

The officer in the lead half-track, urging those on foot kept giving orders to his driver, pointing out the line to take. Two gunners, manning Spandau's, awaited orders. Ron assumed their reluctance to fire was due to a shortage of ammo. He hoped he was right. At three-hundred yards the Germans opened fire, putting two Vickers out of action with their first tentative bursts.

Ron lay in a patch of hay still standing, with Betsy's tracks only inches from his head, loading and firing. Lying hidden gave him some comfort, but a stray bullet, slicing through the corn, would soon put an end to his short life. He snatched at another clip, pushed the rounds into the magazine and slammed the bolt forward. He fired and just as quickly fired again. By now they were two-hundred yards away, but with fewer numbers. Or were they in a dip somewhere, making ready for their final charge? As the clouds parted, he swore he could see the glint of steel. 'Bloody 'ell,' he babbled, 'ta come all this way an' get stuck by a sword wieldin' Kraut.' He fired again and saw a man fall, or had he tripped. He could still hear the rat-tat-tat of Sharpy's Vickers at his right ear, with Ginger feeding the belt. Their next burst took out both gunners on the officer's half-track, peppering the armour with a clatter of rounds. Both silenced Vickers started up again, manned by fresh crews, adding their weight to the clamour of battle. '... This ain't like takin' pot-shots at paper targets, or squeezin' a round off at a big bugger of a bull,' he said tautly. 'God bless ya, Ern. Watch over me, pal.' He kept talking, trying to steady his nerves, keeping his mind on the job in hand. Being so close, he lined up on the officer with his battle sight. 'This is fer you, Ern,' he added as the butt slammed into his shoulder. The officer lurched against the rear of his cockpit and stared at his lifeblood spurting from his chest. A look of disbelief spread across his face when Ron's second bullet struck him in the same place. He slumped down in his half-track just as it blew up, killing his crew and taking two or three others on foot. There was another boom as a second Sherman fired.

With weapons thrown down and hands placed on heads, the beaten, traumatised grenadiers stumbled towards their equally shocked victors. 15 Platoon had come off lightly, with two slightly damaged Brens, one dead and seven wounded. Once again Betsy's crew came away unscathed.

Mr Lyle moved the men around, making sure each Bren was manned and ready for action. They carried on their way, brushing the whole episode off, taking it in their stride. It was not until later that the full force of what had happened would hit them. They drove past the wrecked half-tracks and massed bodies of freshly killed, brave soldiers.

Ron now had his answer. He knew what it was like to kill someone. While it was happening, there was no emotion, no shock, no shame, no regret, only the cold bloodied certainty that the man had to die, at his hands. Once his blood had cooled the knowledge of what he had done struck him hard. There was no feeling of pride in the way he had acquitted himself, even though he had passed the ultimate test, just sadness, shame and disgust.

Having retrieved their damaged Bren, they leaguered at Couture-Saint-Germain, only two miles from the battlefield of Waterloo. To a man, they were shocked by what had happened, but at the same time, mighty glad to be alive. The severely wounded were taken to a CCS and would soon be homeward bound. The rest were patched up at the RAP and returned to unit, ready for their next mauling.

Major Sloan, anxious about their well-being and state of mind, spoke to them the next morning, saying how proud he was at the way they had squared up to a much bigger force. At the end of his fatherly chat, he asked if they needed anything. Mr Lyle said their rum jar got smashed and could they have another. Once they'd finished their evening meal, they had a triple ration of rum. The supposed broken bottle had been hidden away. All agreed Cloddy should get a medal for his coolness under fire and his gall at asking for more grog. Without doubt, he was one of the lads, and they all told him so as they supped their rum around an open fire, toasting the souls of their feet and warming their hearts.

It was a great feeling to be alive.

A report came through from O Group, saying there was no Boche within a ten-mile radius of the leager. A short while later a shell whistled overhead, nearly parting Lofty Shaw's brown wavy hair.

They all dived for cover, cursing the inept recce wallahs.

Mr Jamieson sent out a sergeant and three riflemen to check forward of their position, hoping they would be more successful in finding out Jerry's disposition. They soon returned. The sergeant said a couple of 88s were dug in on the edge of a thicket some two-thousand yards out. As he gave his report, he hopped from one foot to the other while rubbing his backside. Mr Jamieson asked if he'd sat on an anthill. The sergeant promptly dropped his trousers and pulled down his blood-soaked underpants, showing where a bullet had nicked his left buttock. As the officer tended his wound, the sergeant gave the rest of his report. His mates watched as the captain dabbed at his plump, white buttock. This touching scene, showing an officer as mother and nursemaid, brought tears to their eyes, or was it having iodine rubbed into a lucky nick that would soon heal?

Major Sloan arrived just as the 88s started up again. Ron got to work and passed the readings to the major. As three Priests pounded the enemy, Sergeant Meyer from 16 Platoon, a miner from Kimberley, South Africa, directed Vickers fire from four guns. They were shooting at long range, but it didn't matter because they just wanted to make a noise and throw a bit more lead at Jerry.

Sometime later, Freddie and Ron saw the knocked out 88s and a half-track and a couple of soft-skins laden with all manner of kit. Not to mention a dozen or so dead grenadiers and the mangled remains of each gun crew.

The Fifth was once more on the move, heading north, skirting Brussels and linking up with the brigade at Sterrebeck, ready for a thirty-mile dash to Antwerp.

L Company and 14 Platoon, five or six miles ahead of the main force soon found themselves in the suburbs of Antwerp. The jubilant welcome made it impossible to move through the massed crowds.

The rest of the Fifth, having caught up, skirted all the furore and pressed on towards the dock area, where snipers were holding up in several tall buildings. As well as snipers, the city was peppered with booby traps. Two soldiers were injured when one went off outside a café, severely wounding both and killing three civilians.

They set up their leager beside the harbour, disturbed only by the occasional shell from the other side of a canal. A small force was tasked with silencing the guns, but a company of South Wales Borderers had to come to their rescue. They too got in trouble and were forced to withdraw, leaving it to a squadron of Mustangs to sort out these well-entrenched troops.

The only thing to bother them now was a light dusting from German coastal batteries on the other side of the straights.

Peace and quiet cloaked J Support as it settled into the grounds of a large chateau. Being only a couple of miles from the city centre, off-duty riflemen could feast their eyes on this lively city, with many savouring its pleasures to excess.

The lightning advance of this now-famous armoured division, with its endless columns of tanks, overcame all resistance. Their swiftness and dogged determination saved Antwerp and its harbour from certain destruction.

Fun and humour abounded on the streets and in the bars, showing how grateful the locals were. They welcomed these tired, dusty heroes with open arms, taking them to their hearts and homes and letting them want for nothing.

Battalion headquarters was in the middle of all manner of bivouacs and canvas shelters, giving a measure of order over the somewhat errant riflemen. New faces and those returning from sick leave started to swell the ranks. 16 Platoon was pleased to see back the newly promoted Sergeant Len Farrell, replacing Sergeant Meyer. The forty-year-old Kimberley man had been killed by a booby trap while checking over a dead German. There was also a rumour that Sergeant Wally Frazer would soon be fit for duty.

During the long hard dash, Ron and his mates slummed it, rarely washing and hardly changing their underwear. Everyone ponged to high heaven. Though it did have its upside, keeping love-hungry females away. At times they could be a blithering nuisance, especially when you had a job to do. A pretty face, offering it to you on a plate, can be one hell of a distraction. And for just a fraction of a second, your mind is somewhere else. The unwritten rule for most was to keep such things to off duty periods. However, a few rampant buggers had fallen foul of this and had paid the ultimate price. The niceties of being clean were of little importance, only the desire to end each day in one piece. Having time on their hands, they could clean themselves up, do a bit of dobieing, shaking and airing blankets and getting rid of the damn lice. A lit cigarette down the seams kept them at bay for a few hours, but they would soon return, worse than before.

Pack rations and compo were consigned to the toolbox, ready for when they were on the move again. Fresh food made a welcome change. Beef, chicken, mutton, pork, eggs, fresh bread, cheese and vegetables, not the tinned variety they had lived on for months, were in plentiful supply. Beer, cigarettes and tobacco were free for the asking. Many nearly smoked themselves – and others – to death. Naafi goods were also given out, along with mail which had once more caught up with them. Everyone had letters, some having a whole bundle. The post-corporal also retrieved parcels from his special hiding place, handing them to eager riflemen like a doting maiden aunt.

Ron received three letters from his mum, nine from Betty and a parcel. Crammed inside were three two-ounce tins of Havelock tobacco, six packs of Rizla cigarette paper and two packets of fig rolls. He also found a knitted scarf from Betty and four half-pound bars of Cadburys Fruit and Nut from his mum and gran. His uncle moreover included a few essentials to make a soldier's lot a bit more tolerable: razor blades, soap, tooth powder and toothbrush, Izal toilet paper, a couple of Penguin books, penknife, pencils, three pocket-sized notebooks and a brown paper package containing two dozen Durex. There were also Christmas cards and a letter from Jack.

His brother explained that his wound had healed up nicely, and he was once more working his way up the west coast of Italy. Ron already knew about his injury, having been on leave when he was flown home from Gibraltar. Wounded at Monte Cassino, Jack passed through various dressing stations, finally ending up on a hospital ship in Valetta Harbour, Malta. A piece of shrapnel had fused itself to the main artery in his upper right arm, and they wanted to get him home before operating. While waiting for a ship, the wound became badly infected. They gave him massive doses of penicillin in his backside every six hours.

The morning he was given the all-clear they told him to get ready for moving to a French Red Cross ship. For some bizarre reason, which he could not explain, he was loath to get on that ship and asked the officer if he could go on the next one. The MO reluctantly agreed to his strange request and gave his place to a pilot officer in the next bed. This change of plan pleased Jack because Matthew had just heard that his wife had given birth to a daughter and he was chomping at the bit to get home. Lucky for Jack, but not for the badly scarred fighter pilot and the other poor souls on board the ship was sunk three miles off Gozo. When he heard about the sinking, he dashed a letter off to his mum, telling her not to worry. The letter arrived the day before she received a telegram from the War Office, saying her son was missing, presumed drowned.

Flying into RAF Uxbridge, he passed through Woking General, where Kathy and his mum visited him, then on to Leeds infirmary. Later he found himself in a Blackpool hotel to pile on the pounds. They then transferred him to a rehab depot near Halifax for physio. Nine weeks after being wounded he was at the Cameronian's (Scottish Rifles) depot in Hamilton for fitness training. Before leaving Hamilton, he was required to pass several physical tests. He had to run a hundred yards in full kit, jump an eight-foot-wide trench, scale a six-foot wall and carry the sergeant PTI on his back for a hundred yards. He was quite scathing when it came to the staff sergeants from the Army Physical Training Corps. In their zeal to push soldiers along they would help them in any way they could. But they soon declined his offer to leave their cushy depot posting, with its sleeping-out-passes to come and join him at the front. From there he returned to Woking. He then languished at a holding depot for another month, awaiting a posting.

He further explained he had problems with his pay for some time. When a soldier goes missing his mates would say where they last saw him going into action. Until they can prove, one way or the other through the 'body removal squads' or a military hospital, his name would remain on the 'pay suspended' list.

Ron tucked the letters in his trouser pocket, for a more leisurely read later.

The lads attended their first pay parade in months. They now had plenty of money, enough to paint the town red, ten times over. Soon they would be visiting the bars and *estaminets* as they poured out their lively tunes and lightweight pilsner beer. Each needed a bit of fun and excitement, to rid them of the dreadful feeling that seemed to plague each waking hour.

Chapter 19

'Towards the Rhine'

The last few months ordeal paled as Ron and Ginger lounged at their pavement table, stuffed by a half-decent meal and two bottles of vintage wine. They soaked up the atmosphere of Antwerp, happy to be alive on this bright and breezy autumn evening.

Having mulled over the fact they still had another week before returning to the fight, Ron raised his glass in salute to those who would never sup with them again. 'Life's fer livin',' he said, dragging on an after-dinner cigarette. He tipped his glass back, draining the last drop. '... 'Ave ya swigged it all ya little red 'eaded gannet?' he finally added, staring at the empty bottle.

'No!' Ginger countered. 'We divvied it out, equally. You guzzle yours like the greedy pig you are. Good wine needs savouring, like a pretty woman.'

'Idealistic pillock,' Ron retaliated before ordering two beers. '*Deux Pils s'il vous plait*, Sunshine.'

'*Oui Monsieur*,' said the waiter, mincing between packed tables.

'That stuff makes me piss,' Ginger said, taking his last sip of Château Margaux. 'Give me a pint of pale ale any day. Though I have to admit this stuff slips down a treat.'

'It should do fer six bucks a bottle. Bloody butchers ...'

As they sipped their cold beers, half a dozen Royal Tank officers strolled by, eyeing each place. Settling on the one next door they made themselves comfortable at a pavement table and ordered three bottles of wine. One officer got up and made his way over to Ron and Ginger. They quickly took their feet off the chairs opposite and sat up straight, like good little swaddies, waiting for a bollocking for letting the side down. Few officers made a fuss these days about such things, but there were always a few manic types who liked to crack the whip whenever they got the chance.

The officer, scarred from hairline to chin, sat down and stared at

Ron's flushed face. 'Hello, Deak,' he said, picking up the empty bottle. 'Nice wine.'

'Stone'a bleedin' crows,' Ron said in surprise. 'Beggin' yer pardon, Sir. ... Well, knock me over with a ... Aitch. I mean, Sir.'

'Aitch will do,' Harry Lowton said, grinning, 'but keep your voice down, Deak. I told my boss I was coming to see an old pal. A stickler for the rulebook is Squirty. Officers and rankers should rarely mix. He's a queer—'

'Squirty?'

'Major' – he turned to make sure he wasn't listening – 'Pisco ... pisser of a name, isn't it?'

'I wouldn't' 'ave believed it,' Ron said, again shaking his head. Amazed at meeting up with his first and best-ever platoon NCO. He chuckled to himself, pleased to see his old sergeant

'What ... seeing me as an officer or bumping into me in Antwerp's red-light district?'

'Last time I saw you, ya was wavin' as we marched out o' Wilchester barracks. 'Appy ta be rid of us.' He paused, trying to recall a few of those precious moments. But too much had happened of late and such thoughts were temporally washed away. 'It seems a lifetime ago.'

'It *was* ... *is* ...' Harry Lowton said, again looking at the bottle. 'Well, aren't you going to buy a pal a drink?'

'Sure,' he said, looking for the waiter.

'Are you and Ernie Price still together?' he asked, trying to find out about some of the others. 'You two spent so much time together, Jinksy and I thought you were joined at the hip.'

'What ... me an' Ern? Oh ... Christ!' Squirty looked at them and raised his glass in salute to the other ranks, to which Harry Lowton had once belonged. '*Une autre bouteille de vin*, pal, *et un bon millésime encore*,' he said, ordering another bottle of wine. He paused, trying to find the right words to explain what had happened to Ernie. Talking about it always made him sad and mostly he kept things to himself. Playing for time, he raised his glass towards

Harry's fellow officers, trying not to let the word Squirty appear on his lips.

'You're a natural at the lingo,' Harry said in praise.

'Ernie were killed,' he suddenly blurted out.

'Oh, I'm sorry, Ron. You and he were good mates. He was an all-round decent guy.'

'Yes, we was … the best. Ernie Price,' he said, looking at Ginger, 'an' me were in same trainin' platoon, along with Joe an' Oz. … Sorry, Aitch, this is Ginge … Pat Iverson … Ginger to 'is mates.'

'What else!' Harry said, looking at his shock of red hair.

'Hello, Sir.'

'Aitch were our platoon corporal before they made 'im sergeant. Now look at 'im … polished up, little officer. He used ta run us ragged, 'im an' Sergeant Bevan. But they knew their stuff.'

'Basic training taught us a lot,' Harry Lowton said, evading talking about George Bevan. One death was enough for this impromptu meeting.

'An' give us bloody sore feet, don't forget.' He was thrilled to see his old sergeant, swapping stories, finding out how he'd fared in the last four years.

Strained laughter escaped when they got around to the last few months. Harry Lowton, now a tank commander, had had his share of near misses in Normandy's early clashes.

He must have a charmed life they both thought as he spoke of having two tanks brew up beneath him, both destroyed. His first lucky break was when his Centaur Mk IV's fuel tanks ruptured, filling the confined space with hot, acrid smoke. Troopers spilt out of what would soon be a blazing inferno, ears ringing, and all exposed skin and hair seared by the heat infused air. Proof of this was a livid scar down the right side of his face, with hair growing back, paler than his walnut brown. An AP shell hit the second, punching clean through its armour and out the other side, taking off the driver's head and gravely wounding his gunner. Those still alive, and able to, bailed out covered in blood and robbed of their hearing for weeks.

Harry Lowton was resolute, saying he preferred to ride into battle with the turret locked, rather than risking his life in the open. Ron and Ginger shook their heads, smiling, saying he could have *them*, with their thanks. They further said tanks were healthy to be around, but not necessarily inside, having seen too many fall prey to armour-piercing shells. It was plain to see they had made him an officer because he was your typical tank wallah type and would instil trust and confidence in his crew.

After handshakes, slaps on backs, promises to meet up after the war, and good wishes for the future they finally parted, leaving Lieutenant Lowton to return to his officer class.

Strolling back to their relaxed way of life, they looked forward to six more days of pure heaven. On their return they were caught up in an air of trepidation as vehicles from 14 Platoon were put to bed, with gear already loaded.

They should have known better when drivers were ordered to stay behind for special duties. What should have been a nice long break was soon over. At least all this urgency meant the end of the war was getting nearer, and, just maybe, it would be over by Christmas. What a thought? Turkey lunch with trimmings and then listen to the king's speech around the coal fire, toasting His Majesty as well as your cheeks. Ron's mum used to bank up the fire, causing everyone to push their chairs away as it got hotter and hotter. When it was roasting the door would be opened to cool down the parlour. Ron and Jack would sometimes go into the yard, or on the doorstep for a smoke. They talked about the possibility of peace by Christmas but soon remembered the lads in nineteen-fourteen said very much the same. Best not to count one's chickens they both agreed. Take each day as it comes was everyone's maxim these days.

Sharpy had his blanket tightly wrapped around him to keep out the pesky bugs. The humid weather had brought them out in their thousands. He also had a piece of netting about his head for good measure. Squiffy, Deakin and Iverson made their way through the gloomy tent, stepping over their sleeping mates.

'Sorry, Fred,' Ginger said, grinning as he caught him with his size twelves.

'You will be, especially if my line dies out through no fault of my own. You nearly minced my bollocks with your great clodhoppers.'

'What's up?' Ron asked, staring at Sharpy's cigarette. '... Touch that on chuffin' nettin',' he added while lighting up, 'an' you'll do up like a Bengal match.'

'It's the big push towards the Rhine,' he answered, puffing like a chimney. '... There's some tea in the billy. It might be a bit stewed, but it'll soon kill the taste of what was probably a nice meal and a few bottles of plonk. ... You'd better get some shut eye. It's an early start.'

Ron, hot and sticky, told him of their meal and about meeting Harry Lowton.

'Sweet dreams you lot,' Ginger said as he snuggled down.

'Bollocks, carrot top!' they all exclaimed.

A string of lights along the path formed vivid patterns as they danced on a fresh breeze. Curses and caterwauling from soldiers trying to find their bivvy added an air of tension to the proceedings. One or two of the more sober types were wishing goodnight to their mates on guard duty. 'Wotch ya, Nob,' one was heard to say.

'Did ya get yer leg over, Bert,' his mate asked, cradling his rifle.

'You bet!' Though the nearest he got to sex was groping the arse of a waitress in a classy bar. For his pains, he got a stinging slap in the face and was bodily thrown out by an irate father. 'Best bit o' rumpty-tumpty I've 'ad in ages.'

'Lucky bastard, Bert.'

No one was going to get any sleep until these riflemen had been tucked up in bed.

Waiting for sleep to take him, Ron's thoughts flitted from one ex-girlfriend to another and then back to Betty. As they flashed before his eyes, the feeling in his groin grew tenfold. What he wouldn't give to be in the tender embrace of Maggie Kenna right now or cuddling Betty on the rug in front of a roaring fire, with the little terrace house to themselves. And a quickie with Mavis was a dreamy prospect, or one of those ladies in the red-light district, pertly exposing themselves. Some swaddies would risk a dose for the sheer hell of it. Twenty minutes in a seedy hotel room would give them a taste of heaven, after all the evil they had seen. Close, intimate contact with another human being would remind them they were still alive. And why worry anyway about catching a dose of clap. They might be dead this time next week. He began tossing himself off, but soon stopped when he heard his mates around him, snoring and farting. The longing soon faded to be replaced by a less urgent desire. His eyes closed, but his dreams, one which was as wet as a summer cloudburst were some of the horniest, he had ever experienced.

The Guards Armoured Division led the advance, with the 50th Northumbrians on the left flank and the 5th Battalion, The Rifle Regiment, on the right. The Fifth was soon ordered to take over the defence of a bridge over the River Meuse from a Dutch regiment called the Princess Irene's. Within an hour they were attacked by a large force of Waffen-SS. After a few attempts to take back the bridge, they were finally broken at little cost to themselves.

Just before dusk, J Support crossed the bridge. They set up their leager amongst the scenes of battle, giving the Fifth time to recover. Machine gunners sighted their Vickers by the light of blazing vehicles. Stunned SS were rounded up from a desolate battlefield, strewn with dead.

An hour before dawn 15 Platoon was put on standby when a woman ran from a nearby house, saying she had seen German soldiers heading their way. The early morning mist cleared to reveal a couple of dozen grenadiers, some with Spandau's and two or three with *panzerfausts*. Sergeant Cox told them to wait until they had committed themselves fully. When there was hardly any cover, they opened fire, pinning down the grey hoard.

There were only three walking wounded, shuffling along with hands on heads. One was a *Hauptfeldwebel*. The sergeant major's English was perfect, with a hint of black country. His birth certificate, folded in his service book said he was born in Dudley, son of a coal merchant. This was a further example of the strangeness of war.

Two days later, with help from the 3rd British Infantry Division's bridgehead and an intact rail bridge over the Meuse-Escaut Canal, Ron crossed into Holland for the first and not the last time.

Reaching Geldrop, east of Eindhoven they dug in ready to defend their forward lines until more troops could be moved forward to strengthen the sector.

16 Platoon took over a railway station, training its guns east along the tracks. It turned out to be a quiet night. The same, however, could not be said for K Company's mortar platoon. They soon realised they were in an exposed position that had already been counter-ranged. Their folly in not digging in and building a fire to roast a haunch of venison cost the life of two riflemen and an NCO. At the height of their festivities, Jerry gave them a wicked pasting. The officer in charge was duly court-marshalled for 'dereliction of duty' and spent the rest of his war under the watchful eye of Sergeant Major Dawson.

That same night Ron's platoon leaguered behind an old farmhouse, using the house and barn for shelter against foul weather. Once he had reserved himself a pitch, Ginger started laying out his bedroll, when suddenly there was an almighty bang and a blinding flash. He ran outside and saw a column of fire reaching skywards, making it appear like daytime. The source of this blast had been two L Company Loyds, loaded with incendiary grenades. In this stonk, nine men from one platoon were severely burned. One of them being Alfie Neil from their Wilchester days. This now only left Sharpy, Ron and Ossie serving in the Fifth.

When on the move again a force of heavy tanks attacked their vanguard, causing the death of N Company's second in command, two NCOs and seven riflemen.

15 Platoon found themselves under heavy fire on a bridge across a gorge. Not able to advance or retreat they faced incessant mortar fire without a single casualty. Some lay flat on the ground, up against the pillars and balustrade, using their vehicles to shield the blasts. Others crawled beneath their Brens or cringed inside with bedrolls over their head. As soon as the firing stopped, they carried on their way, putting the whole episode behind them.

They re-formed, licked their wounds and counted their steady growing losses in men and equipment.

Sergeant Freddie Cox set up his Vickers on the canal bank, giving him a perfect field of fire. Len Cash – strangely known as Bob – a fresh-faced lad in his late teens, acted as number two. At the same time, Ginger and Ron crouched beside Betsy, ready with reserve ammo. All other gunners were similarly set up, guarding a front of some eight-hundred yards.

Within minutes shell after shell came over, growing in intensity with each salvo. Most landed in muddy water to their rear, drenching them in green gunge. The smell, like an abattoir in the height of summer, clung to their uniforms for weeks.

N Company came up against heavy tanks, backed up by hundreds of grenadiers, many armed with *panzerfausts*. The major ordered them to dig in and defend their position at all cost. They suffered a great many casualties and were put under immense pressure from a much larger force, but slowly whittling them down. A troop of Sherman Fireflies, close at hand came to their rescue and eventually saw off the enemy. It was a close-run thing, nearly costing the battalion one-fifth of its strength.

Once the fighting was over the main street of a nearby town became choked with all manner of vehicles as they strove to advance into the open country beyond. While sorting themselves out, heavy shelling toppled buildings on both sides of the road. As it turned out, not a single vehicle was hit. With the only mishap being a corporal cutting his finger on a tin of Californian peaches.

One mortar platoon, frustrated by lack of progress, stopped at a deserted farmhouse. The officer and some of his NCOs had a lucky escape when an AP shell punched clean through the kitchen wall, where they chanced to be brewing up. The round missed the fair-haired lieutenant by inches, hit a stout doorframe and landed at the platoon sergeant's feet as he was spooned in his sugar. They got out so quickly, many said their reactions bordered on superhuman. A Royal Engineer second lieutenant later confirmed it was a dud and said they could have stayed and finished their tea. Even though he was an officer, they still told him what he could do with his monkey wrench.

War has its humorous moments, but it doesn't seem so at the time. Tommy Atkins though can find humour in most situations.

A few days later they were five miles east of Deurne, on the edge of a bombed-out village. Orders were given to dig in and prepare for an attack because this sector had already seen heavy fighting.

After spending all night working on their defences, the Fifth grudgingly handed them over to a battalion of US Rangers, moving to De Rips, a village north-east of Helmond. They heard that airborne troops, battling for their lives at a place called Arnhem were trying to withdraw from what had turned into a hopeless situation. Ron and the others gathered around wireless sets, hanging on to every snippet of information, knowing only too well the dreadful plight that these poor souls found themselves in.

An American armoured division, tasked with aiding the British

2nd Army, was being shadowed by some doughboy supply units. One of their Dodge's stopped at a fuel dump where 15 Platoon happened to be refuelling.

Seeing what they could cadge, Ron and Ginger made their way over to the master sergeant in charge. 'We need some clean stuff, mate,' Ginger said at the head of a bunch of jostling swaddies.

'Shucks, fellas,' the Stetson-wearing cowboy said in his mid-western drawl. 'Nah problem. Ma pleasure.' He handed out piles of laundered shirts, sand-coloured towels and socks still in their Macey Stores wrappings. 'Ah've got scads an' scads. Ah'm sick an' tahed o' carryin' this trashy stuff about.'

Making their leager a couple of miles from the fuel dump 15 Platoon dug in and set up their Vickers. Ron filled out a range card for each gun, logging all likely trouble spots.

At first light next morning, a German foot patrol received an early morning salutation from four Vickers, with screams showing how accurate their fire was. They found no bodies, but there were trails of blood leading to a nearby wood. They passed this intel onto the infantry, who later confirmed that two dead SS grenadiers had been found in a cave, along with a large quantity of stores and ammo.

Betsy's section was ordered to set up a recce post a hundred yards forward of their lines. It turned out to be the dullest watch imaginable.

'Bugger this fer soldierin',' Ron cursed as he sat, knees under his chin, jawing with Ginger in their trench. 'I need a taste of civilisation.'

'Fancy a pint of pig's ear?' Ginger teased. Rhyming slang tripped easily off his tongue. Living day in and day out with East Enders you soon picked up the lingo. He smacked his lips, forcing this clear, fanciful brew down his parched throat, trying to conjure up its taste.

'Fer Christ's sake,' Ron said, thinking of all the ale's on offer in London Town, 'turn it up, Ginge.'

'Don't you fret? It's my turn, Ronald.' He pressed on with his wicked charade, teasing him even more. 'I'm buyin'—'

'That's noble under bloody circumstances.'

'—and this time we'll have clean glasses,' he said, making to get up.

'Bomb 'appy, that's your trouble.' He kicked his ankle. 'Ya poor deluded sod.'

The Fifth's headquarters company came under attack from a large force of Waffen SS and massed armour, causing more than a few deaths and many wounded. Even the Luftwaffe made its presence felt, adding its dwindling resources to stem the tide. Luckily there was a battalion of Welsh Guards close by who helped repel the attack, quickly sorting things without too much trouble. In this melee, the colonel's half-track was hit, killing the driver and wounding the CO in his left eye. He stayed at his post the whole time, coordinating their defence. Once the threat was over, they rushed him to the nearest ADS. Major Courtney ordered all companies to leager and await his return.

While they waited, 'stand-to' periods, the vain of every British Tommy, was raised to a punishing level. The pressure of these extra duties tested each man to breaking point. Mr Lyle had the bright idea of placing trip flares around the farm. But free-roaming livestock set them off, bringing everyone 'to order' at a minute's notice. Sharpy, having endured two watches in eight hours, put his feelings succinctly, saying he didn't know whether to shit, shave or have a haircut.

At first light, to the dismay of the man on guard duty, two grenadiers gave themselves up. They cockily walked up to him, leant their Russian Mosin-Nagant sniper rifles against a fence and placed their hands on their head. They said they had been hiding in a nearby wood for three weeks and were slowly starving to death. Once fed and sent down the line, the platoon sergeant searched the wood. All he found were rabbits, which made a refreshing change to the pot.

All joked that the snipers must have been townies and wouldn't know the difference between a rabbit and a rat.

Forty-eight hours later, the colonel returned, minus his eye.

Twenty miles west of Eindhoven the battalion came across a German ration dump, overrun with vermin. Because of the changing weather, for the worse, and because of their lightning advance and drawn out supply lines, it was decided to put it to good use.

'I'll never moan again,' Sharpy cried in disgust. 'We're hungry, but not that fuckin' hungry.'

'Sling the bastard lot,' Ron cursed angrily. 'If I clock so much as one-piece of that shit in our box, I'll do me fuckin' nut.'

Once these rank foodstuffs were issued, there was a further spell of rest and refit in De Rips. Far enough from any fighting to make it a proper break. Time away from combat was surreal, making everything seem strangely calm and soothing. This was soldiering at its best. When it was like this, one could easily imagine making it one's life.

A few guys were picked for a visit to Brussels, but Ron, Sharpy and Ginger had to settle for a good old blanket shaking and a bit of dobieing. For a few others, there was to be a screening of Rita Hayworth and Gene Kelly in *Cover Girl* at a picture house in Eindhoven. Ron's platoon was one of those chosen, and they went wild in anticipation. Menus were planned, choosing their best-loved meals, along with a bottle or two of plonk that now graced most toolboxes. With food simmering and corks pulled for a pre-dinner snifter, the men's craving for food soon vanished when they saw Sergeant Cox addressing his section leaders. The best way to kill a soldier's appetite was to see his platoon sergeant placing a clenched fist on his head, a sign to gather around and listen to his latest orders. Their desire to eat would soon vanish, and a tetchy nervous state would take over, robbing them of any thought of food. Soldiers would remain in this fitful state until the action was over. Only then would their juices flow freely, letting them eat without gagging. This time there was no need to worry because Freddie just wanted to update them on the current situation.

Back from the pictures, Ron and the others watched as several beer barrels were being taken off the back of a three-tonner by Mr Dawson and his staff sergeants. They got to work setting up a dry area and a small stage on which an ancient 'upright' would soon take pride of place. The reason for this precipitous spree, once they had been refreshed by what turned out to be a somewhat decent brew, with a good head was to have a good old singsong. The favourites of London Town were aired, at least three times over, along with those sad goodbyes of Vera Lynn, to conjure up thoughts of home sweet home.

At ten minutes to midnight, the sergeant major ordered what little beer remained to be poured away. To stop a few gannets boozing all night. A sweet-natured lad from Port Talbot, juiced to the nines struck up a much-loved favourite, causing everyone to howl with delight:

'Private Jones came in one night
Full of cheer and very bright
He'd been out all day upon the spree
He bumped into Sergeant Smeck
Put his arms around his neck
And in his ear he whispered tenderly

Kiss me goodnight, Sergeant-Major
Tuck me in my little wooden bed
We all love you, Sergeant-Major,
When we hear you bawling, 'Show a leg!'

Don't forget to wake me in the morning
And bring me 'round a nice hot cup of tea
Kiss me goodnight Sergeant-Major
Sergeant-Major, be a mother to me

Once the Welshman had finished his ditty Mr Dawson warmly smiled and said, 'Come on, you scabby buggers, piss off to bed an' dream of home.'

There was a resounding cheer, and everyone would remember this occasion for years to come. The lads drifted off to their bivvies, content and thankful to be alive. Two 'old sweats', having served in India before the war started playing Crown and Anchor on a makeshift board made from a purloined ADS sign. It was still against King's Regs for rankers to play the game without supervision, but because of what the future held, officers tended to turn a blind eye these days. There were more important things to worry about than a harmless game of chance.

Next day, with heads as thick as planks Flying Fortresses and Liberators passed overhead to support an attack along the Maas. Two days later Venray was taken by an infantry brigade, the last stronghold west of the Maas.

The Fifth said goodbye to De Rips and took part in a small advance eastward to link up with the division at Westerbeek. The roads were dreadful, churned up mud, slowing everything to a snail's pace. It took a whole day to do five miles. As soon as they arrived at Merselo, they were ordered eight miles further east.

No peace for the wicked!

Not willing to stay and fight Jerry kept his pursuers at bay with the occasional salvo. Roads, little more than tracks and cratered, strewn with felled trees and in places waterlogged, became impassable to all but tracked vehicles. The ever-faithful Sherman, Bren and Loyd trundled on. Hampered by 'moaning minnies' the crews would bail out, diving for cover and getting up again caked in mud. The change in the weather seemed to herald an early winter, sometimes bringing things to a complete standstill. Long gone were the fifty miles a day, pressing ahead in brilliant sunshine, chasing a fast fleeing enemy that sometimes fought a rear-guard action. Those harum-scarum days, when there was a chance of tagging onto a Jerry column, especially at night could be nerve-racking at the best of times.

At last, they arrived at Merselo and bedded down for a well-earned rest.

With the help of flail-tanks J Support crossed a minefield and finally reached the main road to Venray, where scores of captured Germans were interned in POW cages. They resumed their easterly advance once more, finding things hard going. Owing to lack of supplies, the Fifth was ordered to stop and wait until replenished.

14 and 16 Platoon leaguered in an orchard at Leunen. While setting up their defences a shell scored a direct hit on a partially finished trench, killing one and wounding several others. The perils of staying above ground for more than a few seconds was again brought home to them. More stonks followed, causing a further death. They soon named it the 'orchard of death'. A complex system of trenches quickly took shape, with life becoming more tolerable, despite having to crouch in six inches of muddy water. Enemy patrols came in close at night, but Ron and the others were told not to give away their position. It was tantalising to see them moving about, clueless to their neighbours and watchers. The waterlogged ground meant they had to pitch their bivvies over muddy slit trenches. They slept fitfully, with machine guns sited on a small rise.

Everyone was shocked when Captain Jamieson stepped on a mine while checking the forward lines. His death cast a cloud over the entire company, causing everyone to go around with long faces for weeks. Irish had been a likeable officer, and the loss of their number two would be a significant setback for J Support.

To make life even more wretched, some dipstick of an artillery wallah dropped a couple of rounds on the orchard. It was lucky no one was hurt … a miracle with everyone so tightly packed together.

Next day a Scots armoured battalion relieved the Fifth. J Support was ordered to report to a place called 'prisoner's corner', where they were split up and quartered in several farms. They took up a role as foot-slogging infantry, which Ron was not best pleased about.

14 and 15 Platoon found themselves in what had once been a dairy farm, bedded down in the farmhouse and byers. Company HQ and 16 Platoon were billeted in another farm a mile or so away. Life for a short time was snug and idyllic and thank God dry, barring the smell of silage that seemed to permeate the air at every turn.

The lads feasted royally on pork, mutton and chicken. Ron's talents as a butcher were put to good use. He took great pride in turning his hands to something other than killing Germans and had lost none of his skill to dispatch and quarter an animal.

Out of all the patrols they went on they encountered nothing more threatening than a mangy German shepherd called Heidi, so her collar said. Feeling sorry for the poor wretch they gave her a home and their leftovers. She never wanted for anything. It was only when she started putting on weight that they realised she was having pups. Sadly, she was killed during a raid, causing everyone to mope about, missing their flea-ridden, four-legged friend, wondering what sort of mother she would have made.

While on patrol they mostly roughed it, sleeping in the rain or on the frozen ground. Sometimes Ron and the others struck lucky, finding a disused barn in which to bed down. The highlight of every patrol was to return to the safety and comparative warmth of their billet. But before doing so, they first had to get passed the trigger-happy sentries without being shot. It was essential to remember the password, which changed daily and not to stutter or have a lapse of memory at a crucial moment. Having overcome this hurdle, they could then look forward to their daily rum ration and catching up on lost sleep.

'Lovely stuff,' Ginger keenly said, smacking his lips. He cupped his mug, hoping its warmth would wash away the memory of what had been a dreary and mind-numbingly cold patrol. Steaming, sweet, strong tea, flavoured with a hefty quota of Navy Rum leached into his bones, floating-away the jitters. 'Bloody lovely,' he furthered before taking another sip

'This'll put ink in your pen,' Freddie joined in, squatting beside the others on a groundsheet.

'Luvly ta be lyin' on warm, dry Rory O'More,' Ron said, taking off his wet boots and snuggling down for a kip. 'I need ta give me ole plates a rest.' He lay on his right side in a foetal position, rubbing his feet and yawning. 'Don't bother ta wake me?' he sighed, closing his eyes and pulling a blanket over his head to cut out his current way of life.

At the start of November, J Support moved back to Leunen. This time it was 15 Platoon, and company headquarters turn to leager in the 'orchard of death'. The rest took over a small hamlet a mile away. Within an hour of arriving, they were subjected to 'friendly fire', causing more than a few wounded, though nothing serious. Each was given first aid and returned to their unit.

Everyone thought this would be a posting for some time. Then out of the blue they heard they were being relieved by a battalion of Coldstream Guards. A rumour had been doing the rounds for weeks, saying they were due for a well-earned rest in a properly run reserve centre.

The Guardees, arriving in a matter of days, started taking over from the Fifth. The usual banter when units changed over, sprinkled with a plethora of four-letter words flowed like water between the 'other rank's'.

'Fuck yer luck, kiddo,' Ron said to one scrubbed up guardsman. 'Taint like Bucks ya know?' He winked at the fresh-faced lad who didn't look old enough to shave. 'Keep yer bleedin' Uncle Ned down, Sonny, or some sausage eatin' Kraut'll knock it orf fer ya. Give us a touch, mate,' he furthered, taking a light from the guardsman's cigarette. He gathered up his gear and slung it into the Bren, ready for a quick getaway. 'Nuff said, Sonny, yeah? Good luck. You'll bleedin' need it.'

At long last, they arrived at a ramshackle village eight miles south of Nijmegen, called Beers. All the previous reports of the Airborne's terrible plight were clear to see, with rows of freshly dug graves and widespread destruction.

The rest camp, large and rambling like back home had newly built Nissen huts, real beds, proper mattresses, white sheets and clean blankets, an uplifting change from the damp, mouldy variety they had slept in for the last five months. He could hardly believe it, only five months. It seemed more like five years.

Deloused and dressed in freshly laundered clothing, he nearly cried at the feeling of being clean and warm. The thrill of queuing at mealtimes, being given hot tasty food that someone else had cooked also made a refreshing change. Unbroken sleep and letters from home were things once took for granted. Likewise, the relief of being able to walk above ground, without feeling threatened in any way, was wholly uplifting.

It was pure heaven – and it lasted two whole weeks.

Chapter 20

'Winter Woollies'

Any hope of an early victory had now faded, even though Allied gains had all but reached the borders of Germany. Before mounting the spring offensive, they first had to build up vast reserves to take the fight to the very heart of Germany. In advance of this, it was necessary to have a northern supply route. Antwerp, captured intact, being the most northerly port in the Allies hands, with its inland docks was an obvious choice. However, its small islands, sea routes, headlands and shorelines needed to be under Allied control, while at the same time winning over the hinterland.

Furthermore, German coastal guns currently ruled the sea-lanes to Antwerp's safe anchorage. Likewise, remnants of fleeing German forces, having crossed the straights to reinforce other strongholds also had to be eliminated. After a great many costly landings by Canadian infantry and British commandos, coupled with Crabs, Crocs, Terrapins and Buffalos from the famed 79th (Hobart's) Armoured Division all resistance ceased.

With its channels to Antwerp swept clear of mines and a shorter route now open, work could get underway to supply this voracious army. Using this port would be a deciding factor in bringing about an end to a war that had plagued Britain for five long years.

J Support moved back to their old ground at Leunen. For weeks they endured long-range shelling and incessant rain, engulfing trenches and shell holes with muddy water. Roads were once more impassable and most vehicles, even the ever-faithful Sherman found it hard to get through this morass. Supplies were now being brought up by the new M29 Weasel, a robust full-tracked workhorse. Designed for snowy terrain, it raced ahead as other vehicles sat around waiting for tank-dozers to pull them to solid ground.

German troops seemed to thrive in such weather, throwing everything at the Allies as they reeled under the weight of so much mud. When Jerry was on the offensive, guards had to double up, causing much dissent from the 'rank and file'.

'What ... bleedin' 'ell, Corp?' Rifleman Shadman grumbled when woken by his section NCO. 'Fer Christ's sake give us a chance ta ger me friggin' kit orf. I've only just chuffin' ended me shift. Do us a favour,' he quickly added, 'sort out bloody Wilkie. It's 'is bleedin' turn.'

'About time someone sorted that skivin' bastard out,' said one half-sleeping form. ''E's the one cockin' everythin' up ... lyin' there as if 'e were fast asleep. Scabby little toe-rag.'

'Right, Wilkinson!' the corporal yelled, kicking him in the butt, angry at having to rouse such torpid buggers. 'On yer bleedin' feet ya shiftless sod!' he added, shaking him hard. 'No dawdlin' you loathsome tosser.' Wilkinson's so-called mates laughed at his derision. 'Let's be' 'avin' ya,' his corporal furthered. 'Otherwise, you'll be on guard duty until end o' fuckin' war.'

His mates laughed again, scornfully.

Wilkinson struggled with his pouches and webbing, grabbed at a rifle and picked up his helmet. With eyes half-closed, he adjusted his chin strap and pushed forward to take over from the old guard. A loud whooshing made Wilkinson and the corporal drop to their knees. A high explosive shell landed with a dull thud a dozen yards away, slithered into a trench and came to rest against Eddy Shadman's foot. In recent weeks more duds came their way. And thank God they were, thought Shadman and his mates. War at best was a lottery, and it was good to have the odds lowered occasionally. A hairsbreadth of a second, six inches, either way, or a chance fluke could mean the difference between living and dying. The strangeness of war at times could be baffling to the uninitiated. Fully awake, Wilkinson started his tour of duty from what he hoped was a safer place.

Ron was also on guard duty, wearing his new winter issue long johns. He felt warmly encased, despite their itchiness. 'As snug as a bug in a rug,' he chuckled, easing his back up and down an ADS sign.

'God bless the Duke of Argyll,' Sharpy added, just as pleased with his new underwear. He watched Ron and his antics. 'Blimey, Deak, you're chatty already.'

Just after dusk, two sections from 16 Platoon were ordered to open fire. With it being below freezing the Vickers cooling system froze solid. Twenty minutes in front of a fire, and they were ready for firing. Each gunner fired a full belt and reported his gun nicely warmed up.

The temperature climbed around midnight and rain fell heavily, causing trench sides to collapse, filling them with muddy water. The officer, taking pity allowed half of each section to move into a nearby house. The Germans, somehow aware of this, brought their patrol in closer than usual. They fired on the nearest trench, slightly wounding Lieutenant Nathan, 16 Platoons officer, who was in the process of doling out the men's rum ration. One lad having spilt his tot during this exchange lobbed a couple of Mills grenades to deter the wily Krauts, sending them back to their lines like rats homing in on a sewer.

Payback was meted out on Jerry the next morning when both machine-gun platoons pumped belt after belt into their lines. Not put off in the least they retaliated with pinpoint shelling and mortar fire on headquarters company. In this exchange two vehicles were knocked out, killing one rifleman and wounding several others. A burning scout car, next to where the lead platoon was billeted, started licking at a barn. Soon it was a raging inferno, flames reaching for spruce trees, threatening to make matters worse. Riflemen raced back and forth as they rescued their gear, storing it away from the fire.

'Go on, mate,' one irate corporal shouted, shoving a rifleman in his back, 'don't fart about! Get the lead out of your boots!'

'Get bleedin' beddin', Dick!' someone was heard to yell above the furore.

'If there're any of you idle buggers doing nothing,' added the corporal, taking an armful of blankets from a rifleman, 'you'll taste the leather on my toecap, jacksie way up.'

While J Support stayed behind under the watchful eye of an infantry brigade, the rest of the Fifth pushed northwards to Arnhem. Major Sloan's orders were to defend the west bank of the Maas, digging in and covering a two-thousand-yard front. Thinly spread they guarded a blown road and rail bridge and the far bank where pockets of Germans were dug in, intent on making a stand.

Three days of rain caused the river to break its banks, flooding fields on either side like the Nile's yearly inundation. With their position swamped they withdrew to a dry ridge some five hundred yards to the rear. Dirt roads leading away from the river disappeared under the rushing torrent, bogging down vehicles and in places drowning them like Pharaoh's chariots in the Red Sea.

Tank-dozers were useless under the circumstances. They just had to wait until the weather improved. It took over a week for the river to return to its natural course before vehicles could be retrieved. As soon as they had dried out, with one or two engines stripped down to get rid of the gunge, J Support once more took up station on the west bank. When the roads were passable, they crossed the Maas via a Bailey bridge, courtesy of the Royal Engineers. They made light work of the defenders, but more troops were rushed forward to plug the gap and tip the balance. These were also routed, with the loss of just one man and a vehicle.

J Support re-joined the Fifth's motor companies in their cut and thrust patrols in and around a sprawling town. Slowly they fanned out, mopping up what little resistance remained. Having cleared the area, they leaguered on a recreation ground, with some platoons billeted with locals. HQ Company set themselves up in the middle of a field, behind the burgomaster's house.

During their stay, many friendships were made. These hospitable people organised a party in the town hall on Saint Nicholas's day. With Christmas only a few weeks away, carol sheets were given out, and everyone sang with gusto:

'Silent night, holy night,
all is calm, all is bright
round yon virgin mother and child.
Holy infant, so tender and mild,
sleep in heavenly peace,
sleep in heavenly peace ...'

The village hall echoed to *J'attendrai* and *The White Cliffs of Dover*. Plus, many more that took their fancy. Just as dawn broke the national anthem of both countries echoed around the hall, causing many tears and hugs of solidarity. Revels over they exchanged gifts and keepsakes, items to be treasured for years to come, in memory of a special evening.

Sharpy, Ginger, Ron, Freddie and Corporal Squires were billeted with a doctor and his young family in a village which somehow had escaped the ravages of war. Richly furnished with triple gables and large bay windows in all six bedrooms it was an elegant house. There was no furniture in their room, but that didn't matter, so long as it was warm and dry. Water was always piping hot, and the bathroom had the largest bath Ron had ever seen.

Charlie, now a full corporal – promotions tended to be rapid these days – was back in his old platoon. He was once more teamed up with Ron and Ginger; and sharing the driving with Sharpy. Freddie was now with George Belcher and Mr Lyle. Ron and the others got on *so* well together. There was rarely a cross word between them, but for the vicious banter that flowed like whisky at an Irish wake. They were like a family, knowing each other's moods and tuned in to when one needed a bit of space or just wanted to talk.

A significant event happened when Major Sloan visited brigade headquarters at Patrol Farm. The farm and its many buildings was a holding camp for fresh troops and those returning after recovering from wounds. Just by chance, the major was with the adjutant when this NCO reported for duty. Major Sloan called in a few favours, and Wally Frazer was once again senior sergeant in his old platoon. There were only a dozen or so who were acquainted with him – the rest being replacements – and to a man they were thrilled when he arrived back in their midst.

'Morning, Deakin, Sharp,' he said as they cooked breakfast in the orangery at the bottom of a rambling garden. They both got up, pleased to see their old sergeant. 'I thought I'd find you two buggers still in each other's pockets. Things never change ... thank God!' He shook their hands, pumping each one in turn.

'How are you, Sarge?' Ginger asked, now shaking his hand. 'Wound healed?'

'Fit as a fiddle, thanks, son. I was lucky. As you so rightly said, Deak ... "a flea bite".'

'How's Mister Bowkett, Sarge?' Charlie asked.

'Blimey! Corporal Squires!' he said, clocking his tapes. 'Well, I'll be blowed! Been suckin' up to officers, son?'

'I earned 'em, Sarge.'

'Course you did, Charlie,' he said, shaking his hand. 'They don't give *them* away for being first in the naafi queue.' He smiled and slapped him on the back. ... 'I was only pulling your pisser, Corp. Mister Bowkett's fine. He was lucky. Though he'd lost a lot of blood. You can hardly apply a tourniquet to *that* nether region. A piece of shrapnel – he showed it to me, a good two inches long and as sharp as a razor– missed his old man by a whisker. He's at home now. I don't think he'll be back before this lot's over.'

'If Ron has his way' – there were a few smirks – 'he'll have plenty of time to see action again,' Sharpy swiftly added. They all laughed. '... Mister Lyle's set up a sweepstake on when the war'll finish. Each of us picked our own date. He's holding the pot. A sizable one too, over thirty quid.'

'What date did Deak pick?' Wally asked, knowing full well it would be something ridiculous.

'June sixth, nineteen forty-six!' they all exclaimed, again laughing.

'He's hoping this fun'll carry on a *lot* longer,' Ginger added. 'Mercenary bugger.'

'Always the sceptic, Deak,' Wally said, smiling. 'You never change, dipstick. And thank God you don't,' he added, once more shaking his hand. 'I appreciated what you said that night, son. It's good to be back.'

'An' ... an' it's nice ta ... ta 'ave ya back, Sarge,' Ron said, the lump in his throat tying up his words.

There seemed no end to this God-awful weather. Everyone was more than a bit cheesed off by the drab scenery of Eastern Holland, with all its mud.

To lift their spirits, Mr Lyle told them that there was a chance of a few days in Brussels for a lucky few.

'What ya fink, Ron?' Charlie asked.

'It's on the cards, Chaz,' he said, punching his arm. Charlie was matchless, as Ernie had been. Many would resent a mate being promoted and having to take orders from them. But not Ron. He was more than happy with the situation. It felt good having him around again. 'Just fancy, me ole China plate,' he furthered, 'if we 'ave it off together—'

'Ain't ya got out o' the habit yet?'

'Wot ya mean?'

'Talkin' dirty.'

'We could 'ave a regular booze up,' he carried on, ignoring his harmless quip.

Charlie nudged him in the ribs. 'A nice bit o' totty on our lap,' he chuckled, 'gettin' blotto, an' forgettin' abahhht this blasted war.'

'Sounds bloomin' great ta me, Chaz. ... Let's get packin'.'

They had been staying with the doctor for three weeks, disturbed only by the occasional long-range shell. At the start of their fourth week, a runner warned Ron to report to company headquarters.

'Good news, Deakin,' Sergeant Major Dawson said, grinning all over his face. 'You've got forty-eight hours in Brussels. Report clean and tidy tomorrow at 0630. Transport will be waiting to take you and the other lucky beggars to the fleshpots of Brussels.'

He was over the moon at the prospect of spending his leave in such a delightful city. The round trip would take ten hours, sitting on metal benches, but he didn't mind in the least. It would be worth all the discomfort.

Next morning a party of fifty mixed ranks lined up outside the transport pool. Full of high spirits, clean and spruced up in their best SDs they climbed aboard the Bedford's. They began their journey back across the border and on to Belgium's recently liberated capital. Each three-tonner, led by an RMP motorcyclist drove at speed, swerving in and out of all manner of traffic. Arriving at the city, they weaved through a maze of cobbled streets and at last pulled up in front of one of Brussels' largest hotels.

They stood gazing at a grandiose building, now used as a Salvation Army hostel for the military. The doorman dressed in maroon frock coat and matching peaked cap made everything seem unreal. Looking so out of place, he saluted and beckoned them up the steps. One by one, they made their way through a glass and chrome revolving door, approached an expansive art deco desk and were greeted by a middle-aged woman wearing pebbled glasses. She checked their names off a list, gave each a key and pointed at a bank of lifts.

Ron found himself in room 116 with Bill Ritchie from his own platoon. It had two single beds, clean white sheets and pillowcases, with a small wardrobe for each. Best of all, though, was an en-suite bathroom with ample hot water. A large bay window looked out on the *Grote Markt* (Grand Place) and Brussels' Town Hall.

Both had a good long soak, got dressed and processed like Lords down the grand staircase and made their way into a spacious, well-appointed lounge bar. For an hour, they sat watching people as they came and went, drinking their ice-cold schnapps and milking the moment for all it was worth. A gong warned them to go to the dining room for what turned out to be a tasty, well-served meal with waitresses flitting amongst densely packed tables. Bill and Ron sat with two NCOs, Corporal Jim Nightingale from Beaconsfield and Sergeant Ken Tranter from Forest Gate. Having shared a meal together, these new friends decided to team up and stroll around the *Grote Markt*. They sized up a dozen or so bars and, in case any fancied a bit of female company in the wee small hours, asked where the red-light district was.

A crowd of soldiers gathered around a small fountain down a side street from the *Grote Markt*. Once the crush had thinned, Ron and the others went to see what all the fuss was. A small statue of a boy in guardsman's uniform was emitting a stream of water from his penis. A Cameron Highlander, in best kilt and bonnet explained the legend of this little misbehaving boy, calling him *De Manikin Pis*.

In one of the lively bars around the *Grote Markt*, they found Corporal White and beefy, cherry-faced Rifleman Bream from 14 Platoon, sampling its pale Pilsner beer.

'What's it loike, Corp?' asked Bill.

Chalkie smacked his lips and nodded as a waiter stepped forward to push two tables together. He soon returned with six tall glasses of beer and assorted nibbles. The beer slipped down like velvet, and the relaxed, easy chatter flitted from one thing to another: families, football, pubs, girls and sex. Though the one subject they stayed clear of was the war. The last thing they needed was reminding of what they had to go back to once this dream was over.

An old Wurlitzer filled the bar with Rina Ketty singing *J'attendrai*. In memory of what this song meant the locals were singing along, sometimes wiping tears from their eyes. Bill Ritchie, an out and out extrovert accompanied them in English. In France, Belgium and Holland this song was akin to Vera Lynn's *We'll Meet Again*. Proving so popular the Germans outlawed it, but that didn't stop them filling their homes with its sad lyrics.

They stared in wonder as Bill chatted up a couple of girls in Flemish. Yakking away, perhaps sharing some secret or other with them he overtly stroked the thigh of a rather cute girl no older than sixteen. What possible reason could there be for this raucous Cockney speaking so fluently with the locals in their own language? Later they questioned him on his ability to speak the lingo. He told them his father fell in love with a girl from Ypres in nineteen-sixteen. Bill's Belgium grandmother from Douai looked after him for the first half of his life and Flemish had been his first language for many years. In thanks for being their very own linguist, Major Sloan gave him leave to visit his grandmother. Bill showed them an envelope addressed to *Madame B Lerclec, 14 Rue du Pont, Le Cavins, Douai, Belge*. Sadly, he never delivered it because she died of natural causes six months earlier. He carefully placed the unopened letter back in his battledress pocket, a poignant reminder of the woman who had played such an important part in his life.

Time passed quickly, with hearty meals being served so amicably. Moreover, the crisp white sheets, offering a silky balm against coarse, hairy blankets – making it hard to get out of bed – and female company for the asking was a perfect recipe for a memorable time.

However, all good things must come to an end. Having locked their room for the last time, they made their way down the grand staircase, handed in their key and queued to enter the revolving door. Soldier after soldier pushed his way outside, heading towards the parked Bedford's.

Ron slung his valise up to Bill and then pulled himself aboard by a thick rope hanging from the roof frame. Sitting beside Bill, he looked at the hotel one more time, watching as a Ford Dodge pulled up. A dozen or so GI's jumped down as the doorman saluted and gestured with a sweep of his hand for them to enter. They trooped up the steps and made their way inside, one at a time.

'Come on, Ron,' Bill said, passing him a cigarette. 'I'm sure some other poor bugger was hankering for a couple o' more days, same as you when *we* arrived.'

'No ... jus' thinkin' ...' Ron said, pausing to light up. 'Once this lot's over an' done with, I'd like ta come back 'ere one day, once the city's recovered from its wounds.'

They took one last look at the cobbled street and the rushing figures as they went about their business, sighed and stirred their mind back into battle mode.

Mr Lyle announced that the whole brigade was going back to Belgium for a refit. With Christmas only a few weeks away the thought of spending the festive season amongst old friends in warm, peaceful surroundings put everyone in a cheery frame of mind. More importantly, though, every vehicle needed a damn good overhaul, having travelled over some of the roughest ground in some of the worst weather conditions.

A short while later, Sergeant Cox barged into their room and announced, 'Change of plan, lads. We're now heading for a place called Dinant, fifty miles south-east of Brussels. No rest and no refit. Not quite yet.'

'Come on, Freddie!' Ron exclaimed, thinking he was joking. 'For Christ's sake, yer pullin' our pisser?'

'You've gotta be kidding,' moaned Ginger.

'I wish I were,' Freddie swiftly answered. 'Be by Betsy at 1400, fully packed and ready for a long drive.

'What's so bloody urgent,' asked Sharpy.

'Fritz has broken through at a place called the Ardennes. We're linking up with the brigade south of Brussels. All armour has been put on instant readiness, just in case he attacks from the east, through southern Belgium.'

Chapter 21

'Christmas be buggered'

Within seventy-two hours armoured regiments from the brigade were in Dinant on the Meuse. As soon as J Support arrived, they were ordered five miles east to take up a 'standing patrol' with a troop of Sherman Fireflies. They wasted no time digging in and setting up machine guns and six-pounders to cover the flat, featureless landscape. A thousand yards to their front was a company of US Rangers in a small village.

The lads were kept busy vetting a steady flow of civilians, making their way west, away from the advancing Russians. They frisked each one, looking for weapons and any signs that they were military personnel. Passing themselves off as civilians could only mean one thing, they had something to hide. Once all servicemen were singled out, and arms seized, the rest carried on their way.

At 2100 hours two machine-gun sections moved closer to the village and set up a roadblock. Ron and the others positioned their Vickers in shallow ditches either side of a dual carriageway, running east towards a blackening sky. Each section was given a PIAT, with enough ammo to stop a small army. So long as they rolled over and played dead at the first sign of a rocket. Once their defences were complete, two Fireflies joined them, making everyone feel a whole lot happier.

Just after midnight, they heard heavy tanks and the squeal of tyres. Freddie Cox brought them to order as three Dodges raced towards the roadblock. A giant of a Texan, standing on the running board of the first truck said enemy tanks, along with a company of grenadiers had taken back the village. Once the Rangers were through the roadblock the two sections then took it in turns to watch and wait, sensing an attack might come any moment. Despite everyone's panicky state, the night was peaceful, except for a lone owl on the edge of a small wood, its hooting regaling these anxious riflemen.

When heading back to their leager, they chanced upon an enemy half-track full of field grey figures, a dozen at least. The driver headed across a field like a bat out of hell, with Ron and the rest giving chase, letting off burst after burst. They pulled up when they saw more troops on the edge of a village. No doubt worried about having the tables turned on them they broke off their attack and quickly withdrew, taking another route back to the leager. Ron checked his map, worked out the coordinates and gave them to Mr Lyle. Twenty minutes later, shells screeched overhead, giving Jerry a wicked pasting. The outcome of this barrage was not seen for some days. The sight that greeted them in this once peaceful village shook them more than any other. A sea of bodies, many limbless and in bizarre parodies of death were in places as thick as flies on a piece of rotten meat. They found no armour, only three half-tracks, a couple of scout cars and a tented compound complete with a field kitchen. He felt physically sick, realising he was partly to blame for this slaughter. He hardly said a word as they drove through the village, finally taking up station two miles away on a small hill.

Anti-tank guns, AFVs and machine guns were arrayed in an arc, making a daunting curtain of fire should Jerry decide to attack. The previous evening's warning of Panzer tanks in the vicinity made everyone nervous. A scout car from N Company was sent out on a recce patrol, and Ron and the others were ordered to stay put. By first light, the car and its crew had failed to return, and each feared the worst.

In the distance, there was a road running at right angles across a ridge, with a few wooded areas that might well hold a Panzer brigade. A German staff car with three passengers raced from right to left and was soon gobbled up by the next clump of trees, giving little time for the Sherman's to fire. Seconds later a line of four Panthers followed in its wake. This time they fired, but it proved ineffective because of their range and speed.

A report came through that enemy infantry had been spotted five hundred yards to our front. The troop commander moved off and started engaging them with his Browning machine gun, while at the same time ordering 15 and 16 Platoon to do the same. They rushed into the fray, firing as they pressed down on the enemy. Misreading the situation, the troop commander found a force bigger than anticipated, many armed with *panzerfausts*. Within seconds one of 16 Platoons carriers exploded, flinging its crew about like so many rag dolls. He ordered everyone to halt and then fired a dozen or so high explosive rounds to keep Jerry occupied, giving them time to retire without further mishap.

J Support was guarding a rail and road bridge over the Meuse with scores of American infantry-wallahs. During the night it dropped well below freezing, causing their Vickers to ice up. 16 Platoon lit a fire in the kitchen of a nearby farmhouse with wood from a bombed privy. Sorting suitable pieces from amongst human waste proved hazardous, with volunteers being somewhat thin on the ground.

Half of Ron's platoon found themselves in a small village that some weeks earlier had seen heavy fighting. Each house was a pile of rubble, with a few dead Germans scattered around in varying degrees of decomposition. Betsy's crew took up station in the cellar of what was once a greengrocer's, with their Vickers poking out of a wooden delivery chute. The other guns similarly placed gave a field of fire which would prove devastating if Jerry decided to mount an attack.

'Talk about *Old Bill in a better hole*,' Ginger said, grinning at Freddie as he sat crossed legged, leaning against the cellar wall. He looked the epitome of Bruce Bairnsfather's irascible caricature, with his bushy moustache, balaclava, hand-knitted scarf, greatcoat and blanket wrapped around his shoulders.

Old Bill was alive and well, back in his hole!

''O were smart-arse that said it were Christmas Day,' Charlie mumbled.

'Mr Lyle,' said Freddie.

'Well, *'e* should know,' quipped Ron, "*e's* an officer.'

'I'm bleeding froze,' Sharpy said, putting in his pennyworth. He blew on his hands. 'Christmas be buggered. What a soddin' life.'

'It might be,' said Charlie, 'but yuv gotta be alive ta gripe abahhht it,'

'Philosophical bugger!'

After twenty-four hours in the draughty cellar, they were finally relieved by the rest of the platoon. This enabled them to get their Christmas meal and grab a few hours kip. With three helpings of beef stew and a double ration of rum in their belly, each platoon member crawled away and sorted out a space on the dry straw. They just had time to take off their boots and wrap a smelly, mildewed blanket around their dog-tired body. Soon their dreams were of peace and home. The next few days proved to be a blissful time, sleeping and living in a straw-laden barn ... best Christmas present *ever*.

J Support set about overhauling each Bren, trying to squeeze a bit more out of the tired workhorses. Some were in a dreadful state, breaking down every few days. However, for a few, salvation was at hand. A section from each platoon coaxed their worst vehicles to a motor replacement pool and got given reconditioned Loyds. The Brens were soon cannibalised by a REME officer and his men, removing serviceable parts and towing them to a large field behind a derelict café. They dragged a tarp over each, leaving them until after the war. Betsy mercifully escaped such callous treatment. Sharpy and Charlie doted on the old girl, heaping love and attention on her at every turn, changing worn parts, greasing and keeping her in tip-top condition. Not all drivers were so attentive.

15 Platoon took up station on a hill two miles west of a medium-sized town. Lieutenant Lyle's orders were to observe and report on enemy movements, without giving away their position. In the event of an attack, he was further ordered to support AFVs in any way the troop commander saw fit. They leaguered on the other side of the hill, out of sight, preparing food and brews below and then carrying it up to those on duty. They set up their Vickers in the margins of a small thicket, with Charlie and Ginger on the first watch. The others prepared compo porridge, Lyle's Golden Syrup and sweet tea, strong enough to strip paint.

With the ground so hard they gave up on trenches and instead built walls of snow as if preparing for a snowball fight. With the enemy in retreat, they would be safe enough sleeping above ground, so long as they didn't freeze to death. Ron and Joe found a drift of virgin snow, scraped out a large hole and triple lined it with groundsheets. They prayed it would stay well below freezing because if it rained, it would be the last straw. A couple of blankets, snow walls and a dryish, makeshift hole with a tarp on top and huddled together for warmth would give them a modicum of comfort. Though roughing it like this was playing on everyone's nerves.

'Fuck-fuck-fuck!' Ron fumed as he spilt the compo, choking the flame. 'Wot I wouldn't give for bacon an' eggs right now.'

'Orders are orders,' Wally said as he hunted for his own spot to bed down. 'Iron rations for the duration of the patrol, Deakin.'

'I bloomin' know, Sarge,' he said, using another tablet, 'but I can dream.' The tablet flared, giving off enough heat to replace the overfull mess tin. With fingers like icicles, Ron cupped the tin as the bland, tasteless mixture bubbled away. The trials of the last few months paled compared to this. Never had he felt so cold in his life. His teeth chattered, his balls ached, and his eyebrows were caked in ice. As snow blanketed his head, he swore he could feel ice running through his veins. He shivered and pulled his greatcoat collar up. His balaclava and Millwall scarf from Betty, wrapped around his head like an Arab sheikh, hardly kept out the icy wind that whipped in from the borders of Germany. A bad omen if ever there was. This was the lowest point of his war, so far.

'Ah!' Wally exclaimed as he prepared his bed. 'To sleep, perchance to dream ... aye, there's the rub.'

'Oh Gaud,' Sharpy said, throwing a handful of snow in his direction. 'He's off again.'

Wally took up the invite as he scraped away the snow. 'Thus far into the bowels of the earth ...'

'In point of fact, Sergeant,' Mr Lyle said, rebuking him, 'it's "land". Richard the Third. Act Five. Scene Two.' They were as bad as each other, quoting Shakespeare at the drop of a hat.

'I know, Sir, but "earth" sounds better.'

'Philistine,' Mr Lyle parried.

'Very nice, Sarge,' Sharpy humoured as he opened a tin of golden syrup. 'Now, do you want some of this, or not?'

'No thanks, Sharpy, lad. I'll have same as Deak. Bacon and eggs'll do nicely.'

Ron punched the snow wall. 'Do you know, Sarge!' he said in frustration. 'Sometimes ya get on me wotsit?'

'That's why I was put on this earth, lad,' he said, throwing a snowball at him. He launched off again. '... This blessed plot, this earth, this realm, this England ...'

'Is *that* yes to burgoo?' asked Sharpy.

'Yes! And plenty of syrup, Mistress Quiffy!'

Ron laughed when Wally used his nickname for Joe. He looked at his mate and mouthed, 'If ya see anyone in a white coat, darlin',' – he looked around – 'ya know what ta do?'

'And *that is*, butcher boy?'

'Run like Gypsy Nell.'

'Bollocks!'

They endured a most dismal night, overlooking no man's land and the distant town. In due course their sister platoon turned up, giving them leave to stand down for a spell, eating, sleeping, resting and thawing out.

J Support was once more in reserve, staying in Dinant for the second time. Both machine-gun platoons found themselves in seventh heaven, taking up station beside the Meuse, acting as an anti-parachute patrol. They also plumped for a choice billet, a deserted villa with a well-stocked wine cellar. Company HQ and 14 Platoon were housed with civilians in a nearby town. They filled in as family members, cooking and sharing each other's food. They spent some memorable days in these peaceful, friendly surroundings.

For over a month it had been bitterly cold, rarely going above freezing. Icy winds made the simple task of going for a tomtit a nightmare. The boon of using a lavatory, an everyday thing once taken for granted, being able to close the door and not have an icy blast around your arse was pure heaven. Add to that the kindness shown by those opening their homes to soldiers, a cheery, welcoming smile, the best seat and a glass of something warming, and you had a recipe for utter bliss. This unbridled generosity made the recent hardships seem like a bad dream. It's remarkable how quickly Tommy Atkins can put such horrors behind him and start living again, instead of *just* surviving.

This spell of rest and relaxation ended all too soon.

With further attacks through the Ardennes now highly unlikely, the Fifth was ordered back to south-east Holland, close to the German border. They started their long trek north in freezing temperatures and driving snow, proving arduous for both men and machinery. Morale was at an all-time low. The roads were in a dreadful state, with fresh falls on compacted snow and ice, making driving perilous. It took guts for drivers to keep going, especially those in lorries and half-tracks. 14 Platoon was unfortunate to have four personnel carriers and their guns in the same ditch all at once. Manna from heaven came in the form of an American wrecker. The titan picked them up like Matchbox toys, placed them gingerly on the road and then let them carry on their way.

Breaking their journey J Support made their headquarters in a school next to a convent, with riflemen once more finding their way into people's homes. They welcomed these tired warriors with open arms, letting them relax and feel at home and at peace. Major Sloan called for a belated Christmas celebration. The sisters of mercy worked relentlessly to prepare tables, laundering clothes, and ensuring each rifleman had a hot bath. The company cooks took over the convent's kitchen. With some local produce, pork, beef, chicken and a few scrawny turkeys they gave a banquet fit for a king. Once Christmas pudding and lashings of Birds custard had settled in the dark recesses of their stomachs a pantomime was put on by the divisional concert party. The Mother Superior, howling at bawdy jokes became the leading entertainment and joined in the party spirit like a trooper. Born in County Antrin, she was as tall as her girth and had a laugh like a bull elephant at full tilt.

Social life left nothing to be desired, with dances, parties and cafés serving ice-cream in hot red wine, a much-loved favourite of Tommy Atkins. They planned trips to places of interest and organised ice skating on a large lake. It was their first proper break for ages and the holiday spirit prevailed the whole time they were there.

At the end of January, an advance party was sent to the Menin area, suggesting their leave would soon be over. Everyone was reluctant to leave, wishing they could see the war out with their new friends. As it turned out, the move never went ahead, giving them a further six days of absolute heaven.

The locals not wanting the go turned out in their hundreds to wave the goodbye. The 'red flag' went up and they moved off to cheers and farewells from many love-struck girls. Friendships had flourished, and many promises were made to return as soon as they could.

They pushed northwards into Holland and eventually became a reserve unit with the Airborne Division. This time they billeted in a timber-framed priory and were ordered to hold a sector on the Maas at Venlo. The Franciscans, denying them cooking indoors because of the danger of fire, were quite prepared to put up with these lost souls. Dating back to the fourteenth century they never had proper heating or lighting, other than oil lamps, candles and a large hearth in the great hall. The lack of such comforts was soon sorted by the REMEs, bringing light to every corner, even the monk's cells for which they were truly thankful. Installing a generator in the basement, techies ran cables all over the place. Electric plates were added, allowing them to cook indoors. Before that, cooking took place in the cloisters, which offered little protection from the foul weather that seemed to be sweeping across Europe in the first few months of nineteen forty-five. This made life a bit more tolerable for the cheesed off riflemen, who were denied smoking indoors. Chain smokers – there were more than a few these days – forgoing the luxury of living indoors settled for bivvies in a windswept orchard.

The foul weather, forcing everyone to stay indoors persisted for ten days. Ron and his pals were bored out of their mind, wiling away their time as best they could. Once again, card schools were the chief pastime, but even they had lost their lustre. Grubby paperbacks changed hands until they had been read at least twice. Then they were put on one side, ready for swaps with other units. They repaired clothes, cleaned weapons until they gleamed, lay around smoking, writing and rereading letters from home.

Ron received a letter from his Uncle Fred, giving him all the news. Food shortages were still the main topic of conversation, with queues growing longer and longer as rations got smaller and smaller. Those at home were quite upbeat about the war news, hoping victory was only a few months away. His Auntie Dot's boot factory had been destroyed by a V2, with the loss of most of the night shift. Fortunately, she had been on days at the time. Betty was now a frequent visitor at 144, staying over on a couple of occasions and sleeping in his old room. This gave Ron a nice warm feeling, knowing she was in his bed. He was missing her dreadfully and had got into the habit of writing two or three times a week. Everyone was in excellent health, and while Jack was in Palestine, Kathy was planning their wedding. His uncle's letter was upbeat, making him feel close to his family and at the same time homesick.

The mood lightened when the sun showed its face, chasing away their blues. Bright and warm the ground dried enough for a kick around. The less energetic settled for leisurely walks or fishing in the dykes through ice holes.

The Fifth was put on standby in early February, ready for a move back into the spearhead of the Allies. They made the long trek northwards to Nijmegen, where there was a palpable buzz. The spring offensive was only a matter of weeks away and to herald the fact the weather took a turn for the better.

Yet again they found themselves staying with the locals, who again showed an excess of warm, boundless hospitality. The only thing to spoil their quiet life was the endless stream of flying bombs, growling overhead on their way to Antwerp and other targets in Belgium. The gunners set up Ack-ack guns on their flight path, showing an innate ability at cutting short their journey of death and destruction.

On the move again, they stopped three nights at an Abbey, crossed the Maas and threaded their way across endless dykes. They finally arrived at a place called Hatert, between the Rivers Maas and Waal, only six miles from the Dutch-German border.

16 Platoon joined M Company in Groesbeek, while J Support and the rest of the Fifth linked up with Canadian and British field artillery wallahs. 14 and 15 Platoon set up their guns along the edge of the Maas-Waal canal with each platoon looking after a five-hundred-yard stretch. Field guns, howitzers, rocket launchers, Ack-ack and Canadian 140mm artillery pieces formed a solid wall of fire. This made everyone feel confident, whatever Jerry cared to throw at

them. A line of houses next to the canal towpath became their new billet, giving them a few local delicacies (food and female) and home comforts.

SS units on the other side of the canal were giving a good account for themselves. At the slightest noise, Spandau's fired on their forward lines, forcing Ron and the others to keep their heads down. J Support guarded a road and rail bridge against attacks from frogmen and midget submarines, or any other Heath Robinson contrivance that might make a 'death or glory' raid.

'If ya see anythin' with webbed feet,' Ron joked, 'you'd better shoot it ... fish, fowl, friend or foe.'

'That's half the British Army!' Sharpy countered, aghast. 'I used to take nine, but my last pair of boots were ten. And I'm sure I've got skin growing between my toes.'

'That's Athlete's Foot, dunder'ead,' he kidded, gently cuffing him behind the ear. 'But it might be bloomin' worse than that. Me Uncle Fred said nastiest thing ya can get were trench foot. In its early stages ya gerra unpleasant decayin' whiff as yer skin rots. As it worsens ya feet swell up like balloons. Ya get blisters an' open sores, followed by ulcers. If left untreated, it can turn ta gangrene. At that point, yer toes drop off. Same with the clap.'

'That's novel.'

'What is?'

'The clap affecting your toes.'

'Oh, knobs.'

'Anyway, Doc, you're a cheery bugger tonight.'

'Just givin' ya facts. If ya toes start goin' numb, you'd better pop an' see ole Sawbones. Yer feet are past smelly stage. 'Ard ta tell when yuv got yer boots orf.'

A searchlight played up and down the river, lighting the glassy water, giving Jerry more target practice. Spandau's chattered, causing Ron and Sharpy to duck down behind the high bank.

'I'm only tryin' ta cheer you up ya miserable bugger,' he finally said, lighting two cigarettes. 'Ya sorry sod.' He handed one to Sharpy as they sat with their backs against the bank.

'I'll let you know when I need cheering up, butcher boy.'

'Wot's on menu, Quiff?' he asked, digging him in the ribs.

'But I've already told you, more than once.'

'I know, but what else is there ta talk about, other than our stomachs? So, humour me, grumbly guts.'

Sharpy sighed and then yielded, soothing his highly-strung pal. 'Oxtail soup for starters, followed by Turkey Rissoles and diced veg—'

'Luvly.'

'—then vanilla caramels and custard—'

'Scrummy,' he promptly added, smacking his lips.

The joy of being attached to the Canadians was their rations, which all ranks agreed were by far the best. Ginger had a fruitful morning, doing swaps.

'—and a bottle of Chateau farmyard.'

Another burst of gunfire doused the searchlight. A few yards away Mr Lyle peered through his recently purloined Zeiss binoculars, trying to pick out Jerry's observation post. The most likely place was a church spire that Ron had already ranged at fourteen-hundred yards. A corporal from 14 Platoon asked if he could have a go at it with his six-pounder, to make sure it was in working order. Five rounds were fired, with three finding the target, causing the spire to vanish from the skyline.

Stags prevailed the whole time they guarded the bridges, chiefly because the SS was so close, watching and waiting for a chance to turn the tables. However, these were short stags, two hours on and two hours off and the most gruelling for a tired and hungry swaddy. Sometimes you had to decide if you wanted food or sleep. Furthermore, if your body craved food, then sleep usually ruled, giving your stomach leave to partner your snoring in a tuneless duet.

With sleep clinging to their eyes, in a half-drugged state, Charlie and Ginger relieved the other two, giving them leave to get something to eat and have a few hours rest. They could hardly remember the last time they had a decent night's sleep. Nothing is more fractious than being roused, feeling scruffy and ratty after a fitful, fully clothed kip in the bottom of a watery trench. It can produce some of the foulest language imaginable, just before dawn, half asleep and waiting in dread for a new day.

'Cheer up, Chaz,' Ginger said, slapping him on the back. 'It could be worse.'

'Hard ta friggin' believe it.'

'The shift will be over soon.'

'Best news I've 'ad these five years,' he put in. 'Role on me bloomin' ticket.'

The battalion headed north to Arnhem to join up with their armoured brigade, now refitted with Comets, the forerunner of what would be known as the Chieftain. Each was given a guided tour around this beast by one of the wacky tank-wallahs. It was vital to know as much as possible about the armoured vehicles you were there to protect and to understand how they could protect you. Weighing in at thirty-three tons, her armour in places was five inches thick. She had a top speed of thirty-two miles an hour and a 77mm anti-tank gun and two Besa machine guns.

Quartered in a quaint village some in the school and others in houses, they stayed for just over a week, relishing this special attention, so warmly bestowed by the locals. The weather was glorious, and there were hardly any parades, except for the odd vehicle check. The locals arranged lively parties and the love-hungry females fell over themselves to make their stay as memorable as possible.

But all too soon everything came to an end.

The spring offensive was about to begin. The first sign that things were hotting up was when they saw vast numbers of bombers, their contrails streaming lazily in their wake. This intense bombing campaign was undoubtedly a prelude to stepping into the wolf's lair.

Ron and his pals could taste victory.

Chapter 22

'The jaws of hell'

For weeks British and American bombers pounded the east bank from Rees to Dinslaken, carpet bombing from dusk until dawn. A tactic they hoped would weaken Jerry's ability to mount any serious opposition to the Allies crossing of the Rhine. This stretch of the river was to be the main focal point for Operation Plunder, and its success would be crucial in bringing about a swift end to the war.

On the night of twenty-third of March, Wesel, thirty miles north of Dusseldorf was all but flattened by wave after wave of bombers. South of Wesel was to be the crossing point for a combined American, Canadian and British assault. In advance airborne troops would land and create havoc from the rear, paving the way for the main force. At first light on the twenty-fourth, three thousand guns laid down a barrage, blasting to pieces any troops within a thousand yards of the bank. The night before, engineers worked relentlessly to construct Treadway rafts to take AFVs across once the barrage lifted. At airfields around Paris over sixteen-thousand airborne troops and paras were loaded aboard Dakotas and gliders. Operation Varsity's landing zones were around Hammenkein and Wesel. Their primary objective was to capture both towns, build a solid bridgehead and then link up with the main force.

Forty-eight hours later the Fifth crossed the Rhine two miles south of Wesel on a pontoon bridge three hundred yards long. The building of this bridge, an incredible feat was achieved in just six hours by a US Armoured Battalion. As they touched down on the far bank, Ron stared at the shambolic sight and utter waste of life, then back at the safety of the west bank and in awe at the mighty Rhine. This river, but for a few minor ones snaking through Germany was to be the last major obstacle between *them* and their final goal.

'We've made it,' Ron said, staring at a dozen or so Horsa's which had overshot their landing zone. A couple, broken apart on impact showed bodies nearby, laid in a well-ordered line, covered by gas capes. One glider, tail reaching skywards, still held the pilot, his body strapped in his seat like a headless sentinel. Another, flipped on its back, showed a gaping hole in the starboard side, a jeep half in and half out, pinning a body beneath. 'I thought they'd 'ave arranged a reception committee fer us,' he finally added. Very few troops were around, having mustered and marched off to their first objective.

'There's not much sign of Fritz either,' Sharpy said, checking his map. 'We must have caught him with his pants down.'

'We give 'im enough warnin'.' Charlie orientated the map to his compass. 'That way,' he said, pointing at a pall of smoke on the horizon. Harry Benthall's Bren could be seen bombing down the road, heading towards the chaos of battle. Charlie gave Sharpy's helmet a loud rap and ordered him to catch up with Benny.

A 'people's car' suddenly pulled out from a lane and took the Bren's full weight on its right side, crumpling like a paper bag. Betsy ground to a halt, giving them time to gawk at this scrunched-up ball of metal. Someone thrust a hand through what was once the side window, thumb up, telling them to be on their way. There was none of the usual slanging between drivers, trying to apportion blame, just a wave of goodbye. It was yet another casualty of war.

'I 'ope yer insurance is up ta date, Grim Reaper?' Ron quipped as they drove away.

'Bollocks, butcher boy.'

They headed for their rallying point, a small village three miles south of Wesel, where they planned to bed down. There was little point taking over the houses, as they didn't exist anymore, having in their turn been flattened by weeks of bombing. When fighting in occupied territory, one did one's utmost to respect people's property. But now they were in the land of those who had started all this madness and henceforth Tommy Atkins would give little quarter. He would press on regardless until Germany was finally crushed, never to rise again.

On the edge of the village was a military compound. There were half a dozen burned-out huts, a guardhouse, now a pile of rubble and a motor pool with two wrecked Daimler armoured cars. Mr Lyle said they must have pulled out before the bombing started because there was no sign of bodies or burials. Watching from the margins of the camp were a dozen or so stunned civilians, homeless, too shocked to move away from their former homes. They all had the same look, dazed, beaten with a resigned acceptance of their fate. A few soldiers took pity, trying to talk to them while handing out tins of food, but were either too stunned or too proud to take them.

Slowly they drifted away.

Once more, Ron had to remind himself that these poor wretches were the enemy.

The armoured brigade to which the Fifth was attached, poised to exploit Jerry's confusion – to harass and chase them to the very gates of Hades – took up position on the right. They then headed for their primary objective, Dortmund, forty miles away.

The might of the German Army seemed to melt away before their very eyes, making things seem far too easy. What were they up to, the high command asked? Were we being sucked into a trap, a trap of our own making? They rarely stopped, set on getting everything over and done with, once and for all. They drove through village after village, burning up the miles. People lined the roads, staring in stony silence, hardly able to comprehend what was happening to them. In the last few weeks, the tables had been turned. Seeing these confident, cocksure troops racing by, unopposed, could only mean one thing ... the end was near.

14 Platoon was again deployed with a motor company, leaving J Support to poodle about at the rear with battalion headquarters. Now and again machine-gun platoons would slip off to mop up pockets of resistance. They made light work of these demoralised troops, rounding up survivors and hauling them off to POW cages that had sprung up all over the place.

Each time they stopped, and people's homes were still standing, they commandeered several, forcing the inhabitants to move in with neighbours. Most soldiers respected people's homes, not causing wilful damage. But a few saw it as an opportunity to trash someone's home, just for the sheer hell of it.

Once 15 Platoon was billeted, the duty officer ordered Mr Lyle to check out an abandoned mental asylum on the other side of town. Ron's section, along with a sergeant medical orderly arrived to find the place in darkness. Hearing voices raised in anger they stormed the building, weapons at the ready. They found several men dressed as civilians. Having missed their chance to escape in the flotsam of war they grudgingly gave themselves up, giving their name, rank and service number. This tidy little haul bagged one *Kommodore*, four *Kapitän zur See*, one *Generalarzt*, two SS *Oberstleuntnant's* and one *Konteradmiral*. Relieved that their war was now over they resigned themselves to waiting with their guards for a Royal Navy intelligence officer and a squad of marines.

As they thrust deeper into Germany, a frenzied madness took hold of the hard-pressed defenders. Battles became fierce and bloody, ending with many dead on both sides. The Fifth endured delay after delay as its spearhead thwarted the enemy's attempts to forestall their inevitable defeat. It now took days to do a few miles, where a week ago they were happily rolling along, ever closer to their final objective.

Several aircraft hampered the Fifth's crossing of the Dortmund-Ems canal. The combined firepower of machine gunners and Ack-ack crews made life difficult for them, bringing down a Heinkel 111 and a Stuka. The dive bomber smacked into a hill two miles away, to a round of cheering from Ron and his mates.

Pushing forward again, Jerry fired from well-camouflaged positions in the wooded countryside, never letting them draw breath. Their defences were manned by a hotchpotch of reservists and a small number of regulars, with an occasional NCO or aged officer. Others were the 'do or die' schoolboy soldiers of the Hitler *Jugend*, doing the Fuehrer's bidding ... to fight to the bitter end. Armed with *panzerfausts*, more than a few found them impossible to aim and fire with any degree of accuracy. The rest was made up of *Deutscher Volksturm* and civilians, with a few zealots to spur them on to make the ultimate sacrifice.

A dozen or so survivors found themselves herded together, ready for marching to a POW cage, away from the front. 'Hendon fucking hock, you toady bastards,' Ginger growled at the youngsters. 'Get 'em up you slimy scumbags.' The young soldiers – they were young, some as young as twelve, but old enough to kill and maim – did as ordered and shuffled towards a field on the other side of the road.

'An' you, Hansel and Gretel,' Ron said, seeing two more in a ditch, hoping to escape in all the confusion. When they saw him point his rifle at them, they got up and ran to catch up with the others. Their numbers increased, but the dead far outnumbered the living.

There was a sharp crack, and a bullet missed Ginger by inches, smacking into Betsy, chipping paint and leaving a shiny patch of metal. Nothing is more certain to put a soldier in a frenzied state than to realise someone was shooting at him. There was a louder bang and a fair-haired youngster was driven back by the impact of a .303 bullet at point-blank range. In his death throes, his heels drummed the ground, and his teeth chattered like castanets. Two or three others eyed the Luger, gauging how quickly they could pick it up and carry on where their friend had left off.

Vickers and rifles were turned on them. The tension grew. No one moved, too shocked to do or say anything. Mr Lyle ended the stupor by picking up the Luger and telling them in German not to do anything silly. There had been enough killing for one day, and for *them*, the war was over.

Charlie was next to speak. 'Right, you bleedin' lot!' he shouted, taking charge. 'On yer bloomin' feet! Get yer 'ands on yer 'eads. The first ta give me trouble will be 'anded over to a squad of Russian women I saw earlier.' Very few understood what he was saying, but the word 'Russian' clearly registered. 'An' they won't be 'avin' 'anky-panky wiv ya. Make a line. ... Right, we'll start wif you, Grandad.'

The whiskered *Gefreiter* placed his hands on his head as ordered. Dusty Miller started going through his pockets. He then ran his hands along his arms, around his chest and waist, over his backside and down his legs, checking for concealed weapons. The other platoon members started doing the same until every man was checked. They then lined them up in front of Betsy, hands still on heads. Ginger watched them like a hawk, Vickers loaded and ready to shred them if anyone so much as farted. Charlie and Ron got them to raise their hands so they could check for watches. The GIs had started a craze for wearing three or four on each wrist. They then walked up and down the line, hoping to find a Breguet or an Omega. With weapons and valuables seized they were finally marched away to be handed over to the infantry.

K Company and a troop of Hussars with Cruiser Mark IIs took the full brunt of the attack. Jerry sent in grenadiers armed with *panzerfausts* and a handful of light tanks. These were soon dispatched without much trouble. They then attacked with Tigers, Panthers and a mélange of other AFVs, backed by yet more grenadiers. A company of Royal Warwicks were sent forward to tip the balance. Fighting was hard, and Jerry took a frightful beating, leaving many burnt-out vehicles, plus hundreds of dead. Those remaining drew back to regroup, trying to forestall their defeat.

As they resumed their advance, the battlefield turned into a blazing inferno, reminiscent of hell itself. Soldiers and civilians stood side by side to make their final stand in makeshift trenches. The Germans hardly had any armour left, so it was bullets and flesh versus shells and tanks. Their nerve soon crumbled and the living, beaten but still arrogant were quickly rounded up and marched off to POW camps.

Once they had tended their wounded and buried the dead, there was another long drive to leager near a labour camp, where hundreds of Russians had been released. No doubt these half-starved creatures would soon seek revenge on their captors and any civilians who happened to get in their way. The adjutant ordered everyone to stay clear of towns and villages, without exception.

First thing next morning despatch riders relayed orders to each commander, saying forward troops were about to take several crossing points over the Weser, on a thirty-mile front. The Fifth's proposed bridge, however, was blown just as a squad of sappers were making it safe, with the loss of a sergeant and two privates. A company of doughboys came to their rescue. They rigged up two sections of a pontoon bridge, ready to ferry J and M Company across as an advance party. Their orders were to secure the far bank and protect the building of a Bailey bridge. Two anti-tank sections from 14 Platoon stood by, waiting to cross first. Each section's guns were loaded and hauled to the other side. While all this was going on the Warwicks crossed in rubber dinghies. As the six-pounders were dragged into position, all other troops dug in, ready to repel any possible attack. The Yanks then ferried across a further two hundred men, which gave a combined front of some fifteen-hundred yards.

The Americans promised that the crossing would be ready by first light the next morning. With the far bank secure they started unloading a Bailey Bridge, laying it out like a giant Meccano set. During the night they suffered a great many losses from artillery and rocket fire, resulting in the bridge not being completed on time.

J and M Company, having to hold out until relieved stood half their force down on three-hour cycles. Doing so at least meant they could get some sleep, but it's surprising how quickly three hours can pass when your bushed. On J Support's sector grenadiers started attacking in large numbers across open ground, using the cover of early morning to mask their attack. Mr Dawson roused everyone amidst grumbles and curses. Machine gunners were ordered to hold fire. The Royal Artillery, given wrong coordinates, dropped their ranging shots amongst the Warwicks. A quick adjustment and a pinpoint barrage, some four-hundred yards away halted the attack and forced Jerry to withdraw. A few weeks earlier, they would not have been seen off so easily. Within an hour M Company was also attacked, with them coming to within two-hundred yards of our forward lines. Another call and the barrage, though frighteningly close once more broke up the attack and forced Jerry to retire with his tail between his legs.

A commando unit, crossing ten miles upriver routed the heavy guns and rockets that had caused so much trouble, giving the Yanks leave to finish what they started. At last, the Fifth joined the two companies that had borne the brunt for thirty-six hours. L Company's mortar platoon was attached to the commandos, to assist in the capture of a village which they skirted around during their rapid advance. After a successful night's work, Ernie's old platoon rejoined the rest of the company.

Two sections from 23 Mortar Platoon were ordered to deploy on the outskirts of a large town. While sighting their mortars a Wehrmacht light field gun lobbed a couple of rounds in their direction, causing everyone to dive for cover. Another mortar section from N Company on the other side of the road, having sighted their tubes sent up a couple of ranging shots that proved bang on target. The section then peppered Jerry with a dozen rounds, causing him to retire, leaving the gun and two or three wounded.

Just after dawn, sentries spotted several dozen Germans heading in their direction, using what little cover there was to mask their advance. The artillery again missed their mark, giving the Warwicks another light dusting. The gunners reset their aim, and shortly a textbook stonk straddled the enemy, causing widespread panic amongst their ranks. A few stragglers were picked off by small arms fire as they tried to take cover in a nearby churchyard. They were soon plastered with mortar fire, giving them little quarter. Before long, Jerry countered with *Nebelwerfers*, pounding our forward lines, causing considerable chaos. It was evident our position was listed on someone's range card because their rounds dropped with incredible accuracy. The enemy pulled back, but not before sending in a fighting patrol against K Company headquarters, who were pinned down in a school playground. Major Courtney's number two, Captain Swan, was killed during this exchange, along with several others.

As L Company moved forward to link up with the Fifth, they got into a firefight with scores of hardened troops. 15 and 16 Platoon, coming to their rescue, deployed their guns in a solid wall of fire on the edge of a large park. What followed was wholesale slaughter, mowing down three-quarters of their numbers. It was so like those foolhardy charges during The Great War, when hundreds of men, line abreast, walked into ripping fire. Sixteen Vickers on such a narrow front can dish out an immense amount of damage to a human body. But they came on bravely, fighting and dying where townspeople had once courted and played.

A couple of hours later both machine-gun platoons helped a commando unit capture a firmly held command post. During this action, Lance Corporal McBain took a bullet through the right eye. With eyelids now closed – looking so serene – you could hardly tell he was so despoiled, except for a rictus grin and waxy sheen to his face. Sergeant Len Farrell was wounded for a second time when he got his arm caught in the tracks of a Bren after stumbling over a long-dead German. To add to all this, they also took heavy fire from a couple of 88s at the main junction of what had once been the town's commercial heart, where buildings now showed bare bones.

Heavy fire once more added much confusion, forcing several riflemen to take cover in a bunker on the corner of what would have once been a busy shopping area. Within seconds an AP round punched through the wall, killing two and wounding several others. For Cyril (Nancy) Lee, this was his third wound in as many weeks.

He was destined never to return to active service, or his job as a postman, suffering years of ill health.

Blackie (Alfred Coleman) and his mate, Dicky Welby, both from 14 Platoon were unlucky when a German lobbed a stick grenade out of an upstairs window into their Loyd. It landed at their feet, killing them outright and shredding them below the thighs. During all this confusion a mortar platoon officer captured a high-ranking German officer, complete with maps showing troop movements within a fifty-mile radius. He saw the folly of carrying on and ordered his men to lay down their arms. A few hours saw much of the town transformed into unholy bedlam. Orange flames shot skywards from a gasoline bowser, dimming the sky and charring the naked body of a Yank just a couple of feet away. Bren carriers slewed about in front gardens in a frantic bid to sort out a place of vantage. Well-appointed semi-detached houses, once cherished homes were now nothing more than piles of rubble. Others, doors smashed during this welter of madness, showed nothing could stop a strong-willed soldier.

Forty or so prisoners were rounded up, but it was impossible to number the dead. Enough to say the trails of violent death can leave a wealth of poses, fouled by the carnage of war. Still, a soldier must move on, pushing such images from his mind. A machine gun was trained on the prisoners, leading them down the line. 'You can't trust the bastards,' Ginger warned, giving the ammo belt a firm tug. 'Keep just behind 'em, Chaz,' he further warned, tapping Charlie's helmet. His careworn figure squatted low in the driver's seat, with Ron by his side. It was policy to hand over all captives to a POW cage as soon as possible, making sure they didn't stray and create further trouble. Even though it was nearly all over, they still had a defiant air about them.

'Little bastards,' Charlie hissed, creeping forward to nudge a brick-shithouse Waffen-SS *Oberfeldwebel* up the arse.'

'Droopy Drawers is a charmer compared to that ugly shitehawk,' Ron said, passing Charlie and Ginger a lit cigarette.

Just think, bein' caught by that evil bastard,' Charlie opined, taking a drag. 'Ya wouldn't stand a dog's ...' There was a rumour doing the rounds that the Waffen-SS took no prisoners, and it was further said they got promoted on how many they had killed face to face. 'Come on ya motherless fucker. Move yer friggin' arse!' he screamed, giving the *Oberfeldwebel* another heartless nudge.

Betsy and their section's other Bren were ordered to escort them down the line. They dropped their charges off at the nearest POW cage and made their way to the meeting point, a partly blown bridge over the River Leine.

For two days they waited while sappers rebuilt the bridge.

J Support, leading the Fifth away from what would always be known as 'the jaws of hell' was first across. As soon as they were on the other side, three SS officers, waving a flag of truce walked up to Major Sloan's vehicle. They said there was an outbreak of typhus in a camp nearby and they wanted some transport to take away the extremely sick. They further said their high command had told them to ask for help from the first Allies they came across. The colonel was informed, but he refused to let them have so much as a bicycle. He did, however, agree to send his senior medical officer to check out the camp. With the SS officers under guard two sections from battalion headquarters, along with the MO and adjutant, drove in the direction indicated. A message soon came back, saying they had found a vast camp in need of help. That same afternoon orders were sent out from the senior medical officer for the 2nd Army, telling all units in the vicinity to give assistance to the inmates. They were in an awful state, starving to death and dying in their hundreds.

While on the way to their leagering point, the rest of the Fifth drove past the camp's main entrance. Ron, absorbed by his thoughts, smoked nonstop to mask the awful smell which seemed to permeate every pore. The air, still and quiet – no wind or birds sounds, just an eerie silence – was heavy with the sickly-sweet bouquet of death. The sights that greeted him as they drove by belied belief. What he saw and heard would leave an indelible imprint on his psyche, disturbing his sleep for years to come.

The camp perimeter, guarded by armed Hungarian and Slavic troops, who until recently had ably played their part in persecuting Jews and Russians, was in lockdown. Inmates were forbidden to leave, to minimise the spread of disease and access was restricted to the Allies only. Both sides had obviously sanctioned these unusual arrangements. It was an odd decision, using these thugs - many of whom had previously worked in the camp - instead of the Wehrmacht troops that were incarcerated only a few miles back. However, the Allies were taking no chances, with two or three soldiers watching over them every fifty yards or so.

Ron and the others leaguered on the outskirts of a village called Bergen, only a mile from the main gate, shocked and outraged by the stories of wanton cruelty. The men and women involved in the liberation of Belsen and other such camps were touched and appalled by the immense suffering. They would carry the mental scars to their grave.

Richard Dimbleby, a War Correspondent with the BBC, succinctly summed up what many had seen and felt when they first entered this 'hell on earth':

> '... Here over an acre of ground lay dead and dying people. You could not see which was which ... The living lay with their heads against the corpses and around them moved the awful, ghostly procession of emaciated, aimless people, with nothing to do and with no hope of life, unable to move out of your way, unable to look at the terrible sights around them. ... Babies had been born here, tiny wizened things that could not live. ... A mother, driven mad, screamed at a British sentry to give her milk for her child, and thrust the tiny mite into his arms, then ran off, crying terribly. He

opened the bundle and found the baby had been dead for days. This day at Belsen was the most horrible of my life.'

Chapter 23

'Victory Farm'

Each village they came to showed posters of Joseph Kramer, the 'Beast of Belsen' and Irma Grese, the 'Whip Woman', the cruellest and most despicable of his guards. Along with their mug shots, dark, surly and wicked was a list of atrocities committed at Belsen in the name of National Socialism. Within a year both would be hanged by Britain's chief executioner, Albert Pierrepoint, along with others found guilty of crimes against humanity.

The roads thronged with people from all over Europe, moving east and west. The crush of orphans, displaced persons, rancorous soldiers and bemused camp inmates in their striped suits were everywhere. No street, city, town or village was exempt. The steady flow stretched miles, with all manner of transport bearing their worldly possessions. Europe was on the move, and it hardly seemed possible anyone in this crazy world was settled.

As J Support picked their way around hundreds of people, three horse-drawn wagons stopped in front of Mr Lyall's carrier, refusing to let him pass. A mishmash of soldiers and civilians got down and stood with hands-on heads, freely giving themselves up. The world had seemingly gone mad. They were searched and then marched away for questioning and internment in a camp somewhere. Their horses, still tethered to the wagons, heads hung in abject misery, were led into a field. The soldiers, taking pity on them undid their harnesses, bathed their sores and picketed them together.

'I have three at home,' said Mr Lyle. 'Two hacks and a gelding called Caesar. Father gave me Caesar as a year-old colt.' He rubbed the horse's nose and made clicking sounds. The horse tossed his head and whinnied. 'I miss them dreadfully, as you see.'

The other horses, two sturdy cobs, had light chestnut markings with white mane and tail. Ginger and Sharpy, along with a couple of others were feeding them iron ration biscuits. They stroked them, giving them names and treating them kindly. The British had always had a liking for horses, founded through years of amity. Furthermore, they also had a love of animals in general, protecting those less fortunate than themselves. They perked up with all this attention, nuzzling their newfound friends.

Once leaguered, Mr Lyle ordered his sergeant to check out several houses where men had been seen acting suspiciously. They approached the partially bombed buildings, keeping an eye open for trouble. A Krupp 88mm anti-tank gun was poking out of one of the downstairs windows, covering the street opposite. In the first house, they found a dozen or so half-starved men huddled together in the basement: Russians, Poles, Slavs, a couple of German Jews and an American. The American pilot said they had escaped from a nearby camp. Sergeant Frazer and two sections headed for the camp, with the American showing them the way. After a couple of miles, they came across a food store guarded by several soldiers. Ron and Ginger loaded Betsy up with sausages, hams, a flitch of bacon, cases of wine, cognac, champagne and hundreds of cartons of Chesterfield cigarettes. The *feldwebel* in charge said this stash was for the private use of officers. They then carried on to the camp, now visible by goon towers above the trees.

A lone sentry stood guard at the main gate. About to run away, Sergeant Frazer yelled at him to stay put. The jumpy youth dropped his rifle, causing it to discharge. A handful of soldiers ran from the guardroom. They stopped in their tracks, stunned, nervy, unsure what to do. There was yet more shouting from the sergeant, and his men turned their rifles and machine guns on them. The soldiers swiftly threw down their weapons. A quick roundup gave rise to a couple of dozen Wehrmacht troops, now sitting in the road, smoking and prattling like a load of fisherwomen. Some had brought their kit bags with them. The rest asked if they could go back for theirs, but they were told to keep quiet and stay put.

'What do you think this is!' the sergeant yelled. 'A bleedin' picnic?' They pleaded, but he was adamant, saying if they didn't shut their gobs, he would hand them over to Ivan at the first opportunity. The thought of being in *his* vengeful hands soon quelled any further protests.

An early start next day brought them to a town where K Company was dealing with further delaying tactics. 15 Platoon was ordered to attack the left flank. They slowly made their way across a ploughed field. Suddenly there was an almighty explosion. Ron turned and saw Mr Lyle sailing through the air, dead before he hit the ground. His driver, George Belcher, lost both feet, dying on his way home to his wife and daughters. Fortunately, Freddie was in the next vehicle.

Peter Lyle had been a likeable officer and took a keen interest in his men's welfare. Sugar Plum as he affectionately became known in the Fifth would be sadly missed. He was a born leader and a shining example to his men and fellow officers. Silently they took it in turns to dig his grave. They wanted to do more than just leave his body by the side of the road. And anyway the 'body removal squad' would ensure he was given a proper burial. As Ron dug the spade in, he thought of *that* night, so long ago. He would gladly give every blanket in the British Army just to have him back again, leading his platoon. How many more of his friends had to die before this blasted war was over? As they gathered around the shallow grave, a trickle of Germans drifted in from the recent battle, with hands aloft. It was easy to spot the bona fide soldier. Though stunned and battle-weary they still wore their badges of rank and unit insignia. These were a marked contrast to those who removed their collar tabs and discarded their helmet with its tell-tale SS emblem. For those on the lookout for members of the dreaded 'death squads', it would be abundantly clear these men had something to hide and would warrant closer inspection.

Soon after crossing the Ortze, another of Germany's rivers, they came across a prisoner of war camp, the first of many in the weeks ahead. Being mobbed by overjoyed POWs – some in captivity for five years – proved a moving experience. Hugging and kissing their saviours, they were openly crying at the thought of going home. Returning them to their loved ones would be a top priority for the Allies. In the case of British, American and Commonwealth troops, they would be flown to England at the first opportunity.

A few miles from the camp massed anti-tank guns, backed by regulars and a handful of heavy tanks checked their advance on the outskirts of a medium-sized town. The machine-gun platoons were ordered to draw back and mop up any pockets of resistance. It was always advisable when advancing to make sure no one remained in your rear to give trouble for you later. When they were confident that the only enemy was to their front, M Company and two troops of Sherman Fireflies formed up, facing the town. The rest of the Fifth was in the second wave, with yet more armour. 15 and 16 Platoon rejoined J Support and took up station on a hill further back, prepared and ready. It was a splendid sight, seeing tanks deployed with motor platoon carriers in support, primed for a full-scale assault. Two miles further back was a battery of 155mm Long Tom's, waiting to add their weight to the barrage.

Shell after shell whistled overhead, raining down terror on what was once a peaceful town, ripping to pieces both soldier and civilian alike. The order came to advance. However, it was clear that Jerry, stunned by the immense firepower was offering only token resistance. They gave up in their hundreds, walking out with hands aloft, unnerved, broken and glad it was over. They had seen enough fighting for one day. Soldiers on both sides just wanted to live.

Along with their big brothers, the Fifth accounted for eleven hundred prisoners and many dead. Altogether they destroyed seventeen 88s, four Panthers, two Tigers and a hotchpotch of light armour and ordnance pieces.

J Support set up their leaguer by the light of flames from the shattered town, making it like daytime. The sound of shells going off in a munitions dump made everyone Jumpy. What a grim place to bed-down, with endless bangs and whizzes as the fire, out of control, spread to a nearby fuel dump.

A small number of soldiers rummaged through the pockets of dead Germans, searching for something of value. Some went much further in their efforts to line their pockets, knocking out gold teeth or removing a bloated finger to get hold of someone's wedding ring. Soldiers had always done this sort of thing during the Wars of the Roses, the English Civil War and the Napoleonic war. However, it was not carried out with quite the same enthusiasm as it was in those days. In today's modern army, the precise nature of this practice was viewed by many with some distaste. Nevertheless, it still went on, in many forms. Conquerors had always taken from the vanquished, and it would always be the case.

Once the town was secure, Major Sloan sought out the *Bürgermeister*. He ordered all cameras, binoculars, watches and weapons to be made available in his house, ready for inspection. The mayor objected, saying he would instead use the town hall, but the major was insistent, telling him to do as he was told. Having muddy soldiers – some more uncouth than others – traipse through his home would be a humiliating experience for him and his wife. Each time they took over a town or village, this became the norm. It was done under the guise of confiscating anything that might prove a threat to the Allies or just took their fancy.

Today the honour went to 14 Platoon.

On his travels Ron had got hold of a Mauser 7.65mm pistol in a brown leather holster. It fitted snugly under his battledress blouse, ensuring he was always armed. Expecting trouble, he had it cocked and ready in his trouser pocket. The *Bauernführer*, refusing to have anything to do with him objected to the British taking over his farm. In no uncertain terms, he told Ron and the others to get off his land, or he would set the dogs on them. A heavy-set man with arms like tree trunks walked about the yard with three rabid looking Alsatians, watching the heated exchange between farmer and soldier. When questioned by Charlie, he admitted to serving in the SS on the Russian front. Once discharged, owing to wounds, he was assigned to farming duties. He was your archetypal SS soldier, stern-faced with cruel eyes, a callous brute of a man. Ron took out the Mauser and waved it under the farmer's nose, and all protests ceased, with the soil darkening around his feet. Along with his wife, daughters and the ex-soldier he was told to leave and not return for several days. They could then have their home back, so long as it was not being used by someone else. The Russians would not have been so obliging. 15 Platoon took over the farmhouse, while their sister platoon bedded down in a ramshackle barn. Ron and Ginger gave the kitchen a damn good clean, probably the first time in years. They then dispatched six chickens and set about making a tasty stew.

'Wot ya know, Bob?' Ron said to the elderly post corporal as he hovered on the doorstep, watching their domestic doings.

'Not a lot, son.' He tossed a bag on the now clean table. 'Mail up,' he said, sitting down and taking a sip from a discarded mug.

Corporal Joe Hicks took charge, shouting out names. 'Rifleman Cash!'

''Ere, Corp!'

'Letter from yer sweetheart, Bob,' he said, flicking it into his waiting hands.

'Rifleman Thomas!'

''E's gone ta bog, Corp,' someone answered.

'Lance Corporal McBain!' he resumed.

A cloud settled over them. Each thought about Mac, his rifle pushed into newly turned earth with his helmet on top. 'Dog tags' and AB64, wrapped in his gas wallet inside his mess tin were placed next to his head, so the 'body removal squad' could record his untimely death.

Ginger and another guy each received a parcel. The noise of crackling paper soon lifted everyone's spirits.

'Cor, Ginge, that's a bit of orl right,' Charlie teased as his mate unwrapped a cake from his mum, so big it must have taken their entire rations for a month. 'Come on, Deak, let's be 'avin' a brew. Who's fer a piece of Ginger's homemade?' Soon his sword was working overtime, giving each a sizable wedge.

'Bit of all right this, Ginge,' Ron said, grinning all over his face.

'Glad you like it,' he replied, snidely, 'and kind of you to let me have a piece.'

Sharing with one's mates was the expected thing to do. Ginger stared at the piece of cake Charlie had given him, the biggest slice – well, it was his cake – and watched as his mum's fruitcake disappeared before his very eyes. Next time someone got such a treat, he would be sure to do a 'Charlie' on them.

'Oh yeah, what's this bleeding lark!' Joe Sharp exclaimed, clumping downstairs. Needing no invitation, he got his slinger and helped himself to what was left, crumbs and all.

Before the mail arrived, Ron and Ginger were poring over last Monday's *Daily Sketch*. On the front page, it showed black arrows driving towards Berlin, closing the gap on Hitler and his henchmen, between east and west.

'Won't be long now,' Ginger ventured. 'I reckon it'll be over within the month. Adolf's luck has finally run out.'

By the end of March, the Fifth was on its way to Lübeck on the Baltic Coast. Skirting Winsen – fifteen miles south-east of Hamburg – in the dead of night they crossed the Elbe, Germany's last river in artificial light, courtesy of the Royal Engineers. There was hardly any opposition, but for a few diehards and an occasional long-range shell, fired indiscriminately. It was only a matter of time before it was all over.

They embarked on what would be a long and arduous trek. Frustrated by never-ending stopping and starting, dragging things out interminably, a certain solace lay in the fact that this was the last leg of a journey which had taken five years. They carried on heading north, driving through the night. If they did stop, it was mostly because of a broken-down vehicle, which the tank-dozers quickly pushed out of the way. Brief stops made it impossible for drivers to get any proper sleep. Though it was heaven for Ron and Ginger, curled up either side of the engine housing, with the rocking motion keeping them in dreamland. At the first sign of a lengthy break, Joe's studded size tens would thrust their way towards his snoozing mates.

'Come on you lazy bastards, it's my turn,' he would shriek at them. 'Move your arse. Let's have a kip.' Within seconds of changing places, he was snoring his head off.

Freddie Cox and Charlie in the lead Bren drove down a quiet country lane, bounded by tall hedgerows. They stopped when they saw a knocked-out Panther, half blocking the road, despoiling this peaceful setting. Charlie gave the blackened tank a wide berth, churning away at the muddy verge. A massive explosion from a Teller mine flipped their Bren on its back, with bogie wheels still grinding away. By another freak of war, Freddie and Charlie crawled from under the wrecked carrier, suffering no more than loss of hearing and minor bruising. The Vickers mounting frame had saved their lives. Wild-eyed and reeling they made their way to the RAP, thankful to survive yet again. Very soon the upturned tanks ignited, and seconds later belts of ammo started popping.

'Get moving you lot!' Sergeant Frazer shouted, frantically waving at Sharpy and the next carrier while walking ahead, showing them which path to take. Ron and Ginger got down and started walking some distance behind. They refused their mates lippy request to remount, choosing to wait until he was well past the danger point.

'You bastards!' Sharpy yelled over his shoulder as he leant forward, trying to follow Wally's frantic signals.

Ten minutes later they climbed aboard and were greeted by their mate, speechless and scowling.

'Come on, Joe,' Ron said, shrugging his shoulders. 'It's bloody crazy fer us all ta ride an' cop it.'

Sharpy ignored him, lit a cigarette and pulled away, cursing under his breath. Ron of course was right. But it still hurt that they had abandoned him in such a way, leaving him to fend for himself. He knew it was the right thing to do, under the circumstances, and he would have done the same. He would not hold it against them. These days life was too short to bear a grudge.

There was another hold up while a single artillery piece shelled the road. As J Support waited for it to be silenced, Corporal Davis from 16 Platoon spotted a Daimler scout car parked some hundred yards away, down a track on their right. Along with Rifleman Harris, he went to check it out, leaving his driver with the Bren. Within seconds two shots rang out. The scout car reversed at speed, skidded across the road, smashed into Betsy's rear-nearside and started driving away. Corporal Davis's driver opened fire, killing all three occupants with a prolonged burst from his Vickers. Both his mates who he had been with for three years were dead.

Further down the road, a German medic sat with his back against a wall, fiddling with his medical kit. For him, the war was over, as it was for two SS officers sprawled untidily next to him, a bullet hole between their eyes. Behind them were plumes of gore artily splayed across the whitewashed wall. A line of civilians, some injured came down the road. Suddenly the medic got up and made his way over to them, administering first-aid to those who had been injured by a shell from the rogue artillery piece.

Once they were on the move again, rumours started spreading that Germany was making overtures of peace. Was it possible the war would soon be over? What heaven it would be! No more killing. No more living in fear of being seriously wounded. They didn't mind dying, they were ready for it. At times they felt as if they were dead already and just waiting to be reborn. Pain from dying would be short-lived, and peace would be eternal. No more, dirty, stinking, damp clothes. No more rotting corpses. No more kipping in a muddy hole which tomorrow could be your grave. Oh, what heaven it would be. The only thing left would be the memories – memories of hard-fought battles and lost friends. In years to come, they would remember those who had died in the name of freedom.

A second lieutenant took over 15 Platoon, and a short pep talk ensued during one of the many brew-up stops. Their new officer turned out to be a bright twenty-three-year-old called John Phillips, halfway through his law degree and youngest son of a coal miner from Atherstone. He said he would ride with Deakin, Sharp and Iverson in the lead Bren. They made room for his bedroll and kit. A few moments later, having checked the whys and wherefores of Betsy, he lifted the battery box cover beside Sharpy's head and placed a carton of cigarettes inside. It further followed there would be a delivery every other week from his tobacconist in Bristol.

'Help yourself, lads,' he said, tapping his pipe against the Vickers frame.

'Yes, Sir,' they all agreed, pleased with this new arrangement.

That same night they halted in a residential part of town jaded by war, waiting for Sergeant Frazer to return from the company commander's briefing. As soon as he was back, he told them to commandeer several houses. No one bucked at such an order, even though it always resulted in a slanging match with the locals. Still, it was improper for victorious soldiers to bed down in the road, among the garbage of war.

Nobby, the only other rangefinder in J Support, approached the first house. He started hammering on the door. '*Guten Abend werte Dame,*' Rifleman Clarke said as a woman in her mid-fifties opened the door.

A different sort of war ensued, one of words and arm-waving. The woman, far from impressed, told him to stop bothering her and go away. Ron and the others held back, grinning, waiting for Nobby's eventual defeat. With tears in her eyes, she gave in and allowed them inside. She started removing things from the larder, loading them in an old pram, helped by her crippled husband. When ready, they left through the back door, out into the yard, ready to make their way to wherever. Suddenly her husband tapped the window with his crutch. '*Bitte geben Sie mir das Bein,*' he said, pointing at his stump. Ron looked around and saw his false leg leaning against the wall. He passed it to the white-haired man through the window and then returned to his chores, keeping an eye on a battery of saucepans. The downstairs was made up of four rooms and furnished in a cheap austerity style. Ron looked at the small but clean kitchen, pleased to be making their evening meal indoors for a change.

The occasional shell, some miles off was the only thing to disturb this peaceful setting. Nobby's rendition of Charlie Kunz's *Love Walked In*, even though his touch on the keys was far from polished, only added to this domestic scene. Staring at him on the 'upright' was a photograph of a *Kriegsmarine* officer, postulating on the conning tower of a U-boat. He took his right hand off the keys and knocked the officer off his perch, sending him scuttling across the floor. 'Best place for you, mate,' he said, launching into *A Star Fell Out Of Heaven.*

The next day they were on the move again, heading north towards Lübeck. There was little opposition to their advance, meaning it was only a matter of time. Everyone could now breathe a sigh of relief.

News started spreading that the Fifth had found a warehouse full of champagne and vintage wine and vast quantities had been squirrelled away, ready for the forthcoming celebrations.

Ron, Sharpy, Ginger and Sergeant Frazer, plus two sections from 16 Platoon were picked for a raiding party. An hour later they had rounded up at least fifty Luftwaffe personnel (male and female) from a radar station. As they lined them up more joined their fast-swelling ranks, plus countless *Kriegsmarine's*. They checked each one for arms and watches, with riflemen lechering over the women as they frisked them.

A stern bull necked *Konteradmiral* marched up to Wally Frazer, as if on the prow of his flagship. He saluted, yielded his sword and Luger, handed over his charges and formally surrendered. The rear admiral bowed, saluted again and returned to mixed ranks of sailors and airmen. More *Kriegsmarine's* came out of a nearby wood, with scores of Wehrmacht soldiers, swelling their numbers even further. By now, there were well over four hundred, formed up and ready for marching to the nearest war cage, where they would be examined to see if any should answer to war crimes.

An *Oberst* with Luftwaffe lapel patches was saying goodbye to his lady friend. '*Mein Liebling*,' he soothed fondly, kissing her while eyeing Ron. '*Alles kaput*.'

'Come on, ya ... getta bleedin' move on,' Ron mouthed as he gazed at the wheelbarrow, loaded with kit, scabby root vegetables and other unpalatable foodstuffs. It was probably all he owned in the world, and he was one among many.

'Say goodbye to Nellie Dean,' Sharpy jeered from his driving seat, gunning the engine. 'Get a move on, Adolf.'

'Russkies fer you, matey,' Ron warned, pointing east. 'If ya 'ang 'round 'ere much longer you'll end up in Siberia. You'd better start walkin'. Leave the *Fraulein* with us. We'll look after 'er.' He winked at Ginger. The officer refused to move. 'Wot about Coventry, Warsaw, London?' he shouted, prodding him in the ribs with his Lee-Enfield. 'Get lead out yer boots, Uncle.'

Sharpy edged forward, yelling, 'Move it, Fritz!' The Bren caught him at the back of his legs, pushing him along with his wheelbarrow.

A machine gun was trained on them from the lead Bren, loaded and ready to fire. Betsy followed up the rear, pushing them along. They hurriedly marched away, keen to put as much distance as they could between them and the advancing Russians. Ron saw a small boy of no more than ten, proudly wearing his *Deutsches Jungvolk* uniform, walking with his elders to a prison camp somewhere. Within a few miles, they handed them over to a sergeant major from the Durham light infantry.

It was dark when they found the others on the outskirts of Lübeck. Parked on muddy lawns of a dozen semis, having churned away hedges and prim borders, they were brewing up. Ron reported to Wally, who assigned a bedroom in one of the houses and gave him a bottle of bubbly.

'We'll toss fer the bed, Joe,' Ron said sportingly.

'You're on,' he replied, taking a penny from his breast pocket. It was one he had carried with him since leaving Tilbury ... a lifetime ago. He threw his loose change to the kids as they drove to the docks, but this penny was caught in the lining of his battledress. There was nothing special about it, apart from the fact it was dated the year of his birth. At the time, it seemed a good omen, and it became his lucky charm. He'd never been superstitious before, but the last five years had changed him in many ways.

Ron quickly made his bed on the floor, settled down and popped the cork. Within seconds of taking a mouthful, he was fast asleep. In the early hours, he was woken by someone coming into the room. He rolled on his back and looked up the hem of a sheer nightdress at a pair of female legs, bare and knickerless, stepping over him. It was the lady of the house, eager to retrieve something from the bottom drawer of a tallboy. He watched as she removed a flowery chamber pot. He knowingly smiled. This was probably her most prized possession, and no Tommy was going to take it from her.

The next day there was *fantastic* news!

The war was over!

Monty accepted the surrender of German forces on Lüneburg

Heath, with *Generaloberst* Alfred Jodl signing on behalf of the German High Command.

At their billet, named Victory Farm in celebration, both machine-gun platoons took over an enormous straw-filled barn. The long-awaited party got underway. Officers, having taken over the farmhouse, could be heard drinking and making merry.

Vast amounts of champagne and vintage wine were shared out between ranks. Small parties sprang up all over the place, in barns, outbuildings and workers' cottages. By early morning, when most parties were in full swing, Ron, Sharpy, Ginger, Charlie and Freddie lay in the clean hay, wrapped in fresh blankets, secure content and happy. Each had a bottle of champagne, toasting each other. Charlie started the proceedings off with a bottle of Martell, the one Ron gave him months ago.

Was it for real or was it a wishful dream? Everyone was in a state of shock, finding it hard to believe. They had spent so long living from one day to another, hardly daring to think about tomorrow. And now it was here, peace – blessed peace. Just maybe, within a matter of weeks, some would find themselves going home. They would be looking to the future, feeding off their memories and trying to adjust to family life and a job that may not suit them anymore. They spoke about the possibility, fearing the change, just as they dreaded reporting as civvies all those years ago. And it felt like 'all those years' because they'd done more living in five years than they would eventually do in their entire life.

Someone was making their way up to the hayloft. 'Well, look who's here,' Sharpy said breezily. 'It's good old Mister Phillips.'

He was well and truly plastered, reeling towards them. It was a miracle he hadn't broken his neck climbing the rickety ladder. 'Where ish, my lovely boys?' he slurred. 'Come on out – *hick* – you scabby buggers.' He stumbled over the empty Cognac bottle, fell on his face and then crawled towards them, straw all over him. He pushed himself up and grinned, just like a baby would do when sitting up for the first time. Let's 'ave a drink – *hick*. ''Ere ... 'ere,

Ron, fill 'em up – *hick*.' He took a bottle of Black and White from his valise and tried to open it. 'Let's – *hick* – 'ave a sup. We'll soon be back in Civvy Street with thousands of other miserable ... *hick*.' He started to sing. '*Bless 'em all, bless 'em all the long and the short and the tall* ... Do you know – hick,' he went on, giving up on the song, 'I've got the worst ... worst fuckin' – *hick* – platoon in the whole fuckin' battalion?' He burped, finally opening the bottle. 'I've also got the worst bloody NCOs in the – *hick* – 'ole fuckin' army.' He saw Freddie lying with the others. 'An' that ... that goes for you – *hick* – Freddie Bartholomew Cox. Ya wan—'

'An' we've got the worst fuckin' officer ... *SIR!!!*' they all piped up before he could say more.

'I'll ... I'll drink to that,' Mr Phillips said, taking a hefty swig before passing out.

Ron grabbed the bottle before too much was spilt, patted him on the head and raised the whisky in salute. 'An' good health to you ... John,' he said, chirpily, 'an' the best o' health to us all.' He took a deep draught and then added, solemnly, 'An' ta all those who can't be ... God bless 'em!'

Chapter 24

'Peacetime Soldiering'

An advance party from the Fifth was already at their new home, sorting out quarters and meeting with the Red Cross and newly formed *Stadtrat*. While they waited for orders to go, rumours were rife about the battalion's future. Despite all this guesswork things could only improve, with the prospect of some long-awaited peacetime soldiering.

The booming voice of Company Sergeant Major Dawson echoed around the square, bouncing off metal buildings that served as their current billet. 'Officers on parade,' he shouted, 'dis-miss!' Each man turned to their right, saluted, paused and faced the front again.

'Stand at ease.' Sergeant Frazer ordered. 'They're all yours, Sir.'

'Stand easy, lads.' Mr Phillips took his war-torn pipe from his trouser pocket, knocked it against his hand and smiled as he added, 'And don't bust a gut.' They snickered at his carefree attitude and customary habit of cocking a snoot at authority. He turned around, making sure the CSM and major were nowhere to be seen and again smiled at the platoon as he filled his pipe. 'You will be pleased to know,' he went on, 'we'll soon be leaving the bicycle shed.' Their latest billet was a disused bicycle factory, two miles from Brekendorf. 'Our new home is a draughty castle in Schleswig,' – he tamped down the tobacco with his thumb – 'north of here. I've also been told that you get a nice stiff breeze from the Baltic. All good soldiering stuff. I'll give you more when I know more. Thank you, sergeant,' he said, lighting his pipe. 'Let them go to tea.' Keen to discuss something with Ron and Sharpy he called them over before they had a chance to scarper. 'I have a job for you two reprobates,' he said, drawing on his pipe. 'At first light tomorrow, pack our kit on Betsy. Rifleman Dingley will be with you by 0600. We're picking up three horses to start a riding school. Dingley and I will ride them back to Schleswig. You two will carry our kit and spearhead our little party. You're to sort out places on-route to eat and sleep.' Mr Phillips grinned as if contemplating a wicked prank. 'There's bound to be some kind-hearted soul who'll lend us her range and bed in exchange for some proper food. Hopefully, there won't be too much fighting on this trip. Unless some wart infested *hausfrau* with crotch critters takes a shine to me. It should be a cushy little number, something to wind down to, ready for demob. I've also heard the rumour, and as far as I know, it's true.'

Next morning Ron and the others reported as ordered. Mr Phillips spread out an ordnance survey map and asked, 'Who's the map reading wizard?' Sharpy volunteered Ron before he could open his mouth. 'Right,' he continued, pointing at the map, 'we pick the horses up here at 1300 hours. We'll then we take our time as we head for Schleswig, via this route.' He traced a finger north of a large lake and fiord. 'We'll stop here for something to eat and then carry on to this village, where we'll billet. I've further been told that the natives aren't too hostile, so we shouldn't be told to piss off too often. Before we get going make yourself some breakfast,' – he pointed at a box with a dozen eggs and enough bacon to feed an army – 'and we'll get going at 0800. A mess orderly will be here shortly with a few bits and pieces to sustain us on-route. Store them in the toolbox, along with these.' He handed Ron two bottles of Black and White. 'We'll use them as barter, along with any surplus food. I'll see you at 0800,' he further added before making his way to the officer's mess.

They travelled north for a few miles then struck out east. In the distance were a lake and a rambling city nestling beneath a tranquil summer's sky. Ron checked his map and told them it was Schleswig. The road, with few travellers and hardly any vehicles, snaked through an impressive landscape. They soon arrived at the long body of water, stretching as far as the eye could see and turned right. Passing through village after village, untouched by war, Kosel, Bohnet, Riesby they finally arrived at Kappeln. After picking up the horses, they drove through the town and over a large bascule bridge. Once more they headed into the countryside, admiring the splendour of Schleswig-Holstein.

They arrived tired and hungry at the place they planned to stop for lunch. Each house, shuttered, appeared to have been empty for years. They made their way out of the village, intent on finding a kindly *hausfrau* who would let them use her range. Coming across a wooden, slatted farmhouse, close to the road, with smoke curling above the chimney, they halted beside a five-bar gate. A sign on the gate said *Willkommen auf Zuhause Bauernhof.* Both agreed Home Farm somehow conjured up thoughts of Blighty.

Ron took a large box out of the Bren, nudged open the gate and made his way up a cobbled path. He paused at a freshly painted door, rapped three times and wondered what sort of reception he would get. The door was opened by a flaxen-haired beauty, neatly framed in a halo of light from the kitchen window.

'*Guten Tag, Fraulein,*' he said, giving her his best smile.

As he marshalled his thoughts, the young girl waited. He subsequently asked if there was any chance that he could use her kitchen to prepare lunch for four soldiers. He said they were willing to pay, showing her the box with heaps of sausages, well-scrubbed potatoes and dozens of eggs.

'*Ja, komm herein*, Tommy,' she said, holding the door open while inviting him into a spacious, quarry-floored kitchen.

Standing in front of a vast range was an older woman and a girl in her early teens, busily making lunch. The woman, attractive in a Teutonic way, hair in plats, full-chested with broad-shoulders frowned, unable to understand why these British soldiers had invaded this wholly female domain. The older girl explained what he wanted and pointed at the food. '*Ja, ja, junger Mann. Kommen herein,*' the *hausfrau* said, her manner changing for the better. She pulled out a chair, took the box and drooled at its contents. Guessing Ron had not been knocked on the head and thrown down the well, Sharpy walked up the path, knocked on the open door and waited to be invited in. '*Du auch, junger Mann,*' she greeted the newcomer, pulling out another chair. She thrust a slice of strudel and a mug of *ersatz* coffee into their hands. They took one sip, made from toasted, ground acorns, ran outside and spat out the foul mixture. They shortly returned, bowing apologetically to the woman. Sharpy took a tin of American coffee from behind his back and handed it to her.

'*Wunderbar. Bohnenkaffee, sie Liebling,*' the older girl said, planting a sweet-scented kiss full on his mouth, sucking the very life from him.

The woman peeled back the foil from an eight-ounce tin of Hills Brothers coffee and lifted it to her nose. '*Paradiesisch,*' she said, eyeing Ron.

'What did she say?' asked Sharpy.

'I think it were 'eavenly.'

'What, you or the coffee?'

What followed was the best cup of coffee they had ever had, along with Mr Phillips's cigarettes.

'Roy Rogers'll be 'appy,' said Ron.

'Why?'

'No warts.'

'Ah, but what about the rest?' Sharpy ventured, handing him another cigarette.

'That's fer 'im ta find out. I ain't 'is batman, ya know.'

What barriers remained were soon lowered as they tried their best to converse with the girls, Angelika and Kristin and their mother, Kita.

Sausage, egg and chips were timed nicely for when Mr Phillips arrived on his sleek, chestnut brown stallion. Dingley onetime stretcher bearer with headquarters company rode one of two placid bays.

A pleasant meal was had, provided by Ron with Kita's bewitching help. Her brown shoulders and arms and heaving breasts with plunging cleavage seemed to dominate his world as she doled out more strudel, mug after mug of coffee and a hearty tot of plum brandy. Ron persevered with his German, but it was only a matter of time before he put his foot in it. When asking for another cup he mistakenly asked this bonny, sweet-smelling ex-enemy for a kiss, causing bursts of laughter from Kita and her daughters.

'*Das ist eine Tasse, keinen Kuss,*' Kita said, holding a cup under his nose. Everyone howled with laughter. She handed it to him then kissed him full on the mouth, her breath tasting of cinnamon and plums.

Meal over, dishes washed and dried, Mr Phillips gave them what was left of the food, along with another tin of coffee.

'She were a brahmer,' Ron said, climbing in beside Sharpy as he gunned the engine. Lost in his thoughts, after the pleasant interlude with doe-eyed Angelika, he ignored his mate, focusing on his driving to the exclusion of everything else.

Mr Phillips waited until they had driven away before mounting his mettlesome steed. Bob Dingley quickly got his bays in hand and trotted after the noisy Bren.

'Yes,' Sharpy finally replied. 'She was a bonny wench, and she'd certainly got the eye for you. And her daughters were corkers.'

'I bet you'd liked ta 'ave rubbed yer hands through Angelika's flaxen 'air, Quiffy?'

He smiled while keeping Betsy running straight and true as the steep, gorge edged road crested a tree-lined summit.

Mr Phillips, getting used to his horse, caught up with them. He pulled up beside Betsy, gently tugged at the horse's ear and made clicking sounds as it walked beside the trundling monster. 'A good find you two,' he said, tightening his reins. 'Let's hope we're that lucky tonight.' He heeled the horse and galloped away, burning up the long, straight road as his mount defecated in its wake.

'Where's Tonto?'

'About a hundred yards back,' said Ron. 'clip cloppin' along as if 'e ain't gotta care in the world.'

'Strange ...' Sharpy said, smiling.

'What is?'

'Well, six months ago, we were dodging bullets. Look at us now ... dodging horse shit.'

'About par for the course.'

Knowing they had time on their hands, they stopped for a natter with a bunch of khaki bonneted Argyll and Sutherland Highlanders. The sergeant offered them a strong, sweet brew, laced with Captain Morgans and a Spam wad with real butter. A pleasant hour was spent, talking about each other's war and what their prospects were for the future if the Far East lot didn't end soon.

Back on the road again, Mr Phillips and Dingley cantered by, horses pricking their ears and jinking away from the noisy Bren. They stopped, turned, galloped back and pulled up sharply. Both were seasoned horsemen, keeping their mounts on a short rain. Each time they came near the clanking tracks, their mounts seemed less nervous.

By the time they reached Taarstedt, the rain was falling steadily and what little light remained was fading fast. The village, quite large meant the prospect of finding somewhere was good. However, they needed to find a place for three horses as well as themselves. So, they went in search of another farm. They soon came across one about a mile outside the village. This one had no welcoming sign like the other. Except for that, it could have been the same place, but for a more weather-beaten appearance.

Ron walked up the dirt path, going over what to say, getting his German just right. He knocked, hoping the lady of the house would be as obliging as Kita and her daughters. '*Guten Abend, Mein Herr,*' he said, smiling at the white-haired old man. He explained they wanted accommodation for four soldiers and three horses.

'*Nein!*' the man said, shaking his head. He mulishly stood his ground.

Ron tried again, but once more, he said no and slammed the door in his face. He returned to Betsy and waited for Mr Phillips. Shortly their officer came into view, holding his lean, glossy-coated mount on a tight rein. Getting down he handed the reins to Ron, went up to the door and hammered on it. The same man answered, and a brief exchange took place, with the man becoming amicable, especially after being given a bottle of whisky.

The farmer took them to the outbuildings, put the stallion in a stall and gave the Bays the run of the barn. However, things got somewhat heated when his granddaughter refused to let them sleep indoors, saying German soldiers always slept outside. Later, after a few glasses of whisky, the girl said she was an ardent Nazi. It turned out to be a long night, passing in an atmosphere of tension and dislike.

As they moved off next morning, five Russians banged on the farmhouse door. Eager to make tracks to Mother Russia, they would make short shrift of anyone standing in their way. Not wanting to get involved, Ron and the others ignored them and quickly drove away. Inwardly, though, they had serious misgivings for the family's safety, especially the hate-filled *Fraulein*.

A couple of hours later Mr Phillips tried to coax Ron into having a ride, hoping to ease his saddle sores. 'You'll be fine, Deakin?' he said, handing him the reins. Ron's face quickly drained of colour. 'But keep him on a close rein. It's like riding a bicycle without peddles.'

Ron noted the stallion's eyes as if it somehow knew there would shortly be a change of rider. 'Not on yer nelly, Sir,' he firmly replied. He had seen some of the caper's horses got up to in the lanes around Wilchester, prancing, snorting, and growing unruly. 'An' anyway, Sir, I ain't ridden a bike either. ... Not bloody likely. I'll stay with Betsy. I know where I am with 'er. You carry on, Sir. Yer doin' a fine job.'

The roads became more and more crowded as they neared the end of their journey. Ex-combatants, displaced persons, orphans in their hundreds, former camp internees, confused beyond belief, added to the chaos on the roads, despite the MPs efforts to keep things moving.

Arriving at Schleswig, twenty miles from the Baltic, a stiff breeze whipped across the lake, reminding everyone how close they were to the Arctic circle. At the far end of a wind-swept shoreline stood a cathedral, standing like a sentinel over the city, its red-tiled roof shining like a beacon in the midday sun. A surfeit of boats lined the water's edge, giving a picturesque feel.

They made their way down the lakeside, heading towards their new billet and what, all being well, would be their last before demob.

Crossing a drawbridge over a weed-choked moat they found themselves not in front of a castle as expected, but what looked more like a stately home. Each of the four sides, perhaps a hundred yards long were in places seven stories high. Throughout the war, *Schloss Gottorf* was used as a foreign workers' camp and had a reputation for cruelty and want. They made their way through an ancient gateway, topped by a portcullis, into a courtyard where a motor pool was set up. Mr Phillips and Dingley quickly left, leaving Sharpy to park Betsy between two Bedford's.

Having traipsed all over the castle, they eventually found 15 Platoon in a long draughty room on the third floor, above the gateway. Ron and Sharpy picked an empty bunk bed and hefted their kit on to stained, shabby mattresses, ancient springs twanging in displeasure. A check of each locker gave rise to several items left behind by the previous occupants. These included a framed photograph of *Reichsführer* Himmler, a large manila envelope, a beer stein with SS crest on one side and a swastika on the other, a small amount of unwashed kit and a few bits of worthless trash. The room NCO gave Ron a greying pillowcase and told him to empty both lockers. As they dumped the remains of someone's service life, they checked each item, in case it had some worth.

Sharpy picked up a forage cap with its 'deaths head' badge, plonked it on his head and started giving a noisy rendition of Hitler. '*Achtung! Achtung!*' he shouted. '*Zer* German people vil be *glücklich!*' He started marching up and down, screaming at the top of his voice while throwing out his arm in a Nazi salute. '*Zer* enemy *ist kaput*! Any von disobeying *zer* order by *glücklich* being *glücklich* vil be shot!"

'Okay, Sharpy, you half-baked-barrel-load-of-horseshit, turn it up,' Jonah pleaded.

'Give it a rest, clown-head,' said another. 'People are tryin' ta get some shuteye over 'ere. We ain't all spent last few days prancin' 'round wif Wild Bill Hickok.'

'Spoilsport!' someone yelled from further down what used to be the long picture gallery. 'We could do wif a bit o' prancin' in this crap 'ole. Ya could 'ave more fun in a knockin' shop wivahhht bints.'

Having dumped most of the stuff, Ron picked up the envelope and saw Gustav Friedmann in pale blue ink on the front. He sat on the bed and tipped out the contents. A collection of photographs showed an SS *Hauptmann* in his early thirties, tall, good-looking, chiselled features with closely cropped fair hair. The black and white photos, perhaps forty in total, had officers posing with a few 'rank and file'. Some were of a domestic nature, soldiers cooking, washing clothes, sleeping. One showed a dozen men standing around an open grave, heads bowed in prayer. They looked just the same as Tommy Atkins, but for a different uniform. Others showed street fighting, utter ruin, dead horses, bloated to twice their size, lines of wrecked vehicles, Panzer tanks and SS troops marching down dusty roads. Three photographs were being kept separately in small cellophane envelopes. The first showed Erwin Rommel, looking through a pair of field glasses mounted on a tripod with an officer by his side. Next was Hitler and *Generalfeldmarschall* Wilhelm Keitel, leaning over a table, looking at a map. The last showed two Polish officers, seated, with four German officers standing behind them as they signed some official-looking document. He placed the photographs back in the envelope and tucked it in his large valise, along with other keepsakes.

The foreign workers had been moved months ago, along with their guards. A few SS stayed behind to clean up their mess and carry out menial tasks around the castle. Despite the promise of better food, their torpid behaviour persisted. At times they had to be firmly persuaded that we did not need any more fires lighting or any more damage to the billet. A few personal items went missing, but some rough justice soon sorted the problem.

Each member of 15 Platoon settled into a routine, reliving the events of the last eighteen months. Ron and the others, never quite tired of retelling them, talked about what the future had in store, especially with the Far East War still going on.

The numbers in Schleswig had grown more than expected in recent months, putting immense pressure on the Allies and *Stadtrat*. Hundreds of ex-combatants returned to bombed-out homes and missing relatives and friends, not knowing if they were alive or dead. They still wore their ragged uniforms, with all badges removed, bringing officer and private to the same level. Their days were spent looking for work and handouts and clumping – many with missing limbs – their way through the city. Their presence was a stark reminder of the price many had paid for their country's transgressions.

With little to do, other than roam the streets and beg, violence was rife. Fights broke out between locals and floating population over the slightest thing. In most cases, they were simply protecting themselves and their property. Many were settling of old scores or just wanton cruelty against the populace. A gang culture emerged, fuelled by black-market, illicit stills and mob rule. Shootings were commonplace, and life was once more held cheaply.

To try and curb this violence, the Allies introduced a gun amnesty, despite age and condition. At a given time, everyone was required to hand in all weapons to the senior officer present. Tables were placed outside the *Schloss*, with 15 Platoon manning them under supervision of the adjutant. All manner of modern and ancient was handed in: Browning's, Lugers, Mausers, shotguns, muskets, even a couple of cased duelling pistols. The diverse mix of weapons included some homemade guns and knives, along with daggers and swords. Most were brought in by locals, with some from the floating population. But few Russians paid little attention to the order.

'Look at this beauty, Bert,' Ron said, showing a musket to the dour Geordie.

The owner, an elderly man, dressed in Prussian garb and sporting a bushy moustache and duelling scar down his left cheek, stood erect as Ron fingered the musket.

'Family heirloom, Grandad?' Bert asked, taking it from Ron. An anxious look on the man's face at having to part with this well-cared for museum piece showed in his steel-grey eyes. Bert weighted the .69 calibre Charleville musket, put it to his shoulder and sighted down the long barrel. He turned it over in his hands, again looked at the man, shrugged and dropped it on the steady growing pile. 'Sorry, Pops,' he added, smiling apologetically. 'Orders are orders.'

Altogether they amassed over fifteen hundred weapons and enough ammo to start a small war. There was likely more of the same hidden away in people's homes, much of it in the wrong hands. For a while, things quietened down, but as more people drifted into the city, the problems started up again. Particularly with the Russians, who thought the war owed them something. Patrols were assigned in case of trouble, with a company placed on standby to put down any riots that might flare up, mostly to do with the distribution of food.

'Right you lot, outside in five minutes,' Corporal Hicks ordered, breaking up a game of three-card brag.

Flash, Donny, Ron and a lanky kid named Carroll finished their hand, gathered up their webbing and bondooks and made their way to a parked vehicle. The Loyd, bucking and whirling around the streets finally arrived at a shabby high-rise on the corner of Schyby and Flensburg Strasse. Joe Hicks made his way up a dark flight of stairs, followed by Carroll, Ron and Flash, real name Samuel Brightman.

'What's bleedin' trouble' ere?' the corporal shrieked, forcing his way between three Russians and two women, screaming at each other in their own tongue. The Russians could see no earthly reason why they should not take a table and chairs from the women's home, to make their own billet more comfortable. This fracas was right-up Joe Hicks's street, having been a council bailiff in Stepney. The rough, burly East Ender, in no mood for trouble, quickly propelled them downstairs, telling them to drop everything.

'*Tovarich*,' the ringleader said, hinting it did not matter after all. Though clearly showing he was about to loot the flat.

'*Da, Da*,' one of his cohorts added, eager to get out of what had turned into a ticklish situation.

'Yeah, yeah. If ya say so, Ivan,' the corporal scowled. The ringleader haltingly made his way downstairs. 'Come on faggot brains,' Hicks taunted, 'gerra move on!'

He turned on the corporal and gave him a mouthful of guttural Russian while slipping a hand in his trouser pocket. The corporal levelled his rifle, pointing it at the man's chest. 'I'm only goin' ta say this once,' he said, thumbing the safety catch. 'If ya don't do what I say ... I'll shoot.' He paused then added, 'Turn 'round. Go downstairs. Return to yer quarters. ... Do ya understand what I've jus' said?' The Russian nodded, with all bluster gone. 'Good. Now piss off!' Without saying another word, they left.

Both women remained quiet during this altercation, not wanting to make matters worse. The older one, stern-faced and as broad as an ox was not the sort of person you would want to cross swords with. She smiled at Hicks and said, '*Ich danke Ihnen sehr, sehr viel*, Tommy.'

'*Es ist alles Ordnung, frau*,' he replied, saying it was all right.

Outside with the vehicle, Donny, playing with two small boys, turned when he heard the noise. Marching down Flensburg Strasse was rank upon rank of Russians, arms raised across their chest with legs kicking out, comparable to a German goose-step. They were singing a marching song about Stalin ... the glory of battle and victory against all the odds. The Russians looked an oddball bunch, close-cropped heads, dressed in pre-nineteen-fourteen German dress uniforms and a strange mix of trousers with badly worn footwear. As they advanced their deep throaty song told of the struggles of Leningrad and Moscow.

Just before reaching the building, where Ron and the others were waiting in the lobby staring in wonder – indeed sheer fright – as the men wheeled down a side street. Their booming voices, singing in perfect harmony, sounded like a well-balanced male voice choir at The National Eisteddfod.

'Jeez, Deak,' Donny said as the others joined him. 'I thought I were a gonna. Saucy buggers.' They all watched as the rear files disappeared around the corner. 'Gerra load of 'em,' he added, exhaling deeply.

When making their way back to the castle, they saw three MPs trying to restrain a Royal Marine who had got his hands on some bad hooch. All manner of stuff went into this fiery, gut-wrenching brew: methylated spirits, metal polish, battery acid, boot polish, plus anything else that came to hand. Elicit stills, making variants of whisky, vodka and schnapps had mushroomed all over the city.

The soldier thrashed about, possessed it seems by some evil entity. With arms and legs flailing, kicking, gouging and biting, he struggled to be free. He lashed out with his hobnailed boot, catching an MP below the knee with a sickening crack. His friends, trying to incapacitate the marine before he did more harm set about him with their long white truncheons.

He now lay inert in the road, cuffed and ready for dumping in the jeep with two others.

The sound of shelling and the fear of being seriously injured slowly faded, to be replaced by a nervous tension which persisted for some time. All it took was the sound of a door slamming or a lorry backfiring, and they were whisked back to their worst nightmare. Living a regular life away from the horrors of war slowly restored frazzled nerves. Concentrating on other things, other than what they had recently gone through, helped bring about a more balanced existence.

Needing to keep everyone occupied, headquarters set up a social committee and arranged a programme of activities. These included sailing, rowing, fishing, swimming, football, rugger, cricket, boxing and amateur dramatics. For a bit more relaxation, they visited the naafi, Red Cross and CWL canteens, which bought some relief from the drabness of living at the *Schloss*. However, spreading their wings and in need of some excitement, each time they sought out a *wirtshaus*, the locals would greet them with stony silence and indifference. In consolation there were plenty of lovely walks on the fringes of Schleswig, trekking through the woods and climbing the pine-clad hills with their scudding clouds. Walking by the lakeside on a Sunday morning, along with locals, made them feel alive, reminding them of better times to come. But zealot MPs soon put a stop to any thought of fraternisation. Which was mostly ignored by Ron and his mates. Wandering through the city, with beggars on each street corner and gazing at boarded-up shops and banks was also something to be avoided. Most soldiers kept their ambling to daylight hours. If they were abroad after dark, usually up to no good, Toms and black marketeers would flood the streets, like rats deserting a sinking ship.

All manner of folk dealt in the black market, and no nationality was exempt. Everything was to be had at a price and not in Deutsch marks but US dollars, the only currency trusted in post-war Germany. A bottle of Haig, two-hundred Senior Service and an eight-ounce tin of Maxwell House realised ten dollars each. This set the price by which everything else was measured.

Army life had changed much in recent months, with less bull and fewer guard duties. This led to Tommy Atkins having more time on his hands, a fact that almost sent him around the bend. Ron and his mates willingly stepped forward when volunteers were sought, the opposite of Tommy's typical mindset. Guard duties such as the *Bahnhof*, railway crossings, bridges, public buildings, food markets and bakeries were highly sought.

Most hated living in the castle, preferring the homely feel of a Nissen hut. The occasional guard duty gave them the chance to mix with the locals and chat up the girls, without having an MP breathing down their neck. They were further ordered to turn a blind eye to black-market dealings, and not to antagonise the populous any more than necessary.

The drivers, not able to tinker with their precious engines anymore, were likewise bored stiff. Just twenty vehicles were maintained in good working order by a REME platoon, with the remainder stored in what was once the foreign workers compound. A few Bedford's were always on hand for trips to places of interest, along with the bi-weekly 'mail-run' to Neumunster. The 'mail-run', as it was loosely termed, sixty miles each way and needing an overnight in one of their grottiest hotels took place every second Friday. This allowed those picked to make a long weekend of it. Officers now gave the 'rank and file' more leeway, not keeping close tabs on them like they used to.

Since arriving at Schleswig, Ron regularly put his name down for the 'mail-run', but this was the first time Mr Dawson had chosen him. He rode in the back, Mauser cocked and ready, hemmed in by mail bags, some containing gold coins and US dollars. Ron felt like a millionaire, surrounded by so much wealth. His driver, dark, swarthy Bill Chater from Spalding, threw the three-tonner along at top speed to get to Neumunster so he could spend more time with his girlfriend, Gisa.

German roads were lauded as some of the best in Europe, but for their edges which fell away into loose shale, making them lethal to the unwary. Because of being fast roads, drivers drove at top speed, with little regard for others. Poorly maintained vehicles could be a death-trap at the best of times. To meet a charcoal burning lorry travelling in the opposite direction, towing a couple of whipping trailers, was a hairy experience and had been the downfall of many an army driver.

To pass the time they organised trips to all manner of places in Schleswig-Holstein, inland and on the coast. It was strange seeing bases that had once housed the German Navy, a force that nearly brought Britain to her knees. Trips included naval bases at Flensburg and Rendsburg, where *Kriegsmarine's*, under the watchful gaze of a Royal Marine sergeant, ferried these happy band of sightseers around the harbour in an E-boat. A few months earlier it would have been blown to pieces on sight.

How their world had changed.

Another outing was to Kiel, to see their submarine pens. Months ago, the workers left in great haste, leaving behind their tools on workbenches either side of two irreparably damaged U-boats. They boarded the heavy cruiser *Admiral Von Hipper*, with dire warnings not to venture below deck because of water and diesel in the hold. Waiting to be repaired, she was bombed four days before the end of the war. A massive bomb scored a direct hit on her forecastle, forward of the main battery. The crew, unable to move her had no choice but to scuttle their beloved ship at its moorings. Once more a *Kriegsmarine* motor launch, its blue and white flag fluttering at the stern cruised around Kiel harbour. Several armed merchantmen turned turtle had received direct hits from the RAF. They now cluttered up the harbour, making navigation somewhat perilous.

On one trip they sailed in a motor launch, purported to have belonged to Adolf Hitler. They visited various inland waterways around the coast, viewing its castles and scenery from the craft as it cruised by, almost touching the jetties of these once-grand estates. On their way back from this trip, Mr Phillips told them the Far East war had ended in a cataclysmic way. It was not until much later that they learnt of the complete destruction of two cities, flattened by enormous bombs and the atrocious loss of life. On this occasion, the Allies had indeed surpassed themselves. Still, the end of *that* war was great news. They could now breathe a sigh of relief, knowing full well being posted to the Far East was out of the question.

Within days of Mr Phillips being made up to Lieutenant, he and Major Sloan were ordered with four other officers to attend a victory parade in Berlin on the seventh of September. Each platoon member took a piece of his kit and dagged it up to a high-guard-mounting-standard. Without a doubt, this was the first time a whole platoon had been involved in their officer's par-excellence turnout. Such was the love of one's officer! Sharpy, acquiring some hair clippers and a pair of half-decent scissors gave everyone a trim, including Mr Phillips and the major. While dagging-up their own officer's kit they also worked on theirs, ready for *their* victory parade.

A few days later the 5th Battalion, The Rifle Regiment, marched at a lively pace, quickened by a band from the County of London Yeomanry. The people of Schleswig turned out in their thousands to watch as column after column of khaki marched around their city. They stood in stony silence, showing no dissent, only a grudging acceptance that nothing would ever be the same again. This parade was 'showing the flag' like no other. Each man marched as he had never marched before, almost cocking a snoot at the locals. The British soldier can never be accused of being arrogant. Still, there was such a thing as regimental pride and honour.

The lads were shocked, pleased and saddened when Major Sloan did not return from Berlin. They had given him command of the 1st Battalion. Major Courtney was also offered a peacetime commission. Still, he turned it down in preference to returning to the family farm in Cumbria.

Things were changing. More than a few moved to the 1st and 2nd Battalion. Well-earned promotions followed, and everyone wore their newly issued campaign ribbons, with medals following later.

Those still in Schleswig awaited their return to Blighty. And for most that day could not come quick enough.

Chapter 25

'Homeward Bound'

Risking his life each day, seeing one of his mates die, kipping rough in a muddy hole, and hardly daring to think about the future, soon became the norm for a soldier on active service. He must take such anguish and hardships in his stride, without faltering. This is what being a soldier is all about. But once the cut and thrust of war ends and peace cloaks the battlefields, it can be a shock to his system. Like when he saw his first dead body, killed a man, or held a dying pal in his arms. Worse though, and this does gall him more than anything else, is when his world is filled with endless hours of inactivity.

For Ron and the others, there are only so many times they can play a hand of poker, write a letter or read a book. Time hung heavy on their hands, and they were anxious to get home, once more with their loved ones. Though some might have to wait up to a year before being demobbed. Particularly if they were late joining up, single or under twenty-five. They were guests of His Majesty's armed forces, and their release was at his discretion. And while they waited, more than a few went out of their mind.

In the closing weeks of nineteen-forty-five, nearly everyone's self-esteem was at an all-time low. To lift morale, trade and hobby lectures were introduced. This would have the threefold effect of filling the empty hours, teaching them a skill and giving them the confidence to return home. More than a few dreaded the prospect of once more being in civvy street. The 'powers that be' were also concerned that when back home, away from their pals and once more with family, who in no way could understand what they had gone through, many would find it hard to adjust. So, a new skill, hobby or interest may help them make the transition from soldier to civilian to family man.

The adjutant checked every record card, finding out what each man did in civilian life. He was amazed by the skills and experience in the ranks. They might have served king and country for the last five years, but first and foremost, they were cobblers, bakers, chippies, plumbers, brewers, tailors, teachers, lawyers, farmers, artists and writers. Nearly every walk of life was there, from common labourers to professionals.

The lectures covered many trades, languages, a broad mix of hobbies and coaching in most sports. They sourced teachers, including Ron on butchery and put lists on notice boards. It was a great success, with many being oversubscribed within a matter of hours. One such class was life drawing. Its popularity was somewhat influenced by the fact that local girls would be brought in as models. Before anyone could enrol, they had to complete three sketches for the teacher, to attest they were serious about joining the course and not just out to ogle the girls. Ron also signed up for woodwork, so he could help make scenery for Wally Frazer's forthcoming production of *Twelfth Night*. He had got to know him well in the last few months, drinking together and calling him by his first name. Once the fighting had stopped, he happily became one of the lads, up to a point. Sharpy put his name down for car maintenance. With Ginger and Charlie, he also joined a brewing class which was being run by an older guy from Banks's in Wolverhampton. As expected, this proved quite popular, with do-it-yourself demijohns sprouting all over the place. With Ron's busy schedule, he gave it a miss but said he would be more than happy to sample their wares so long as it passed muster and did not kill him. Ginger, having gone with Mr Phillips and Charlie to pick up three more horses helped ride them back, joined the riding school, and along with Donny and Carroll looked after the horses. Under the tutelage of Mr Phillips and Bob Dingley, the school took off in a big way and turned out to be one of the most popular classes.

Warm days and balmy nights at *Schloss Gottorf* made it a pleasant enough place to live. But with winter coming it would soon be unbearably cold, with little heating to be had. By mid-December, what had been a bracing summer breeze was now an icy wind that howled through the castle, down corridors, under doors and across rooms in a most intrusive way. Snow disguised everywhere, while the wickedly cold blast once more reminded everyone how close they were to the Arctic Circle.

On freezing days most stayed in bed, giving them a haven of warmth to reflect on their looming demob. During the daytime, things were bad enough. Though at night it was far worse, dropping well below zero, freezing pipes and bursting joints and resulting in no running water for weeks. Fire buckets were used to collect human waste, with German orderlies taking them away and spotlessly scrubbing them before putting them back. This gave rise to many 'shitty' jokes at the German's expense. Such as: 'How many SS does it take to clean a fire bucket? Depends on how many toothbrushes you have.'

One extremely cold day, with little to do other than reading about Hubert Wilkins's last trip to the North Pole, Ron lay in bed, trying to keep warm. He had his greatcoat, serge blouse and trousers weighing heavy on him. He was already wearing his long johns, angora shirt, fatigues and both pairs of socks. His hands sheathed in gloves with fingers cut out numbly turned the pages. He paused at one photograph, showing dogs huddled together for warmth and shelter, caked in ice and snow, lying next to a fragile, windswept tent. He shivered at the thought and snuggled down the bed, trying to blot out the cold and the fact he was dying for a piss.

'Do us a favour, Ginge,' Ron said, turning towards his snoozing mate.

'No,' Ginger abruptly replied.

'But I ain't bloomin' asked yet.'

'It's still no ... whatever it is.'

'Wot ya want, Deak?' Ossie asked. His own platoon having been disbanded was now amalgamated with the others.

'This cold's playin' 'avoc with me waterworks. I'm dyin' fer a chuffin' piss.'

'So!'

'Ya couldn't bloomin' go fer me, could ya, Oz?' No answer. '... I'll buy ya a pint of Truman's when we ger 'ome.'

'Ya bastard,' Ossie hit back. 'Ya know 'ow ta get a guy goin'. Now *I* wanna piss.'

'Me too,' piped up Flash.

A couple of others said they were also dying for a leak, tipped over the edge by Ron's cruel quip.

They put on their greatcoats and dashed to the only lavatory on the third floor. Once finished they made their way back, fumbling and feeling along draughty, cold, dimly lit passageways. They started racing each other, slipping and sliding on newly polished floors. Once in their billet they jumped into their sacks and griped about the cold and the battalion's demise. A few weeks earlier, the colonel told them the Fifth was to be disbanded at the end of March. Those left behind would be demobbed or absorbed into the 1st or 2nd. Cruelly they kept them in the dark as to their fate, which did little for morale.

Along with his Christmas parcel was a letter from Uncle Fred, saying a builder had offered him a job as a bricklayer, ready for his demob. During one of his leaves, he and his uncle talked about the possibility of wangling an early discharge, and this was the ruse they came up with. With all the bomb damage the army would probably let him go before his 'age and service release group' came around.

He also received a letter from Betty, saying she had set the date. In a recent letter to her, he had popped the question. Over the moon when he got her reply, he wrote back straight away, telling her to arrange a date sometime in May. All he wanted now was to get married and start that family he had dreamed about during the worst times.

Along with the builder's application for Ron's early release was a letter from his mother. She said he was now the principal breadwinner and needed his release as soon as possible. Jack and Kathy had recently got married and would shortly be moving to Slough, where he was joining his father-in-law as a painter and decorator. However, Ron still intended to return to his job as a butcher. His mother spoke to Dick, and a new striped apron and white cow gown were hanging in his usual place, awaiting his return.

By Christmas week there was no sign of his discharge papers. Sadly, he would have to wait for his 'age and service release group' to come around. Placing his future on hold, he set his mind to the coming festivities and what all being well would be a fitting end to his army career.

Wally's long-awaited production of *Twelfth Night* was to take place on Christmas Eve. Against his better judgement, Ron was coerced into playing the part of Olivia's jester, Feste, by an ex-Wehrmacht *Feldwebel* clerk. Gerhart Mueller, a lover of Goethe and Shakespeare, also signed up for a role that Wally was finding hard to cast.

While on his way home to Hamburg, Gerhart broke his journey at Schleswig. During most of his war, he was based in Denmark and used to visit the city on leave. Schleswig offered him some much-needed refuge with friends he had made during his time there. As it turned out, the only one he found was a Jewish wine merchant, who during the war passed himself off as a tap-room-man in a *wirtshaus*. By the time he arrived in Schleswig, Gerhart was so thin that many thought he was an inmate from a labour camp.

Day after day he visited the castle guardroom in the hope of finding work. Each time they sent him away empty-handed. In the end, his persistence paid off. The battalion admin warrant officer happened to be in the guardroom during his next visit. He asked about his military service and what he had done in civilian life. Gerhart said most of his war was spent in Aalborg at a seaplane station. In late forty-four, they sent him to Silesia, North Prussia. Furthermore, in perfect English, he said he worked as a solicitor's clerk in Hamburg before being drafted in forty-one.

They served Christmas lunch in what had been the banqueting hall, now doubling as an 'other ranks mess' and battalion recreation room. Tables ran the full length, dressed and prepared with wine glasses, homemade crackers, paper hats, a Havana cigar and a twenty pack of Senior Service at each place setting. Along with those from the Fifth, a few trusted Germans were also invited. Ron sat opposite Charlie, with Sharpy on his left and Gerhart on his right. Ginger, Ossie, Freddie, Wally, Carroll, Flash, Donny, Bert Moule and Joe Hicks made up this happy bunch. The mess staff and a few locals set the tables with decorations, along with swags garlanded across the hall, giving it a proper festive feel.

It was always the custom in the armed forces for officers to serve the men their Christmas lunch, a ritual that raised a few ribald comments from the 'rank and file'. To see officers acting as mess orderlies, doling out Turkey and Christmas pud was looked forward to with great glee. Each officer took care of his own men, attending to their wants like a doting mother.

By the time the colonel arrived, he and his officers were the worse for wear from their revels. Things eventually got underway, with junior officers racing each other to the kitchen supply hatch. They soon returned with plates piled high as soldiers cajoled them into getting a move on because they were dying of hunger. The senior officers, steering clear of such a menial task, mingled with the men, pouring drinks and slapping them on the back.

J Support's new commander, acting Major Mainley, juiced to the nines, made his way behind each man, shampooing him with a bottle of biddy. They did not mind in the least, laughing and joking.

With red wine dripping down his neck, Gerhart turned to Ron and quietly said, 'I have a surprise for you, Ronald.' He looked at the others, making sure no one was listening.

'After your bloomin' debacle last night, nothin' would surprise me.'

'This will,' he said, moving closer. He briefly paused and then added huffily, 'Besides, I thought my Viola was memorable.'

'It were ... fer wrong reason,' he said, kicking his ankle. 'Anyway, my little German pumpernickel ... what bloomin' surprise' ave ya got fer me?'

'Orders have just come through for number twenty-five 'service release group'. Your name is on it.'

He could hardly believe his ears.

It was the best Christmas present, ever!

At the prospect of his early release, Ron went to say goodbye to an old friend. As he wandered around the foreign worker's compound, the snow started falling heavy. Tarps were stretched over each carrier, making it hard to find Betsy. For some obscure reason they had also whitewashed out the unit badges and vehicle numbers. Weaving his way between carriers, lifting each tarp, he looked for the damage done to her rear when Lance Corporal Davis and Rifleman Harris were killed. It was not until the last row he found her parked against one of the foreign worker's huts, alone and bereft. He looked for something to clear the snow so he could see her one last time, in all her glory. She had been his constant companion for four years, and it felt like she was part of him. He found a bass broom in the hut, leaning against a line of disgustingly filthy urinals. The cheerless hut stank of human bodies, shit and piss. There was also an underlying hint of disinfectant, but not strong enough to wash away the aura that would resonate for years to come. Down both sides of the hut were deep shelves, three high with a ladder nailed to the top shelf every few yards. He instinctively knew this was where the workers had slept and died. He shivered at the thought and swore he could hear voices at the far end of the hut ... or was it his mind playing tricks?

As he swept away the snow, he breathed in the sweet, crisp air. Having untied the tarp, he dragged it out of the way. She looked tired and shabby, with metalwork rusting, where once she was green and virginal, like the day Captain Jamieson showed him his new carrier for the first time. He saw a small dent where the bullet meant for Ginger had slammed into her side. Climbing aboard, he wondered how many times he had settled down in the old girl? Hundreds, maybe thousands? He took his old seat, lifted the battery box cover, and saw a half carton of mouldy cigarettes. The memories broke over him like surf on a beach. The time he nearly got killed by a strand of wire running along the top of a hedge, Joe bombing down the Pickering to Kingsthorpe Road, Monty standing on Betsy to address the troops, and when they touched French soil for the first time. *I should write it all down*, he thought, *to remember each thing as clear as it is today*. In the years to come, the edge would be taken off his memory, making it hard to recall the small but essential details of his war. Such as where they were when Second Lieutenant Phillips first sat in Betsy, with his regular supply of cigarettes. His tobacconist, true to his word sent a carton every other week, without fail. Mr Phillips rarely partook, favouring his battered old pipe. Liking the rebellious youngster, they called him Pip. They never referred to him as Cloddy. It seemed like tempting fate after Mr Lyle's death.

He went to the toolbox, thinking of Tommy Danks and his little friend Sidney, thrilled with their tea and chocolate. It seemed so long ago, but, at the same time, like it was only yesterday. He opened the box and found a pack of iron rations, half a dozen eggs and a bar of Fruit and Nut, all encased in a block of ice.

He replaced the tarp, patted her one last time and wiped tears from his eyes, leaving the old girl to her uncertain future. 'Thanks, Bets,' was all he could say.

Ron reported to Battalion HQ for his release papers and a thorough going over by the medical officer, which he passed A1.

The bad weather held up all transport for ten days, forcing everyone to stay glued to the sky, hopeful of a smudge of blue to burn away the grey-leaden clouds. On the last day of January, things improved, and his time for departure finally came.

Ron and Joe Hicks were carried in army blankets to the transport line, where a fleet of Bedford's waited to take them to Kiel railway station.

They passed from friend to friend, saying their goodbyes.

'Drop us a line, Deak,' Sharpy said, slapping him on the back. 'And don't forget us.'

'Sure, Joe ... An' first thing ya bloomin' do when ya ger 'ome,' he said earnestly,' is give yer ole man a hug. Because 'e ain't always gonna be around. Make yer peace with 'im. Life's too short for that. We should know ...'

Sharpy sighed as Ron's words struck home. He was just about holding himself together. When he was alone – and how he was dreading the prospect – he would have a good old blub.

'Tarrah fer now, Ginge,' Ron said, pumping his hand. Ginger cuffed his eyes and walked away, too overcome.

Charlie was next. 'Ya load o' wimps! Yer goin' soft in yer chuffin' old age. We'll all be sharin' a pint in bloomin' boozer wivvin a couple o' months,' he chirped. 'Mister Phillips' – he winked at him – 'has everyone's address an' will send us each a list. So, stop yer blubberin' an' let this lad ger 'ome to 'is Ma an' sweet'art. An' good luck ta you, Ron. Yuv bin a good mate,' he finally added, sniffling. ... 'I'll tell ya one thing though, this chuffin' place'll be death o' me. I'm sure I've gotta cold comin'.'

They all laughed.

Ron shook hands with the rest, dreading not having them around, thinking of those he could not say goodbye to. His mates who would never grow old and would always be with him in the years to come, a constant reminder of the treasured friendships they had shared so briefly. As they gathered around him, he felt a lump in his throat, recalling all that had happened in the last five years. He smiled, tears welling in his eyes, looking from one to another, trying to express his innermost feelings to those whom he may never see again. His thoughts were all over the place: happy to be going home, sad to be leaving his friends, angry at all the waste and furious that they had robbed him of five years of his life. In the years to come, when worldly-wise and long in the tooth, he would realise these lost years were, in fact, the most important of his life. And what a five years' they were!

He was finding it hard to break free, being held by an invisible thread attached to his heart. Perhaps he would never be free, tied to the past forever? In truth, he was sad it was over. He and others gave so much for the cause – a cause that proved just.

Three senior officers, and Mr Phillips, giving the other ranks time to say their goodbyes, joined the lively crowd: Lieutenant Colonel Jonathon Courtney, CO of the soon to be disbanded 5th Battalion, The Rifle Regiment, Major Mainley and Company Sergeant Major Dawson.

The colonel, wearing the grubby mackintosh that marked him out as K Company's Commander, chided the departing rifleman. Waving his swagger stick like a conductor of a symphony orchestra, laughing and joking, he seemed reluctant to let them go. They were part of his family, and he felt honour bound to look after them, as they had looked after him. Shortly they would not be subject to his commands, and he too within a matter of months would be free to take up his former life. He stopped and chatted with each of the soon to be civilians, talking about home, work and family.

'Well, Deakin,' he said, shaking his hand, 'you'll soon be home.'

'Yes, Sir.'

'What are you planning to do?'

'I'm gonna be a brickie,' he said, carrying on with the pretence. Fall at this hurdle, and he might never go home.

'Well, there's plenty of building to do, in more ways than one. That's for sure. You won't be short of work.' He smiled. After a brief pause, he added, 'Slept with any officers lately?'

'What do ya mean, Sir?'

'Exactly what I said ... "slept with any officers lately?"'

He grinned. 'How did ya know, Sir?'

'You snore like a bull elephant on heat.'

'But I don't snore.'

'Believe me, Rifleman Deakin, your snore is enough to wake ... And that's the last order I'll give you.'

'You should have chucked me out, Sir.'

You were sleeping so peacefully. I thought, in the months ahead, you wouldn't get too much of that.'

'Did anyone else know?'

'Oh, yes, the whole battalion knew. Everyone knew about Rifleman Deakin sleeping with officers. It was talk of the mess for months. Took our minds off ...'

They both laughed, remembering the moment like it was yesterday.

Ron said his farewells and climbed aboard. As soon as he took his seat beside Joe Hicks, the Bedford's sprang into life. With a heartfelt tug, tears started rolling down his cheeks. There was no shame in crying because most were likewise stricken. He turned and looked at his yowling mates as the convoy drove over the moat and then made its way along the lakeside. He would miss his platoon, his army family, the little band of crazy, beloved guys.

*

After a back-jarring drive, they finally arrived at the transit camp a couple of miles from Kiel. As soon as they debarked, they were marched to the mess for stew and suet dumplings and rock-hard jam tart with watery custard slopping all over the tray. Once their meal was out of the way, they were given a quick travel update by an acne-faced second lieutenant, barely out of short trousers. He then showed them to a freezing billet with no palliasses, pillows or blankets. Ron lay on the bare springs, fully clothed, waiting for the morning train. During the long, bleak night, only the happy thought of being homeward bound kept his freezing spirits up.

He started the new day with a piping hot bath, a scalding mug of strong, sweet tea, two helpings of bangers and mash and Heinz baked beans with lashings of HP sauce. Later they trooped on to the platform and were crammed into half a dozen clapped-out German carriages with no corridor and a bucket in each compartment. They were so tightly packed that to get to a trouser pocket, they had to stand and then jemmy themselves down again.

The train journey was long and tiring. But there were plenty of stops for rations and the chance to stretch their legs and empty the overflowing bucket. They travelled over the northern plains of Germany, through Minden and Munster. There was a brief stop at Dortmund for a proper meal, then onto Dusseldorf and ultimately Brussels. They were billeted at the same hotel that Ron had stayed at with Bill Ritchie, another pal who would never grow old.

At length, they reached the last transit camp at Tournai, just two hours from Calais. They were put up in a seedy hotel, given some Belgian francs and told to find somewhere to eat. A pleasant evening was had, eating, drinking and browsing the shops that had reopened just before Christmas. As they strolled around, they had to decline the tempting offers of local, good-time girls, out to make their last night on the continent a thrilling and memorable experience. Though maybe unforgettable for the wrong reason.

The crossing from Calais to Dover was a far more relaxed affair than the overcrowded troopship eighteen months before. A slow train took them to St Pancras Station, where each soon-to-be-civilian was told to make his way to the Army Demob Centre at Olympia. No one was going to hang around, especially with the promise of money in their pocket and the chance of swapping army serge for a fine-worsted suit. For many, this would be the first time they had worn civilian clothes since being called up.

He joined the queue, awaiting his turn. It was nearly six years since he had gone through this process, from civvy to soldier. He chuckled to himself, thinking the whole thing had been a terrible mistake and the army was only just making amends for their error.

With the weather so chilly he was asked by the corporal if he wanted to keep his greatcoat. He shook his head and started to get undressed. In no hurry, he carefully placed his beret, greatcoat, webbing belt, battledress blouse, gaiters, trousers, braces, best angora shirt, socks and boots on the counter. These were the only things he could bring with him, except for his small valise with toiletries, pyjamas, a change of underwear and a few personal effects and keepsakes. The corporal asked if he wanted to keep something as a reminder of his time in the army. Ron picked up his beret and placed it back on his head. A Montague Burtons tailor then started running a tape measure over him.

He now found himself in the famous exhibition hall, laid out with seemingly enough civilian clothes to equip the entire British Army. Still wearing his beret, he was fitted out with a double-breasted suit, two shirts, a tie, two pairs of socks, raincoat, leather gloves, shoes and a brown felt fedora. Any other items were placed in a stout cardboard box, along with his AB64 part one and demob papers. It was like a production line. Soldiers entered through the back door and civilians left by the front on to Kensington High Street, shaking hands with two NCOs manning the entrance like commissionaires at the Odeon Leicester Square.

Ron crossed the road and queued outside the Prudential Assurance building. He received eight weeks 'demobilisation and leave pay' and ration allowance for eight weeks at three shillings a day. In total, they gave him thirty pounds. They also told him that a gratuity of sixpence a day for 'time in service' would shortly follow from the regimental paymaster. This would amount to a further fifty pounds. Eighty pounds in all, a goodly sum.

Not wanting to part company with the army quite yet he took them up on their offer of a meal at the hotel next door. A mild-mannered girl brought him a three-course meal with beer or cider. Looking around the packed dining room, he chuckled to himself. Each ex-soldier was wearing the self-same navy pinstriped suit, making them look like Chicago mobsters at a national convention. He had only swapped one uniform for another.

The man next to him kept wittering about his trousers being unfriendly. When asked what he was blathering about, he said they were keeping their distance from his feet.

Within an hour he was standing outside 144, looking up at the terraced house, sweeter than he ever remembered it. The drizzle had turned to heavy snow, with a brisk breeze swishing and swirling the flakes about him. Chilled to the bone, he pulled up the collar of his raincoat and hunched his shoulders. Apprehensive, Ron paused, waiting for what, he didn't know, shrouded by the unlit street like a stranger.

Someone pulled back the curtain from over the door, and a welcoming arc of light flooded across the pavement and half the road. The door was opened by Ron's mother. She stared at him, hardly daring to speak.

He said something, but his words were whisked away by the wind.

Holding her arms out, like only a mother can, he stepped into the hall and warmly embraced her. She spoke, but her words were for him alone.

Before following her down the narrow hall, he closed the door and drew the curtain, turning the street into a dark, hostile place.

He felt safe once more, truly safe, the first time in years.

THE END

Editor's Notes

My father returned home on 16th January 1946, where he once more took up his job as a shop manager at Foster Brothers Clothing Company Limited. Being thirty-two at the time and married with a four-year-old daughter he would have been entitled to early release, rather than wait for an 'Age and Service Release Group' to come around. Over the next thirty-three years, he managed several shops in and around Birmingham. When he retired in 1979, he set about recording his wartime experiences in this novel.

Being the eldest of thirteen, he was already married to my Mum, Elizabeth (Maud), when he was called up. She is referred to in his story as Betty, a petite auburn-haired girl with shapely legs, orphaned and working in a shoe shop. Perfect in every detail. Also, the account of them meeting did happen the way it's told in 'Chapter Ten – Jonnie Doughboy'. I do so hope Ron's dalliances with Mavis and Maggie were a figment of his imagination to spice up the story. Though, he did tell me, once it was finished, not to let Mum read it. So, who knows what was fact and what was fiction? If only I had read his story while he was alive. I could have asked him so many questions that remain unanswered.

By February 1941 he was a corporal, but due to an altercation with an officer he was demoted to Rifleman. This is referred to in 'Chapter Ten – Johnny Doughboy', when Ron's platoon are on an exercise, and the officer in charge cossets himself away in a Bren carrier with all the blankets. This officer was sadly killed a few weeks before the end of the war. He wrote about this in 'Chapter 23 – Victory Farm', when a Teller mine kills Lieutenant Lyle. He wrote kindly of this officer, showing him as a decent sort. So, I assume my father held him in high regard, even though he had been responsible for his demotion. A few weeks before D-Day they offered him his tapes back, but he turned them down. Moreover, during his initial training he was put forward for officer training but declined, saying he preferred to remain part of the 'rank and file'.

When I first read his story, I couldn't get over the many references to food. It must have been an important part of a soldier's life, and my father was no exception. I was instantly whisked back to our many holidays, when my wife and I would sit in my parent's hotel room, having a pre-dinner whisky and going through the menu. He always liked to know what he was going to eat before sitting down at the table. Old habits die hard, and this mindset must have been fostered during his army service.

One thing that did confuse me a little, was the way he named Ron's place of training as Wilchester and called his regiment The Rifle Regiment, when (in dad's case) it was Winchester and The Rifle Brigade. I toyed with changing it back but chose to leave well alone, because first and foremost it is his story. He also changed some place names, more so at the start. I've also left those as they are. However, he got into the habit of naming the actual places: Thetford, Freckenham and Aldershot. During the campaign itself, he swapped letters around to disguise the town or village, but it was obvious what the places were. So, I unravelled them to make the battles more factual. While editing his manuscript, I came across a few tantalising clues as to the possible locations where my father served during his service life. I took the liberty of including the actual places: Netheravon, Lowestoft, Bridlington and Pickering.

His story roughly follows the progress of the 8th Battalion The Rifle Brigade from its mobilisation in 1940 to its eventual disbandment in March 1946.

Dad was wounded in the upper right arm at Presles on 3rd August 1944 and was not fit for active service until later that year. This photograph, taken at Lübeck, had written on the back:

'LUBECK 3 or 4 days before the end of
the war, with a couple of mates. Yours
truly towering above the others.'

I have lived with this photograph for most of my life, but it was
only when tidying it up for this book that I noticed each has a
revolver, just like Chicago mobsters showing off their Tommy guns.
My father is holding a Mauser 7.65mm, which he referred to in
'Chapter 23 – Victory Farm', and 'Chapter 24 – Peacetime
Soldiering'.
Jack's injury at Monte Cassino in 'Chapter 18 – The Ultimate Test' is
my father's account of what happened to him, even down to my
grandmother getting a telegram, saying her son had been lost at sea,
presumed drowned. My father asked that any bad news should go to
his Mother. To help fill in the gaps for the months that he was out of

the war, he referred to this booklet, sprinkling it with his own experiences from early and later periods during his war:

Published in January 1946 there is an Editor's Note, but no Author's name. The Foreword is by A.P. Rowan (Major), who, I assume, was E Company's last CO before they disbanded the 8th Battalion in March 1946.

My father spent many hours typing up his story, and I felt it was something that needed saving for future generations. I have stayed true to his work and his memory and have kept all his original storyline. I have taken one or two liberties (not being there myself), and, as a result, it may not be 100% accurate, historically, but it's as near as 'damn it' is too swearing.

For me, this has been a labour of love, and I have felt my father's guiding hand as I have lovingly worked through his manuscript. It was a task that I have taken immense pleasure from, living his war through his eyes.

His account will live on!

Paul Talbot

I hope you enjoyed reading my dad's book. I would be grateful if you would consider leaving me a review on Amazon.com or/and Amazon.co.uk with a few words on what you thought of his story.

Thank you, Paul.

Cockney Rhyming slang and East End dialect explained

Rhyming slang is a high-spirited linguistic form that tends to flourish in confident, outgoing communities, such as the East End of London. It is a way of obscuring the meaning of what is being said from outsiders and is furthermore a way of increasing bonding of the users during times of stress or exuberance. The way rhyming slang works tends to exclude those not 'in the know' (including not just the listener, but the reader as well). The substitution of one word for another often relies on reference to a key phrase or places, which both parties are familiar with. For example, to get from 'Barnet Fair' to 'hair', one must first be aware that Barnet is a London borough and holds an annual horse fair dating back hundreds of years.

It seems a bit nonsensical to use two words when one will do, but rhyming slang, or none rhyming, has been around for a long time, and not just in the East End of London, but also places like Glasgow, Liverpool, Dublin etc., as well as all over the world. Used excessively in creative writing it can be frustrating for the reader, so it has been used sparingly in this novel. It is reserved exclusively for banter (look that one up) between East Enders. Dad dedicated his book to the people of London and wanted to bring alive the humour and spirit of the East End. It would hardly make sense writing a book about Londoners and not using the language of the people. If you find the use of it grates and takes something away from the story, I apologise, but it was my father's wish to include it, along with the dialect, and I have stayed true to his wishes.

airs and grace/s   – for –   Face/s
almond rocks   – for –   Socks
ball of chalk   – for –   Talk

Barnet Fair – for – Hair
bees and honey – for – Money
Billy and Dick – for – Sick
bird lime – for – Time
boat race – for – Face
brown bread – for – Dead
Butcher's hook – for – Look
China plate – for – Mate
daisy roots – for – Boots
dicky dirt – for – Shirt
Donald Duck – for – Luck/Fuck
fillet of cod – for – Sod
George Raft – for – Draft
golden dove – for – Love
Gypsy kiss (Gyppo) – for – Piss
Gypsy Nell – for – Hell
Hampton Wick – for – Prick
Kate Karney – for – Army
Khyber Pass – for – Arse
kidney punch – for – Lunch
mince pies – for – Eyes
nickel and dime – for – Time
oily rag – for – Fag
pen and ink – for – Stink
pig's ear – for – Beer
plates of meat – for – Feet
rabbit and pork – for – Talk
raspberry tart – for – Fart
Rosie Lee – for – Tea
Rory O'More – for – Floor
Rob Roy – for – Boy
septic tank – for – Yank
skyrocket – for – Pocket
Sidney – for – Kidney

sorry and sad	– for –	Bad
sugar and spice	– for –	Nice
thumb sucking	– for –	Fucking
toby jug	– for –	Mug
tomtit	– for –	Shit
trouble and strife	– for –	Wife
thrupenny bit	– for –	Tit
turtle dove	– for –	Love
Uncle Ned	– for –	Head
whistle and flute	– for –	suit

What follows is my interpretation of an East End dialect, from listening to recordings of East Enders and researching the subject. It is not a definitive list of rules and is how I interpret the accent. In some cases, I have made it fit my rules, for the reasons explained below, and in advance, I apologise to the reader if this has caused confusion or offence in any way. If by any chance I have got something wrong, at least I have shown consistency in my error and hope the reader will forgive me.

- Sometimes omits 'the' before a noun.
- Often omits 'h' at the beginning of words,
- Often omits 'g' at the end of words and sometimes within a word.
- 'My' sometimes sounds like M'. Example: 'It weren't my car but m' Dads.' This would be confusing, so I have used 'me' instead of 'my'.
- 'Was' sometimes sounds like 'w'. Example: 'John w' me mate, and I w' 'is.' This would be confusing, so I have turned 'w'' into 'were'.
- Also, 'th' is often omitted in words. Example: bovver for bother, brovver for brother, annovver for another, fink for think etc.
- Sometimes confuses 'were' and 'was'.

Other words included

aahhht – for – out

aahhr – for – our

abahhht – for – about

agin – for – again

ain't – for – have not or haven't

bin – for – been

brahn – for – brown

daan't – for – do not or don't

fer – for – for

Gaud – for – God

ger – for – get

gerra/getta – for – get a

gerrin – for – getting

gertcher – for – get you

gotta – for – got to

gonna – for – going to

loike – for – like

nah – for – no

nuff – for – enough

orl – for – all

orf – for – off

ta – for – to

wanna – for – want to

wif – for – with

wiv – for – we have or we've

wot – for – what

wotch – for – watch

ya – for – you

yer – for – your

ya're – for – you are or you're

yud – for – you'd

yuv – for – you've

Some character's East End dialect is more pronounced than others. Charlie, Ernie, Alfie and Ossie adopt most of the above, with Ron and other Londoners to a lesser degree.

Army terms, jargon, slang, and London colloquialisms

A.D.S. — Advanced Dressing Stations are generally staffed by medical officers, medical NCOs, orderlies and stretcher bearers for the evacuation and immediate treatment of battlefield casualties. Traditionally the first step in the evacuation process for wounded soldiers, who are assessed and then either returned to unit after treatment or transferred to a Casualty Clearing Station. In WW1, A.D.S posts were generally the closest medical aid to the front, and many C.W.G.C. cemeteries are located close to where an A.D.S was.

A.F.V. — Armoured Fighting Vehicle.

A.P. — Armour Piercing shell.

A.R.P. — Air Raid Precaution warden.

A.W.O.L. — Absent Without Leave.

A.B.64 *(part one)* — Personal records, description, next of kin details, training records, kit issue etc. Was always carried in the top left-hand pocket of a soldier's battledress blouse. (AB = Army Booklet)

A.B.64 *(part two)* — Record of payments and credits. Always kept with A.B.64 Part One.

Ablutions — Washhouse.

Alakefic — Arabic word used to express equal preference for several options.

Allies — Countries that fought in the Second World War against the Axis forces. First referred to as the United Nations (U.N.) by President Roosevelt in January 1942 and ratified on 24th October 1945.

Army Parlance — Language used by a soldier that can often be full of jargon and not readily intelligible to non-military personnel.

Arsenal — Place for storing weapons and ammunition in huge quantities, and a place where ammunition is manufactured.

Atlantic Wall *(the)* — An extensive system of coastal defences built by Nazi Germany between 1942 and 1944 along the coast of continental Europe and Scandinavia.

Axis Forces — Countries that fought in the Second World War against Allied forces. Known also as the Axis powers.

B.E.F. — British Expeditionary Force. Part of the British Army in Western Europe from 1939 to 1940. Commanded by General Lord Gort. The first troops who fought in France in 1914 were also called the B.E.F.

Bags — Trousers.

Banger — Sausage.

Bahnhof — German for railway station.

Bakelite — One of the first plastics (invented in 1907 by a Belgian-American chemist, Leo Baekeland) made from synthetic components. Bakelite was used for its heat-resistant properties in electrical insulators, radio and telephone casings and such diverse products as kitchenware, jewellery, pipe stems, children's toys, and firearms.

Barmpot — North English term for an idiot or foolish person.

Barracks — Building or group of buildings used to house military personnel.

Bascule Bridge — Bascule bridges are the most common type of movable span (i.e. Tower Bridge, London) because they open quickly and require relatively little energy to operate while providing the possibility for unlimited vertical clearance for marine traffic.

Battalion — Normally made up of four or five companies with 700-800 men. Commanded by a Lieutenant Colonel.

Bauernführer — German farmer in charge of a cooperative farm.

Bed down — Having a nap or sleep.

Bed pack – Blankets with sheets in the centre, folded into a pack that sits at the head of the bed, with a pillow on top and kit displayed around it.

Bengal match – Much like a firework sparkler but was classified as matches rather than fireworks. The head was larger than a normal match and when ignited burnt bright green or red for about 15 seconds, before turning into a normal flame.

Biddy – Cheap red wine.

Billet – Place where a soldier lives, hut or tent.

Bint — Derogatory term for a female.

Birdbrain — Silly or stupid person.

Bivvy/Bivvies — Tent/Tents.

Blanco — Staining fluid to rub into webbing *(white or khaki)*.

Blathering — To talk long-windedly without making much sense.

Blighty — Informal term for Britain, used by soldiers in the First and Second World Wars. Also, a wound *(a Blighty)* that would get a soldier repatriated back home.

Blind *(a)* — A term given to a shell or grenade that fails to go off.

Blooming — Used to express annoyance or for emphasis.

Bluejackets — Royal Navy sailors.

Bob — One shilling – twelve pence.

Bobagee — Army cook.

Boche — German person, especially a soldier in World War One or World War Two.

Bodger — Female/girl.

Bomb happy — Scared of explosions through long-term exposure.

Bondook — Rifle or best friend.

Bottle *(got the)* — Having grit or guts.

Brahmer — Excellent or perfect.

Brass monkey — Cold enough the freeze the balls off a brass monkey.

Bren carrier — Lightly armoured personnel carrier, armed with a light or medium machine gun. Normally has a crew of three or four. The Bren-gun Carrier, as it was sometimes called, came into being in 1934 and was originally designed to carry two Bren guns.

Brigade — A brigade contains four or five battalion-sized units, around 4,000 to 5,000 personnel, and is commanded by a Brigadier General.

Bubble — Shake with anger at something.

Buckshee/s — Free gratis or plentiful.

Buffalos — Amphibious assault vehicles.

Bully — Corned beef.

Bung — Cheese.

Burgoo — Porridge.

Button it — Keep quiet.

C.C.S. — Casualty Clearing Station. A military medical facility that is used to treat wounded soldiers who will not be immediately returning to duty. Usually located beyond the range of enemy artillery and often close to transportation facilities for movement to a rehabilitation/recovery centre or for repatriation home.

C.O. — Commanding Officer.

C.S.M. — Company Sergeant Major.

C.W.G.C. — Commonwealth War Graves Commission. The Commission was founded by Major General Sir Fabian Arthur Goulstone Ware K.C.V.O., K.B.E., C.B., C.M.G., and became constituted through Royal Charter in 1917.

C.W.L. — The Catholic Women's League (CWL) is a Roman Catholic lay organisation founded by Margaret Fletcher aimed at women in England and Wales.

Cat in hells chance — Has no chance of achieving something.

Cadge/Cadging — Borrowing something.

Cakehole — Mouth.

Cha — Tea.

Charabanc — Early form of single-decker bus, used typically for pleasure trips.

Charlie *(turning)* — Getting scarred, losing one's nerve or bottle.

Chassis — Body.

Chatty — Feeling dirty, or worse, lousy with lice or fleas.

Cheesed off — Feeling annoyed, bored, or frustrated with something or somebody.

Chit/Chitty — A receipt or ticket to be exchanged for something.

Chuffing — Used for emphasis or as a mild expletive.

Churchill — British infantry tank with 75mm gun. A crew of five (Commander, gunner, loader/radio operator, driver, front gunner).

Clap *(the/dose of)* — Army slang to describe a dose of Venereal Disease.

Clock/Clocked — To see or have seen someone or something.

Clod — Stupid or dull person.

Cloddy — Officer.

Cockney — The name given to a Londoner who was born within three miles (the sound) of St Mary-le-Bow – 'Bow Bells'.

Comet — British cruiser tank with 77mm gun. A crew of five (Commander, gunner, loader/radio operator, driver, front gunner).

Company — Normally made up of four or five platoons with 120-150 men. Commanded by a Major.

Compo — Tea, sugar and powdered milk. All mixed together ready for quick preparation.

Comtesse — French for Countess.

Coppers — Coins. Farthing, half pennies, penny and thrupenny bit.

Cor blimey — Is an exclamation of surprise and is a euphemism (specifically a minced oath) derived from 'God blind me'. First used in the 1880s.

Corps — A field fighting corps is a formation of two or more divisions, potentially 50,000 personnel, or more, and commanded by a Lieutenant General.

Costermonger — A street seller of fruit and vegetables.

Counter-ranged — Ranges and degrees recorded of your current position from a possible withdrawal location, in case the position needs to be evacuated, allowing artillery to shell the new occupants.

Cowson — English term for 'son of a bitch'.

Crabs — Flail tank for clearing mines.

Craven Cottage — A football stadium located in Fulham, London. It has been the home ground of Fulham Football Club since 1896.

Credits — Pay outstanding. Money held back for payment to the soldier on demobilisation or paid to next of kin in the case of death.

Crocs — Flamethrower tanks.

Crotch Critters — Slang for a sexually transmitted virus, bacterium or other microorganisms, particularly pubic lice.

Cromwell — British cruiser tank with 75mm gun. A crew of five (Commander, gunner, loader/radio operator, driver, front gunner).

Crown and Anchor — Game that originated in the 18th century. Still a popular game in the Channel Islands and Bermuda but is strictly controlled in the forces and may be played, legally, with an officer controlling the game. Played with dice and is like roulette.

Cruiser — The cruiser tank was an inter-war British tank. Designed to function as an armoured/mechanized cavalry unit with a two-pounder gun and 7.9mm machine gun.

D.D.'s — Light swimming tanks nicknamed Donald Duck's.

D.U.K.W. or Duck — Amphibious vehicle.

Dag or dagging — Cleaning with spit and polish.

Datum line — A line to which dimensions are taken from.

Denim Fatigue — Khaki clothing used in battle conditions or when carrying out fatigues.

Defaulters — Those who have misbehaved or broken army rules and are given fatigues.

Deutsches Jungvolk — A separate wing of the Hitler Youth for boys aged 10 to 14. Through a program of outdoor activities, parades and sports, it was meant to indoctrinate its young members in Nazi ideology. Membership became compulsory for eligible boys in 1939. By the end of World War II, some had become child soldiers. In 1945 after the end of the war the *Deutsches Jungvolk* and its parent organisation the Hitler Youth ceased to exist.

Diddycoy — People who live like Gypsies but are not Romany's.

Digs — Someone's lodgings or a place where they live temporally.

Dipstick — Stupid or inept person.

Division — A division is a formation of three or four brigades of around twenty thousand personnel, commanded by a Major General.

Dixie — Large food trays from which several meals are served.

Dobie/Dobieing — Wash/washing of clothing. A naval term for a wash. It is generally used with other words such as Dobie-dust or Dobie-powder meaning washing powder.

Dog end — Nub of a cigarette, cast away and squashed on the floor.

Dog tags — An informal term for the identification tag worn by military personnel. Called 'dog tags' because of their resemblance to animal registration tags. Usually has name, service number, blood group and religion.

Dollop — Lump or blob of some substance: i.e. dollop of mud, stupid dollop *(person)*.

Double — Run twice as fast as you march.

Draft — Troops going overseas.

Ernest Bevan — Started conscription for young men to work in coal mines during WW2. British statesman, trade union leader, and Labour politician.

Estaminet — French for small café, selling tobacco, alcoholic drinks and snacks.

F.S.M.O. — Full-Service Marching Order.

Falaise Gap — This is the Battle of the Falaise Gap, after the corridor which the Germans sought to maintain to allow their escape from South West France. Sometimes referred to as the Chambois Pocket, the Falaise-Chambois Pocket, the Argentan–Falaise Pocket or the Trun–Chambois **Gap**.

Farrier — Specialist in equine hoof care, including the trimming and balancing of horse's hooves and the fitting of horseshoes.

Farthing — One-quarter of a penny.

Fatigues — Jobs *(sometimes quite dirty and arduous)* given out to defaulters by provost staff or platoon NCO.

Feldwebel — German equivalent to sergeant.

Flicks/fleapit — Picture house/cinema.

Fizzer — Being put on a charge.

Forage cap — A small cap worn on the right side of the head. It's called a 'cheese cutter' in the Army and a 'chip bag' in the R.A.F.

Free from infection check — Inspection of troops to check if any have Venereal Disease or any other transmittable diseases, ready for movement onwards.

Frigging hell — Express anger, annoyance, contempt or surprise.

Full kit inspection — Checking the inventory of what a soldier has against their AB64 *(part one)* kit issue record.

Funnies *(the)* — 'Hobart's Funnies' were several unusually modified tanks operated during the Second World War by the 79th Armoured Division of the British Army, or by specialists from the Royal Engineers. The 79th was formed by Major General Percy Hobart.

G.I. — General Issue. The term given to United States troops.

Gaiters — Khaki webbing strapping around the ankles.

Gams — Legs *(usually used for female legs)*.

Gander — Look at something.

Gefreiter — German equivalent to lance corporal.

Gen — Information.

Generalarzt — The lowest general rank of the Joint Medical Service or the military medical area of the *Bundeswehr*.

Generalfeldmarschall — German equivalent to Field Marshall.

Gestapo — Secret State Police of Nazi Germany. Headed by Heinrich Himmler.

Ground Action — The order given to go to battle stations and to prepare to defend or to attack.

Glasshouse — The use of the word Glasshouse originated at the military prison in Aldershot, which had a glazed roof.

Gobshite — Stupid, foolish, or incompetent person.

Grog — Rum or any spirit

Guinea — One-pound sterling and one shilling.

Guardees — A informal term for Guardsman.

Gunfire — Cup of tea.

Gunwales *(packed to)* — The upper edge of a ship's uppermost side.

H.E. — High Explosive shell.

Hack driver — U.S. taxi driver. From the word, Hackney cab driver *(London)*.

Harbour — A besieging army's camp *(also known as a leager)*.

Half a Crown — Two shillings and sixpence. Also, known as a tosheroon. A crown was five shillings.

Half a Dollar — Two shillings and sixpence. During WWII five shillings was worth one U.S. dollar.

Hanover *(bleeding)* — Shock or surprise at something.

Harry Champion — Music hall entertainer who made the song *Any Old Iron* famous.

Hauptfeldwebel — German equivalent to sergeant major.

Howitzer — Artillery piece that is characterised by a relatively short barrel. Uses comparatively small propellant charges to propel projectiles over relatively high trajectories with a steep angle of decent.

Heath Robinson — William Heath Robinson (1872-1944) was an English cartoonist and illustrator best known for drawings of ridiculously complicated machines for achieving simple tasks.

Hussif — A variant of the term housewife. Usually given to items that are associated with housewife duties, such a sewing kit.

Iron Rations — Blocks of concentrated food that can be grated and boiled up to provide a high-energy meal.

Irons *(eating)* — Knife, fork and spoon.

Jankers — Term for being confined to barracks, and additional fatigues.

Jerry — A term that was first coined in 1916 to describe German soldiers. Jerry is the British slang for a chamber pot, and the German helmet that came into being in 1916 looked like one.

J'attendrai — French translated into English as 'I will wait'. This song in France, Belgium and Holland was their equivalent of Vera

Lynn's *We'll Meet Again*. During the occupation, the song became immensely popular and was outlawed by the occupying forces.

Johnny Doughboy — Doughboy was an informal term for a member of the United States Army or Marine Corps.

Johnnycake — North American unleavened bread made from maize flour and baked or fried on a griddle.

Jugs — Slang for female breasts.

K-ration — Combat rations supplied to the U.S. troops.

Kapitän zur See — German for 'Captain at sea'. The naval rank of someone commanding a ship-of-the-line or capital ship.

Khazi — Slang for lavatory/toilet.

Kings Regulations — A collection of rules and regulations in use within the British Armed Forces.

Knocking shop — A brothel.

Knocker-upper — A knocker-upper's job was to rouse sleeping people, so they could get to work on time, and was still happening as late as the beginning of the 1950s. They would tap on bedroom windows with a long pole to wake people up.

Kommodore — The German equivalent of a navy Commodore – equivalent to Colonel in the army and Group Captain in the RAF.

Konteradmiral — German equivalent to rear-admiral.

Kriegsmarine — Navy of Nazi Germany from 1935 to 1945.

Kybosh — An end to something, dispose of decisively.

Latrines — Communal lavatories/toilets.

Leager — A unit's temporary camp during an offensive. Taken from the Afrikaan word *laager*: for a defensive encampment encircled by armoured vehicles and wagons. In Dutch/German called a *leger*. *(also known as a harbour)*.

Leave of Absence — Official permission to be absent from duty for a given period.

Liberty Ship — A class of cargo ship built in the United States during WW2.

Light Aid Detachment Platoon — A unit for recovering vehicles and repairing them.

Loftus Road — A football stadium in Shepherd's Bush, London, which is home to Queens Park Rangers from 1917.

Lolly — Money.

Lousy as cuckoos — An idiom to describe something that is crawling with fleas or lice.

Low Countries — The European Low Countries are the coastal regions bounded by the North Sea and the English Channel, i.e. Netherlands, Belgium and North/West France. Referred to as the Low Countries because of their low position above sea level.

Loyd — Fully tracked British armoured personnel carrier. Came into to service in 1939 and went out of commission in early 1960s. In design, like a Bren carrier.

Luftwaffe — Aerial warfare branch of Germany during WW2.

M.O. — Medical Officer.

M.P. — Military Police.

Malarkey — Meaningless talk – nonsense.

Mashed *(tea)* — Leaving the tea to brew for a long time.

Meuse/Maas *(River)* — In France and Belgium, it is called the Meuse, while in the Netherlands it's referred to as the Mass.

Moaning Minnies — German *Nebelwerfers*, a multi-barrelled rocket launcher which rained down terror on Allied troops with a horrible screaming noise.

Mulberry — The mobile harbour that was towed to Normandy from England to help with the unloading of equipment and supplies. Parts of it remain on the Normandy coast.

Mullock — Rubbish, refuse or something dirty.

Muster — Assemble (troops), especially for inspection or in preparation for action.

N.A.A.F.I./naafi — Navy, Army and Air Force Institute shop/canteen.

N.C.O. — None Commissioned Officer.

Napper — Head.

Nellie Dean — A name inspired by Gertrude Astbury, an early 20th-century music hall singer whose signature song was 'Nellie Dean', later the title of a musical in which she starred.

Nissen *(hut)* — Hut made of prefabricated steel, made from a half-cylindrical skin of corrugated steel. Originally designed during WW1.

Nobby *(nickname)* — Those with the surname Clark/e would sometimes be called Nobby. Clerks (pronounced clark or clerk) in the City of London used to wear Nobby hats, a type of bowler hat.

No bottle — No courage or daring.

No man's land — Land that is unoccupied or is under dispute between armies who leave it alone due to fear or uncertainty.

Nosh/ing — Food/eating.

Oberfeldwebel — German equivalent to sergeant.

Obergerfreiter — German equivalent to corporal.

Oberst — German equivalent Colonel.

Oberstleutnant — German equivalent to Lieutenant Colonel.

O.H.M.S. — On His/Her Majesty's Service.

Old Bill — Fictional character created in 1914–15 by cartoonist Bruce Bairnsfather. Old Bill was depicted as an elderly, pipe-smoking British 'tommy' with a walrus moustache.

Old sweat — A senior soldier with long service, some of it in action.

Other Ranks Mess — Dining hall and social area for all 'other ranks' – corporals and below.

Overlord *(Operation)* — The operational name for the Normandy landings on 6th June 1944.

Oxford Bags — Loose-fitting baggy trousers favoured by members of the University of Oxford.

P.I.A.T. — Projectile Infantry Anti-Tank Gun.

P.T. — Physical Training.

P.T.I. — Physical Training Instructor.

P.X. *(store)* — Referred to as a Post Exchange (PX) in the U.S. Army. Exchanges on Army and Air Force installations are run by the Army and Air Force Exchange Service.

Pace stick — Hinged **stick** used by drill instructors to measure the pace of marching and static soldiers.

Panther — Medium German tank with 75mm gun. A crew of five (driver, radio-operator/hull machine gunner, commander, gunner, loader).

Panzer — The German word for armour.

Pat *(butter)* — A small piece of butter enough for one slice of bread.

Paws — Hands.

People's car — *Volkswagen* is German for 'people's car'.

Peelers — Peelers was the name given to the first police officers. They were named after Sir Robert Peel who introduced them first in Ireland and then in England. They were also known as Bobbies in England.

Pee Wee Herman — North American term for penis.

Pell Mell — Disorderly, headlong haste, in a recklessly hurried manner.

Picket Duty — Picket refers to a soldier or small unit of soldiers maintaining a watch. Origin: 17th century in which a soldier was ordered to do guard duty with a pointed stake. 20th Century (WW1/WW2) they would use a pickaxe handle.

Pillock — A stupid person.

Plain jane — A woman who is regarded as not pretty or good-looking.

Platoon — A troop of thirty or so men. Commanded by either a Second Lieutenant or Lieutenant.

Priest — American self-propelled artillery vehicle, Armed with a 105 mm Howitzer 17 pounder gun. A crew of five (driver, radio-operator/hull machine gunner, commander, gunner, loader).

Provost staff — Regimental Police.

Pukka — Genuine, proper or authentic.

Q.M. *(Q.M.S.)* — Quartermaster *(Quartermaster's Stores)*. Responsible for supplies.

Quicksilver — Moving, acting or occurring with great speed.

Quad — A field artillery tractor (half-track) used by the British and Commonwealth forces during WW2, to tow field artillery pieces, such as the 25-pounder howitzer and anti-tank guns, such as the 17-pounder.

R.A.P. — A Regimental Aid Post advances with the regiment/battalion and are normally staffed by the unit's medical officers, medical NCO, medical orderlies and stretcher bearers, and is for the immediate treatment of battlefield casualties. Traditionally the first step for wounded soldiers, who are assessed and either returned to unit or forwarded onto an A.D.S or C.C.S.

R.E.M.E. — Royal Electrical and Mechanical Engineers.

R.M.P. — The Royal Military Police is the corps of the British Army responsible for the policing of service personnel, and for providing a military police presence both in the UK and while service personnel are deployed overseas on operations and exercises.

R.S.M. — Regimental Sergeant Major.

Rabbiting — Talking at a fast pace.

Rack and Pinion — Steering system of a jeep or lorry.

Ragamuffin — A child who is dressed in rags and is usually dirty and poor.

Ration — One's allowance.

Recce — To oversee or appraise.

Regiment — Made up of three battalions in peacetime with 1800-2000 men. Commanded by a Brigadier General.

Red Flag *('up' from the lead vehicle)* — Prepare to move.

Rocker *(off his)* — Someone who is crazy, silly, nutcase etc.

Rooty — Bread.

Rum Ration — Daily rum ration, or 'tot', consisted of one-eighth of an imperial pint (70 ml) of rum at 95.5% proof. The last rum ration was on 31 July 1970 and was known as Black Tot Day.

Run and Walk — A forced march. Marching for so far then running the same distance. Then alternating between run and march until completed.

S.D. — Service Dress. Uniform or boots of best quality kept for special parades.

Saida Bint — Middle Eastern woman. Derogatory term.

Sam Browne *(belt)* — General Sir Samuel James Browne VC, GCB, KCSI, came up with the idea of wearing a second belt which went over his right shoulder and held the scabbard in just the spot he wanted.

Sarnie/Sarney — A sandwich.

Sawbones — Slang term for a doctor or surgeon.

Scabby — A person, loathsome or despicable.

Scads — North American slang. A large number or quantity.

Schemes — An army slang word for exercises and manoeuvres.

Schutzstaffel or S.S. — A major paramilitary organization under Adolf Hitler and the National Socialist German Workers' Party *(NAZI Party)*.

Scrotum — Testicles.

Scrubber — A promiscuous or vulgar woman.

Sgian-dubh — Gaelic word. A small, single-edged knife worn as part of traditional Scottish Highland dress along with the kilt.

Shakedown — Relaxing or taking it easy.

Shell-like — Has been used to mean a person's ear since the late 19th century – because if the ear looking like a shell.

Sherman — Medium American tank with 75mm gun (17-pounder). A crew of five (commander, gunner, loader, driver, co-driver).

Sherman Firefly — Medium American tank, fitted with a 76mm (17-pounder) anti-tank gun as its main weapon. A crew of 4 (Commander, gunner, loader/radio-operator, driver). Anti-tank gun modification by the British and used primarily British and some commonwealth formation during WW2.

Shilling — Twenty shilling in each pound sterling and twelve pennies in a shilling.

Shiner *(old)* — Person or thing that shines.

Shitehawk — Unsavoury character.

Shot *(the)* — Aldershot, Hampshire.

Shrapnel — Fragment from a shell or change in your pocket.

Shufti — Look or reconnoitre, especially a quick one.

Shufti Cush — Arabic term for the act of sexual intercourse.

Shultz — German private soldier.

Silver — Coins other than copper coins: sixpence. Shilling, Florin, Half a crown and crown.

Skint — Having no money or short of cash.

Slinger — Mug.

Small kit — Term given to PT clothing.

Smoke *(the)* — Term for the city of London.

Spanish archer — Cockney for elbow (El bow)

Speaker's Corner — An area where open-air public speaking is allowed. The original and most notable being on the north-east corner of Hyde Park Corner in London.

Spondulics — Money.

Spotted Dick — Savoury, suety pastry rolls with dried fruit.

Stadtrat — German for Town Council.

Stag — Period of guard duty.

Stone'a crows — Shock or surprise at something.

Stonk — Artillery bombardment.

Stuart — British light tank with 37mm gun. A crew of four (Commander, gunner, driver, assistant driver).

Swaddy/Swaddies — Soldier/s. Similarly referred to as a 'squaddie'.

Swan/Swanning *(to/along)* — Drive or walk along, unopposed.

Tad — A small amount, or a bit.

Taking the mickey/Michael/piss — Teasing someone or pulling their leg.

Tanner — A six penny piece/bit.

Tap — To scrounge.

Tarp — Tarpaulin.

Terrapin's — Amphibious vehicles.

Teller *(mine)* — Explosives sealed inside a sheet metal casing and fitted with a pressure-actuated fuse. As the name suggests *('Teller' is the German for a dish or plate)* the mines were plate shaped. Because of its rather high operating pressure, only a vehicle or heavy objects passing over the Teller mine would set it off.

Territorial Army/TA — Part-time volunteer army formed by Parliament in 1907. Though the term, territorial, goes back a lot further.

Thrupenny bit — Three penny piece.

Tiffy — The Hawker Typhoon was a British single-seat fighter-bomber.

Tiffin — A light meal, especially one taken at midday or in the afternoon.

Tiger — Heavy German tank with 88mm gun. A crew of five (commander, gunner, loader, driver, co-driver).

Toe-rag — A beggar, tramp: from the pieces of rag they wrapped around their feet.

Tojo — A derogatory term used to describe Japanese soldiers. Tojo Hideki was the Japanese Prime Minister who ordered the attack on Pearl Harbour.

Tom — Prostitute.

Tommy *(Tommies)* — British soldier. Also known as Tommy Atkins.

Tommy cooker — Compact, portable stove, fuelled by a solidified alcohol or gel fuel.

Topee — A lightweight cloth-covered helmet made of cork or pith. Warn in warm climates. Also known as a pith helmet.

Tosheroon — Two shillings and sixpence piece. Also, known as half-crown or half a dollar.

Tosspot — A British English, English insult, used to refer to a stupid or contemptible person, or a drunkard.

Tracer — Bullets that are built with a small pyrotechnic charge in their base. Ignited by the burning powder, the composition burns very brightly, making the projectile trajectory visible to the naked eye during daylight, and very bright during night-time firing.

Trollop — A sexually disreputable or promiscuous woman.

Twat — A vulgar term for a woman's genitalia.

Upright *(piano)* — Upright pianos, also called vertical pianos, are more compact because the frame and strings are vertical. Generally used in small areas, bars, clubs, small rooms etc.

Urchin — A playful or mischievous youngster.

Valise — Webbing backpack for holding one's kit.

W.R.A.C. — Women's Royal Army Corps.

Wad — Sandwich.

Waffen-SS — Armed wing of the *(Schutzstaffel)*. Its military formations included men from Nazi Germany, along with volunteers and conscripts from both occupied and unoccupied lands.

Wakes Week — Up until the 1960's, this was a holiday period in England and Scotland when the manufacturing industry closed down on mass.

Wassock — An idiot or daft person.

Wallah/s — Fellow/s.

Warrant Officer/W.O. — The highest group of non-commissioned ranks, holding the King or Queen's warrant, rather than a commission.

Waypoint — Waypoints are sets of coordinates that identify a point in physical space, i.e. the navigation points of a battle group.

Webbing — Strappings, rifle sling, pouches etc.

Wehrmacht — The unified armed forces of Nazi Germany from 1935 to 1946, combining army, navy and air force.

Wet canteen — A canteen where alcohol can be bought.

Whizzbang — WW1 term. A small, high-speed shell whose sound through the air arrives almost at the same instant as its explosion.

Made in the USA
Columbia, SC
28 December 2020